Praise f

'A delicious second-chance
It's an episode of *Paranormal Investigations* but with more
sass and the Winchester boy of your dreams. A spooky
delight!' **Steffanie Holmes, author of *Fangs for Nothing***

'Spooky, swoony and sexy, *Ghosted* made me want to believe
(in love).' **Jodi McAlister, author of *An Academic Affair***

'Equal parts heart-racing thrills and heartwarming
moments, it gave me all the best kinds of chills. Amy
Hutton is a master of spooky romance.' **Karina May,
author of *That Island Feeling***

'A perfect blend of spooky and romantic. Lovers of
paranormal romance will devour this.' **Alexandra Almond,
author of *Thoroughly Disenchanted***

'Spooky, funny and sexy! *Ghosted* had me guessing – but
the romance kept this scaredy-cat from jumping out of
her skin. Cosy up, this is the perfect spooky season read.'
Melanie Saward, author of *Love Unleashed*

'Atmospheric, spooky, pacy romance . . . For those who like
their romance with a side of adventure, action and eerie
haunted houses.' **Clare Fletcher, author of *Love Match***

'This book cast a spell on me! *Ghosted* is a page-turning,
genre-bending delight full of sizzling, slow-burn chemistry,
second chances, and a mystery that will keep you guessing
(and swooning) right to the last page.' **Natalie Murray,
author of *Lights, Camera, Love***

AMY HUTTON
GHOSTED

ATRIA BOOKS

New York   Amsterdam/Antwerp   London   Toronto   Sydney   New Delhi

GHOSTED
First published in Australia in 2025 by
Atria Books Australia, an imprint of Simon & Schuster (Australia) Pty Limited
Level 4, 32 York St, Sydney NSW 2000

10 9 8 7 6 5 4 3 2 1

New York Amsterdam/Antwerp London Toronto Sydney Melbourne New Delhi
Visit our website at www.simonandschuster.com.au

For more than 100 years, Simon & Schuster has championed authors and the stories they create. By respecting the copyright of an author's intellectual property, you enable Simon & Schuster and the author to continue publishing exceptional books for years to come. We thank you for supporting the author's copyright by purchasing an authorised edition of this book.

No amount of this book may be reproduced or stored in any format, nor may it be uploaded to any website, database, language-learning model, or other repository, retrieval, or artificial intelligence system without express permission. All rights reserved. Inquiries may be directed to Simon & Schuster, 1230 Avenue of the Americas, New York, NY 10020 or permissions@simonandschuster.com.

© Amy Hutton 2025

All rights reserved. No part of this publication may be reproduced, stored in a retrieval system, or transmitted in any form or by any means, electronic, mechanical, photocopying, recording or otherwise, without prior permission of the publisher.

ATRIA BOOKS and colophon are trademarks of Simon & Schuster, LLC.

This book is a work of fiction. Any references to historical events, real people, or real places are used fictitiously. Other names, characters, places, and events are products of the author's imagination, and any resemblance to actual events or places or persons, living or dead, is entirely coincidental.

A catalogue record for this book is available from the National Library of Australia

ISBN: 9781761424878
Cover design: Mallory Heyer
Interior design: Midlands Typesetters, Australia
Printed and bound in Australia by Griffin Press

The paper this book is printed on is certified against the Forest Stewardship Council® Standards. Griffin Press holds chain of custody certification SCS-COC-001185. FSC® promotes environmentally responsible, socially beneficial and economically viable management of the world's forests.

*To Mum and to Hazel
for always fiercely believing in me and this story.
And to Holly and Callum
for being so patient.*

This one is for anyone who's ever felt like they didn't fit.

CHAPTER ONE

Pain sears through my cheek, my shoulder, my back. I'm sprawled across the floor, my face pressed to the boards and my hip lodged painfully against the fireplace. I wince at the pounding in my head, so furious it's like a tiny person's inside there, attempting to jackhammer their way out. My eyes cautiously flicker open, and I blink, trying to focus. The last thing I remember is hollering a string of Latin at a pissed-off ghost as it heaved me skyward and tossed me across the room. After that, nothing.

'Ms Daniels, are you with me?'

The voice oozes into my consciousness as if filtered through pudding. I will my mind to clear, squinting against the stabbing in my eyeballs, and take a quick mental sweep of my body. Feet, legs, arms, hands. It all hurts, but it all seems to be working.

'I'm fine, Mrs Tyler.' I wobble as I stand, barely containing a groan. It's not as if it's the first time I've been thrown into a wall by an angry spirit. You'd think I'd be used to it by now.

Mrs Tyler puts a hand to her heart. 'For a moment there I thought you were dead.'

'I'm not that easy to get rid of.' I offer what I hope is a reassuring smile and not the pain-filled grimace I suspect it is.

'I'm glad to hear it, dear.' She grips my arm. 'But did your spell work? Is the spirit gone?' Then she whispers, 'Did you see it? Please tell me it wasn't my darling Alfred.'

This is the part of the job I hate the most. The part where I lie. The ghost *was* Mrs Tyler's darling Alfred; I recognised his leering face from the photo beside the older woman's bed. His suit was even the same.

Most people think ghosts are vaporous and floaty, or that they glitch like the spirits in horror movies. But for me, that's not how they present. The ones that I confront, the ones that don't move on after death, just look like humans. Humans with something a little off about them. Something in their appearance that looks . . . well . . . dead.

Mrs Tyler's husband – or rather, his spirit – has been tormenting her for months. But there's nothing to be gained by telling her that; it would only break her heart even more. So instead, I squeeze her hand and tell her what she wants to hear.

'No, it wasn't him. And yes, it's gone. I sent it on to the next plane. It'll be at peace now.'

That's what I tell all my clients because it seems to comfort them. It could be true; honestly, I don't know. I have no idea where the spirits I rid the world of are sent. Heaven, hell, outer space – I really don't care. One less dead person hanging around past their use-by date is all that matters to me.

'Do you have someone you can call to come and sit with you, Mrs Tyler? You've had a bit of a night. Or I can book you an Uber if you'd rather stay somewhere else?'

I pull my phone from the pocket of my backpack. My eyes flutter closed at the text message that greets me. The one that came through just as I was heading out tonight. The one that's probably responsible for the break in focus that sent me into a wall. The one from Callum Jefferies. Paranormal investigator, podcast host, and – what was he? Ex almost boyfriend? I press my lips together, take a deep breath and turn back to Mrs Tyler with a smile.

'Don't worry about me, dear,' she says, 'I'll be fine. There's no one to call anyway. My family moved upstate some time ago, and my friends are all dead, or so old they wish they were.' Her face crinkles with a resigned smile.

I study the woman smiling at me. She's immaculate. Despite everything we've just been through, her silver bun is still neat as a pin and her pants as crisp as if they just came off the hanger. Wealth practically drips from her. Her apartment on New York City's Upper East Side is so large my tiny East Village condo could tuck inside it three times over. But Mrs Tyler doesn't have a single person she can turn to. Not a living soul.

The shock of realisation hits me so hard I wobble on my feet. This is how I'm going to end up – completely alone.

I try to recall the last time I spoke to someone other than a client, the barista at my favourite coffee spot or the Uber driver who delivers my pho. If I dropped dead tomorrow, would anyone notice? Weeks could pass before my body was discovered rotting on my apartment floor, my bones gnawed on by rats. And that is all on me. What else can I expect when I shut everyone out? I take a breath. If I don't make a change, my existence will be reduced to . . . well, this. I'm going to have to rejoin the world of the living, no matter how frightening that prospect might be.

Mrs Tyler clutches my arm again, and I'm so lost in my thoughts I jump.

'Sorry dear. We're both a bit jittery.' She laughs lightly. 'I just want to confirm that you're absolutely confident the spirit is gone.'

I pat her hand. 'I promise it's gone. That ghost won't bother you again. Trust me – this is what I do, and I never fail.'

Back at my apartment, I stare at my phone on the coffee table, Callum's message staring back at me. I need do something about it, because apparently frowning at it won't make it go away. I could ignore it, I've done that before, or I could delete it – I've done that too. Or I could be a professional and answer him. It's not like he's just saying hi. He's messaging me about a job.

I press a pack of frozen peas to the bump on my forehead, hoping it'll quell the jackhammering in my skull, and read the message one more time. My nose scrunches up at his easy tone.

> Hi Holly. Hope you're good. I have a job you might be interested in. Feel like teaming up again? I could do with your help. C

Callum and I haven't spoken for nearly two years. What could possibly be so compelling that he'd ask for my help after all this time? Especially given how whatever it was between us ended. I sigh. I guess there's only one way to find out.

> What's the job?

Three dots appear as he types a new message. Then disappear. Then reappear. Then . . .

> Can we discuss over coffee? There's a lot of detail.

My stomach lurches. Coffee?

Seeing Callum is not something I'd intended to ever do again. Sure, I've wondered what it would be like to see him. I've rehearsed what I would say to him over and over. I just didn't think it would happen. At least, I knew I wouldn't be the one to make it happen, so . . .

I tap my finger on my phone as I think.

If it's a real haunting, I should probably look into it. If he's asked for my help, there must be a good reason. *Tap. Tap. Tap.* We can meet, talk over the job, then I can decide what to do. *Tap. Tap. Tap.* And if someone is being harassed by a ghost, I should help, regardless of my feelings about the situation. That's my job. I nod to myself. Right. I'll meet with him and see what he has to say.

Anxiety quickly takes hold making my whole body clench. I exhale a breathy groan. I'm being ridiculous. Why am I the nervous one? He's the one who screwed everything up. I tap out a frustrated message.

> Can meet at my office tomorrow, 10 am. Do you need address?

I put my phone on the coffee table and try not to stare at it. When a new ding comes almost immediately, my stomach lurches again.

> I've got the address.

Another ding.

> I'll bring coffee. See you then.

CHAPTER TWO

I'm in a dimly lit musty room, the earthen scent filling my nostrils. Iron sconces along the wall hold candles that throw long shadows across the rough-hewn beams of the ceiling.

In the middle of the dirt-covered floor, a young girl kneels. She can't be more than sixteen. The cloth of her simple grey dress is clutched in her fist and blonde hair pokes messily from beneath her white bonnet. Three men tower over her, their faces shrouded by their black wide-brimmed hats.

Her cry rips through the air.

'Be still,' the first man says, almost gently. 'We know what you are.'

The girl's wail quietens to a whimper. 'I am nothing, sir. I swear it.'

'Liar,' the second man growls. His voice is deeper and filled with contempt. 'You are an abomination.'

The girl wails again, furiously shaking her head.

'An abomination which must be struck from this earth,' the third man adds. He says it so calmly, matter-of-factly, that a shiver runs the length of my spine.

'No, sir. No.' She looks up at him, pleading.

He reaches out and touches her cheek, and for a moment I think her entreaties have swayed him. But then a glint of candlelight bounces off a silver dagger, its blade decorated with a strange engraving, its heavy wooden hilt gripped tight in his fist.

I gasp and cry 'Stop!', sure of what will happen next. But no one turns, because no one hears me.

The girl calls out too, her eyes widening in terror. 'Please!'

But the man lifts his arm high in the air and swoops the weapon down.

She screams as the knife plunges into her breast, her hands pawing at the wound, her dress quickly turning scarlet as her life spills out of her, soaking the material and spreading over the floor.

I want to go to her, but my feet won't move. I'm frozen and mute. All I can do is watch in horror as the girl's cries slowly become a gurgle.

One last pleading sob slips past her lips, then, with a soft exhale, she slumps to the ground, her terrified eyes now glassy and lifeless.

The men step forward and huddle over the girl's crumpled form, their heads bowing as they mutter a chant I cannot hear. Then the room darkens, and the men vanish. In the silence that follows, I hear a voice.

'Holly. Let us in.'

The dream rattles me. I'm used to nightmares, they come with the job – battling ghosts does not bring a peaceful night's sleep. But something about this one feels different.

Like I was there, but not there. A silent audience, bearing witness to something so grisly and real . . .

I pull on my boots and tie the laces as I try to shake off the dream, but I can't get the image of the girl out of my mind, nor the voice, and the way it said my name. *Holly. Let us in.* A disembodied voice that somehow knows me personally? Yeah, that's not creepy at all.

I rub at my head, still tender from colliding with Mrs Tyler's wall. And all the muscles that ached last night ache twice as much today. I'm so tired, I could fall asleep standing up. And if that's not enough to make me edgy, I'm due to meet Callum. Butterflies swarm my stomach as I close my apartment door.

I tug my leather jacket closer to shut out the fall chill as I march along the leaf-strewn sidewalk, it's golden litter grubby from the city grime swishing around my boots. I need to figure out exactly what I'm going to say to him.

Hi, Callum. Casual, with a smile. *Callum.* Surly, with a frown. *Hello, Callum.* Cool and professional. That's it. This is about a job; the best way to handle it is to be cool and professional, to be at my desk looking busy and one hundred per cent composed when he arrives. *Hello Callum, please take a seat.*

But he's early. As I round the corner to my office, he's already there, leaning against the wall. Well, shit.

He's scrolling through his phone with one hand while balancing a cardboard tray holding two large coffees in the other. His sunglasses are pushed back over his light brown hair, which he still wears short, and the sun shimmers on the pale skin of his cheeks. I don't know what I was expecting but he looks the same, dressed head to toe in black, right down to his motorcycle boots – the ones he always wears even though he doesn't ride a motorcycle – and totally at ease. That was something I always admired in him; he exudes easiness. Always open, cheerful and relaxed. Three things I'm not.

He suddenly shifts his stance, pushing off the wall and rolling his shoulders, and I dart into the closest doorway before he can spot me.

I scrunch my eyes closed. This is not a good start. I considered cancelling my meeting with Callum around three hundred and eighty-two times this morning. Back and forth, back and forth. I just don't know if it's a smart move to put myself through this. I guess I could still text him and pull out. Or I could just hide in this doorway until he's gone. But what if he walks past? That would be awkward.

I *tsk* at myself. I'm being ridiculous again, and cancelling on him last minute is not who I am and not who I intend to be, no matter the circumstances. We're only discussing a case. Besides, I face ghosts for a living, I can face Callum Jefferies.

With a deep, steadying breath, I square my shoulders, set my jaw, step onto the pavement and call his name.

Callum glances up, and the most spectacular smile lights up his face.

My butterflies flap wildly.

'Here she is. My favourite ghostbuster,' he says, slipping his phone into the back pocket of his jeans.

My butterflies turn into angry bats. 'Don't call me that. You know I don't like it.'

'Sorry. Let me start that again. Hi, Holly.' He gives me a cheery wave teamed with an even broader smile.

'Hello, Callum.' My cheeks prickle with warmth.

'I see you're still wearing your ruby slippers.' He nods to my cherry-red Doc Marten boots. 'I always loved the way they perfectly matched your hair. You cut it shorter. It suits you.'

My hair used to fall past my shoulders, but now I have a choppy bob that sits just below my ears.

'I cut it a while ago.' I fuss with my windswept bangs, then lift my gaze to meet his eyes. Big mistake. They're greener than I remember them – vibrant, and strikingly bright, with gold flecks that circle the pupils.

When I first met Callum two years ago, his eyes were the first thing I noticed about him. Not just their extraordinary colour, but their kindness, and the way they danced with humour and mischief. A perfect reflection of who he was. Who I *thought* he was.

I wiggle past him, easily ducking under his arm, and unlock my office door. I inherited my office from my grandmother. She was my mom's mom and her name was Jenny. Grandma Jenny was a fortune teller. The kind that dot the streets of downtown New York; neon signs in their windows. Growing up, I didn't have a lot to do with her. My family didn't like how she made a living, believing she took money from 'desperate fools happy to believe her lies'. But they were wrong about her. My grandmother's abilities were genuine.

I was so grateful when I discovered that truth, because that meant I wasn't the only *freak* in my family.

Grandma Jenny's store resembled something from the movies, with crystal balls, runes and smudging wands, and colourful beaded scarves draped over lamps. She always said, 'Might as well give them bang for their buck.' When my grandmother suddenly died, her store became mine. The first thing I did was get rid of the kitschy fortune-teller vibe. The people who come to see me are often traumatised. Being haunted can do that to a person. I wanted to make sure my office was calm and peaceful – everything hauntings aren't. The only thing I kept, besides a few books and a well-worn set of tarot cards, was a red and gold wing-backed chair. I call it my throne. It's my little piece of Grandma Jenny.

My gaze follows Callum as he wanders around my office, picking things up and breezily commenting on them. He examines one of my grandmother's books on near death experiences, excitedly telling me he also owns a copy and smiling in a way that makes my stupid stomach flutter. Was he always this tall? Has he been working out?

'Large and strong enough for you?' he asks.

I jolt. 'W-what?'

'The coffee. Large latte, extra strong. That's still your order, right?'

'Oh, yeah. It's perfect. Really, really . . . great.' I trail off, cringing as I take a quick sip.

'Good,' he says, apparently oblivious to my awkwardness. He drops into the chair opposite me. 'This was your grandmother's place, right?'

I nod. 'She left me this and her condo when she died. Well, she left the condo to me and my sister. I'm saving up to buy Maggie out. But the store she left to me.'

'I like it. It's got a nice feel. Peaceful. Though you could use a plant or two. I know this great place in Chelsea if you ever—'

'I'm not good with plants,' I say, shaking my head. 'I'm not good with anything living.'

He chuckles. 'Yeah. I remember.'

I can't stifle my gasp at the sting in his flippant comment.

'Shit,' he says, 'I didn't mean that how it came out.' He leans in. 'I only meant that you're great with the dead. With ghosts. You're great at what you do.'

'Right. Okay.' I turn away to cover my hurt, open my desk drawer and rummage for some painkillers. I toss back two with another mouthful of coffee.

'Headache?' he asks.

'I had a job last night that turned a bit ugly, then I didn't sleep very well. Weird dream. It was as if . . .' I shudder as the voice rings out in my mind again. *Holly. Let us in.*

'Was it a nightmare?'

'There was a fair bit of blood, so yeah, you could say that.'

'I get it. Goes with the job, right? Some of my dreams, man. All I can say is I'm glad they're not my reality.'

His eyes fill with an understanding that catches me off guard. Understanding is not what I was expecting and it's not what I'm used to. Barely contained horror is the look I normally get.

'And that?' He points at the angry red bump on my forehead. 'Did your ghost do that?'

'More the wall it threw me against.' I prod at the bump and wince.

'Don't poke at it.'

He reaches across the desk and pulls my hand from my face. Warmth rushes up my arm from his touch, as that intangible thing I felt from the moment we met stutters in my heart. I quickly snatch my hand away.

The realisation of what he just did flashes across his eyes, and he wiggles back in his chair. He clears his throat.

'So, this dream of yours. What was it about? Last night's job, or something else?'

'Not job related. I don't know what it was, just that it was . . . different.'

'Do you think there's anything to it? I know your magic never worked like that before, but it's been a while since we've seen each other, so I wasn't sure if—'

'I'm not comfortable with the term "magic", it sounds witchy. I just see ghosts and, given the chance, cease their existence. That's all I can do.'

'*All* you can do?' He chuckles. 'I still haven't met anyone else like you, and believe me, I've looked. Magic or not, you've got to admit you're something special, Holly Daniels.'

I scowl as I shuffle some papers on my desk. 'Something special' was not how he last described me. 'What's the job you need help on?' I ask, bluntly. Time to move this conversation along.

'Yeah, okay, onto the job. Hang onto your hat. It's . . .' He plays a drumroll on the desk with his fingers. 'The Western house.'

I blink. The name means nothing to me. 'Should I know what that is?'

His shoulders droop. 'It's only one of the most famous haunted houses in New York State. Possibly America.' He sits back again.

I shrug.

His eyebrows shoot up. 'Seriously? The Western house. It's the holy grail of paranormal investigation, Holly. The holy grail.'

'Ohhh. Okay.' I don't get as excited about ghosts as Callum does. Mainly because I hate them. And I don't need to go looking for hauntings, they come to me. 'But as I haven't heard of it, maybe you could fill me in.'

'Fine,' he says with uncontained exasperation. 'It's out on Long Island and has reportedly been haunted for generations. But the Western family are notoriously reclusive, so no one knows the truth. They've declined every request from every paranormal investigator and ghostbusting show around. The house is currently vacant, has been for a while. I guess the Western who owns it now is too creeped out to live there.'

'If no one's living there, there's not much chance of it being an active haunting.'

'You don't know that.'

'I do know that, and so do you. People always think ghosts haunt buildings, but in my experience, they haunt the people who live there. That's why most of the places you investigate turn up empty – because they're deserted buildings. If the people are long gone, the ghosts will be too.'

His eyes narrow as he slumps further into his chair. 'There are a lot of stories about this house, and in *my* experience, where there's smoke, there's nearly always fire. I know about this shit, Holly. It's a famous haunting.'

'Which has never been investigated.'

'That doesn't mean the stories aren't true.'

'Or that they are.'

'Which is why they've decided they want it investigated.' He glowers at me. 'Are you deliberately trying to push my buttons?'

'I'm giving you my opinion. Isn't that why you're here?'

His still-narrowed eyes study me. Then he sighs and relaxes. 'Yep, of course, sorry.'

A beat of guarded silence hangs between us. I quicky fill it.

'So, how did you end up talking the family into giving you permission?'

Callum instantly perks back up. 'That's the best part – I didn't. They contacted me. Let me find the email.' He scrolls through his phone for a second, then hands it to me before snatching it back. 'Just don't go looking through my photos. I'd hate for you to see more of me than you bargained for.'

I grab the phone from him. 'Believe me, Callum, I'd hate that too.'

He chuckles, and it's deep and husky, and I'm instantly transported back to the times we sat in his office watching

YouTube clips, laughing at the hosts of other ghost shows overreacting to every creaky floorboard. Laughing about ghosts. I remember that being a first for me.

The spark of something I've tried to convince myself was long extinguished flickers with warmth inside me. A memory of happiness, a tickle of past hope. Then I think about *the last* time I saw Callum, shove the feelings back down and focus on the email.

> Dear Mr Jefferies,
> I have been asked to commission you to investigate the disturbances reported at the Western home in East Mill, Long Island. Mr Edward Western, the owner of the property, believes you have the necessary background to assist him, and is eager for you to be involved. Please call me to discuss. We'd like to move forward as soon as possible.
> Sincerely,
> Albert Rosing, on behalf of Edward Western

'So this Edward Western man must know you specialise in investigating rumoured hauntings,' I say. 'Is he a fan of your podcast?'

'He's not a subscriber, I checked, and he's not on my mailing list. Maybe he's just heard of me, or came across me on YouTube, did a Google search. I don't know. Anyway, I called this Rosing dude. He was weirdly evasive for someone who supposedly wants to give me a job. I asked when I could meet with his boss, and all he said was Western is out of town. So, he'll be the point of contact for now.'

Callum removes the lid of his coffee and licks off the leftover froth on the underside of the plastic, before running his tongue over his lips, gathering a smudge of chocolate. I try not to stare but it's really hard not to. So I steal a glance at his tattoos instead. Dark ink against pale skin, weaving up the muscles of his forearm. A series of interconnecting Celtic knots he once told me honoured his family. When I look up again, he's watching me.

I promptly lift my wastepaper basket. 'Are you quite finished with that coffee?'

He tosses the cup inside. 'The froth is the best bit, don't you think?' One brow quirks.

I look away, drop the basket to the floor, and ignore his question. 'What do you know about the haunting?' I ask.

'Right. Okay so, at least two different ghosts have been reported, sighted multiple times. One is a young woman with long fair hair seen wandering the grounds. She's never been named, but I assume she must have died on the estate. So maybe staff and not family? She's said to wear a white dress, and rumour has it she may have taken her own life after being jilted by her lover. But given that no one knows who she is, I'm not sure where that story comes from. The other haunting is more specific. It's believed to be Margaret Western, who would have been Edward Western's great-great-grandmother. She would have been alive sometime during the 1800s, likely died in the house. She's been seen throughout the building, but most often lingering around the staircase.'

'Are any of these encounters recorded as violent?'

'That's something we should ask. There's not a lot of info out there.'

I note his use of 'we' and ignore it. 'Then where are these stories coming from?'

'The family and staff who've lived and worked in the house, I assume, and local residents of East Mill.'

'So the family wants you to debunk the stories or confirm they're true?'

'Yep, and once I've done that, I'll brief Edward Western and he'll decide how to move forward. I'll then be free to discuss the investigation as part of my podcast. I've already started teasing it. My subscribers are going crazy. Unfortunately, Western has said no to any video or audio recordings at the property – did I mention they're reclusive? – so I won't be taking a crew. It'll be just you and me.'

'I haven't said I'm coming.'

'Yet.' He grins. 'Google the house.'

He lugs his chair around to my side of the desk and wiggles in beside me as I log into my laptop. He's close, very close, and he smells of chocolate and coffee and something else, a scent I remember as being just him.

'The most recent info I could find about the family was an obit on Brendin Western,' Callum says, 'Edward's uncle and last resident of the house. There's also an article in the local paper about the Western house being left vacant after his death. A town committee wanted to take over management of the place, because of its historical significance, but Edward Western refused – I assume because he wants to live there. I couldn't find much on him, other than the occasional mention of his name. The guy is a ghost. No pun intended.'

'You didn't find *anything* on Edward Western?'

'Like I said, a mention here and there, but other than that . . .' He shrugs. 'He must keep one hell of a low profile. I've asked Rosing to send through any information about the house and the family that might be useful while I wait to interview Western.'

I click on an image of the house and the back of my neck instantly prickles. There's something oddly familiar about it. The heavy gate and iron fence, the silhouette of the building hunkering down behind it. I feel as if I've seen it before. But I'm sure I've never been there. I can't remember a trip out to Long Island while Mom was alive, and there's no way Dad would have taken me and my sister out there after her death. Family vacations went to the grave with Mom. I click on another photo, then another. The house is two storeys with a rambling wraparound porch and a widow's walk that rings the pitch of the shingled roof. The windows are shuttered, and the garden beds surrounding the house have been left to go wild. The photo is dated 2019.

'Have you gone out there to look at it yet?' I ask.

'Nope. You can't see much from the street, and I couldn't see the point of peering through the fence at the place if there was no chance of getting in there.'

I nod. 'When was it built?'

'The Westerns have maintained a house on that parcel of land for close to four hundred years. The original house burnt down. The one you're looking at now was built in 1872.'

I click on another photo. This one looks to be older. The shutters on the windows are wide open and the garden beds are in full flower. This time the hairs on my arms stand up.

'Brendin Western passed away seven years ago,' Callum continues. 'Died in the house. He was ninety-five. No one's lived there since. I spoke to Ola Hutchings at the East Mill Historical Society. She said she's happy to help, and that we're welcome to go through their collection. Unfortunately, they're not online yet, though the process is underway. We're going to have to go old school, head out there and dig through their files, Mulder and Scully style.' He elbows me playfully.

'Except we both believe,' I say.

I'm studying an old grainy newspaper photo when something in the open attic window catches my eye. I zoom in, squinting to see what it is. Suddenly it's like the air is being squeezed from my lungs. My throat tightens, and fear bubbles inside me as if I'm recalling a memory that isn't mine. I press at my chest anxiously.

'What's happening?' Callum moves in closer, his breath tickling my cheek. 'Are you okay? What is it? Are you sensing something?'

The strange feeling vanishes as quickly as it began. I draw in a deep, easy breath.

'Nothing,' I say, dropping my hand to my lap.

'That didn't look like nothing. You sensed something.' He grabs the mouse and zooms further into the photo.

'I don't sense things from photos. I'm not that kind of psychic.' I snatch the mouse back and quickly close the image of the house.

I can feel him studying me, his eyes roaming my profile. I turn and face him, hoping he'll look away. But he holds my gaze steady, his startling green eyes full of suspicion. Then he gives me a small shrug and rocks back in his chair, his focus finally off me.

I blow out a quiet breath. I'm not sure which was more disorientating, the weird sensation from the photo or the intensity of Callum's stare.

'Ghost photography is a real thing,' he says. 'Not that I've ever caught much on camera. But I've seen photos that I believe are the real deal. If the photo was taken when the spirit was present, could that be what you were sensing?' He folds his hands behind his head, his jacket falling open and his T-shirt riding up.

I blink at the glimpse of flat, pale stomach and the thin line of dark hair that runs from his belly button down beneath the waistband of his black jeans. I quickly turn away as my heart starts an annoying tap dance routine in my chest.

'I *said* I didn't sense anything. And . . . you can move now.' I point across the desk.

'Right. Sorry.' He picks up his chair and plonks it, and himself, back opposite me. 'So? What do you think?'

I scramble to gather my thoughts, which are split between the sensation I got from the photo and how annoyed I am at these stupid Callum feelings.

'I think we should wait until Edward Western gets back to town and talk to him in person before we commit to anything.'

'You said we. Does that mean you're in?'

'I never accept a job or even go to the property until I've met with the client.'

'But this isn't your job, it's mine.' He tilts his head.

'Then why ask me the question? What is it you want from me?'

He stares, his Adam's apple bobbing, and I suddenly realise how that sounded. That's not what I meant – or maybe it is. What is he hoping for here? Why, after nearly two years, has he reached out to me? Is it just this job, or is it . . .

Callum takes a deep breath, letting it go with a heavy sigh. 'I . . . ah . . .' He stops and clears his throat. 'I believe in what I do. I believe the sounds on a spirit box and EMF readings can indicate a haunting. But they're never going to be one hundred per cent. You will be one hundred per cent, and you'll be able to identify the ghost. This job is a big deal, and it's been entrusted to me. I need you there. I have to be sure, and you'll know for sure. If there really are ghosts there, you'll *see* them.' He sighs again. 'Look, I understand this is not your usual kind of gig, and it's not how you usually work. I also realise you might not want to team up with me again. If that's how you feel, that's cool, just tell me and I'll be on my way.' He pauses, his teeth tugging at his bottom lip, his gaze locked to mine. I stay silent.

'How about this then,' he says. 'East Mill is only a few hours' drive away. Let's go out there, interview the locals, check out the historical society and get eyes on the house. Maybe you'll see a ghost standing in the front yard and we can come straight back home again.' He shrugs, then adds, 'I should probably mention the job is good money.'

I lean in. 'Define good.'

He laughs. 'I'm thinking maybe we see if we can get . . . 20k.'

'So 10k each?'

'Plus expenses covered.'

I'm sure my eyes go so wide they're the size of my head. 'Are you serious? That's a lot of money.'

'We're worth it don't you think? It could go towards paying off your condo. Get you closer to making that apartment your own.' His brows lift. 'What do you say, Holly? Aren't you even a little tempted?'

I've never really done my job for the money; it's more an unwanted calling. That's not to say I'm not paid and paid well. I offer a specialist service, and my fee reflects that. But that fee also depends on who's being haunted. I'm never going to turn someone away because they can't afford me. Pro bono ghost work happens more often than I'd like. $10,000 is a lot of money for me, and it sure would help put a dent in what I owe Maggie.

I turn back to my laptop. Then there's the Western house. I study the photo again. Something tickles at the edges of my senses. Something I shouldn't be feeling. I see ghosts and I exorcise ghosts, which is weird enough. But I don't get strange vibes from photos, and I don't have dreams with disembodied voices whispering my name, and I don't know why, but I feel like those two things are connected.

With a slow breath out, I seek the feeling again. It comes quickly – energy rippling across my skin, the sense that I know this house. I must have seen it before; there's no other answer. Or maybe it's just because I'm tired and stressed and the guy sitting opposite me is still giving me feels that are just plain irritating and I can't get my bearings. It's like I'm being ganged up on by the universe. Am I tempted?

'I tell you what,' Callum says, not waiting for my answer. 'How about we go get some breakfast right now? My treat. As I recall, you like to eat.' I scowl and he laughs. 'We can discuss the case some more and then hopefully with a full stomach, you'll decide to come on board.'

'Callum, are you bribing me with money *and* food?'

'Maybe, or maybe I'm hoping you won't be able to resist the lure of a spooky getaway with me.' He grins.

I splutter out an incredulous laugh. 'Spooky getaway? Really? In your dreams, Jefferies.'

'My dreams aren't usually that good, Daniels.'

He unfolds himself from his chair and shakes out his long legs. 'I remember how surprised I was when Celeste first introduced us. You were nothing like I thought you'd be.'

I prickle. 'Why, what did you think I'd be like?'

'I dunno. More like the psychic from *Poltergeist*, and less—'

'The eighties *Poltergeist*? You thought I was going to be a four-foot, fifty-year-old woman?'

'Possibly.' His eyes tease. 'But I was glad you weren't. Though, I still think you should finish every job with . . .' He throws out his arms and says, 'This is house is clean,' then grins. 'You should do that.'

'I doubt my traumatised clients would appreciate it.'

He shrugs and opens the door for me. 'I'm glad I reached out to you about this job, and I'm glad you decided to answer. I wasn't sure you would . . . after Celeste, and well, everything . . .'

'I wasn't sure I would either,' I say. 'To be honest, I'm still not sure why I did.'

He stares down at me, eyes narrowed, teeth jagging his bottom lip. Then he softens, and grins again. 'Is it because you remembered I was irresistibly charming?'

I don't answer. I just slip under his arm and out the door.

CHAPTER THREE

Callum leans on the cafe counter as the young woman serving him twists her long blonde hair around her fingers. We're supposed to be doing research on the Western house. And Callum is supposed to be talking me into going with him. I push a forkful of pancake into my mouth as I watch him laugh with the server, their heads thrown back.

A flirting difficulty of five point five, I think.

I'm always astonished by how effortlessly people can talk to each other. How strangers can strike up a conversation in the supermarket or on the street and connect like it's the most natural thing in the world. It's never been that way for me. At least, not since I saw my first ghost, when I was eight. Life got weird after that, and it was easier to withdraw into myself than see the suspicion and doubt in my family's eyes. Easier to shut myself off than to listen to my classmates calling me names like Holly the Freak. God how I hate that word. *Freak.* Scrawled across my locker. Whispered behind my back. *Freak, freak, freak.* I even started calling myself that, the word became so tangled up with my sense of self. Carved into my heart.

When I met Celeste in college, she helped me to see I was more than that word. She became my friend, something I thought I'd never have until I met her. Celeste was a sensitive who couldn't see spirits but knew when they were around. She told me to stop fighting my gift, to learn to control it and find a way to use it to my benefit. She made me practise shutting my mind to the spirits, until I could open and close it to them at will. When she hefted in a big book of spells one day, I laughed. But we tried some out, mostly for fun, and then one day, *boom*. I uttered some Latin words neither of us understood, while holding a rosary we'd picked up in a thrift store, and a ghost I'd been struggling to block just vanished. That moment changed everything. I felt like I finally had control of my life.

The satisfaction of watching a spirit leave this plane never gets old. They all exit in a different way – some go quietly, others howl and some just flick off like a light – but each is just as gratifying. On a good day, it feels like a sweet deal watching the things that plague my life vanish from it. But then there are the bad days.

Callum turns and waves at me, giving me a smile. I shake my head at him, look away and concentrate on my pancakes.

I need to be careful here. I'd forgotten how easy it is to be around him. How normal he makes me feel. The memories of what it was like when we worked together keep knocking at my heart, and I find myself wondering if I could bury what happened between us and go back to what we almost were. No confrontations, ugly truths or excuses. No reliving what happened. Which would probably suit me fine, because

I'm great at hiding from my feelings and avoiding confrontation, unless it's with a ghost. Except I can't do that, because I'll always have that doubt when I look into his eyes.

I open my photo roll and scroll until I find a selfie of me and Celeste lying on the grass in Central Park, laughing and squinting into the sunshine. That was the day she introduced me to Callum. I'd already heard of his podcast and had checked it out. I liked the idea of this guy who believes in the paranormal so completely that he's made it his mission to debunk fake hauntings and the fake ghost hunters that promote them. It didn't hurt that he was witty and charming and wasn't bad to look at. But watching him on YouTube didn't prepare me for meeting him in person. I think my chin actually dropped. He just glowed from the inside out.

Callum asked me to join his paranormal investigation team, and I shocked myself by agreeing. His enthusiasm was contagious, and the thought of being around like minds and souls was irresistible to me. I felt the spark between us from the very beginning; the air practically ignited whenever we were around each other. He made me feel a part of the world I'd always felt separate from. We had so many late-night conversations over burgers and fries and Cheetos in the small studio where he recorded his show. About why he loved ghosts and why I didn't. About my powers and how fascinating he found them, and about his passion and how baffled I was by it. He enjoyed teasing me, and I liked him doing it. He made ghost hunting fun, something I'd never thought possible.

After a couple of months of getting and closer and closer, he asked if I'd like to meet for a drink. I met him at a bar in SoHo and we spent the night laughing and flirting, something he is an expert at. Around him I was the kind of person I'd always wished I could be, relaxed and funny and maybe even brave. That night he told me how much he liked me. He said he was happy to take things slow, that he didn't want to rush me, he wanted me to feel comfortable. He knew I sometimes struggled around people, I'd told him that much during our late night talks over Cheetos.

And I had said, 'Maybe don't take it *too* slow.' I couldn't believe the words came out of my mouth. I still remember how much that had made him laugh. 'Next time, we'll go on a real date,' he'd promised. 'I'll take you to dinner, because I know how you like to eat.' I remember whacking his arm and laughing, and him grabbing my hand and holding it. He made me dare to wonder if I could have a normal-ish life. One that included acceptance and love, unconditional and non-judgemental. At the end of the night, he leant in and pressed a tender kiss to my cheek. I felt the promise of so much more in the warmth of his lips on my skin. But the next day, that promise vanished like the ghosts I exorcise.

I close the photo of Celeste, then watch as the server takes a coffee card off the pile on the counter, scribbles something down and hands it to Callum. He slips the card into his back pocket, draws himself up to his full, impressive height, then saunters back to me.

'Coffee is on the way,' he says, sliding into his seat.

'Did you just arrange a hook-up for later?'

A smirk settles on his lips. 'Looks like you enjoyed your breakfast.'

I narrow my eyes and stuff the last forkful of pancake into my mouth. 'I was hungry,' I mumble through the food.

'I can tell.'

'You don't get to judge me. You can't resist flirting; I can't resist pancakes.'

'I wasn't judging or flirting.' He leans back in his seat, piercing eyes still on me.

The server arrives at our table with our coffees. She pushes her hair behind her ear as she gazes down at Callum.

'So, I might see you there?' She touches his shoulder and gives him a shy smile.

'I promise I'll try, but it depends how long I'm out of town. But hey, break a leg, okay?'

A little nod and another smile and she swishes away.

He stares at me staring daggers at him. 'What?' he says, looking affronted.

'Yeah, no flirting at all.'

'She invited me to see a play she's in.'

'Mm-hmm.'

He picks up his teaspoon and starts stirring his coffee. 'Ms Daniels, if I didn't know better, I'd say you were jealous.'

I scoff. 'Oh please. Don't be ridiculous.' I quickly avert my eyes and focus on my cup.

We've been in the cafe for a little over an hour, and I'm on my third coffee. I'm buzzing from head to toe, which I'm almost certain is from the caffeine and not from the way Callum keeps looking at me, all intense eyes and quiet smile. We've both got our laptops out, and we've been sifting through the stories surrounding the house.

'Here's one,' he says. 'Something about . . . Oh, it's just about the town wanting to access the land for historical tours and the family saying no.'

'It sounds like the Western family aren't particularly nice people,' I say. 'Which is another reason we should wait and talk to Edward Western in person. In my experience, asshole people become asshole ghosts. We need to know what we're walking into. Not being prepared can get you killed. I shouldn't have to tell you that.'

'Holly, what happened to Celeste was an accident. It wasn't anyone's fault. You understand that, right?'

'I know that.' I pick up my cup, disappointed to find it empty again.

'It wasn't *anyone's* fault.' He squints at me.

'I said I know.'

'Alright, then . . . why don't we just drive out there? We won't do anything until we've spoken to Western or Rosing. We can check out the house – keeping our distance, have a look around East Mill. You never know, it could be fun. We could visit the beach or . . . I hear the restaurants are pretty good.'

'Reminder: we are not going on a spooky getaway.' He chuckles. 'But okay, fine. I'll do it. I'll see if I get anything from the house. From a distance. I mean, 10k is 10k. But before we head out there, make sure you let this Rosing guy know that I'm coming too. He should understand what I do, in case they want me to move their dead relative on.'

'No need,' Callum says. 'He knows what you do.'

'What?'

'We talked about you.'

'I don't . . . when did you talk to him about me?'

'When we were talking about the job. I was told to bring backup. Another ghostbuster. Specifically, a psychic.'

My heart sinks. I had thought he'd reached out because he wanted to. But he only needed me because this Rosing man insisted on him bringing a psychic. Why does this upset me so much? This was always just a job, and that's all I want it to be. Isn't it? My breath hitches, and Callum hears it and sits forward.

'Obviously, if I need a psychic, you're the first person I'm going to think of.'

'Obviously, because I'm the only one you know who can actually see ghosts. You already told me that. Were you even going to let me know I was just one half of a package deal?'

'You're not just part of the deal, but why would it matter if you were?'

'Because it matters.'

'Holly, I didn't think I'd be telling you anything, I'm shocked you're even here. I never thought you'd answer my message.' He rubs his fingers across his forehead, a dark frown hardening his face. 'You ghosted me for two years. Disappeared without a word. Ignored all my calls. Radio silence.' He shakes his head and looks down into his empty cup, his knee bouncing so violently it rocks the table.

My pulse pounds in my ears. Of course it was going to come up. Of course there'd be a confrontation. How could I be so stupid? I knew this was a bad idea. I knew I should have deleted his message. He's blaming me for *his* behaviour. Like *I* did something wrong, when he was the reason for . . . everything. But I don't want to go there. I don't care how many times I've rehearsed what I want to say, it's not worth it. I suddenly wish I was at home, alone, where it's safe.

Callum reaches across the table and touches my hand. 'Hey.' His voice is gentle again. 'I didn't mean to say any of that . . . I'm sorry.'

I pull my hand away and fuss with my napkin, folding it into a tiny square. 'Um . . . I need to think this over some more.'

He sits back again, his arms across his chest. 'Which part? The job or me?'

'You made it seem like you actually wanted to work with me again. But it turns out you just can't do this job without me.'

He nods, slow and deliberate. 'Is that right? So, you don't think I can conduct an investigation on my own? They contacted *me* because they wanted *me*. You were just backup.'

My anger flares, quickly replacing the hurt. 'Oh please. You've got book smarts, some useless gadgets, and a YouTube channel, sure but—' I stop, sucking back a gasp at the bitter tirade that just tumbled from my lips.

'Fuck.' He says the word through a mirthless laugh. 'Tell me what you really think, Holly. Just because I don't explode ghosts with my mind doesn't mean I'm not a good investigator.'

'I don't explode them with my mind, I use an incantation. And they don't explode, they . . . vanish.'

'Mm-hmm. Still, let me get this straight. What you're saying is you're better than me, and I'm basically useless without your . . .' He does air quotes. 'Special gift?' I flinch. 'This might come as a complete shock to you, Holly,' he goes on, 'but I know what I'm doing. I have an excellent reputation. A hell of a lot of people subscribe to my show and ask for my help.'

'I wasn't questioning that. I didn't say you didn't have *any* abilities.'

'Ah, yeah, you did.'

'Well, I didn't mean to. I know you're good at what you do. It's just . . .' I shake my head. 'I just think . . . I can't.'

He nods. 'Got it. You don't have to say anything else.' His eyes, so soft earlier, are now hard chips of emerald.

My hands tremble. 'I should go.' I grab my backpack from under the table.

'Stay there.' He runs a hand through his hair. 'It's okay, Holly. To be honest, I'm kind of surprised we got as far as we did. I guess I was hoping . . . I don't know what I was hoping.' His chair slides back with a scrape, and he stands and drops some money on the table. 'I don't understand what I did to make you ghost me like you did, and I'm not asking you to tell me, though I hope one day you will. I'll be heading to East Mill to poke around, because that's how I do my job. If you'd like to come along, the offer stands.' His teeth graze across his bottom lip as he looks down at me.

'Callum—' My voice is so low it's barely a whisper.

'It was good seeing you again,' he says. 'Take care, okay?' Spinning on his heel, he stalks away, walking out the door without a backward glance.

I press my pack of frozen peas to the nasty red bump on my head again and flop onto the couch. With last night's ghost attack and now everything that happened today with Callum, my brain is thumping.

It's been hours since Callum stormed from the cafe. I didn't mean to lash out at him. No matter how much he hurt me, I didn't want to be cruel. That's not who I am. I didn't even believe what I was saying. I think he's a great investigator, I know he is. I was just so disappointed that he only contacted me because he needed a psychic, and not because he wanted to. I'm so mad at myself for feeling like this. I'm even madder about walking away from all that money. I want to buy Maggie out. She's not pressing me for it yet, but who knows when she might need the cash herself. I'd be so happy if I could surprise her and give her $10,000 in one big chunk. She could go on that trip to the Grand Canyon she's always going on about. And then there's the Western house. Why can't I stop thinking about it? I need to be part of Callum's investigation if I'm going to find out.

So I grab my phone. My hands are actually shaking. I've got to get it together. It's just a job. A very well-paid job out of town with Callum. Oh god.

I type up a message and send it before I have second thoughts.

> I'm sorry. I didn't mean what I said. I'm not good with the living, remember? I want to take the job. If you still want me?

I toss the peas onto the coffee table, flip open my laptop and do a photo search for the Western house. Regardless of what happens with Callum's investigation, my curiosity is piqued. The house gives me a weird feeling and I need to know why. As I flick through the images, I'm hit again with the same sensation. The feeling that I *know* the house, that I've seen it before. A buzz of familiarity. A pull.

I grab my phone again and type up another awkward message, this time to my sister.

> Hey, did we ever go to East Mill when we were kids?

> Sorry, what? I haven't heard from you in two months and now you're asking me about happy family holidays? Maybe you should ask Dad. Oh wait . . .

I cringe at her salty response. I deserved that. Dad's still mad at me about his Labor Day cookout, so I won't be asking him. I go back to staring at the house, even more miserable than before. It's as if it's calling to me, begging me to go there, and I find that disturbing, even though I deal with disturbing things every day. But if there's really a centuries-old ghost so powerful I can sense it through photos,

I have to check it out and send that spirit on its way. Isn't that what I was put on this earth to do? To move the dead along. What other reason could there be for this nightmare of a 'gift'?

I scribble a few notes in my journal, then slam my laptop closed and slouch against the cushions. I'll give Callum another hour and then I'll call him. Maybe. No, I'll definitely call him. Probably. I huff, pick up the soggy peas and scuff mournfully across my small living room and into my kitchen.

You're a coward, Holly Daniels, I tell myself as I toss the peas back into the freezer. *And you're going to die alone and be eaten by rats.*

I take a half-finished Meat Lover's pizza out of the fridge and give it a quick sniff, shove it into the microwave and drop heavily onto a kitchen chair. That's when I hear the ding. I rush to the living room, swearing loudly as I stub my toe on the ottoman, hopping the rest of the way to the coffee table. I grab my phone and instantly fumble it, juggling it midair. When it's finally clasped safely in my hand, I stand perfectly still, squeeze my eyes shut, and take a deep breath. Then I check the screen. My heart skips a beat.

> Hi Holly. Of course the invitation's still open. Give me a call and we can talk details.

I read his message three times, then hover my finger nervously over his name. *He told you to call him.* I put the phone down. *You're just talking details.* I snatch it back up again. *You face ghosts, you can do this.* With a determined breath, I finally press call. Callum answers before I even hear it ring.

'Holly, I didn't mean you had to call straight away.'

'Oh.' *Oh shit.* 'Sorry, I'll—'

'It's okay,' he says through a laugh. 'We can sort it out now.'

'Actually, before we do that, I just wanted to say that I do respect the work you do, and I even think some of your gadgets are . . . you know . . . um . . . cool.' I chew a nail as I wait for his response.

He takes a beat, then chuckles quietly. 'What do you say we start today again? You're just lucky I'm such a pushover, Daniels.'

The way he says my name makes my stomach attempt an Olympic-level somersault. 'So, East Mill. What's the plan?' I say excessively cheerily. He huffs out another quiet laugh and I cringe at how obvious and awkward I am.

'I was thinking about heading out there tomorrow,' he says. 'I'll probably stay out there a few days.'

A few days? I thought he was kidding about the spooky getaway. My stomach continues its gymnastic routine. 'Oh, um. Yes. But no. I mean.' *Breathe, for god's sake.* 'I can't do tomorrow. I have a job booked.'

'Then how's Sunday?'

'I can do Sunday. Should we take my car? I'm assuming you still have that old junker of a truck.'

'Are you intent on offending me today? I'll have you know that truck's a classic. But it's also the most uncomfortable car in history. So yes, let's take yours. Besides, I do love to be chauffeured.'

The microwave suddenly announces that my pizza is ready with a loud *bing*.

'What's for dinner?' he asks.

'Pizza. Meat Lover's.'

'Meat lover, huh?'

The innuendo drips off my phone like the grease from my pizza.

'Oh my god. Was that your attempt at a sex joke? To think a minute ago I was feeling bad for you. Send me your address. I'll text you Sunday morning when I'm on my way over. Jesus.'

He laughs. 'See you Sunday, Holly.'

CHAPTER FOUR

My focus keeps slipping, and now there's a ghost harassing me on the subway.

This is the second time today that a spirit has wormed its way through my protections. The first was at the bodega this morning. Mrs Hernández was sitting in the corner of the store reading her newspaper and ignoring everything else, including her customers and her husband, just like she did when she was alive. I asked Mr Hernández how he was coping – his wife died only a few months ago; there are still tributes to her behind the counter. He said he's doing okay – that he feels as if his Katalina is still there with him, and that's comforting. So I left the ghost of Katalina alone, making a note to check in with Mr Hernández again, in case that comforting feeling turns into something less pleasant.

Now there's a dead businessman staring down at me, his waxy skin shimmering and his red tie askew.

He'd been holding onto a grab handle like it was a normal workday, standing near a woman who kept shifting uncomfortably, as if she knew something was there and it was making her skin crawl. His wife maybe, or a work colleague, or perhaps just a woman he always shared a subway ride with. Then his head snapped around and his cold, dead eyes locked onto mine and *whoosh* – he was right in front of me.

I blame Callum for this. I haven't been able concentrate since I saw him yesterday. I still can't believe I agreed to work with him again. I'm filled with a mix of apprehension and a disturbing level of excitement and it's throwing me off my game. This spirit would normally be safe from me, because unless I open my mind to them, they remain locked out. But to keep them locked out, I need *focus*, which apparently, I don't have, so this spirit is about to have a very bad day. He can blame Callum too.

The woman sitting beside me rubs her arms, feeling the chill of the dead hovering over us. The ghost opens his mouth, his jaws stretching unnaturally wide, and I wince, preparing myself for what comes next – a screech so shrill I put my fingers in my ears. Why do they always have to yell at me? Luckily, on the New York subway no one looks at you twice if you pull out a rosary and start muttering Latin. A few moments later the spirit fizzles away with an anti-climactic 'pop'.

I get off at Christopher Street, ducking around a woman who must have died in the eighties if those massive shoulder pads are anything to go by, thinking *focus, focus, focus,* as I head to the Trattoria where I'm meeting my client. We can't meet at her house because she won't go anywhere near the place.

'Haven't you ever seen *A Tale of Two Sisters*?' she'd asked me.

'Is that a horror movie?'

'A Korean horror movie. We know how to make horror movies.'

'I don't watch many horror movies.' Why would I, when half the time I'm walking around in one?

I wave to Maria as I enter the restaurant, a trail of fallen leaves blowing in behind me. She's at a table with two glasses of red wine.

'Thank you for squeezing me in on your weekend,' she says. 'I know I should have done this straight away, but every time I thought about it, I freaked out. I'm not usually one for hiding my head in the sand, but it's a lot, you know?' I nod. I do know. She takes a sip of wine. 'I mean, there's a ghost in my house,' she whispers. 'I'm nervous just being this close.' Her house is around the corner. 'Do you need a drink before you go in? I got you one.' She gives me a very stressed smile.

'No, but thank you.'

She hands me her keys. 'Will you be okay?'

'I'll be fine. But if I'm not back in an hour, call the police, just in case.' Maria's eyes saucer.

The house on Washington Street was built at the end of the nineteenth century. It was once a hospice run by the Sisters of Camillus de Lellis, until the building was sold off by the church. Maria lived there happily for three years before there was even a hint that something wasn't right. It started with cold spots, which she excused as bad heating, then bumps and creaks she attributed to the old building moving.

But then objects started to shift around. A cup magically moved from the coffee table to the kitchen counter, a bathrobe hung behind the door when she was sure she'd left it on the bed. When she began catching a dark shape in the corner of her vision, she called me in. As soon as I stepped into the house I sensed it. I didn't need to see the presence to know it was there. When I told Maria, she nodded once, picked up her handbag and walked straight out. That was nearly two weeks ago.

The spirit's energy hits me as soon as I unlock the door, along with a heavy, musty scent that I don't think is due to the house being closed up. I climb the two flights of stairs to the open plan living space and kitchen. I can sense the spirit, feel its energy, but it's not in this room. I head up to the next floor, where the TV room and master bedroom are, but they're both empty too. I grumble impatiently; of course this thing would make me walk up four flights of stairs. The temperature drops a few degrees as I climb to the top floor, and that's where I find the spirit. It's in one of the bedrooms, kneeling beside the bed, hands clasped in prayer. I blink, then blink again. It's a nun. She must have lived in the house when it was the hospice. But why wouldn't a nun move on? Nuns believe in heaven; you'd think they'd be excited to get there. While I'm trying to make sense of what I'm seeing, the nun turns and looks at me. She's an old woman, her waxen skin heavily wrinkled. I pull out my rosary.

The spirit's attention turns to the string of onyx beads clasped in my fist, then she shows me her hands. She's holding a rosary too. Is this ghost trying to bond with me?

No that can't be . . . Whatever. I have a job to do. This old lady is dead, and Maria doesn't want to share her house with the dead.

The nun's jaws open wide, her lips stretching across yellowing teeth. She releases a ghastly wail that rings in my ears. The same musty stench I noticed downstairs overpowers the room. I cough and gag. Then she's moving towards me and she's fast, her rosary across her open palm, her lifeless eyes locked on me, her long white habit billowing. I back away with an embarrassing squeak, stumbling over a rug and banging into the wall, thumping my funny bone in the process.

'Fuck!' I cry out.

The spirit stills, the dark voids of her eyes widening. She scowls at me. Then she hauls back and wails again.

I do a classic double take. Did this ghost just tell me off for swearing? No. No, that's impossible. The sprits never engage with me except to bellow. I'm just all over the place today.

I concentrate my energy on the apparition, using my mind to hold her at a distance, then take a quick breath and start to whisper the Latin words.

Ego te spiritum expello. I drive you out spirit. Tuum tempus hic fit. Your time here is done. Virtus mea te ex hoc plano percutit. My power strikes you from this plane. Dominium habeo. I have dominion. Desine esse. Absum. Cease to exist. Be gone.

There's a soft glow that starts in the spirit's chest, a radiant light that slowly spreads, rising out of her and glinting off the silver crucifix that hangs from her neck. Then, bit by bit, her body dissipates until only her face hovers in midair. We stare at each other, the nun's disembodied floating head and me. That's when she smiles, and then she's gone.

'I'll have that wine now,' I say to Maria as I drop into a chair. That had to be the weirdest exorcism I've ever performed.

Maria pushes a full glass of red towards me and I swallow half of it in one gulp.

'What happened?' she asks. 'Did you do it?'

'Did you know a nun?'

'Yes, Sister Genevieve. She worked at the hospice for years, and I think she missed the place. She'd catch the Staten Island ferry over once a week and I'd make her tea. She died four months ago. Oh no! Don't tell me it was her?'

'I think it might have been.'

'Oh, I would have let Sister G stay.'

Too late now. 'I think the spirit was happy to move on,' I say. 'She . . . smiled.'

'I should probably have guessed it was her. You know the moving cup and bathrobe? She always straightened up for me when she visited.'

Oh great. It was a kindly tidying nun. Still, it never goes well when a ghost lingers too long. The living have their time, and the dead need to move on when that time is done. Sister G's time was done four months ago.

'Do you think she's in heaven now?' Maria asks.

'Absolutely,' I say. I finish off my wine with another large gulp. 'I'll send through my final invoice when I get home.' I hand her the keys thinking, *I'm adding a weekend surcharge for that job!* When she looks reluctant to let me leave, I add, 'And I checked the whole house before I left. You have nothing to worry about, it's definitely clean.'

I can't hold back my grin. This house is clean.

CHAPTER FIVE

I'm standing in front of the old house, its hulking silhouette cloaking me in its shadow. The air has a bitter chill, and I wrap my arms around myself and shiver. Stepping cautiously onto the uneven stone path, I make my way past the dried-up flower beds, stopping at the steps that lead up to a wide porch. I consider the shuttered windows, peeling paint and worn boards. The house appears to be empty – as dead as the plants that surround it. But I can sense life behind its walls. Energy pulses through every crack. Pain seeps through every fissure. Old pain. A torrent of pain.

A wave of agony slams against me, sucking the breath from my lungs. I lurch backward, gasping as I stumble into a man – tall and striking, his hair glistening like cords of silver and his skin aglow with the moonlight.

'Don't listen to what they tell you, Holly,' the man says. 'The witches all lie.'

I shrink away from him. There's something terrifying in his pale, golden eyes.

'W-who are you?' I ask. 'What witches?'

A hand rests softly on my shoulder, and I spin around to find Callum smiling down at me.

'Don't be scared, Holly,' he whispers. 'No matter what happens, you can trust me.'

I stare at the buzzer to Callum's apartment. My insides vibrate with anxious energy. I had another dream last night. This time it was at the Western house. Which makes sense, given I was thinking about it before I went to sleep. It also makes sense that dream-Callum would ask me to trust him, because I don't know if I can or ever will again. But what was that horrible pain that ripped through me, and who was that man? I shudder at the memory of his strange-coloured eyes and how scared of him I was, as if an old fear was rising inside me. Everything was so clear; more like a vision than a dream, just like the dream of the murdered girl in the windowless room a few nights back. Except I don't have visions, I've never had a vision, I'm not that kind of psychic, not in the same way my grandmother was. Still, I can't stop feeling as if there's more to it.

I flick out my hands to shake off my nerves, then press the buzzer, chewing on my thumbnail as I wait for Callum to answer. The intercom comes to life with a beep.

'Yep?' His voice crackles.

I yell into the speaker, 'It's me. Um. It's Holly.'

'Come on up.' The door buzzes beside me.

When the elevator slides open on Callum's floor, he's waiting for me in the hallway. His hair is wet like he's just jumped out of the shower, and his hands are shoved casually into his pockets as he lounges against his doorframe, smiling easily. My gaze trails his body before I can stop it. Black T-shirt snug on his arms, black jeans low on his hips, tattoos popping against his skin. My heart is suddenly doing all sorts of manoeuvres it shouldn't. Damn heart. Damn him.

'Welcome.' He says it with a sweep of his arm.

I nod and slip past him, ignoring the smell of soap and something else that makes me want to stop and take a deep whiff of his skin. I've got to get it together. This is a job, and I'm determined to focus on only that today. None of the other *us* stuff. That's done with. It's ancient history. Then I step into his apartment, and I have to stop from awkwardly gasping, 'Wow!'

The room is huge, and surprisingly elegant, with two overstuffed couches and floor-to-ceiling bookshelves with books piled in every direction, propped up by an assortment of curiosities. An eclectic art collection adorns the walls, modern splashes of colour, paintings from other cultures and even some religious iconography.

'This is . . . very . . . nice.' I struggle not to sound shocked.

'What were you expecting? That I lived like some frat boy sleeping on a futon surrounded by empty pizza boxes and beer bottles?'

'No! I don't know what I was expecting, but not that. Besides, you're way too old to live like a frat boy.'

His eyebrows shoot up. 'How old do you think I am exactly?'

'I don't know, I haven't actually thought about it. Same age as me? I turned twenty-eight in January.' I'd celebrated on my own with egg rolls and the latest season of *Outlander*.

'Damn,' he says. 'When did I start looking my age? Close. I'm thirty. Do you want a coffee?' He pads across the room in his bare feet, his back flexing beneath his T-shirt. 'And take off your ruby slippers, please,' he calls over his shoulder. 'The rug is over four hundred years old.'

I untie my cherry-red Docs, slip them off, then tiptoe across the rug. I'm standing in front of his bookshelf when he returns with two coffee mugs featuring his show's logo on the front in spooky green lettering: *The Debunker*.

'Is that a monkey paw?' I point to an ugly black thing that looks as if it was dismembered from a chimp.

He places the mugs on the coffee table. 'Yep,' he says, moving in to stand beside me. I reach up to touch it. 'Don't touch it! It's cursed.'

I quickly pull my hand away. 'Really?'

'No. I think the guy I bought it from 3D printed it. But he spun a good story, and I thought it looked cool.' I frown up at him and he laughs.

'And what about that?' I point to an unusual ceramic jar.

'That is an antique spirit jar. My aunt's in there.'

'You have your aunt on the shelf?'

'No.' He laughs again. 'I scattered her in Central Park. Were you always this gullible?'

I bite my tongue, so as not to say, *'Apparently. I fell for you didn't I?'*

'That ouija board is interesting though,' he says. He pulls it off the shelf to show me. 'It was used by a famous spiritualist who conducted seances in the mid-1800s. Madam Morana.'

'You know ouija boards are just toys. They don't work.'

He carefully puts the board back with a drawn-out sigh. 'Let's sit down, the coffee's getting cold.'

I spot a series of frames balanced on the very top of the bookshelf as I plop onto the couch. 'Are those degrees up there?' I ask.

'Yep.'

'And they're *all* yours?'

'Yep,' he says again and hands me my mug. 'This might be a bit strong. I use an old-style percolator I picked up in Italy.'

I take a sip. It is strong, and exactly what I need. 'What did you study?' I ask. 'I don't think we ever discussed it.'

'No, we never got around to that.'

He flicks me a side-eye and I quickly glance away. Not going there today.

'Let's see,' he says, 'European and Mediterranean cultures in classical civilisations – I did *not* want to do that one, but my aunt insisted. It turned about to be interesting, though, especially the mythology. Medieval and modern languages – so far not very helpful, except for the Latin. Theology and religion – obviously handy, especially the doctrinal mythology. I really love that stuff. Behavioural science – purely for the parapsychology element of the degree. And that last one is a Diploma in Psychic Phenomena and Modern Demonology from the Paranormal Studies Center here in New York.'

'No way. You're teasing me again, right?'

'Gee Holly, way to make a guy feel good. I skipped ahead a couple of years in high school, which meant I got the jump on college. That made things easier.'

'It made things easier to get . . .' I quickly count them. '*Four* degrees?'

'And a diploma. It's really no biggie,' he says. 'I never did a doctorate or anything. Not even a masters.' He waves his hand towards the certificates. 'They're just your average degrees.'

I think about my one measly 'average' degree in anthropology and religion which I barely passed.

'And you collected all of this?' I gesture at the various pieces of art in the room, beginning to understand just how little I know about Callum.

He shifts on the couch and our shoulders touch. He's solid and warm, and just that brush of him sends a jolt through me. I wiggle away up the cushions a little.

'Some of it I picked up while travelling. The religious pieces are from a deconsecrated church on the Lower East Side that was having a yard sale. The rest I inherited. My mom and dad died when I was a kid. I think I told you that.'

I nod. He did. He shared that with me one night over greasy burgers and fries.

'Some of the art belonged to them,' he says. 'And some to my aunt.' He shrugs. 'The rug I bought on a trip to Turkey. It really is over four hundred years old, so please don't spill anything on it.'

'I . . . wow . . . I didn't know. I mean, I remember you mentioning your parents. But how did I not—'

'You never asked.' He arches a brow.

I glance away again, and studiously examine the logo on my mug.

'The truth is,' he says, 'I didn't get much choice on the education thing. My aunt Aideen took me in after my parents died, and she was pretty firm on me studying. I think she spotted my potential straight away, and I didn't want to disappoint her. She was also interested in a lot of eclectic stuff. That's where my interest comes from. I spent my childhood learning about Irish legends, various religious mythologies and all sorts of paranormal creatures. She had me memorising incantations when I was way too young for that kind of thing. Not that I've ever used them. I don't have those kind of skills. But I did have the most bizarre reading list of any kid I knew.' He chuckles. 'I loved it though, and it just clicked. It seems I'm . . . naturally attracted to the spooky.' He quirks a brow.

'Wow. Callum, I had no idea you—'

'Were so smart?'

'No! I was talking about the other stuff. You're obviously smart.'

He shrugs. 'I don't know, I do tend to hide that part of me. When you're a kid, being into weird stuff *and* being smarter than anyone else is not a great combo. It's easier to pretend that's not who you are, so you fit in, you know? Turns out that's a hard mindset to drop.'

I nod. I know *exactly* what he means. But I'm shocked to learn he ever felt like that.

'Anyway,' he says, slapping his thighs and standing, 'we've got ghosts to bust.'

'Do you need to call Mr Rosing to let him know what's happening?' I ask as I go to grab my boots.

'Already have.'

'You've confirmed with him that I'm on board?'

'Yep. Did that after our breakfast the other day.'

I look up from my laces. 'You mean the morning we argued?'

'Mm-hmm. I was betting your curiosity would get the better of you, and the money of course.'

'That was . . . presumptuous.'

'Or maybe I'm psychic too?' His lips quirk.

'Hilarious. Did he . . . okay the money you asked for?' I've been thinking I could call Maggie and surprise her. Or maybe even go and see her. Are giant novelty cheques really a thing?

'Without hesitation,' he says. 'Which makes me think I should have asked for more. We can add some holy water expenses or something.' He slings a duffle bag over his shoulder. 'I don't suppose I need my "useless gadgets" if I have you.'

I wince. 'Probably not. But bring them anyway.'

'In case you disappear on me again?'

Is this how it's going to be? 'No,' I answer tersely. 'Because this is your job, so you should bring your tools.'

Our eyes lock. My heart pounds.

Then Callum relaxes.

'Okay, Daniels. What do you say, are you ready to do this?' He grins now.

I'm not sure if the sudden thrill that surges through me is excitement or nerves. I never do anything spontaneous, and here I am about to go out of town with Callum Jefferies.

The man I had no intention of speaking to ever again. On a spooky getaway to a haunted house. I hunt ghosts for a living, and this is still probably the scariest thing I've ever done.

CHAPTER SIX

The Western house is set back from the road, concealed behind its formidable iron gate and an array of 'Keep Out' and 'No Trespassing' signs. From the car, I can just see the weathered grey shingled rooftop, and the tips of upper windows secured behind shutters. On a rise in the distance, an imposing oak tree looms, its leaves a mix of yellows and golds, fluttering gently in the crisp sea breeze.

The hairs on the back of my neck prickle as I notice the stone path winding its way up to the gate. The exact path I walked in my dream.

'Now *that* looks like a haunted house,' Callum says. 'The widow's walk, for a start. Creepy.' He points to the small platform bound by a railing on the roof of the house and fake-shudders.

'Aww. Are you scared?' I tease.

'Are you kidding? I live for this shit. I mean, everyone wanted to get their hands on this one and I got it. I can't wait until we can get in there and check the place out.'

I shake my head. We couldn't be more different in our feelings about ghosts.

'The "keep out" signs wouldn't be much of a deterrent,' he says, 'and there's no mention of a security company.' He peers through the window at the gate. 'It doesn't look like they've got cameras either. We should check that with Rosing.'

'Imagine growing up in a place like that,' I say. 'It's huge.'

'My aunt's place was pretty big,' Callum says, still gazing out the window.

'Didn't you grow up in the city?'

He turns to face me. 'Yeah. It was one of those old Upper West Side houses that take up a whole corner. I have no idea where she got her money. I can't imagine it was family cash – me and my folks lived in a tiny apartment from what I remember. I don't think they had any money, at least none that came my way.'

'Your aunt never discussed that with you?'

'Nope, but to be honest, I never really asked. She got prickly about family stuff. It was sort of off limits. It was like it hurt too much for her to talk about my mom. But also I always got the feeling something went on that she didn't want to relive.' He shrugs, then shuffles around in his seat, his knees hitting the gear stick. 'You lost your mom too, didn't you?'

I nod. 'Breast cancer, when I was eleven. I still miss her.'

'Fucking cancer, huh? Aideen as well. Shitty disease. Though I'm glad you got at least a little time with your mom.' He looks away again. 'After Aideen died, I sold the house and took off travelling. There was quite a bit of hype when it went on the market, a big house like that. In the end a developer bought it. Turned it into three apartments, one on each floor.'

He sighs, and in it I hear sadness and regret. I watch him as he studies the house. We have more in common than just our work. We both understand loss and the chasm it leaves in your life. Except I still have a sister and a father, which is more than Callum has. I have a family that I rarely see – I need to fix that. I'm going to fix it.

'So, you're smart *and* rich,' I say. 'My opinion of you is improving with every conversation.' It's a feeble attempt to lighten the mood, but it works, and he laughs.

'Glad you're finally realising I'm a catch.'

His gaze meets mine, deep and shimmering. My skin tingles as heat creeps up my neck and into my cheeks.

'Right,' he says, 'let's go check into Maddison House. That's the B&B I booked for us – it's a converted historic home. Then we can call on Rosing and see if we can get the key to that.' He points to the gate. 'What do you say we come back and have a poke around the grounds? You up for a little adventure?'

'Callum, you promised.'

'C'mon, I know you're as curious as I am.' He leans forward. 'We'll just have a look around. See if you feel anything.'

'We do *not* go inside. Not until we know what we're dealing with.'

He crosses his heart. 'We do not go inside.'

'Fine.' But as I start the car and pull away, the prickle at the back of my neck becomes a creeping dread.

*

My overnight bag is still clutched in my hand as I take in my room. *What. The. Hell.* A vase of pink roses sits on a small white-and-gold table beside the window, and a pale-gold velvet buttoned headboard towers over a fat bed swathed in floral covers. I drop my bag onto the pink-and-white striped French-style couch with a shake of my head. It looks like shabby chic threw up in here.

I unpack a few things, then head next door to Callum's room. It's identical to mine, only in shades of a ghastly mint green.

'It's all a bit . . .' I struggle to find the right word.

'It's not that bad,' he says, 'is it?' He glances around. 'Though I promise I didn't know it was going to be quite so . . . would you call this romantic?'

'Me? Absolutely not.'

'Me neither, then.' He flicks me a lopsided smile. 'This was the only place available at short notice that was close to the house and included breakfast, just for you.' He unzips his duffle and pulls out his toiletry bag. 'Hey, I meant to ask how your job went last night.'

'Easy. Quick. A little weird. The spirit was a nun.'

Callum's brows lift. 'An evil nun?' He briefly disappears into the bathroom.

'Not according to my client,' I call after him. 'She says this nun liked to clean.'

'But you still got rid of her?' he asks as he comes back into the room.

'Of course I did, my client was terrified. She wouldn't even step foot in her house.'

'Do you think the nun went to heaven?'

'I don't know where she went. Do you believe in heaven and all that white light stuff?'

'I mean, it would be nice, right? Especially for our folks. But I don't know. There have been a lot of studies into near-death phenomena, and there are a lot of commonalities in the stories of those who have gone through a near-death experience. The white light stuff being one of them.'

'Yeah, but everyone knows about that, so—'

'What about the people who can describe in detail everyone and everything that happened in the room while they were unconscious? I know you don't care but I think it would be interesting to understand where the spirits you send off end up, don't you?'

Frustration huffs out of me. 'What I understand is that the people who call me in are being terrorised by those things. They're dead. They don't belong here anymore. Now, can we go eat? I'm hungry.'

'More like hangry,' he mutters as he follows me out the door.

East Mill Village is already decked out for Halloween. Jack-O-Lanterns leer from every store window, cobwebs coat the normally stylish shrubs, and pumpkins of every hue nestle amongst the dazzling oranges and yellows of the fall flower beds. The leaves on the maples that line the street have turned a pale gold, and paper bats flutter from their branches, their wings rustling in the breeze. Tourists buzz from store to store in hope of spotting a vacationing celebrity, before visiting some of the historic buildings that dot the small town, or stopping to dine at the plentiful restaurants that hug its foreshore.

We find a park near the harbour, surrounded by the gentle *ting, ting, ting* of yacht rigging tapping against steel masts, and make our way to a small cafe squeezed between a bookstore with a smoking cauldron out front and a store with a window full of colourful Halloween-themed kites.

'I've never got Halloween.' I'm staring at the skeleton propped up in a corner of the cafe with a coffee mug strapped to its bony hand. 'Why celebrate ghosts? It's weird.' Callum looks up from his food. 'I'm guessing you probably love it.'

He shrugs. 'Sure, it's fun. Though it doesn't have much to do with the origins of the tradition anymore, it's more about decorations and candy now. It was originally a Celtic celebration giving thanks for the summer harvest before the winter set in. Bonfires were lit and costumes worn to ward off evil spirits, because the Celts believed that the veil between the living and dead was thinnest on that day.'

'It's always thin, in my experience,' I say.

He *mm-hmms*.

'I never really celebrated Halloween as a kid,' Callum goes on, 'my aunt was not a fan. I've been to a few parties since then though. My buddy had one last year. We went as the twins from *The Shining*.'

'The little girls in the blue dresses?'

'Yup.' He shoves a fry in his mouth. He must be able to tell I'm mentally trying to pull that image together, because then he chuckles.

'So . . . um . . .' I slap my notes on the table and slide them towards him. 'The Western family. I didn't find anything much online outside of what we've already discussed. Nothing about the haunting that could be considered one hundred per cent genuine. There seems to be more speculation than fact. So, if we don't get the story from the source, we'll be on our own and starting from scratch, or going on rumours, which isn't good enough.'

'Hopefully the historical society can help out,' Callum says. 'I wonder why the family keeps the haunting so under wraps?'

'Not everyone loves a ghost like you do.' He shrugs and takes a bite of his burger. I shuffle through my notes. 'Do we have any idea how long the disturbances have been occurring? You mentioned sightings of a spirit thought to be Margaret Western, Edward Western's great-great-grandmother, right?' He nods. 'Are these recent or historic sightings? What about the young woman seen on the grounds?' I think of my dream, and the girl in the bonnet and the men with wide-brimmed black hats. 'The current house may have been built in 1872, but if there's been a house on that land since the mid-1600s we could be talking about the spirit of one of the first settlers out here.'

'Oooh, don't tease me.' He grins. 'And this is why we're here, to find this stuff out. The only way to know for sure about the second spirit is to identify the young female. Hopefully we can get a clue from Western. She must have a connection to someone who lived in the house at some point. But my gut says the hauntings are nineteenth or twentieth century. The original house burnt down, so I don't think a spirit from that period would still be kicking around. Have you ever faced a ghost from another century?'

I shake my head. 'My jobs are almost always contemporary. Fresh ghosts. Usually within months of death. I have a theory that spirits get more and more pissed off the longer they stay past their use by date. Though some were probably just assholes to begin with.'

'There's been research into your angry spirit theory, whether the feeling of being displaced causes the spirit to lash out. Or if they have unfinished business that leaves them frustrated post-death. That's the main theory on why they can't let go. What's your experience?'

'I don't know what their business is, they don't tell me.' I pull my burger apart. 'Anyway, everyone has unfinished business, that doesn't mean we all linger after death scaring the people we supposedly love.' I peel a pickle off the bun, and Callum grabs it, dropping it into his mouth. 'Ew. I can't believe you like pickles.'

'I can't believe you don't.' A soft smile curves his lips. 'Hey, do you remember how much Celeste loved pickles?'

'Oh my god. Those huge ones that come on the side with a sandwich.'

'And fried pickles. She even liked fried pickles.'

I screw up my nose. 'She made those for me one time when I had dinner with her and Max.'

'Do you . . . ever hear from Max?'

'No.' I put my burger back together and take a large bite. 'Me neither . . .'

A shared sadness throbs between us.

I take a deep breath and say, 'Anyway,' quickly moving us along. 'Did you know that during the mid-seventeenth century there were witch trials here? I'd always thought that only happened in Salem.'

'The first witch trials in North America took place right here in East Mill,' he says, nodding. 'Only the town doesn't celebrate or even recognise it the way Salem does, so most people don't know.'

'The thing that really bothers me about all of this is how little information there is about Edward Western, apart from the fact that he exists and now owns the house.'

Callum leans forward, his knees tapping mine. 'I love a good mystery, don't you?'

I shift my knees to the side and wiggle back in my chair. 'No, not really. We should get going. Call your Rosing guy.'

Albert Rosing is a man in his mid-fifties, of average height, average build, average appearance and with very little hair. He wears a nondescript grey sweater and neatly pressed beige pants. I don't think I've ever seen a blander man.

He peers through the screen door, which he keeps conspicuously closed.

'Unfortunately,' he says, 'I can no longer join you at the property tomorrow. I have some business to attend to.'

'Not a problem,' Callum says. 'Are you happy for us to go there on our own?'

'As long as I have your guarantee that you will stay on the grounds and won't enter the house until I can be there too. Mr Western was quite firm on that.'

'You have my guarantee. But if we could sit down with you at some stage after that?'

Mr Rosing nods. 'That should be fine. I'll email through the information you requested, to start with. If there's anything else you need, let me know.'

'There is one thing. Do you have any security we should know about? Cameras or patrols? CCTV can be useful for catching paranormal activity, but we don't want to set off any alarms and have security guards descend on us.'

His eyes fill with suspicion. 'No security staff. And our cameras were vandalised. I'm yet to replace them.'

'And what about Mr Western?' I ask, stepping from the shadows and into the glare of the porch light. 'When can we meet with him?'

'Ah, you must be Ms Daniels.' Mr Rosing finally opens the door and reaches out his hand for me to shake. It's like a wet fish. 'Thank you for agreeing to assist us. I will confirm Mr Western's schedule with you in the next day or so. I'm just finalising his calendar.'

'And if we do find a spirit at the house,' I say. 'Would you like me to clear it? I'm not sure if you're aware that I can do that.'

'Mr Jefferies told me of your specific talents. But we can discuss next steps once you've experienced the house.'

I nod, and he smiles with thin, tight lips. It instantly gives me the creeps.

'I'll go get the gate key,' he says and closes the screen door again, disappearing inside.

'Strange dude,' Callum whispers.

'Very. I get a weird vibe from him.'

'One of your "I'm not that kind of psychic" weird vibes?'

'Ha ha. And no, just your normal "That guy's creepy" weird vibe.' I hiss, 'Shh,' as I spy Mr Rosing approaching.

'You don't intend to visit the property tonight, do you?' Mr Rosing says, withholding the key. 'It's not a place to be at night.'

Callum shakes his head. 'Nope, we'll wait till tomorrow.'

'We'll probably have to go there at night at some point, Mr Rosing,' I say. 'Spirits are often more active at night.'

'We will make preparations for that event,' Mr Rosing says as he hands Callum the key.

'Have *you* been inside the place?' Callum asks slipping the key into his pocket.

'No, I have not. I maintain the grounds, organise maintenance, and do whatever else Mr Western requests of me, but he has never asked me to go inside the house. That's for braver people, like you and Ms Daniels, and I suppose the previous investigators.' Mr Rosing freezes with a sharp gasp, the colour draining from his already pasty face.

Callum and I glance at each other.

'What previous investigators?' Callum asks. 'I understood I was the first investigator out here.'

Mr Rosing shuffles. 'Oh . . . ah . . . Mr Western's attorney organised some others to investigate some time ago, but the job was never completed.'

Callum nods slowly. 'Do you have their names?'

'We probably know them,' I say. 'There aren't a lot of us doing this kind of work.'

'I wasn't involved in their employment,' Mr Rosing says. 'But I'll see if I can find their details for you.'

We walk back down the quiet street towards my car.

'Why did you lie to him about going to the house tonight?' I ask Callum.

'It sounded like he wasn't going to hand over the key if I told him the truth. The bigger question is, why didn't he let me know about the other paranormal team?'

'I don't think he meant to tell us that.'

'I don't think he did either.'

'And I can't believe he wouldn't know the names of the other investigators,' I say. 'He looks too organised not to have that information.' Callum grunts in agreement. 'I don't feel good about any of this, Callum. I think we should do what we told him we would, and go to the house tomorrow.'

'It's not like you to be skittish about ghosts.'

'I'm not being skittish. I just think it would be smarter if our first visit was in the daylight. You heard what Mr Rosing said, it's not a place to be at night.'

'And I heard what you said. There's more ghost activity at night.'

'Fine,' I say impatiently, 'but we stay in the garden. I put out my feelers, and you don't do anything stupid.'

'I can't guarantee that last part.'

'Yeah, I thought that would be too much to ask.'

CHAPTER SEVEN

The night is still, the moon tucked behind a bank of ominously heavy clouds. A row of streetlamps is the only light in the smothering darkness, their soft glow pooling in small circles along the lane outside the Western house. Fall leaves crunch under our boots as Callum unlocks the formidable iron gate and gives it a push. It swings back, surprisingly silent.

'I was at least expecting a creak,' I say.

He glances back over his shoulder. 'You've seen too many horror movies.'

'No, I've *lived* too many horror movies.'

He pulls an electromagnetic field meter from his jacket pocket and studies it. Red and green lights flicker up and down the screen. He looks towards the lane. 'We might be too close to the streetlights to get an accurate EMF reading. Maybe nearer the house.' He squints down at me. 'Don't look at me like that.'

'I'm not looking at you like anything.'

'This stuff works.'

'I never it said it didn't.'

His brows lift.

'Okay, I might have said that, but I also said I didn't mean it.'

I step onto the familiar cobblestone path, the ground uneven beneath my boots, and we slowly make our way towards the shadowy house, the beams from our flashlights bouncing in front of us.

'Stay close,' Callum whispers.

'I'm not some damsel in distress, Callum.' I grab the back of his jacket. 'And this is far enough.'

He passes the beam from his flashlight across the front of the old house, revealing a deep porch. The light glints on the windows beyond it, their shutters surprisingly folded back. The hair on the nape of my neck stands on end as the entirety of the house comes into view, hulking in the shadows, exactly as it did in my dream. I shudder and glance around, half expecting to see the strange man with the frightening eyes standing behind me.

'Are you alright?' Callum asks.

'We should have waited until morning.'

'But you just had to come out here,' he says. 'I was all for going back to the hotel, but—'

I thump him on the arm.

He grins, white teeth and pale skin glowing in the moonlight.

'Let's have a quick scout around,' he says, 'then we can head back.' He lifts his EMF meter and shakes his head. 'I'm not getting anything. Are you getting anything? See any nineteenth-century ghosts wandering about?'

'Give me a minute,' I say.

I draw a deep breath and still my thoughts, blocking out everything around me. Sounds. Emotions. Callum. I allow my mind's eye to drift along the path and up the stairs that rise to the porch. I stop my mental gaze at the impressive front doors, bracing for the same anguished sensation that hit me in my dream, or the same odd feeling that came over me when I first looked at the photos in my office. But there's nothing, and that's strange, because old houses should not be silent.

'It's . . . quiet,' I say.

'That's weird, right? You should be picking up some kind of energy with a house this old. Maybe the spirits are playing possum.'

'Spirits can't play possum with me. If something was here, I'd sense it, and then I'd see it, and then I'd—' A wave of nausea crashes over me, rushing up my throat. 'Oh god.' I throw my hand to my mouth to stop from vomiting.

'What? What's happening?'

I fold over and clutch at Callum's leg. 'Something . . . awful. I'm going to be sick.'

'Shit. Okay.' He makes tiny circles on my back with his palm as he helps me straighten up. 'Let's get you to the car.'

But as we start back towards the gate, Callum stops, turns around and passes the beam from his flashlight across the front of the house again.

'What are you doing?' I grimace as I swallow back hot bile.

His hand drops from my arm. 'I thought I heard a voice, or . . .' He takes a step away from me. 'Holly, do you see that?'

'What?' I peer into the darkness. 'What am I looking at?'

Callum's gaze is fixed on the shadowy building. 'There,' he says, pointing. 'At the window.'

I straighten up and aim my flashlight at the house, squinting towards the feeble beam of light. 'There's nothing there.' I tug at Callum's jacket. 'We need to go.'

'She's right there.' He points frantically. 'A woman. Why can't you see her?' His feet shuffle forward.

'What are you doing?' I grab his hand, but he jerks it free of my fingers and starts to sprint across the yard. 'Callum, no!' I lunge forward, trying to catch hold of him again, but he's too fast. He's already at the steps, climbing them two at a time, before I've even moved. He races across the porch toward the front door. 'Stop!' I call out, staggering after him. 'Don't go—'

An ear-splitting shatter fills the night. Shards of glass explode outward from one of the porch windows, raining down into the garden like tiny moonlit daggers. Callum pitches backwards, his body hitting the porch railing with such force he takes a chunk of it with him. He soars into the garden, arms flailing, then crashes to the ground with a horrific thud.

I freeze, not quite believing what I've just seen. Then I'm off, dashing towards him, landing heavily on my knees beside his inert body.

'Callum!' He breathes out a soft moan. I grab his hand and pull, grunting as I desperately try to hoist him off the ground.

Bile rises in my throat again, and with it a stabbing pain ripping through my gut. His fingers slip through mine as I crumple to the earth beside him. My head rolls towards the house. Pain pours from its walls, drowning me in a tidal wave of suffering. The same suffering I felt in my dream. The same wretched agony slamming into me again and again and again. I have to get up. I have to get us out of here. My muscles tremble as I push up on my knees.

'Callum.' I tap his cheek and he breathes out another moan. 'Get up!' I yell the words, but he still doesn't move. An image of Celeste's broken body flashes through my mind. *Nope. Nope.* This is different. This is his fault. I asked him to do one thing. Not be stupid. And what does he do? 'Get. Up,' I yell again. This time he flinches.

I try to yank him to his feet, but I can't, he's too heavy and the pain that keeps crashing into me is too great. I can't stand it anymore. I need it to end. So, I lift my face to the sky and scream out, 'Leave us alone!'

My nausea instantly stops. The pain vanishes. The house is silent again.

I crawl back to Callum and slip my hand under his head. 'Come on, Callum. I need you to help me here.'

His eyes finally flutter open. 'Holly?'

'Oh, thank god. Can you stand? We need to move and I can't lift you.' I push myself up, grab his hand again and tug, grunting as we somehow manage to get him to his feet.

He lets out a sharp hiss and puts his hand to his side. 'Am I bleeding?' He holds up his palm to show me. 'Holly, I'm bleeding.'

'We'll look at it in the car.'

We lumber awkwardly towards the gate, Callum's tall frame leaning heavily against me.

'What happened?' he asks.

We stumble out into the lane and the comforting glow of the streetlamps.

'You did something stupid.' I prop him against the car. 'We should call Mr Rosing and tell him what just happened.'

'Or we don't. We told him we weren't doing this, remember? I don't want to get us fired on our first night.'

'I remember *you* said we weren't doing this.' I ease him into the front seat. 'I'm pretty sure I had nothing to do with it.' Flicking on the interior light, I push aside his jacket and roll up the hem of his T-shirt to check his wound. 'I'm taking you to the hospital.'

'No hospital. Just take me back to my room, I can stitch myself up.'

'Oh, okay, Rambo. What with, dental floss?' I shake my head. 'There's a lot of blood. You need a doctor.'

'I said, *no hospital*,' he shouts.

I recoil. 'Don't you dare yell at me.'

'I'm sorry. Just, no hospital, okay? Too many questions and . . . I don't like them. The cut's not that bad. I've had worse. Get me to my room, I'll sort it from there.'

I run my hands through my hair, forgetting that they're sticky with his blood. I grab an old towel from the trunk. 'Here.' I press it to his side, and he yelps. 'Don't be a baby,' I say. 'Keep pressure on it, and if you bleed all over my car, you're cleaning it up. Give me the key so I can lock the gate.'

Callum's hand shakes as he digs the key from his pocket. 'Wait, where's my EMF?'

'Just buy a new one.'

'No, it's evidence, Holly. Rosing will find it. I've got to go get it.' He groans as he tries to push up.

'Stop. I'll go.' Before he has time to protest, I turn and dash back through the gate.

I scour the lawn with my flashlight, focusing hard to block out whatever attacked us. I won't allow it to lay me out again. It only gets to do that once. I spot the EMF near a piece of broken railing and quickly snatch it up. Then I look at the house, crouching in the shadows like a beast eyeing its prey. Whatever is in there is sneaky, and more powerful than anything I've ever faced. But that doesn't mean I can't face it.

I turn and sprint away, and as I reach the gate, I hear the voice.

Holly. Let us in.

The little bed and breakfast is deserted. Everyone is either out for dinner or has called it a night. The only person we see is a woman sitting in a lounge chair in the small reception area. She looks up with a smile that quickly drops.

'Is everything alright?' she asks.

I put my arm around Callum's waist and let him rest against me. 'Too much fun.' I roll my eyes.

I groan under his weight as we stumble up the hall.

'Jesus, you're heavy,' I say as we reach our rooms.

'I'm a big boy.' I think he tries to wink, but it looks more like a wince.

I shake my head at him. 'Where's your key?'

'Front pocket.'

'I'm not digging around in your pocket.'

He drops his arm from my shoulder and fumbles for his key, but his hand is trembling too violently to make contact with the lock.

I snatch the key from him, unlock the door, push it open with my foot and help him across the room, unceremoniously tossing him onto his bed.

'Gentle,' he says with a pained hiss.

'I'm not your nurse. If you refuse to go to the hospital, this is what you get. Now, wait here while I find something to clean you up.'

'Wait here? I was planning on going out for a burger and hitting the clubs.'

'Oh, for fuck's sake,' I whisper to myself.

I retreat to my room and lean against the wall with my eyes squeezed shut. My hands shake at my sides, my heart still racing. That could have turned out so much worse. So, so much worse. Another image of Celeste flashes behind my eyes. *Nope, nope, not going there.*

I shrug off my jacket and take a couple of quiet breaths in a failed attempt to calm down, then grab my bag and rummage through it, pulling out the first-aid kit I packed at the last moment. I had a feeling I would need it. I drop my bag back onto my bed, and that's when I notice the adjoining door. It's perfectly camouflaged, covered in the same hideously patterned wallpaper that adorns the walls. But there it is, a door linking my room with Callum's.

You have got to be kidding me.

I click the lock, close my hand around the brass handle concealed within a swirl of gold, and fling open the door.

Callum leaps about a foot off his bed.

'Was this your idea?' I ask.

'I would like to take credit for it, but no. I appreciate it, though.' He gives me a weak smile.

He looks terrible. He's pale, even paler than usual, and he's sweaty and slumped awkwardly on his bed.

'Take your shirt off,' I say.

'That's a bit forward, Holly.'

'Callum, can you take your shirt off or not?'

'I might need a hand.'

I eye him suspiciously, but as he struggles to remove his jacket, I can tell he's hurting.

'Hold on.' I help him slip his jacket off one arm, then the next as he hisses and grunts and groans. I need to get to the wound, but also want to check if he's broken a rib or three, and I can't see how we can get his T-shirt off without a lot of pain, so I ask, 'This isn't a favourite in your collection of black T-shirts, is it?'

He looks confused, his eyebrows bunching.

I pull a pair of scissors from my first-aid kit and begin to cut his T-shirt away.

'Kinky,' he says.

I pause the scissors mid-snip. 'Callum, stop trying to be cute. You don't have to put on a tough act all the time.'

He stares directly into my eyes and says, 'I could say the same to you.'

I squirm. It was a good comeback. I always have my game face on and my walls up. Vulnerability and fear are things I learnt to hide a long time ago. I had to. I wouldn't have survived otherwise.

I breathe out long and slow, relaxing my shoulders, letting my face soften.

'Okay, so both of us can drop the act and be freaked out as much as we want. Now, let's get this shirt off so we can sort that wound. Are you in a lot of pain?'

'I've had worse.'

'So you keep saying.'

I pull the remnants of his bloody T-shirt away, and look around for somewhere to drop it where it won't stain the mint green decor. Balling it up, I take it to the bathroom instead and toss it in the tub.

'Okay, how's it—'

When I step back into his room Callum is facing me, bare-chested, the towel still pressed to his side. I've been so focused on cutting his shirt off, I'm not prepared for what's beneath it.

The stomach I got a glimpse of in my office has muscles I was not expecting, and his now naked shoulders somehow seem even broader. But he also looks anxious and frightened, and I don't remember ever seeing him this shaken before.

He blinks at me, chewing on his lip. Then he forces out a smile.

'Right,' I say, not moving. 'Right,' I say again, this time a little firmer. I sit on the bed beside him and pour antiseptic onto a cotton pad, which quivers in my shaking hands. *Adrenaline. It's just adrenaline.* 'This is going to sting.' I gently dab at the cut that runs just below his ribs.

His lets out a muffled groan and grabs my arm. 'Sorry,' he says, but he doesn't let go.

'Hang in there,' I say. 'I'm almost done.'

I dip my face to check his wound, gently touching the skin around it, now smeared brown with iodine. He's warm. I'm warm. I look up and he's watching me.

'I think you might be right,' I say. 'It doesn't look that bad. Just a lot of blood.'

'I told you it was just a scratch.'

'I still think it could do with a couple of stitches.' I dab at him again and he jerks.

'That stuff stings like a son of a bitch.' A crooked grin twitches on his pale lips. 'You're enjoying hurting me, aren't you?'

I smile and say, 'More than I could ever express.'

I use butterfly strips to hold Callum's wound together and cover it with a non-stick dressing, then clean two small cuts on his arm and cover them with Band-Aids. After some pushing and prodding, and the occasional yelp from Callum, we both agree he hasn't broken anything. The only thing left to do is clean up the nicks on his face.

I reposition myself and, without thinking, rest my hand on his thigh as I pull myself closer. He sucks back a breath, his muscles flexing beneath my palm. Gently placing my other hand under his chin, I lift Callum's face to catch the light. He leans into me and closes his eyes. My heart races. My adrenaline must *still* be pumping from what happened at the house, because it can't be anything to do with how close his face is to mine. Or his lips. Or his thigh under my touch.

He winces again as I clean a tiny cut on his cheek. 'Sorry, nearly done.'

His eyes open and he looks at me.

'No, Holly, I'm sorry. I could've been really hurt tonight. I should never have put either of us in that situation. Especially knowing what you've already been through. It was stupid and thoughtless.'

My hand still cups his chin as he stares at me, his gaze locked to mine. He's so close, just a couple of inches closer and my mouth would be on his.

He breathes out, his tongue swiping across his bottom lip.

Oh shit. I spring to my feet. *Nope. Nope. Nope.*

'I think you'll live,' I say.

I bend to pick up the mess of cotton pads and discarded Band-Aid wrappers from the floor, but I can feel his eyes still on me and I need to be out of this room right now. I straighten up so fast the blood rushes to my head and Callum reaches out to steady me as I wobble. I take a quick step back, putting some distance between us.

'We can sort this mess out in the morning. Do you need painkillers or anything?' Callum's eyes are still on mine as I awkwardly stumble backwards across the room.

'I'm okay,' he says quietly. 'But . . . do you think you could leave the door between our rooms open a crack? I'm kind of freaked out.'

'Oh. Of course. Sure.' Then I remember what he said at the house. 'You said you saw someone at the house tonight. What exactly did you see?'

'I saw a woman.'

'At the window?'

He nods.

'Are you positive?'

'Yeah. No. I mean, I think so. She was looking out the window at us, but when I got closer to the house, she was gone. Then *boom*.'

I frown. 'It wasn't a reflection or anything?'

'Do reflections explode?' His eyes widen. 'You really didn't see anything?'

'I felt something. There's obviously something very wrong at that house. But I didn't see . . . Callum, you've never seen spirits before, right?'

'No.'

'Not on any of your investigations?'

He slowly shakes his head. 'Nope. Never. But that can't be what happened, can it? I must have imagined it.'

'Do imaginary things explode? I think spirits can choose to reveal themselves to certain people because they want something or need something. But it's usually someone with a deep connection to the spirit. Like a husband or a wife. Spirits have no choice with me, I can see them whether they want me to or not . . .'

'But I don't *have* a connection to this place, unless you count wanting to investigate it . . . It doesn't make sense.'

'No, it doesn't.'

A deep crease settles between his eyes.

'Don't think about it tonight,' I say. 'We can go over it more tomorrow. There are a few things we should discuss.' What happened tonight has made me realise that we're dealing with something big, something unknown. And that means I should probably tell Callum about my dreams, the pull I feel from the house.

'Things we should discuss? That sounds ominous,' he says.

'Just try to sleep. I'll leave the door open, call out if you need anything.'

As I flick off the light, through the darkness, I hear him quietly say, 'Thanks for looking after me, Holly.'

CHAPTER EIGHT

I watch the refined couple step down from their buggy. The gentleman takes the woman's elbow while she lifts her heavy skirts to avoid the dirt of the path. As they step onto the porch, he removes his tall hat. She links her arm through his and then they enter the grand house together. Lamp light shines in every window, glowing out into the darkness, and soft laughter drifts on the breeze, rising up the grassy hill towards me.

Whispering from behind the oak tree at my back catches my attention, and I turn and see the lovers, their fingers entwined, their gazes locked.

The girl is young, around eighteen, with light hair she wears loose down her back and curled in ringlets around her face. The man is older, maybe twice her age and dressed in a tailcoat and a white bow tie. Her dress is plainer, a simple cream with a modest neckline and buttons through the bodice. And though both are good-looking, he is breathtakingly so.

He gently draws the girl to him and presses his lips to hers. The kiss is tender, and I turn away, embarrassed to be intruding on such an intimate moment. I look instead back down the hill to the impressive building below. The house seems strangely familiar, and then it suddenly hits me, it's the Western house. Except it's no longer empty. It's full of life and music. A living, breathing, vibrant home.

When the man behind me speaks again, I'm curious enough to turn and listen.

'You are perfect,' he says, his voice soft and rich.

The young girl shakes her head. 'I am far from perfect. You know my truth.'

He strokes her cheek. 'It's your truth that makes you special, and that's what makes you perfect.'

The young girl sighs at the man's caress, his long fingers tracing the length of her pale throat. He's tall and elegant, with eyes the colour of wheat, and alabaster skin that gleams as if he is lit from within. His beauty is so exquisite, I can't stop myself from staring.

'My darling,' he says. 'I have searched so long for someone like you. Tell me, are you happy?'

'I am very happy.'

'Then, if I asked you, would you choose to be with me forever?'

She smiles, and I see that she's trembling. 'I am already yours and yours alone.'

'Good,' the man says.

Then his face changes, light and softness vanishing, as he wraps his hands around the young girl's throat and begins to squeeze.

I'm in the bathroom splashing water on my face, trying to chase away another horrible dream, when a tap at my door startles me. I tiptoe to the bedside table and check the time on my phone. It's 3.15 am. Witching hour. My head snaps around at another tap. I pad over to Callum's room and peek inside. I can see his shape under the covers, so whoever is knocking isn't him. I turn and stare at my door again, then slowly tiptoe over and peer through the peephole.

I step back from the door and shake my head.

Seriously. Is this a joke?

I lean in for another look. There's the spirit of a man in the hall. He's old, with wispy grey hair and a neat brown suit, and he's knocking on doors. A guest steps out of one of the rooms and looks around in confusion. He quickly hugs his arms, feeling the chill of the smiling dead thing standing right in front of him. Another guest appears, looking equally baffled. The men exchange a few words, while the spirit stands beside them, grinning. Then they shrug and return to their rooms again.

I scrub a hand down my face, go to my bag and dig out my rosary. When I open my door, the spirit is straightening a painting.

I lift my rosary. The ghost looks up in surprise and I wait for the inevitable screeching and ringing in my ears. But instead, he just smiles. Then he neatens a doily on a hall table, gives me a friendly wave and disappears.

I blink, staring at the empty hall and the perfectly placed doily. Then I slowly step backwards into my room and close the door.

For a moment I consider reaching out with my senses, forcing the spirit back and dealing with it. But I'm too tired and too confused by that smile and that cheery wave. I toss my rosary onto my bedside table, climb back under the comforter and flick off the lamp.

When I wake for the second time, I'm heavy with exhaustion. I stretch my arms over my head, groaning at the ache across my shoulders, then rub at my eyes with my knuckles.

A tap at the door makes me jump again, but this time it *is* Callum, and this time he's at our adjoining door. It still takes a second for my heart to settle.

'You awake?' Callum half whispers.

'Sort of,' I call back.

He pushes the door open and leans against the frame. He's still in his jeans, but he's pulled on a black sweatshirt with his podcast's logo across the front. His hair is disarmingly messy, sticking up in every direction, and he has that soft, just woke up look about him.

I push up on my elbows. 'This place is haunted.'

'Yeah, I know. Apparently, it's famous for it.'

'You booked us into a haunted hotel? Don't I have enough ghosts in my life?'

'I didn't know it was haunted when I booked it. Just that it was a historic house. If I had known . . . well I probably would still have booked it. I thought you would have sensed the spirit or read about it in the B&B brochures.'

'Well I didn't sense it, and who reads brochures?'

'Everybody. Don't tell me you got rid of the ghost? I think it's one of their big selling points.'

'No, I didn't. But it was weird. He didn't yell like they normally do. He . . . waved.'

'Yeah, the info says he's friendly.'

'They're not usually like that with me.' I shrug. 'Anyway, how are you feeling?'

'I feel as if I got tossed through a railing and off a porch. I might need patching up again.'

He raises the side of his sweatshirt, revealing the bloodied dressing and those muscles I discovered last night. I pat down my bed hair, suddenly feeling wildly self-conscious.

'I'm going to take a shower,' he says. 'Then we can go get breakfast, talk about last night and . . . the other stuff you want to talk about.'

'Okay, I'll get dressed.'

I kick my covers away. He doesn't move.

'I didn't know you were an AC/DC fan,' he says.

I look down at my oversized *Highway to Hell* T-shirt. 'I'm not really. Someone threw it in with my laundry, so I kept it.'

'Serves them right. It looks good on you.'

'It's way too big.'

'It's perfect, Sunshine.'

I stiffen. My face tingling as I flush. Sunshine. I'd almost forgotten he'd ever called me that. According to him, I light up even the darkest, creepiest night. So cheesy and so completely inaccurate. I always told him to stop it, that I hate cutesy names, but the truth is, I might have liked it a little, and I'm ninety per cent sure he knew that.

'Can you please not call me that?' I tell him. 'You know I hate it.'

He chuckles. 'Sure you do, Sunshine.' Then he turns and leaves, closing the door behind him.

I stare at the ugly wallpaper on the back of the door as butterflies take off in my stomach again.

I push the hash browns around my plate with my fork as I try to decide how much to share with Callum. Do I tell him everything about my dreams? Do I tell him about his starring role and how he asked me to trust him?

'What?' Callum asks, watching me. 'What are you thinking?' He winces, his hand pressing against his wound.

'I'm thinking you're hurting.'

He shrugs me off. 'It's nothing. I pulled a few muscles.'

'We should get your ribs X-rayed. They could be broken.'

'You poked them, they were fine. Besides, I've broken ribs before, I know how it feels, and this is not it.'

He picks up a piece of bacon, stuffs it into his mouth, then licks his fingers one by one. I wish he wouldn't do that, it's very distracting.

Wiping his hands on a napkin, he says, 'Do you remember my friend Jason? I think you met him one night at my office.'

I shift uncomfortably. I don't want to talk about those nights in his office, I don't want to sit here and reminisce. I don't know where that conversation might lead, but I do know I don't want to go there.

'Vaguely,' I say. 'Really tall guy, dark-haired, skinny?'

'That's him. Anyway, we were talking this morning. He's coming out here tomorrow.'

'What? Why?'

'Well, I'm a bit banged up right now and might need a day or two to recover. He can lend a hand if we need him, but also, he runs an architecture business with his brother in Connecticut, and they specialise in post-Civil War architectural restorations. He knows of the Western house and offered to help. I mean, if nothing else, he's an expert. He'll be great at deciphering any old blueprints we might get our hands on.'

'Callum, no. It's not safe. We don't know what we're dealing with.'

'Jason will be fine. He's helped me out on the show before, and we've known each other since we were kids; he's not freaked out by my weird shit. He doesn't want to go into the house anyway, not after he heard about what happened last night.'

'You were told you could bring one other person on the investigation, a psychic, and that's me.'

'So we won't tell anyone. Jase could give you a hand for a couple of days. Us. He could give *us* a hand. Be backup. To be honest, I thought you'd be happy about it. This way you're not stuck out here alone with me.'

'Why would you think I'd think that?'

'Really, Holly?' His jaw flexes.

Ugh. I sit back and set mine. 'Fine. He can come.'

'I've already booked him a room.' He shoves a forkful of eggs into his mouth.

'Of course you have. But I don't *need* backup, Callum. You know I do this for a living, right?'

'Can you just humour me? I know you're good at your job, Holly. But this feels different, and . . . Look, I'm a little freaked out, okay? I'm dropping the tough guy thing, like you asked.'

He fixes his gaze on me, and I fold under its intensity with a frustrated sigh.

'We don't let him in the house, no matter how interested he is in post-Civil War architecture.'

'I told you; he won't be going in there.'

'And from now on, he can patch you up, not me.'

'If I need patching, Jase can patch.' He waves down the server to top up our coffees. 'Now, what was it you wanted to talk to me about?'

I recount my dreams; the voice that says *let us in*, the strange man with pale gold eyes, and the two murdered girls. I tell him how the house gave me weird vibes even before we got to East Mill and wonder aloud if whatever is haunting the house is particularly powerful. 'Maybe the older the ghost, the stronger it is,' I muse. 'Have you heard of anything like that?'

Callum shakes his head. 'Nope, but I can dig around.'

In the end, I don't share every detail. I decide not to mention his guest appearance in my dream, asking me to trust him. Because then I might have to tell him why I don't, and I'm not going there.

Callum listens carefully, a crease in his brow getting deeper and deeper.

When I finish he asks, 'That's it? That's what you wanted to talk about? Dreams?'

'And you know, the house and its pull.'

He nods slowly and says, 'Right.'

Oh shit. He thought I was going to talk about us, I realise. He thought I was going to talk about what happened. I scramble for composure.

'Look, I don't know if any of this is important,' I say hastily. 'But I thought I should tell you. You have a lot of experience and all those degrees and that one diploma, I thought you might have some insight.'

He nods. 'Of course. I'm glad you told me.'

'Do you know if there's a cellar in the house? One of the dreams . . . it took place underground. No windows.'

'There'll be plans on record. I'll see what I can find out.' His eyes narrow. 'So, you *did* sense something from the photos.'

'Sorry I didn't tell you at the time. I wasn't sure what was going on. I'm still not sure.'

'What about the "let us in" stuff? Do you ever let anything in? Do you ever channel spirits?'

'I do the exact opposite of channelling – you know that.'

'I don't know what you've been doing. I haven't seen you for two years.'

'I've already told you, nothing's changed.'

'Except you got a vibe off the house.'

I sigh and stare out the window to the street, where tourists wander from store to store, while we discuss death and ghosts and things that would terrify most people.

'The house is haunted,' I say. 'Of course it's going to give me a vibe.'

'From a photo, when you're not *that* kind of psychic?'

I rest my chin in my hand. 'It was definitely a new experience. It was as if something was calling me out here.'

'The voice?'

'Maybe.'

'Are you worried?'

'A little I guess.'

'Okay, well, let's figure out what's happening.'

He motions for the check, his other hand pressing on his wound again.

'You need to rest up,' I say.

He nods. 'Agreed. I'll lay low, dig into the research, nudge Rosing about the info he promised. What will you do?'

'I can go visit your Mrs Hutchings at the technologically challenged historical society. If I'm really lucky, they'll have a microfiche machine.'

Callum pouts. 'Damn it, I love a good microfiche machine. Let me give you a list of what to look for. And don't forget to tell Ola I say hi.'

The East Mill Historical Society is part of a historic estate, the gardens of which now form a park in the middle of town. Elm trees tower in bursts of gold, and lilac hydrangeas, their once bright summer blooms now fading, line the path which weaves across the thick lawn to a simple two-storey white house. A straw cornucopia spews tiny pumpkins onto the steps, and timber pails of bright yellow chrysanthemums frame the entrance way.

A brass plaque on the front wall announces that the building is in the Federal style and was constructed by the Chatfield family in 1802. I wonder if they knew the Westerns, back in the day. I wonder if they could have been at that party in my dream. I push open the door, and a cheery chime announces my arrival. A woman with short, salt-and-pepper hair looks up from her desk, and though she's smiling at me, I quickly get the impression she's disappointed I'm not Callum.

'Are you Ola Hutchings?' I ask. 'I think you've been in touch with my . . . colleague, Callum Jefferies, about the Western house?'

'Yes, that was me. You know, I recognised his name from that ghost show of his. I may have watched it once or twice. I was hoping to meet him. He was delightful on the phone.' She fusses with the rainbow-coloured cord her glasses hang on. 'If I were a younger woman, I'd say he was flirting with me.' Her laughter is almost girlish and her already rosy cheeks deepen with a blush.

I smile; I'm sure he was flirting with her. 'He couldn't make it today, unfortunately – he had a slight accident involving a few loose fenceposts.'

'What a shame.' She casts an appraising eye over me. 'Are you two . . .' She makes a hand movement to indicate 'together'.

'Oh, no. Noooo,' I answer, way too emphatically. 'We just . . . work together.'

'I'm sorry. That was rude of me. I'm a historian, I like asking questions and, well, it's just . . .' she gives me a sly grin, 'he's quite the charmer, isn't he, and dare I say, not bad to look at.' She sighs in a way that I can only describe as wistful. 'Right, enough of that. On to business. Callum mentioned you're investigating the troubles at the Western house?'

The troubles. Interesting term. I nod. 'Yes, but we're having difficulty speaking to the family directly, even though they approved the investigation. Instigated it, actually. So far we've only been dealing with a Mr Rosing.'

'It's a shame you weren't here yesterday; you could have spoken with Edward then. I bumped into him on my morning walk. He hasn't been out to the house for quite some time, so I asked what brought him out here. He said he had some family business to take care of.'

I frown. 'We *were* here yesterday, and we were told he was away. We saw Mr Rosing last night. He didn't say anything about his boss being in town.'

'This was quite early. Maybe he'd left by the time you got out here. I wouldn't make too much of it – and I wouldn't put too much stock in Albert Rosing's behaviour, either. He treats anything to do with that family like it's a state secret.' She shakes her head as if reliving personal experience, then meets my eyes and smiles. 'Now, how exactly can I help?'

I take a seat opposite her and pull out my phone to look at the list Callum typed into my notes. 'We're looking for historic records on the family, their role in East Mill, the names of those who lived and worked at the house, building plans, and any other information you think could help. Mr Rosing has promised us some family photos. All we have so far is a grainy photo of Brendin Western that accompanied his obituary. But if you have any photos of the interior of the house, that could be helpful.'

She hmms, scribbling on a yellow notepad. 'I'm not sure how much I can help regarding a list of staff. Edward would have to supply that. The Westerns have always been very private. Brendin Western kept to himself, he seldom came into town, and Edward is the only family member I know of that ever visited him. He seemed quite close to his uncle.' She jots a few more notes on her pad. 'We have some photos of the interior of the house taken after Brendin Western died, when we were pitching to manage the property. I can scan those for you. If I can find them.' She rests her chin in her hand as she thinks. 'That might take me a while. We're in a bit of a pickle at the moment, trying to get our records online so everything's more accessible. I have a team of volunteers working on it, so some records are offsite. But I can help with the building plans now. I have the plans for *both* houses here, so I can organise those for you straight away. You do know that the current house is the second house the Westerns have built?'

I nod. 'The first one was in the 1600s, it burnt down.'

'That's right. It was built in 1654, and stood for over two hundred years, until it burnt down in the spring of 1870. A Thomas Mulford was taken into custody on suspicion of setting the fire. But it was never proven, and the Westerns never pursued it. To be honest, there was probably a list of suspects as long as my arm who would have torched that house. The family has never been well liked. The house you see now was completed in 1872. I have a copy of the authenticated plans of that house, but we only have replica plans of the original house, which were created many, many years later from archival information, so who knows how correct they are.'

'What happened to the real plans from the first house? Were they lost when that house was burnt in 1870?'

'No they were lost long before that. They were destroyed in *another* suspicious fire. That fire took place in 1659 and destroyed a good deal of the town. The courthouse, the meeting house, the church, most of the official buildings and a few homes went up. It's why we don't have a lot of the original documents from that period, why we don't even have a complete record of the early settler population. It's also why the town centre was moved to where it is now. Here, I can show you.'

Ola takes me over to two framed posters on the wall above the information pamphlet stand. She points. 'Old town. New town.'

'The Western house didn't move.'

'No, their land was outside of the original town centre. Can't blame them for wanting to be near the coast.'

'Can I get copies of these too?'

'Any gift store in the village will have these.'

As I take a photo of both posters, she pulls a pamphlet from the stand and hands it to me. 'You'll also want to visit the East Mill Witch Study Center. They'll have more detailed information relating to the part the early settler Westerns played in the witch nonsense that happened around here.'

'The Westerns were involved in the witch trials?'

'Up to their necks. But I'll let Louise at the Witch Study Center fill you in. She's our local expert. And if you have access to the gardens at the Western house, take a look around the small family cemetery under the large oak tree up on the hill. A fascinating slice of history.'

My skin prickles. The tree I stood under in my dream. I didn't know there were graves below it.

'Is there anything else I should know about the house? Any strange occurrences, aside from the ghost sightings?'

'The house has been vacant for a while now, and I don't know how strange this is, but about a year ago, two workmen were injured at the property,' Ola says. 'They were doing some electrical work and got into some sort of fight. One of them died as a result of the altercation. You should be able to find that on the *Gazette* website if that's at all helpful.'

'Thank you, we'll look into it.'

'I'll sort out those building plans for you now. But I may need a couple of days to pull together the rest of the information.'

I step under the bright orange bunting that spells out 'Happy Halloween' above the doorway of Main Street Gifts and come face to face with an array of ghost-shaped decorations, none of which resemble the real thing.

I breathe out a weary sigh and quickly scan the store until I spot what I'm here for – the posters Ola had on display.

I'm trying to decide whether to buy full-sized or smaller versions when Callum messages.

> How's it going?

> Just on Main Street buying something.

> A present for me? I'm sick, don't forget.

I shake my head, shove my phone back in my pocket and head to the register, taking my small, laminated posters with me.

I pick up a book from the counter called *Local Long Island Legends*.

'A local enthusiast prints that himself,' the woman behind the register tells me. 'If you like ghost stories, you'll love it.'

I don't, but I know someone who does. 'I'll take it,' I say. Then I spot a bowl of touristy magnets. Most just say 'East Mill' with a picture of an old house or the harbour, but there are also a couple of witchy ones in a Halloween display, and one with a ghost that says 'Boo'.

I hand her the 'Boo' magnet. 'I'll take this too, please.'

CHAPTER NINE

Callum is lying on his bed with his laptop by his side and his eyes closed. I start to tiptoe from the room when he calls out, 'Hey, you're back.'

'I wasn't sure if you were sleeping,' I say. 'How are you feeling? Were you awake long enough to do any research, or have you snoozed the day away?'

He pushes himself up with a wince. 'I feel fine, and I'd like to point out that you're the one who told me I needed rest. But I did a little of both. I multitasked.'

'Find anything interesting?'

'I've mostly been reading up on the history of the area. I did find that the current Western house was built on the same spot as the house that burned down. The *exact* same spot.'

'I have the plans for both.' I go to my room and come back with everything I got that day. 'Ola copied these for me.' I shift his laptop and perch on the edge of his mattress. 'This is the original house. These plans are just a replica though; the originals got destroyed in a fire in 1659.'

'I read about that fire. They lost a good chunk of the town.'

'Mm, and a lot of the town records. Here are the plans of the current house. Ola said the master blueprints are in the town archives if we need to access them.'

'I can get Jason to do that if needed. Told you there was a reason he should come out here.'

'She also told me no one liked the Westerns.'

'What, ever?'

I shrug. 'Sounded like it. And I got these.' I show him the two laminated maps of the town. 'By the way, Ola would appreciate it if you visited her next time. I got the feeling I was a disappointment. She thinks you were flirting with her.'

He points at himself with a silent, *Me?*

I ignore him. 'But everything else you asked for might take a couple of days, so it looks like we're not going anywhere soon.'

'Sad you can't get this over and done with and get out of here as quickly as possible?'

His gaze is on me, piercing scrutiny. I shift awkwardly on his bed.

'No. I didn't mean that. You're putting words in my mouth.' He keeps staring, so I quickly add, 'By the way, Edward Western was in town yesterday morning.'

'But why wouldn't Rosing tell us that?'

'Exactly.'

He frowns, then looks at the replica plans of the original house. 'This might be your murder cellar.' He points to a small square at the back of building.

'Maybe,' I say noncommittally.

He pulls the second set of house plans onto his lap. 'Weird. It's not shown on the plans of the current house. I wonder if they filled it in when they rebuilt? We can get Jase to have a look and see what he thinks.'

There's that creeping dread again. I don't want there to be a cellar. I don't want the dreams to be real.

'I got this book too,' I say shaking off the troubled feeling. 'It's by a local, lots of ghost stories and legends. You never know, there might be something in there. I also got this . . .' I pull out the magnet. 'A present for you as requested.' His brows flick up as I press it into his palm.

He looks at it for a long moment.

'Holly, are you calling me your boo?'

My cheeks flush. I should have seen that one coming, 'Of course I'm not. It's gag gift, Callum.'

'Right. Well, thank you.' He puts it on his bedside table. 'By the way, I told the manager you saw their ghost. He said a couple of the other guests asked him about it this morning. Seriously though, don't obliterate it, okay? It's well-loved here.'

I frown. A well-loved ghost? Now I've heard everything.

Callum swings his legs off the bed, grunting in the process.

'Where are you going? I have more to tell you.'

'Let me wash up first,' he says. He looks tired and grumpy; there's no trace of his normal excited enthusiasm, no trace of that glow he always has.

'Are you in pain? Because you seem a bit—'

'Cabin fever. I'll be fine after a shower.' Then he disappears into the bathroom, pushing the door closed behind him.

While Callum cleans up, I read up on the ghost who haunts the bed and breakfast. His name was George Baker, a man who worked at Maddison House until he died on the job at eighty-nine, and apparently he still hasn't retired. George did the early morning wake-up calls, so now his spirit knocks on people's doors at all hours. He's also known to lurk in the guest lounge, which is probably why the manager always keeps the fire burning in there. A ghostly presence often leaves a chill in the air. I look down the page to a smiling photo of George – it's definitely the dead guy from the hall. I reach out and sense his presence right away, the buzzing trail that he's left behind. Why didn't I notice it when we first arrived? *Focus, Holly, focus!*

I never bother talking to ghosts unless I'm swearing at them, because they don't react to anything I say. Except that nun, who might have got upset when I said fuck, and now George, who's smiling and waving at me like we're besties. Oh, what the hell. I close my eyes.

'Listen, George,' I whisper. 'Apparently, they're fond of you here. But if you wake me up again, I'm going to have to deal with you, and you won't like it.'

'I'm going to make an appointment to visit the Witch Study Center, find out more about the family's involvement in the trials.' I've just told Callum that the Westerns were connected to the East Mill witch trials, and he's weirdly unenthusiastic. 'What do you think?' I say, as I look up the Witch Study Center website.

'Oh, sure. Sounds good.' He seems distracted.

I frown and scooch around. He's sitting on his bed staring down at me, chewing his lip.

'What's going on?'

'What?' he says. 'I'm not doing anything.'

'Exactly. You're not doing anything. You're not looking anything up, you're hardly saying anything. What's going on?'

He glances down, his teeth still grating back and forth across his bottom lip. Then he sighs, a little shaky and a lot dramatic. I stiffen. I shouldn't have asked.

'I'm so happy you agreed to work this case with me, Holly. I'm glad you're here and that we're doing this together.'

He's not looking at me. He's looking down, scratching at the fabric of his sweatpants. I wipe my clammy palms on my jeans.

'Which is why I wasn't going to bring this up,' he says. 'I don't want to ruin everything, but . . .' He wiggles forward on the bed. I wiggle backwards across floor. 'I've had a whole day on my own to think about this, and if I don't say something now, I know it's going to eat at me.'

My heart quickens. 'Okay,' I say, even though it's not okay. So not okay.

He nods, more to himself than to me. 'I thought you were going to say something at breakfast this morning. I thought you wanted to talk about what happened with us. It's just . . .'

He looks at me now, and I swear the green of his eyes deepens. 'You know what I'm going to ask you, right?'

I know exactly what he's going to ask me, and I wish the ground would open up and swallow me whole.

Two years ago

I swear I can still feel the touch of Callum's lips soft on my cheek. I'm buzzing from everything he said last night, with the idea that he actually likes me like *that*. What's happening between us seems to be heading somewhere good, somewhere I was hoping it would. I feel this promise of possibility fluttering inside me and it's making me giddy.

I have a meeting with a new client in the West Village, not far from the studios where Callum records his podcast, so I've decided to be brave, grab us both a coffee and stop by and see him.

I find him in an edit suite with his new producer, Peter. The guy worked on one of the big ghost hunting shows on cable and Callum's excited to have him on board. He's hoping he can tap into Peter's experience and grow his podcast and his YouTube channel, maybe even use his contacts for something bigger.

I hover in the doorway on my tiptoes, not wanting to interrupt, peering over Callum's broad shoulders at what they're watching. I'm surprised to see it's footage of me Callum shot the week before during an exorcism I performed. Latin is streaming from my mouth. The lighting is less than flattering.

I look like a character in a low-budget thriller, holding a flashlight under my chin.

Peter pauses the video and zooms in on my face – my mouth wide open, my eyes nothing but pits of shadow. He starts to laugh, and I watch in horror as Callum laughs with him.

'These psychics are all the same,' Peter says, once his laughter has subsided. 'Such fakers. None of them can provide a shred of evidence that they can actually do what they say they do. *Communing with the spirits* doesn't show up on EMF machines? Surprise, surprise.' He laughs sarcastically. 'The audience loves the tech, Callum. Show them the Structured Light Sensor camera, the night vision goggles. You need to be focusing on the science and not this . . . woo woo bullshit. Who is this girl anyway?'

Callum shrugs and says, 'Just someone a friend brought in. We don't have to use the footage for the show.'

'Maybe you should tell your friend to stop dumping freaks like this on you.' Peter nods at my frozen face and starts laughing again.

Callum shuts off the video. He's bright red, as if he's embarrassed to be associated with me. 'Right, yeah sure. No more freaks.'

I swear my heart stops as the years of torment that word has caused me come flooding back. *Freak*. Callum just called me a . . . freak. I spin around, drop the coffees in the trash and walk out the door.

*

With a deep breath I steel myself, look up and meet Callum's eyes.

He swallows nervously.

'Why did you vanish like you did?' he says. 'I called you, texted you, emailed you. Left you I don't even know how many messages. But you never answered. You ghosted me.' He laughs cooly at his choice of words. 'That hurt, Holly. If that's what you meant to do, good job, it worked. I had no idea what was happening, no idea what I'd done. I assumed I scared you away with what I'd said the night before. How I felt. That it was too much too soon or something. Celeste said to just give you time. Time turned into two years.'

I push up onto my knees. 'I . . .' My breath is coming fast. 'I had my reasons.'

'Oh yeah? I'd love to finally hear them. For a second there I thought we might actually have had a future together.'

The flimsy dam holding back my anger bursts. 'A future with the *freak*, you mean?'

He looks confused. 'What?'

'I know what you think of me, Callum. What you *really* think of me.'

'And what's that?'

'That I'm a freak.'

He rocks back and frowns. 'I don't think that. I've never thought that.'

'Oh please. I saw you, Callum. The morning after you'd told me how much you liked me. You were with that new producer, watching video of me exorcising some ghost. He started laughing, and instead of stopping him, you started laughing too, like I was just a big joke to you. Then he called me a *freak* ... and ... so did you. I heard you, Callum. I heard you.'

Callum's face is ashen. He looks down, brows bunched, mouth set in a hard line, his eyes flicking right and left. Then he squeezes his eyes shut and drops his head.

'You were there?' he whispers.

I think I actually gasp. I wasn't expecting him to admit it. I was sure he'd tell me I imagined it; I'd half convinced myself that I had.

'Let me explain,' he says. He shuffles forward and reaches for me. I quickly move away. 'It's not what you think, Holly. I don't think you're a freak.'

'You just admitted it.'

'I know, but I didn't mean it. I mean, I know I said what I said, but it's not what you think.'

'You might say all the right things to my face, but behind my back . . .' My voice hitches.

'Holly, I swear I just wanted Peter to shut up. I was furious, I couldn't believe what he said, but I didn't want to risk pissing him off. We'd only just started working together. I know I should have told him to fuck off, but I felt like I had to keep on his good side, and I didn't know how else to get out of the situation. So, I just agreed with him, to get him to stop.' His pale cheeks are now lit deep crimson, and a dark groove has lodged between his eyes – which are glued to me. 'But I should have had your back,' he says. 'I'm so sorry I didn't. Holly, I'm sorry.'

I stare at him, shaking my head. 'I don't believe you.'

'It's the truth, Holly. I swear. I don't think you're a freak.'

I take a deep breath. 'So you just trashed me to stay on some guy's good side? How is that better? I would never do that to you.'

He buries his face in his hands. 'I know you wouldn't, and I'm so sorry, it was wrong and stupid. But I just wish you'd answered my calls. I could have explained everything. If you'd have just spoken to me . . .'

'I was hurt.'

He looks up. 'Me too.'

It's as if all the oxygen gets sucked from the room. I can't breathe and my pulse rages so loud in my ears I have to stop from covering them. Who needs this? Who needs people? The land of the living? Fuck that.

I snatch up my notebook and push off the floor. 'I should go. I'll let the manager know I'm leaving early and, um, you can have my notes.'

'Running again?' He slides off the bed.

'I'm not running. I'm choosing not to be here.'

'Holly, please. Please don't go.' He takes a step forward; I shuffle back. 'Give me another chance. I will make it up to you, I promise. You're extraordinary. But you're not a freak, and I am so sorry I ever made you feel like you were.'

I glance at the door. Three steps across the room and I can walk through it and walk away.

Callum moves closer. Slowly reaching out again. He carefully takes my notebook from me.

'Please stay,' he says again.

I look up and into his eyes and see hope and fear and pleading. A pang of sorrow throbs heavy in my chest. A weight that I've carried for so long. I have two choices. Go or stay. One is sure to make me miserable. The other one *might* make me miserable . . . but there's a possibility it might not.

The warmth of his fingers brushes my hand, and I glance down at his tentative touch. Then, with a deep swallow I choose possibility, and link my fingers through his.

We perch side by side on the edge of his bed.

'You don't understand,' I say. 'I've heard that word for what feels like my entire life. It's what everyone called me. How everyone sees me. Holly the Freak. Kids chanted it at me at school. Left on notes in my locker. And then you . . .'

'I do understand, and I don't see you like that. I never have.'

'I want to believe you.'

'You can.'

I stare down at our hands, his so much bigger than mine, our fingers still entwined.

'I should have confronted you about what happened,' I say. 'I should have called you out on it then and there.'

'You were hurt,' he says.

'Still.' I shake my head. 'I could have chosen a better way to handle it.'

'We both could have chosen a better way.' He draws a deep breath. 'So how about this – from now on I won't be a dick, I'll always have your back, and we'll talk and won't keep things from each other. Do you think that might work for you?'

I lift my face to his and find a gentle smile.

'Maybe,' I whisper.

'Yeah?'

I nod. 'Okay.'

'Okay,' he echoes.

His smile widens and our eyes lock. My heart races, warmth creeping into my cheeks, then ... *Thump, thump, thump.*

Our heads snap to the door.

'Are you expecting anyone?' I ask.

'No. Jase isn't coming until tomorrow.' He goes to answer it. 'Did you order food?'

'No. But I could probably do with some.'

He peeks through the peephole, turns back to me with a wide grin and flings the door open.

'Come on in, George,' he says with a sweep of his arm.

I leap up. 'Are you kidding me?'

Callum starts laughing. 'I don't know. Is he here?'

'No, but he was. I feel traces of him. What an asshole. I spoke to him about this, too. I told him to leave me alone or—'

'You spoke to a ghost? But you never speak to ghosts.'

'I blame you. You made me read the *About Your Stay* brochure and now I'm talking to *well-loved* hotel ghosts.'

Callum laughs and it's throaty and rich, and it lifts my heart just enough to make me roll my eyes and smile.

'How about I get us some pizza?' he says.

I nod. 'Yes, please.'

'Meat Lover's?'

'It's like you know me.'
'I do, Holly. I really do.'

I find sanctuary in the shower while Callum orders our food, welcoming the alone time to breathe and think. I'm not sure I can completely excuse what he did, but I do understand it a little, and understanding might help me forgive.

I've always felt a tickle of shame for walking away like I did. Shame for not standing up for myself and storming into that room or picking up one of his many calls and letting him have it. I don't think I meant to *ghost* him. It just worked out that way. Celeste asked me to at least let her tell him why, but I refused. I didn't want to relive it. And then she died, and that was that. I chose to believe the universe was sending me a message: *Stay away from the living and focus on the dead*. Because as much as I loathe the dead, they never seem to hurt me in the way the living do.

I wonder what would have happened if I'd let Celeste explain everything to Callum. I wonder what would have happened if we'd talked, or if I'd never walked in on that horrible conversation. Where would we be now? I shake the thought away. That's not helpful. At least we're talking and working together again. It'll be good to have someone to speak to who understands my world. A colleague to share the horrors with. That's all I need. Anything else is too dangerous anyway. I only have to think about Celeste to know that.

But, as annoying as it is, I do like Callum. I *still* like Callum. I don't feel so *other* when I'm around him.

Then his words from my dream come flooding back. *No matter what happens, you can trust me.* I turn off the water and grab a towel. But can I do that?

CHAPTER TEN

'Can I ask you a question?' Callum says, holding two pizza boxes out in front of him. 'If George haunts this place, do you think he ever spies on the guests?'

'What do you mean?'

'Like, if someone's showering. Do ghosts watch people shower?'

'I suppose if a spirit is pervy in life they could be pervy in death.'

He chuckles. 'I love how matter-of-fact you are about that.' He puts the pizzas on the end of the bed. 'What do we need to go over from today?'

I stand awkwardly in the middle of the room. Is this what we do, go on as if nothing has happened, as if we didn't just have a huge confrontation that had be brewing for years? I have no idea about this stuff.

'Holly, is everything okay?'

'I don't know. Is it?'

'Yeah, I hope so anyway. I feel like a weight's lifted. I'm glad we got all that out. Said what we needed to say. We couldn't go on pretending things were fine.'

I probably could have, I think.

'It's going to be a while though, until I stop feeling ashamed of myself,' he says. 'If I ever do.' His brow creases. 'I'll just leave you a pizza and head back to my room. Give you some space.'

I drop to the edge of my bed. 'No . . . stay. I want you to stay. I don't need space.' *I've had years of space.* 'But would you mind if we just watched TV? I'm kind of wiped out.' *And that way I don't have to think, and we don't have to do any more talking.*

'Whatever you need,' he says, then he looks me up and down. 'Cute look, by the way.'

I'm in leggings, an oversized hoodie and chunky grey socks, and my hair is wet. I glower up at him.

He laughs, then says, 'I got us something else,' and disappears into his room again. When he comes back, he has a bottle of red wine and two glasses. 'I thought we might need this?'

'God, yes.' I've never needed booze so much in my life.

He flops onto my bed. I glance sideways at the totally empty ugly striped couch, then with a resigned sigh, wriggle up next to him.

He passes me a tumbler, and wraps his hand around mine as he pours wine into my glass. 'Don't want to spill it on this *beautiful* bedspread.'

'Honestly, I don't think it would even show.'

He chuckles, slowly releases his grip on me and asks, 'What are we watching?'

I take a very, *very* large gulp of wine and hand him the remote. 'You choose,' I say, then reach forward and grab a pizza box. 'Hey, have you thought any more about Rosing not telling us that Edward Western was out here yesterday?'

'Yep. My first instinct is, weird. But I guess if he was gone by the time we got to town . . .' He flicks through the TV channels. 'Not much choice. No premium cable.'

'Do you trust him?'

'Rosing or Western?'

'Either. Both.'

'Can't say about Western. Not sure about Rosing. But next time we see him we can shake him down for info.'

I laugh. 'Shake him down? What, like good cop bad cop?'

'Ooh, will you be bad cop?' He takes a sip of his wine, his lips twitching around the edge of his glass.

I look away, pull a piece of pepperoni off my pizza and toss it in my mouth.

'And what about the spirit you saw at the house?' I ask manoeuvring us back onto safe turf. 'Can you describe her to me?'

His humour quickly disappears. 'I've been thinking about that. I must have got caught up in the moment. Just overexcited. It was probably only a shadow or a reflection.'

'But the window *exploded*!'

'It was probably a gas explosion or something. The house is *old*.'

'Callum, seriously?'

'What can I tell you? You didn't see anything, so I couldn't have. Anyway, I don't want to talk about it. We're watching TV, remember? Your idea.'

I side-eye him. That's some next-level avoidance, and that's coming from me. He's scared; I don't need to be psychic to figure that out.

'Hey, *Alien 2*,' he suddenly says, pointing the remote at the TV. 'You wanna watch this? I think the second *Alien* movie is the best one, it's got more action.' He looks at me, waiting for my answer.

I decide to let his bullshit slide for now; I'll call him out about his ghost sighting another time. We've both had enough confrontation for one night.

'Sure,' I say.

'Right, I remember now, you like action movies, but not horror.'

'Unless the ghost is getting it.'

'I like slasher horror better anyway,' he says.

'Me too. Stabby is way better than spooky.'

We look at each other and laugh.

'How about that,' Callum says, 'we agree on something.' He raises his glass to clink against mine.

By the time the movie finishes, we've drunk the wine and started on the old-school minibar. We're still lying on my bed, but now we're both a little tipsy.

'When did you know you could see spirits?' Callum asks, rolling onto his side to face me. 'I don't think we've ever talked about how it started for you.'

I twist my head to look at him. His long lashes cast spidery shadows on his cheeks. His eyes are almost unnaturally green again, and his skin is flushed with a pink glow.

I'm silent for so long he gently taps my foot with his and says, 'Earth to Holly.'

I blink, pull my gaze away from him, and take a sip of vodka from my tiny bottle.

'I was eight, and sleeping over at a friend's place. I still remember it so clearly, standing in the hallway in my pyjamas pinned to the wall by a screeching man. I told my friend's mom what I saw. But of course, there was nothing there. I was so upset, she called my parents and they took me home. It was awful, especially because no one believed me. After that, it kept happening, but no one wanted to hear about it. My parents thought I wanted attention because Maggie had made the school gymnastics team, and that was taking up every weekend. But it wasn't that. I liked watching Maggie's gymnastics. It was the fact that people no one else could see kept yelling at me. After a while I realised they must be ghosts. They just looked dead.'

'I've never thought about how horrible it must be for you.'

I shrug. 'I've learnt to deal with it. But it was rough going for a bit. When Mom died, I lost my anchor. Dad and Maggie had always been tight, and very anti my ghost thing, whereas I was closer to Mom. She'd started to listen to me too. She might have even believed me. When she was gone, I lost that, and it felt like I didn't have anyone anymore.' The memories come flooding back and I have to stop for a moment to chase them away again. Callum waits patiently. 'Anyway, after that Dad sent me to a paediatric therapist for a while. I don't blame him for it; we were all going through a lot, and he was really worried about me. But that's when I stopped talking about everything – it was easier that way. It got pretty lonely at my place though. I was so happy when my grandmother invited me to live with her. Even happier when I discovered that she really did have a psychic gift. Maybe that's why Mom listened, because deep down she knew the truth. My grandmother's gift wasn't quite like mine – hers was more gentle and helpful. She could read people and sense things about their lives and their futures. I just have angry dead people up in my face all the time. Grandma Jenny saved me, really. I don't know where I'd be if it wasn't for her. Maybe nowhere.' I shake my head. 'Sorry, I'm talking too much.'

Callum nudges my shoulder gently. 'No, you're not. I want to know. I'm interested. Like, when did you discover you could do whatever it is you do now?'

'Oh,' I laugh lightly, 'that was mostly Celeste, and a lot of experimentation. She and my grandmother both told me to trust that there's a reason I'm like this. That made me determined to find out what that might be. Turns out it's helping people who are haunted like I am.'

He gives me the softest smile, and it tingles right through me.

'Celeste was a good friend,' he says with a drawn-out sigh.

'She really was. I found a cute photo of her in my phone the other day. Want to see it?' I grab my phone and pull up the photo of me and Celeste in Central Park.

'When was this?' he asks, looking over my shoulder.

'The day I met you, actually. We stopped and ate in the park on the way. She'd just got that haircut. Do you remember?'

He chuckles. 'I remember she wore a hat for two weeks.'

'I know. Crazy, right? The cut looked so good.'

I smile at her beautiful face smiling out at me, swallow back an ache that never seems to shift, and close the photo again, dropping my phone.

Callum studies me, and I'm suddenly worried he'll want to talk about what happened the night Celeste died. I know he's aware of the details, because I know he spoke to Max. He just doesn't know how I carry it with me.

But he doesn't ask, he just gives my hand a quick and gentle squeeze, then rolls off the bed.

'You must have been one tough kid,' he says, as he goes to the minibar. 'Last two.' He holds up the tiny bottles.

'Our bill is going to be massive.'

'Western's bill is going to be massive.' He grins, cracks the top of the miniature brandy bottle and hands it to me.

'What about you and your family? Is it okay to ask how your folks died? We've never talked about that either.'

'Yeah, it's fine,' he says settling back onto the bed. 'They died in a car accident when I was five. We were living in California and my parents left me with a neighbour while they went to an art show opening, and they never came back. Head-on collision with a drunk driver. They were the same age as I am now.' He shakes his head. 'Anyway, the next day, Aideen swoops in and takes me home with her to New York. My dad didn't have any family, he was an only child, and both his parents were gone by the time he was in college, so it was just me and Aideen.' He knocks back his tiny bottle of whiskey. 'Until she died, I'd assumed she'd left everything my parents owned back in California. But she had a storage unit, and I found boxes and boxes of their stuff in there. Mostly junk, but also a few things I'd have loved to see as a kid. I guess Aideen had it all packed up and sent over at some point but couldn't face going through it. I get that; I still haven't gone through all the boxes either.'

'But don't you want to know more about them?'

'Sure, but the time just never seems right. It's a little overwhelming, to be honest. What if I don't like what I find?' He cocks his head. 'But who knows, maybe you've inspired me. Maybe after this job I'll finish them off.'

He screws the cap onto his empty bottle and tosses it across the room, neatly landing it in the wastepaper basket. He lifts his arms in triumph, then turns back to me and smiles.

'Does your family still avoid the ghost thing?' he asks.

'Completely. We mostly just catch up for birthdays, Christmas, the anniversary of Mom's death, that kind of thing. That's okay, I guess. I'd hate for them to know I'm involved with anything like what happened last night. It would scare the shit out of them.'

'It scared the shit out of me.'

'Me too. Let's not do that again.'

'Deal.' He studies me for another long moment, long enough to make me squirm, then he leans in closer and whispers, 'You know, I was really looking forward to that date we never got to have.'

His eyes shimmer in the light from the TV, and his tiny freckles pop enticingly against the blush of his cheeks. His breath is warm on my face and his lips within kissing distance again and I have to quickly look away in case I close the space between us.

Flushing, I glance at my hands and fidget. His shoulder presses against mine, his warmth seeping into my skin, and the tiny hairs along my arms stand on end, balanced on top of tingling goosebumps. I need to say something. I need to fill the empty air. I take a deep breath and force myself to meet his teasing gaze.

'Do you want to watch something else?' I fumble with the remote. 'Or would you rather call it a night?' I try to sound casual, but I sound awkward.

Callum's gaze stays on me for what feels like an eternity, then he smiles again and rolls onto his back.

'Well . . .' He stretches out his long legs with a satisfied hum and pats the mattress. 'Your bed is comfortable. I vote for another movie.'

The low murmur of the TV creeps into my consciousness. *What time is it?* My head is fuzzy, and my neck aches from resting awkwardly on . . . Oh my god!

I push myself off Callum and jolt across the bed as if a couple of hundred volts of electricity just shot through me. Callum stirs and rubs the back of his hand across his eyes.

'Oh shit. Sorry, Holly, I crashed out. Hey, I think you left a little drool on my shirt.' He smiles at me sleepily.

I wipe my mouth. 'I did not.'

He chuckles. 'It's okay, I won't hold it against you. What time is it?'

I reach for my phone. 'Just before six.'

Callum rolls off my bed, wincing as he puts his hand to his injured side. 'I might take a shower and grab a couple more hours of sleep. Wake me for breakfast?'

'Sure, because I'm your secretary now.'

He yawns, waving a hand behind him as he shuffles to his room. 'Okay, okay, I'll set an alarm.'

I roll over with a groan. My head is pounding. I should get up, take a couple of painkillers and change into my pyjamas. But instead, I crawl under the covers fully clothed. My bed is still warm from where Callum was lying, and I can smell his scent on the pillow. Like a sweet shampoo, mixed with a hint of his cologne. I inhale deeply as tendrils of desire spread through me.

I sigh, warm in a way that has nothing to do with my bedcovers.

CHAPTER ELEVEN

After a few more hours of sleep and a shower, I feel much better. In fact, I feel *good*. Like Callum, I feel as if a weight's been lifted. Maybe finally confronting him about what happened between us was a good thing. Maybe burying everything doesn't really work for me. *Gee, do you think?*

I head down to breakfast and spot a single table tucked into a bay window. I make my way over to it.

'Finally, she's awake.'

I swing around at the sound of Callum's voice. He's already seated at a table in the opposite corner of the room, his laptop open and a mug of coffee in front of him.

'How long have you been up?' I ask, dropping into the chair.

'About an hour. I thought I might have to come and drag you from your bed. I was kind of looking forward to it.' His eyes sparkle, and my face flushes.

Callum waves the server over. 'Can I get another coffee please, and one for my sleepy friend here? Latte?'

'Strong, please.' I take a croissant from the basket on the table, pull at its fluffy centre, and shove a piece into my mouth. 'So, what's the plan today?'

'Well . . . I've been going over the information Rosing sent through last night.'

'He finally sent it?' I grab his laptop and spin it to face me. 'About time. Is it the family history of the house? How far back does it go?'

He spins his laptop back to him. '1832.'

'What about before that?'

He shakes his head. 'I'm guessing the older family records were destroyed in the fire.' Callum pauses. 'One of the fires. But Margaret Western died in 1908, so what we've got should cover her, at least.'

'Still, I feel like we're only being fed half the picture, don't you?'

He grunts. 'Yeah I do. But sometimes the whole picture isn't available, and you've got to work with what you've got.'

'Any clues on the other spirit that's been seen on the grounds?'

'Nothing in this email, but judging from the way she's described and when the sightings started, I'm guessing she died sometime in the late 1870s or '80s. There'll be death records, obits and newspaper articles from that time, if she was news. I'll dig into that.' He rubs his chin as he thinks. 'This isn't the way I like to work. I don't usually research on the run like this. But this job fell into my lap, so I jumped on it without any pre-planning. We're just going to have to pull together any other info we need as we go.'

A woman appears beside us with our coffee order. She puts them on the table with a smile.

'Thanks, Janis,' Callum says, returning her smile.

Her cheeks lift higher. 'Don't forget,' she says, 'the Mill Pond Cafe. Pecan pie with cream, not ice cream.'

'Cream, not ice cream, got it.'

'And make sure you tell them I sent you. They'll give you a little discount.'

'Will do,' Callum says. 'I'll report back later with my verdict.'

She chuckles. Or rather, she titters. 'Well, you two have a nice day. Morning, honey,' she says to me as she turns and walks away.

I stir my coffee very slowly. 'First Ola Hutchings and now Janis?'

'What do you mean?' He looks at me innocently, but his slight smirk betrays him.

'The flirting. I didn't know you were into older women.'

'You keep saying I flirt. I don't flirt.' He grins crooked and mischievous, lifts his coffee and blows across the cup.

I shake my head and laugh. 'Yeah okay, Romeo, back to the case. Did Mr Rosing mention anything about his boss being here the other day, or say when we'll actually be able to talk to the man?'

'He didn't, but I sent him an email about it. He says Western was here to sign some papers last-minute, and was only in town for a matter of hours, which is why he didn't mention it to us. He says Western should be available in a couple of days.'

'It seems ridiculous that he's so hard to talk to, given that he hired you. Let's see if Rosing will meet us at the house today. He can give us an official tour of the grounds.'

Callum fiddles with his laptop. 'Um. Not today. I want to take a closer look at this new information first, and check out that book you got yesterday, see if there's anything useful in there. I also want to look over the town maps and house plans in more detail. I mean, I didn't get to do any research last night because *someone* kept me up half the night watching movies.'

'I believe that was mutual movie watching.'

He chuckles, his eyes alight with humour again. 'Besides, Jason's arriving at lunchtime, so I should make sure I'm around to meet him.'

'Hey, I get it. I'm nervous to go back to the house too. Let's leave it for another day.'

His arms fold over his chest. 'I didn't say I was nervous. I said I want to do more research.'

'Sorry, I guess I was . . . projecting.'

'What are you going to do today?'

'I'll head to the Witch Study Center, get some info on what the Westerns' involvement was in the witch trials back in the 1600s.' He keeps staring. 'What?' I wipe at my mouth in case I have croissant crumbs on my face.

'You're not planning on going to the house without me, are you?'

I scoff. 'Callum.'

'Holly.'

'Of course I won't.'

It's a crisp October morning, but the sun shines bright in the watery blue of the sky, and I bask in its warmth on my skin. I breathe in the fresh air, enjoying the tang of sea spray that hits the back of my throat, and the earthy scent of the fallen leaves. I could be forgiven for blowing off my plans and taking a stroll along the harbour foreshore, checking out the boutiques, or exploring one of the windswept beaches. But that isn't me, even if sometimes I wish it was.

On my way to the Witch Study Center, I decide to take a drive and explore the area a bit. But instead, I find myself turning into the lane where the Western house sits. It's as if the house has drawn me there.

I park behind a white van and walk up to the gates. Everything looks so different in the light of day. Far less ominous. I can now see the grounds are immaculately kept – green and lush, neatly mowed and raked clear of the fall litter, with brightly coloured flowers laid out in well-tended beds. Steeling myself, I close my eyes, seeking out the sickening sensation from the other night. In the corners of my mind, I can sense a faint buzzing. A tiny pulse. This is what I was expecting, not the weighty silence we were met with on our poorly thought-out adventure. Sometimes when people die, they leave behind a residual trace. Like a vibrating trail of spectral energy. Callum calls it a disturbance in the force. I call it a death echo. The rumble of a life still reverberating in this world. It's what Callum's EMF meters are supposed to pick up. I've learnt to tell the difference between these kinds of vibrations and the presence of a fully formed spirit. A spirit's energy fills my entire body. It throbs inside me, knocking at my ribs. An echo is gentler, as if death left behind a lingering breath. This buzzing feels like an echo, but I don't trust the house. Something has a hold of it, and I think it can cloak itself from me. I don't like that.

When I open my eyes I practically jump out of my skin. Mr Rosing is standing on the other side of the gate, staring at me.

'I'm sorry I startled you,' he says.

He doesn't look sorry. He looks suspicious.

I wave off his apology. 'I was just passing and wanted to see if I could get a feel for the place. I hope that's okay.'

'Of course. I have some time now if you'd like to look around the grounds?'

I quickly consider his invitation, remembering my promise to Callum. It takes me about a second to decide. 'That would be great,' I say. Technically, I'm not going to the house. At least not into it.

'Is Mr Jefferies not here?' Mr Rosing asks. He opens one side of the heavy gates, glancing back towards my car.

'He's busy with research today. We decided to spend a couple of days investigating around town before we arranged to come here with you.'

'I did wonder why you hadn't called.' He smiles, and my skin crawls. 'I've discovered some damage to the front of the house, one of the windows and the porch railing,' he says. 'Did you notice anything when you were out here the night before last?'

Sneaky. I compose a suitably confused face. 'We didn't come here that night because you advised us not to.' I pull the gate key from my backpack. 'Which reminds me, I have this. Should I hang onto it or—'

'I'll take it. I can arrange for you to collect it if you ever need to be here unattended.'

He casts an eye over me as he slides the key into the pocket of his beige overcoat, then he smiles again. Oof. I really don't like that smile.

'It's a shame you won't see the house at its best today,' he says. 'Some young vandals, I expect, went a bit too far. Unfortunately, it's not unusual at this time of year, with Halloween looming.' He pauses and studies me again, his eyes shrewd.

This time I arrange my face into a look that I hope mirrors his frustration. 'Will you call the police?'

'No point. Whoever it was will be long gone.'

'Maybe it's time to install new security cameras?' I say, silently thankful that they weren't active the other night.

'Mr Western has decided not to put another security system in. He's concerned someone could hack into it and leak the recordings online.'

'Is that why he won't allow Callum to record out here?' He nods. 'But you're okay with him doing a show about the house.'

He regards me with open impatience. 'If you both do your job, hopefully there won't be anything to interest people anymore.' He glances back towards the house. 'I'm going to circle the building and check nothing else needs my attention.'

We walk down the familiar stone path, stopping about ten feet from the porch. The damage is way worse than I thought it would be. The explosion left a gaping hole.

Shutters hang askew and only a few pointy slivers of glass cling to the cracked timber frame of the shattered window. A broken piece of railing dangles precariously over the garden from where Callum flew through it.

I consider the house, and the dark hole where the window once was. It's almost as if something set a trap, waiting for the exact moment Callum got close enough and then, *kaboom*. A shiver creeps down my spine. I've never witnessed ghost behaviour like that before. I've seen spirits toss objects across the room, including me, but I've never seen a spirit explode anything. Or set a trap for someone. In my experience spirits react, they don't strategise. So what happened here?

'This is as close as I will go,' Mr Rosing says. 'You see how the garden beds nearer the house are dead? I can't pluck up the courage to tend to them.'

'I wondered about that. Negative spectral energy can sometimes cause plants to die off. I thought that might be what's happened here.'

'Nothing so sinister. I'll have to find someone to clean up this mess.' He waves towards the devastation Callum and I caused. 'The window and the shutters are original to the building. They'll be difficult to replace.'

'Why are the shutters on the lower floor open, but not the top floor?'

'The lower floor is quite sheltered from the weather, and keeping them open allows sunlight inside, which reduces the chance of dankness and mould.'

'Oh.' That makes sense, I guess. I shuffle forward a few steps, peering into the void created by the broken window.

'Would it be okay if I went up on the porch, Mr Rosing? I'd like to have a peek inside.'

'I'd prefer you didn't, not with the glass and broken railings. It's unsafe.'

'Then maybe if you have any photos of the interior you could send them through with the ones of the family you're organising for us? We've asked the Historical Society, but their files are in chaos at the moment, so it might be a bit of a wait. We have a copy of the house plans, but we'd like to get a better sense of what it looks like inside.'

'I've already sent some photos through with the information I forwarded to Mr Jefferies last night. Did he not receive them? I assumed he'd share them with you.'

My senses twitch to life. I'd have assumed that too. 'We haven't had a chance to catch up properly this morning,' I lie.

Had Callum not noticed the photos, or did he not get them? Both things seem unlikely. I chew on my lip, an unwanted suspicion needling me, then I turn to Mr Rosing and smile sweetly.

'I'll check with him when I get back. It's such a shame we didn't get to meet Mr Western when he was in town the other day. If you'd have let us know his plans, we could have arranged to come out here earlier.' He visibly stiffens. 'Can we at least call him? It's unusual not to speak to the client in cases like this.'

'You haven't had a case like this, Ms Daniels,' he says pointedly. 'And I have already conveyed all the information regarding Mr Western's schedule to Mr Jefferies. I think you two need to *catch up properly*. Shall we continue our inspection now?'

It takes everything in my power not to punch him in his smug face.

As we walk along the front of the house, keeping a safe distance from the building, he points to the widow's walk on the roof above the attic.

'That was a favourite spot of Mr Brendin Western. He liked to take his whiskey up there in the late afternoon, enjoying the excellent view of the ocean. On occasion he'd invite my father to join him.'

'Brendin Western was the last person who lived in this house, right?' He nods. 'And he was Edward Western's uncle?' He nods again. 'And was your father a friend of the family or did he work for the Westerns too?'

'He worked for them, as did my grandfather.'

'Your family histories are quite intertwined, then.'

'I suppose they are.' He points to an arched window above the grand front door. 'That was Margaret Western's favourite spot. From there she could oversee the entire estate. She was a magnificent woman by all accounts.'

'Edward's great-great-grandmother, right? The rumours are it's her ghost that haunts the house.'

'There are many rumours about this house, Ms Daniels, but I hope that's not what you're hanging your investigation on.'

If you gave us all the information we needed, I seethe silently, *we wouldn't have to.*

I point to the impressive oak looming in the distance. 'Is the Western family plot up there?'

Mr Rosing raises his eyebrows. 'Maybe you *have* been doing your research. You'll find some family members laid to rest there, along with members of the household staff who were particular favourites.'

'Would it be okay if I checked it out?'

'Please do. It's a fascinating piece of local history. I have a little gardening to attend to. When you're done, you'll find me among the rose bushes near the front gate.' He smiles his thin smile and disappears down the side of the house.

I climb the small hill, stopping under the shade of the majestic tree, resplendent in every hue of gold, to look back down the rise. I recognise the view instantly. This is the spot where my dream took place. Where I stood and admired the Western home, glowing in its heyday. Where the beautiful man tenderly kissed the young, fair-haired woman before choking her to death. Having a dream about a case is not unusual, but having a dream about somewhere I've never been before, which then turns out to be stunningly accurate? That's new. Something's happening to me, and I'm sure it's connected to this place. I look to the space beside me where I watched the lovers kiss, and I wonder who they were. Could that young woman be the ghost who's been seen stalking the grounds? Callum mentioned something about a girl with a broken heart who had taken her own life. Maybe that's not what happened. Maybe someone else took it. Of course, that's assuming my dreams are more than just dreams, and I don't know that, no matter how real they feel.

The graveyard is surrounded by a small iron fence. Fleurs-de-lis adorn its rails, some with their points snapped off.

Inside is a collection of grave markers in various states of disrepair. Tiny white daisies dot the ground, and faded, tattered floral tributes sit dried and mouldy among the crumbling marble and stone. On the gate is an iron plaque with the word 'Western' engraved in surprisingly simple lettering. A small triangular symbol sits below the name. I flip open my notebook and do a quick sketch, before swinging open the low gate. It groans and creaks, its old hinges stiff with rust.

Now that's an appropriately creepy gate noise.

Holding a copy of the Western family info that Callum printed out for me, I step over debris, reading what headstones I can and checking off the names. Some of the headstones are very close together, and some even bear two names. I bet if this site was ever dug up, they'd find bodies stacked on top of each other.

For the slabs of stone that have deteriorated beyond legibility, I use a sheet of paper from my notebook to do a pencil rubbing, capturing the letters I can't see. If I find a headstone with a name that's not on my list, I make a note of that too. Two of those names are Rosing.

'I guess you guys were the favourites,' I mutter to the headstones as I jot down the information. I note the words 'faithful acolyte' under the name of the Rosing I assume was Rosing Senior. It seems like an odd word to use. Acolyte. I'll have to ask the current Mr Rosing about it.

After a while, I tuck my notebook away and focus my energy on connecting with any trace of the spirits that might have once lingered here. But when I quieten my mind, I'm met with a silence so heavy it presses down on me. Even the echo I sensed earlier is gone. I've never been to a graveyard where there wasn't at least one ghost hanging around. Most of them are like the Haunted Mansion at Disneyland – ghosts everywhere. Maybe the Westerns are particularly contented dead people. Or perhaps the silence in the graveyard is something more sinister. Ghosts afraid of other ghosts? I make a mental note to mention it to Callum.

I return to the shade of the towering oak, resting against its sturdy trunk as I contemplate the house below. Under today's clear blue sky, the sunshine hits the building in such a way that it sparkles, almost as if it's alive.

I recall my dream, the lamp light glowing in the windows and the laughter floating from the doors. I close my eyes and soak up the history, the family that once lived here, the love and tragedy that must permeate its walls and the grounds around me. I try to sense the murdered young woman who drew her last breath only steps from where I stand, but once again, I'm met with an eerie silence. I can't remember a time when I haven't had at least one spirit muttering to me when I've opened my mind to them, and lately, even when I haven't. But not here, where I'd expect a cavalcade of voices.

This must be what it's like for people who don't have my psychic abilities. Normal people who go about their lives without the dead popping up in front of them. I never stop wishing for that life. Wishing I wasn't the way I am – an anxious, lonely, ghost-seeing freak. I sigh in resignation as I push off the tree and take one last look at the house.

I freeze. Something in the attic window catches my eye. A movement. A shadow. A person? I squint at the building, trying to see past the reflection the sun casts on the glass. That's when it hits me. Grief. Anger. Pain. Despair. Thundering through my body all at once.

Tears fill my eyes, the air around me thins, and I struggle for breath, sinking to my knees, my mouth opening and closing, my lungs gasping for air.

'What . . . what . . .' I paw at my throat as it constricts.

White spots pop in front of my vision as I fall to my side, my breath a wheezing squeak.

Is this how I die?

Another wave of sorrow rises up from deep within.

Does it really matter?

My life comes into sharp focus. My isolation, my otherness. I'm not loved. I'm not wanted. Rejected by my family. My mother and grandmother dying to escape me. Even Celeste chose death over being my friend. And Callum will be next. Because I'm a monster. I'm cursed. Not worthy of love. Not worthy of anything. I'm an abomination.

That's when I hear the voice.

'*It will be over soon,*' it says, rumbling through me, strangely soothing. '*No more pain. Let go. Release it all and you'll finally be free.*'

So, I breathe out, and I don't take another breath back in.

I lie on the hill, the grass cool against my face. The pulse throbbing in my temples slows, and I'm suddenly so heavy I feel as if I will sink into the ground. That the moist dirt will envelop me and drag me down into the earth's warm caress. It feels good, the blackness that beckons. It feels like relief.

'It will be over soon,' the voice says again.

Whispers swirl through the air, a hiss of strange sounds I don't understand.

'Let go,' the voice coos. *'Don't you want to be free?'*

'Yes,' I croak. 'I want to be free.'

As darkness fills the corners of my mind, I hear another voice, this one calling out my name.

I ignore it at first, focusing on the sweet nothingness seeping into my bones.

Then the other voice comes again.

'Ms Daniels, I'm leaving for the day.'

The nothingness begins to recede. Air fills my lungs, and my eyes flutter open. A face. There's a face staring down at me. Floating, blurred, dreamlike. There's something familiar about it, but the more I try to focus, the more the image fades away.

'Who are you?' I say, or think – I can't be sure which. But then the face is gone, and I wonder if it was ever there at all.

With a breath so deep it burns, I push onto my hands and knees and reach for the tree beside me, pulling myself up. I rest my head against the oak, and my arms and legs tingle as life returns to them.

Clinging to the tree, I check around me, then look down to the house. For a moment, I think I see something at one of the downstairs windows, a blur of a shape, maybe a figure, but when I blink it's gone. An intense quake rolls through my body, threatening to fell me again. I quickly clean off the dead leaf mulch clinging to my jeans, and gather up my notebook and backpack, my hands trembling so violently I almost drop them. Half stumbling and half running, my feet slipping and sliding on the grass, I make my way towards what I now know was Mr Rosing's voice. I arrive at the rose garden, panting, sweat dripping down the side of my face.

'Sorry,' I say through a series of puffs. 'I didn't hear you at first.'

'Are you all right, Ms Daniels? You look as if you've seen a . . .' He stops and glances at the house, his face draining of colour. 'I need to know what happened.'

I instinctively shrink away from him. I'm shaking and my mouth is dry, and the nausea that I felt the other night is back. If I don't get out of there now, I'm going to puke on Mr Rosing's bland brown shoes.

'I lost track of time.' I force myself to smile. 'So interesting. The graveyard. Thank you for letting me look around today, it was . . . insightful.'

'Are you sure you're alright? You look ill. Why don't we go—'

'I skipped breakfast, that's all. Low blood sugar. I should head off. Callum will be wondering where I am.' There's something about this man that I know I cannot trust.

He glances at the house again. He looks as sick as I feel.

As I lurch towards the gate, I remember something. 'Mr Rosing,' I call back, 'are some of your family buried in the graveyard?'

'Yes. As I said, particular favourites of the household staff were awarded the gift of resting with the family.'

'And these favourites were known as acolytes?'

He stares at me, his eyes cold and grey. 'A strange word, I agree. The Westerns have a certain sense of humour – something that comes with privilege, I suppose. But the Rosing family has always served the Western family however we are needed.'

I speed away from the house, not knowing or caring where I'm going. My hands are still trembling as they grip the steering wheel, my knuckles white and my palms slippery with sweat. Only when I've put a decent distance between myself and the Western place do I dare slow down. I check the rear-view mirror as if expecting to see someone, or something, following me. Mr Rosing's words float through my mind.

However we are needed.

Suddenly, my foot is hard on the brake as I swerve the car to the side of the road, skidding on the dirt. Fumbling with the door, I fling it open, jump out, lean over the drain ditch and vomit.

CHAPTER TWELVE

I quickly make my way to my room. I need time to catch my breath and process what just happened. I also need time to figure out how to tell Callum. He's going to be mad as hell, and I deserve it. I did exactly what I said I wouldn't do. I push open our adjoining door, sighing in relief to find Callum's room empty, then lock it to ensure I'm left alone. I brush my teeth, rinsing my mouth over and over to wash away the sour taste of vomit. I toss my jacket on a chair, then drop onto the edge of my bed and take a series of deep breaths, enjoying the sensation of the air travelling freely through my body. How could I have been so stupid to go there alone after what happened the other night? I could kick myself for being so arrogant. This is not my usual haunting, and that place is obviously dangerous.

I suddenly remember the accident Ola Hutchings mentioned and grab my laptop. Why the hell didn't I do this before? I'm not thinking clearly. A search brings up an article from the *East Mill Gazette*.

The article is dated nine months ago. Two men who'd been working on the Western property had a violent argument which left one of the men dead. He was beaten to death with a flashlight. The man who survived was found wandering in the lane adjacent to the property, covered in blood. He said he had no memory or knowledge of his coworker's death, and was taken to the hospital for assessment. Upon examination, he was found to have fingernail scratches around his neck.

I rush to the mirror and check my own neck. There's a red welt on one side where I scratched at myself as I desperately gasped for air.

I return to the article, my hands shaking again. Based on evidence from under the dead man's nails, investigators concluded that the dead man had attempted to throttle the surviving man, who fought him off using the flashlight, ultimately killing him in self-defence. That man is now under psychiatric care, awaiting further investigation before a possible manslaughter trial.

I scroll down to the smiling photo accompanying the article and my hand flies to my mouth. These men weren't tradesmen. I recognise one of them. They were paranormal investigators.

I don't even remember falling asleep, but when I wake up my feet are still on the floor, my laptop is still open across my thighs, and Richard Browling's smiling face is still staring back at me. He's a parapsychologist and amateur ghost hunter who's called me for advice a few times. We even had coffee once. He's a nice man – a little naïve and starry-eyed about the paranormal, but nice all the same. He always talked about helping people, that's why he wanted to do the work. I can't picture him beating someone to death with a flashlight, in self-defence or otherwise. He has a wife he adores and a couple of kids he dotes on. He showed me pictures of them.

I slam my laptop closed, groaning at the groggy daytime-nap feeling and the headache accompanying it. Checking the time, I see it's nearly 1 pm. I force myself up, splash water on my face and throw back a couple of painkillers. I knock on our adjoining door, but there's no answer, so I peek inside again. Callum's still not there.

I grab my phone and text him.

> Where are you?

> At the Maddison. Where are you?

> You're not in your room.

> We're in the lounge. Jason's here.

Callum is sitting in an armchair, leaning forward with his elbows on his knees. I vaguely recognise his friend, Jason, sitting opposite him. His legs are so long, his knees are bent up comically high, courtesy of the low couch he's perched on. His skin is fair, though not as fair as Callum's, and his jet-black hair hangs long and messy around his face.

He spots me as I enter the room, and his sudden glance up makes Callum turn towards the door.

'Holly! Remember Jason?'

I nod and hold out my hand. Jason stands and shakes it as I crane my neck looking up at him. He's a beanpole, a lanky six-four at least. His eyes are a piercing blue rimmed with the blackest of lashes, and his smile is wide and warm and makes me like him instantly.

'Nice to see you again,' I say quickly, then I turn to Callum. 'We need to talk.'

He stands, suddenly all business, his own smile vanishing. 'What happened?' he says.

'Don't be mad, but . . .' There's a quiver in my voice. 'I went to the house.'

Callum's jaw drops. 'You did what?' He's mad. 'Holly, what the hell? The place is dangerous! You said you wouldn't go there without me.'

'I know. I didn't mean to.'

'Then why the hell did you?'

'I don't know. I don't even remember driving there. Suddenly I was pulling up outside the gates. And I wasn't alone, I was with Mr Rosing. He was finishing up some gardening and checking out the damage from the other night. Our damage, not that he knows that.'

Callum stares at me, head shaking, his eyes fierce.

'Anyway, he offered to walk me around the grounds. It was all very innocent until, well, I went to check out the family graveyard and something happened.' My knees suddenly turn to Jell-O.

Jason quickly reaches out to steady me as I wobble. 'Woah.'

'I'm okay,' I say, obviously not.

'I've got you,' Callum says, his hand on the small of my back, as he guides me to the couch. He sits in front of me, so close our knees touch. 'Okay.' His voice is gentle now. 'Tell me exactly what happened.'

His fierce eyes have softened, his anger now concern. My taut nerves begin to loosen. I feel safe again, here with Callum, like this is where I should be.

I take a deep breath and tell him the whole story – the bits I remember at least. When I finish, he leans forward with a sigh and places his hands over mine.

'That was colossally stupid of you,' he says. 'My-level stupid.'

'You must be rubbing off on me.' I smile. He doesn't.

'Can we keep it to just one person doing stupid things in this duo? You're supposed to be the smart one.'

'I thought you were the smart one.' This time he smiles. 'I know, I shouldn't have gone to the house, but like I said, I didn't mean to and then with Mr Rosing there I thought—'

'It doesn't matter. All that matters is you're okay.'

His hands encircle mine now, his thumb gently stroking back and forth across my skin. My gaze dips from his eyes to his lips, then down the smooth curve of his neck to the vein that pumps there, its rhythm matching my own heartbeat. Fast. Speeding up with every flutter. Then I find his eyes again, the green seeming to deepen.

It's as if time stops, and I don't want it to start back up. I want to hang onto this moment, revel in his gentle touch, the heat building inside of me with every graze of his thumb.

'Ahem.' Jason clears his throat.

I slide my hand out from under Callum's and sit back full of flutters.

'Are you sure you're okay now?' Jason asks.

'I'm sure. I'm a little frightened, and feel a lot stupid, but I'm okay.'

Callum sits back too, his fingers steepled in thought. 'And this all happened under the oak tree from your dream?'

'The view of the house, everything was the same.'

'And the voice?' he asks.

'I don't know. It was different from the other one.'

'The other one?' Jason asks.

'Holly's hearing voices,' Callum says.

'Just one voice. Or maybe two.' I rub my brow. 'To be honest, the one from today could have been inside my head.'

Callum sits forward again. 'Was it like possession or something?'

'You mean like *The Exorcist*? No. And I've never seen anyone being possessed. Certainly, none of my clients have ever claimed that's happened to them, so I don't know that I believe in it. Do you?'

'You're thinking movie possession,' he says, 'spinning heads and projectile vomiting. Real possession can manifest as a darkness that the victim feels around them all the time. An oppressive energy invading their dreams and thoughts, preventing them from functioning normally, maybe causing them to display violent, anti-social behaviour. There are some pretty well-documented cases of what's believed to be true demonic possession. Of course, most people who claim to be possessed are suffering from a mental health issue, which is why the church rarely condones exorcisms anymore.' He leans in closer. 'But ... there's also spirit possession, which can manifest as either a spirit attachment or the sensation of another entity entering your body. Which could also be called channelling.' He lifts his brows at me. 'I think you know a little about spirit attachment, at least.'

'Well ... I don't think anything entered me. It was more like something tapped into my feelings. Or my fears. I can't remember it all, but it was as if my life was draining away and I was okay with it. Then Mr Rosing called my name, and that brought me around. Thank god he decided to finish up when he did.'

'You might need to change your opinion about him,' Callum says.

'No, I don't think so. There's something off about that man. Anyway, I think it was a warning. Something doesn't want us here.'

'Or something wants us here permanently,' he offers. 'And the face you saw? Was it a spirit?'

'I don't know what I saw.' I sigh, frustrated. 'I was still pretty out of it, and when I could finally focus, there was nothing there.'

'Do you think it could have been the same spirit Cal saw in the window at the house?' Jason asks.

I look from Jason to Callum.

'He filled me in on what happened,' Jason adds.

I frown at Callum. 'So you *do* think you saw something?'

He shrugs. 'I don't know what I think anymore.'

'There seems to be a bit of that going around.' I turn to Jason. 'I'm not sure what either of us saw, but it's odd that Callum saw something and I didn't. Seeing spirts is kind of my thing.' Then I add, without thinking, 'Like the one over there by the fireplace.'

I glare at George, as he warms his dead hands over the flame. If I wasn't so irritated by his sudden appearance, I might laugh. But this spirit has leaked through my defences twice now and this lack of control I'm experiencing is frustrating me. I need to find my focus. I look down at Callum's knees, pressed to mine. That's not helping. I wiggle back further in my seat.

I resist the temptation to get rid of George once and for all, seeing as he's so *well-loved*, and instead focus on shutting down the part of my mind that accidentally let him in. With that, the ghost is gone. I feel his presence lingering, but at least he's out of my sight.

'Holly!' Callum says.

I blink, and see two worried faces staring at me. Well, one looks worried. The other looks slightly horrified. 'Sorry, did you say something?'

'I asked if you were serious,' Callum says.

I look from Callum to Jason. Callum could handle the truth, but I'm not sure Jason can.

'No. Just kidding.'

Callum frowns. 'That's not funny. You scared Jason.'

Jason puffs up. 'I'm not scared.' His eyes dart to the corner of the room.

'Anyway,' I say, 'we have no way of knowing if what went after me today is the same thing that Callum saw at the house. Um, speaking of the house,' I add, trying to sound nonchalant, 'did Mr Rosing send through some photos last night? He mentioned—'

'Yeah, shit. There's not much but I meant to send them through to you. I'll do that when I get back to the room.'

I nod, relieved that's one weird feeling I don't have to worry about anymore.

'There's something else,' I say. 'Do you know a parapsychologist called Richard Browling?'

Callum cocks his head. 'Yeah, I think I met him at a conference I was presenting at. Nerdy, excitable guy, crazy about the paranormal and his kids?'

'That's him. Well, I forgot to mention this before, with everything that's been going on, but Ola Hutchings told me there'd been an accident at the house, some time ago. She said two tradesmen working on an electrical problem had a fight and one of them killed the other one. I only remembered that when I got back to my room today, so I looked it up. One of those men was Richard Browling. I think they were the other team of investigators, the one Rosing accidentally mentioned.'

'Fuck,' Callum breathes out softly. 'Are you sure?'

I pull up the article on my phone.

He quickly reads it, his hand going to his mouth just like mine did.

'Shit. I thought Western must have fired them,' he says, 'because they couldn't give him any answers.'

'Mm. Not so much. This was less than a year ago too. There's no way Mr Rosing wasn't across their hiring. But he acted as if he had nothing to do with it, couldn't even recall their names. I call bullshit. Why wouldn't he tell us what happened? Why would he cover it up?'

Callum scrubs a hand across his chin. 'Maybe he was worried it might scare us off.'

'Maybe. But I don't think we can trust Mr Rosing or the information he shares with us. We need to speak with Edward Western.'

Callum sizes me up. 'You look a little pale. I think I should get some food into you.'

I put a hand to my cheek. 'Oh. Um. Okay.'

'I could eat,' Jason chimes in.

'Dude, you can always eat. You should see this guy eat, Holly. Never stops. That's why he's so lanky.'

'Just because you're short . . .' Jason says.

'I'm six-two.'

'Like, I said short.'

Callum looks at me and rolls his eyes. 'Come on,' he slaps Jason's back, 'Holly and I have found this great little cafe.'

I watch them jostle each other as they leave the room. It's a welcome distraction from the bad feeling gnawing at my insides.

'How's your side feeling?' I ask Callum.

He gives me a thumbs up. 'Fine,' he mumbles, through a mouthful of burger.

I nod at the smear of blood on the inside of his arm, where he's rested it against his shirt. 'I can tell by the way you're bleeding again.'

'Aww shit.' He grabs a napkin and wipes his arm clean, lifts his shirt and presses the waded-up paper to the bloodied dressing. 'It's a good thing I always wear black.'

Jason leans over the table and pokes at Callum's wound. 'You should probably get that stitched.'

'Ow. Stop poking me, man. I'm fine. I'll whack some more butterfly strips on it.'

'He's right, Callum. You need stitches,' I say. 'Please stop being ridiculous. Let me—'

'I said it's okay. Stop fussing, both of you.' He stuffs the stained napkin into his pocket and stands. 'I'd better sort this out.'

'Should I come with you?' I ask.

'I said I'm fine. Finish your lunch and bring Jason up to speed, I'll see you back at the Maddison.' His eyes narrow as they flick between us. 'Just . . . don't have too much fun without me.' He turns and stomps from the restaurant.

'I was only trying to help,' I mutter as I pick up a fry.

'Don't worry about it,' Jason says. 'He's never been great with vulnerability. Years of being picked on, I guess.' He shrugs and bites into his burger.

'He said something about that to me, but I still find it hard to believe.'

'That's how we met. I stopped a group of bullies pounding on him, and we became friends.'

'Seriously? But he's so . . .' I wave my hand, indicating his size and . . . everything else. It didn't seem possible.

'This was before he was . . .' Jason makes the same gesture as I did. 'But he was an orphan and honestly, a bit of a strange kid. He had an oddball aunt, was way smarter than anyone else, always carried around weird books, and was a little slow to grow. He was different. Being different makes you an easy target.'

No shit.

'Once we teamed up and he sprouted, everyone steered clear of us. Except the girls.' He picks up a fry, dips it in ketchup and shoves it in his mouth. 'The girls definitely did not steer clear.'

My cheeks flush in a way I wish they wouldn't.

'He really should get stitches, though,' I say.

'You'll never get him to a hospital, Holly. Not unless his leg is falling off or something. Even then, he'd fight you. Bad associations.' His shoulders rise and fall with the force of his sigh. 'I probably shouldn't be talking about him like this, he wouldn't like it. Anyway, about you and Cal.'

'About me and Cal what?'

'You looked pretty close back there at the bed and breakfast. The way he was touching you, how tuned into each other you seem. I thought you guys might finally be, um . . .'

'I was freaking out, he was being nice,' I look down at my food. 'We're just working together, Jason.'

'Mm-hmm.'

'That's it.'

'Yep.'

I grab my coffee, take a slurp and change the subject. 'How do you feel about a road trip?'

'Where're we going?'

'To see Richard Browling.'

'The murderer? You sure you feel up to that after—?'

'It was self-defence and I'm fine.' It's keep busy or sit around thinking about what might have happened. 'He's in the psych ward at Lakeview Hospital, which it turns out isn't far from here. If Callum refuses to step foot in a hospital, we'll just have to go without him.'

CHAPTER THIRTEEN

Lakeview Hospital is a little under thirty minutes from East Mill. On the drive there, we talk about the Western house and Jason's interest in it.

'It's a curious blend of the colonial style architecture which saw a resurgence after the Civil War, the more decorative Italianate style, which is unusual for this area, and traditional design elements of the summer cottages that popped up along the coast here in the late 1800s.'

'It's hardly a cottage!'

'That's what they called them. They were mostly summer residences owned by wealthy families who lived in New York City and came out here to vacation. Nothing much has changed, really. I'd love to have a closer look at it. My brother and I help plan restorations and extensions on historic properties, protecting the historical integrity of the building. I should leave my card; we could help with the restoration of that window you two broke.'

'You know you can't go in there, right?'

'Cal said not until you've cleared it. How does that work by the way? Do you see spirits everywhere?'

'I can block them most of the time. I'm not sure how it works exactly, but I've met psychics with other skills who do a similar thing.'

'What kind of skills?'

'Read minds. There's a woman in the city I've met a couple of times who can do that. Imagine how noisy that would be if you couldn't zone everyone out. For me, I focus on letting the spirits in and I focus on keeping them out. It's like I can open and close a part of my brain. Like a muscle that I've built up and learnt to use. But sometimes, if my focus is off, the ghosts slip through.'

'What kinds of things knock your focus off?'

I want to say, *Lately, your friend.* 'If I'm tired or stressed or distracted. But also, sometimes their energy is so strong they break through my defences.'

'What do they look like to you? Rotting skin, heads half hanging off and bloodied tattered clothes?'

I laugh. 'No, thank goodness. They look human mostly, but their eyes have no light in them, and their skin shines as if they're made of wax. They're not exactly transparent, but they don't look quite solid either. It's hard to describe. They just look off. Clothes-wise, they wear whatever they wore in life, I guess.'

'Well that's disappointing,' he says. I laugh again. 'And you help these spirits with whatever they need?'

'I move them on. I'm not sure if that helps them or not.'

'Don't they tell you what they want?'

'No, they never speak to me, they just yell. No words, just noise. But even if I knew what they wanted, I'm not sure

I'd care. I just want them gone. My theory is there's life and there's death, and there's no in-between. When you die, your time here is done. Don't be an asshole; move on.'

Jason laughs now. 'That's an interesting way of looking at things. Can any other psychics do what you do?'

'Not that I've met so far. But there's probably someone out there somewhere. I'd like to think so – it would be nice to know I'm not a total freak.'

'You're not a freak.'

'You try going out to dinner and having me suddenly burst into Latin because some waiter who died two years ago still has a beef with the restaurant owner.'

'That's happened?' I nod solemnly. 'Shit. Well, it doesn't matter. You shouldn't talk about yourself like that, Holly. I don't find you freaky.'

'You don't know me.'

'You'd be surprised. Cal's told me quite a bit about you.'

I cluck my tongue at his knowing grin and arched brows.

'Did he show you the plans of the house?' I ask, moving the conversation off me yet again.

'I had a quick look over them.'

'Did he ask you about . . . a cellar?' Why does my voice sound so small all of a sudden?

'Yep. The drawings of the OG house definitely show something that looks to be a cellar, probably a root cellar. They became more popular from the mid-1600s onwards. It looks separate from the house because it would have had an exterior entry on the grounds outside the building.

The drawings don't state what it is, so I can't give you a definite, but my guess would be that yes, the original house had some form of cellar.'

'That people could stand up in?'

He looks confused. 'I mean, sure. People stored vegetables and grain in root cellars, and even butchered animals – they were pretty roomy. I doubt it's still there, though. The plans of the current house are far more detailed and don't show one. The staff quarters cover that area now, so I'd say the old cellar was likely filled in before the current house was built. Does that help at all?'

'I think so.'

That should mean whatever was going on in my first dream, can't be connected to the haunting at the current house. So maybe it *was* just a dream. One of the knots in my stomach releases.

As we travel along the highway, beaches roll past. Spectacular homes rise above the sand, their winding driveways guarded by electronic gates and their grey-shingled roofs blending into the ocean beyond. On the other side of the highway is forest – dense and brushy, a wild explosion of gold and crimson, the ground carpeted in leaves.

Jason tells me more about his work and his family, his brother and his niece. Listening to him chatting away, I understand why Callum has been friends with him for so long. He has the same easy way about him that Callum does, and his life sounds so *normal*. I can imagine Callum craving that, just like I did growing up. Still do.

Jason catches my eye and smiles. 'Have we got a plan for when we get to the hospital?'

'I called while you were sorting out the check at the cafe. The doctor said Richard probably won't speak to me.'

'Even though he knows you?'

'I think he meant he literally won't speak. He hasn't said a word since the police brought him in.'

'What makes you think he'll talk now?'

'It's worth a shot. Richard's been to the property, he may have even been inside the house. He might have information that could help us. Right now, we know far too little, and I don't like that.'

Lakeview Hospital is a long red-brick building, tucked into a stand of pine trees at the end of a twisting driveway. We check in at the gatehouse, then follow the signs to visitor parking. When we arrive at the nurse's station, I explain that I'm an old friend of Richard's, and we're shown into a brightly lit room with long barred windows overlooking a pristine lawn, a picturesque lake shimmering in the distance. In the centre of that room, Richard Browling sits in a lounge chair, staring into space.

'His wife visits once a week,' the nurse says. 'But he doesn't even speak to her, so don't expect much.'

'We just want him to know there are people that care about him,' I say. 'Maybe he'll hear us.'

The nurse looks over at Richard. 'I hope so. We'll be just outside if you need us.'

I squat beside Richard's chair. His gaze is fixed behind me, and I check over my shoulder to see what he's staring at. But it's just a blank wall.

'Richard?' I gently touch his arm. 'It's Holly Daniels. Do you remember me?'

Richard doesn't move, or even blink.

'Holly from New York. I see ghosts. We've spoken a few times, and we had coffee once. You told me about your kids and your wife. Do you remember?'

Still nothing.

'Richard, I've been to the Western house. Something happened to me there. It felt as if my life was being sucked out of me. Did you feel or see anything at the house? The Western house?'

His eyelashes flutter.

'Richard? Can you hear me? Can you tell me what happened to you?'

'Stay away,' Richard says, his voice scarcely a rasp.

My eyes snap to Jason. He looks as shocked as I feel.

I turn back to Richard again. 'There you are. You can hear me.' I rub a hand up and down his arm. 'Can you tell me what happened that day?'

'That place . . . no . . . stay away.'

'Edward Western has asked me to investigate the house. Can you tell me anything that might help? What happened to you there?'

Richard jerks away from my touch and grabs my arm instead. I recoil, almost toppling backward, but he doesn't let go. He squeezes tighter, his fingers pressing deep red marks into my skin.

I scramble to my knees. 'Richard, you're hurting me.'

Jason lurches forward. 'Richard, let her go.'

Richard slowly turns his face towards me, fear etched in every crease, haunted eyes staring into mine.

'Don't let them take you, Holly! Can't let them . . . take you . . .'

His hand drops as he sinks back into his chair, muttering the words over and over, 'Don't let them take you . . .' until he slowly quietens, his blank stare returning.

My heart pounds. 'Don't let who take me, Richard?' I rub his arm again. 'Richard?' But I can see he's already gone.

I stare into Richard's vacant eyes, fear lodging alongside the sadness lumping in my throat, until eventually I allow Jason to haul me off the floor. He stares at Richard too, eyes flick between me and the man now locked in his mind again.

'What the hell was that about?' he asks. The colour has drained from his cheeks.

I take Jason by the hand and drag him to the door. 'I don't know, but let's get out of here.'

There's no chatter this time as we drive back to East Mill. Just a heavy silence that fills the car. I can't stop thinking about Richard. The man I met in the city was a happy man with a lovely family. Now his wife and kids are sitting at home without a husband or a father, wondering what happened and why he would kill someone. What did that house do to him? When Jason finally does say something, it takes me a moment to register the question.

'Sorry, Jason, what did you say?'

'What did he mean, *don't let them take you*? Is that a demon possession thing?'

'I don't know. I just know ghosts. I don't have experience with any other kinds of supernatural things; I don't even know if they exist. Callum's the one with that kind of knowledge. I might swing a rosary and say a bit of Latin, but I'm no expert on theology or possession.'

'But if you deal with ghosts, you must know about the afterlife.'

'The only afterlife I see is the dead clinging on to a life that no longer exists. The spirits I deal with are awful, sure. But they're not usually evil demons from the pits of hell.' I look at Jason. He looks half terrified. 'Anyway, I think we should take what Richard says with a hefty grain of salt, don't you?' Jason just frowns. 'You saw him. Who knows what's going on inside his mind.'

'Why does that not make me feel any better about—'

He's cut short as I hit the brakes, hard. The car screeches, its tyres struggling for purchase. Acrid smoke billows around us as we fishtail across the asphalt, coming to an abrupt stop on the shoulder of the Old East Mill Highway.

'What the *hell*, Holly?'

I nod ahead. 'Sorry, I had to stop for her.'

He squints through the windshield. 'Who? Should I be seeing someone?'

'Nope. This one's for my eyes only.'

CHAPTER FOURTEEN

I slowly approach the spirit on the road. They can move fast when they want to, and they can be strong – I've had the bruises to prove it. The calmer I am, the calmer the ghosts remain, and that makes it easier to do my work.

It's a girl of about sixteen, in a white bonnet and grey dress with a round collar. She opens her mouth and I prepare for the screech as I start my incantation.

'They know what you are,' hisses the girl, her waxy face turned towards me.

The Latin dies on my lips.

I stagger backwards, staring at her, my heart leaping in my chest. 'W-what?' *It spoke. It spoke to me.* 'W-what did you just say?'

'They are powerful, and they know what you are.'

I step forward cautiously. 'Y-you can hear me?' The girl nods. So they *can* hear me. How long have they been able to hear me?

'They slaughtered me and others like me,' she says. 'You must not let them take you.'

My breath catches, my hands trembling at my sides. Those were Richard's words.

'Who are you talking about? Who are *they*?'

'You must let us in.'

Realisation hits me like a bolt of lightning from the sky, rocking me where I stand. She's the girl from my dream. The one in the cellar who was killed with a silver dagger.

'Y-you were in a dream I had. You were murdered in a windowless room. A cellar?' She nods again. 'It was you who spoke to me. It was your voice.' Another nod. I put a hand to my chest; my heart pounds against my palm. 'Why?'

'Because I know *what you are*.' She smiles and goes to turn away.

'Wait.' I foolishly try to grab her hand, like a complete novice, my fingers gliding through her wrist, the chill rushing up my arm. 'What's your name?'

'The dead have no names. But in life, they called me Elizabeth.'

'Elizabeth,' I whisper. 'I don't understand what's happening here.'

But even as my words hang in the air, a puff of warmth against the cold, the spirit begins to vanish. And as I watch the last wisps of her melt away, her voice fills my mind again.

'Do not trust the handsome man.'

I stare at the spot where the spirit disappeared, then rush forward, calling out, 'Please, Elizabeth. I don't understand. I don't know what you mean.' My body shakes; violent trembles rolling through me from head to toe. I've never had a ghost speak to me before. Even as a child when I tried to speak to the spirits, I never heard words in their howls. Why this one? Why Elizabeth? What does it mean?

There's one thing I know it means: my dreams aren't just dreams. They're clues. What's happening to me?

'Holly?' I snap around. Jason hovers beside his open car door. 'Are you okay?' he calls.

I stumble towards him, my knees threatening to buckle. He dashes to my side, but I push him away.

'What happened?' he says.

I glance back at the trees. 'Nothing. Just another day at the office.'

The spirit's words keep rolling through my head. *You must not let them take you. Do not trust the handsome man.* I need alone time. I need space. I need to be away from people so I can think.

'I'm going to head to my room,' I tell Jason when we get back to the Maddison.

He stares at me, his face still pale with worry. 'Shouldn't we bring Cal up to speed?'

As if on cue, Callum bursts into the hall.

'You're back. Fuck. What the hell?' His hands are clasped on the top of his head and he's puffing. 'Where have you been? I've been trying to call you.'

Jason and I glance at each other, confused, then Jason pulls out his phone and shows me three missed calls. 'It must have been a dead spot or something?'

Ironic turn of phrase. I fish my phone from my back pocket. Five missed calls. 'I don't know why, but our phones didn't ring.'

Callum's wild eyes move from me to Jason and back. I've never seen him look like this. He's panicked.

'You . . .' He draws a trembly breath. 'You can't do that to me. You can't disappear like that. I thought . . .' His fists now clench and unclench at his sides. 'I thought something had happened to you.'

Jason whispers, 'Fuck,' under his breath. Then he places his hands on his friend's shoulders and looks into his eyes. 'I'm so sorry, Cal. But we're fine, okay? We came back.'

I watch the interaction between the two men. This is clearly something Jason's dealt with before.

Callum nods, then sighs slowly, his shoulders relaxing on the long breath. 'Where were you?'

'We went to see Richard,' I say.

His gaze bounces between me and Jason again. 'You went without me?'

'He's in a hospital, Cal,' Jason answers. 'We thought you'd prefer to skip it. Don't blame Holly. It was my call.'

'Oh. Right. Okay.'

My eyes catch Jason's with a silent thank you.

'Did Richard say anything?' Callum asks.

'Why don't we sit, instead of standing out in the hall,' Jason says.

He slings an arm around Callum's shoulders and manoeuvres his friend back into the guest lounge. With a wistful glance towards my room, I follow them.

I plop to the couch and sink into the cushions. Callum drops down beside me.

'What happened with Richard?' he says.

My hands ball into fists as I think about the once-happy man I knew and the man I saw in that barren room. 'It was awful,' I say. 'He was just sitting there, staring into space with blank eyes.'

'So, he didn't say anything?'

'No, he did. When I asked him about the Western house he suddenly came to life, just for a moment. Long enough to suggest that we're dealing with more than one spirit here. He mentioned *them*.'

Jason clears his throat. 'What he said was . . . *Don't let them take you*.'

'Don't let them take you?' Callum asks me, his voice tense. 'Who's *them*?'

'I don't—'

Before I can answer him, Jason butts in. 'It sounded like what you were talking about earlier. Possession.'

'Maybe,' Callum says. 'Maybe it's a demon and not a spirit? That could explain the exploding window, they have that kind of power.' He turns to me. 'And why I saw something, and you didn't. It's believed that demons can appear as human, though the Bible doesn't say this implicitly. But there are studies of what are believed to have been demons who took human form to trick someone into trusting them. There's demon mythology in multiple cultures and religions, not just in Christianity. They can also possess objects, like the Annabelle doll.'

'I thought that was just a movie,' Jason says.

'No, no, it's based on a real doll with a terrifying history of causing accidents and death. The doll is still regularly blessed by a priest.'

I rub my temples. 'Okay guys, stop for a minute. I don't think Richard was talking about evil dolls, and he's obviously damaged – he bludgeoned someone to death with a flashlight! Something must have happened to him, but I don't know how much of what he said we can take as gospel, no pun intended. You should have seen him, Callum. It was heartbreaking. His poor wife.'

'His kids,' Callum adds quietly.

I nod. 'Anyway, he shut down before I could get anything more out of him. But if we look at what he *did* say . . . well, whatever we're dealing with, there's more than one of them, and we already know of two ghost stories so . . . I don't think we should be jumping to demonic conclusions. We've been asked to investigate a haunting, and that's what we should do.'

'I don't think we should rule anything out either,' Callum says, his eyes fixed on mine. 'I don't want whatever it is in that house trying to take you.'

Jason clears his throat. 'That's not all that happened. Holly saw a spirit when we were on our way back into town.'

Callum cocks his head, his eyebrows arched.

'What? I see spirits all the time, you know that.'

A headache tightens across my brow. I want to tell Callum about Elizabeth. I want to tell him that she spoke to me and ask him what he thinks it means. Because it's a big deal, it's a very big deal, and I'm freaking out a little. But I need time to process it myself first. I'm not used to sharing everything that happens in my life and opening it up for discussion. If this is what being around people is like, maybe the rats aren't such a bad option.

I stand and stretch. 'It's been a very weird day. I'm exhausted and I need a moment alone to catch my breath.' I look down at Callum looking up at me. 'Let's talk later, okay?'

He nods, eyes wide and worried. I smile and gently touch his shoulder. He reaches up and lays his hand over mine. I linger there, our eyes locked, the warmth from our hands mingling, my heart's beat a little out of rhythm, then I give his shoulder a squeeze and head to my room.

A streetlight throws a long shadow across the ceiling. The drapes are open, and I'm lying on top of the bedcovers, still in my clothes. I haven't even taken off my boots. I shiver as my body becomes aware of the cold, rub my eyes and stumble across the room, cursing as I bang my shin on a small wicker table that appears to have been strategically placed for maximum bruising. I close the window, draw the drapes and turn on the floor lamp, wincing from the sudden glare. I check the time on my phone. It's just after midnight, and I have two unread text messages from Callum.

> We're getting food if you want to come.

Then, an hour later.

> Just checking you're okay. I'm here when you need me.

I pull on a sweatshirt, kick off my boots and slip my feet into a thick pair of socks. I'm ready to tell Callum about Elizabeth. I'm ready to share that she's from my dream – which I now know was more than a dream, though I don't understand how. He's bound to have some insight. Besides, we're supposed to be a team. No more keeping things from each other, that's what we decided.

I pad across the room and put my ear to the adjoining door. Callum's low snores leak through the wood. Oh well, I'll tell him everything tomorrow.

I'm wide awake now, so I grab my laptop and head down to the lounge to do a little research. As well as keeping the fire lit, the owner of the bed and breakfast leaves coffee, tea and snacks out for people who arrive late, or for those of us who can't sleep. I feel the room for George, relieved to find he's not here – probably upstairs knocking on doors. I pour myself an English Breakfast tea, stick a cookie between my teeth and curl up on the couch, flipping open my computer.

'Night owl?' a deep voice asks.

I look up with a start. Jason's leaning in the doorway in trackpants and a hoodie.

'Oh! You scared me.' I wipe a splash of tea from my sweatshirt.

'Mind if I join you?'

I pat the couch in answer. 'Why aren't you sleeping?'

'I'm a little shook about today, I guess.' He drops heavily onto the cushions beside me. 'Why aren't you sleeping?'

'Curse of the ghost business. I do most of my work at night.'

We sit in silence, staring at the flames crackling in the fireplace.

'I'm sorry about earlier,' he eventually says. 'And my big mouth.'

I laugh. 'That's okay. Only, I think it's better to drip feed that kind of stuff to Callum or he might go all knight in shining armour.'

'He does have heroic tendencies.' He shifts a little. 'Can I ask you something?'

'Sure.'

'It's personal.'

'Now I'm worried.'

'You don't have to answer but, I'm not crazy am I? You do like Cal, right? And I don't just mean as a work buddy.'

'Didn't we go over this?'

'Come on, Holly. You're not fooling me. I doubt you're even fooling yourself.'

I look away, the heat of the fire mixing with the warmth of the blood quickly rising in my cheeks.

'Why does it matter to you?' I ask.

'Because he's my friend,' Jason says, 'and his happiness is important to me. He likes you, you know.'

'I know. He doesn't exactly hide it.'

'And you . . .?'

I roll my eyes and nod.

'So, what's the problem?'

God. Where do I start? 'How long have you got?' I joke.

'As long as you need,' he answers sincerely.

'Do you know about why I stopped working with Callum?'

'Yep. He told me today. He feels bad about it. Real bad. He knows there's no excuse for letting you down like that. But, Holly – and I'm not trying to make you feel bad here – I think you should know that when you ghosted him . . . well, you saw his panic today. He has some major abandonment issues going back to his folks. Once he knew you were okay, the fear turned into confusion and hurt.'

I wriggle uncomfortably. 'I meant to call him. To talk to him about what happened. Yell at him or whatever I needed to do.'

'Then why didn't you?'

'Because I was crushed, Jason. Because I didn't want to hear his excuses, or worse, I didn't want to confirm that's what he really thought about me. That I'm a freak . . .' I shake my head.

'Now you've heard his side, can you forgive him?'

I chew the inside of my cheek as I think. 'I'm not sure it matters,' I eventually say. 'I can't have the kind of relationship I think he might want. Or any kind of relationship, really.'

'Can I ask why?'

My eyes drop to the cup in my hands. 'If I'm being honest with myself – which, by the way, I really hate doing – I'm scared of getting involved with someone. Maybe terrified is a better word.'

'At the time, Callum wondered if he'd scared you off. Too fast, too much.'

'No. It wasn't that. I wouldn't have done what I did if I hadn't overheard him that day. Things were different for me then. Until he blew it.' I shake my head. 'I can't believe you guys talk about this kind of stuff.'

'We talk about most stuff. We're like brothers. I'd say I'm closer to Cal than I am to my actual brother.'

'I have a sister, but we're not that close. We haven't been for years.'

'You can't fix it?'

'I probably could. I have a suspicion it's me keeping us apart. Same with my dad. They never got used to what I do, and I never got used to feeling different from them. But I think I could be more understanding, and I want things to be better between us. Especially with Maggie. We used to have a lot of fun together when we were kids.' I sigh at the flash of memories. 'I've been thinking about this a lot lately. About being alone and . . . rats.'

'Rats? I know a good exterminator if you need one.'

'They're metaphorical rats. Never mind. I don't know why I'm telling you all of this.'

'Because I asked.'

Smiling, I unfold my legs from under me. I like Jason. There's no awkwardness with him. None of the tension or heightened emotions I always experience around Callum. Probably because I'm not falling in love with Jason. The thought startles me so much, my teacup clatters in its saucer.

Oh god. I cover it with my hand and sit perfectly still as I process that thought.

'You okay there?' Jason asks.

'Um, yeah. Just clumsy.' I put my cup down and steady myself, curl back onto the couch and pull a protective cushion against my chest.

Jason eyeballs me with his bright blue gaze. 'Why can't you and Cal give it another go?'

'Okay,' I whisper to myself, as much as to him. 'So . . .' I start. 'My friend died not long after what happened with Callum. You know that, yeah?'

He nods. 'Celeste. I never met her, but Cal told me about her. You were with her when she died, right?'

The weight of the memory lands with a thud and I sink further into the couch. I haven't spoken a word about this since I broke the news to Max that his wife was dead. I squeeze the cushion tighter.

'Celeste called and said she needed to talk,' I say. 'She'd had a fight with Max. They were more family to me than my family. Anyway, the night she called, I didn't have time to talk because I was about to head out on a job. So, she said she'd come along. It had been a while since we'd done a spiritual clearing together and . . . well . . . I still don't really know what happened. I only know Celeste and Max had fought earlier in the day. I told her we'd grab a coffee once we were finished and talk about everything then, but she couldn't stop going on and on about their argument, rehashing every tiny detail.'

Jason pulls one long leg up under him so he can face me, and pushes his floppy hair back. 'What was the fight about?'

'That's the thing. It didn't even seem like a big deal to me. It was something about Thanksgiving and Max accepting an invitation before discussing it with her. She was so mad at him about it. I kept saying we'd talk later, asking her to be quiet, to keep calm. If we kept calm, the spirit would be calm. But she was so wound up, and that energy was pouring out of her.' I take a sip of my tea, preparing myself for the next bit. My hands tremble a little.

'You don't have to tell me the rest, Holly.'

'No. I want to. I've kept it in for too long.' I breathe deep. 'It happened in a split second. I felt the energy in the room shift and spun around to see the spirit closing in on Celeste. She couldn't see it, but I could tell she could sense it was there. She was up against the landing railing trying to steady herself, but in her panic she lost her grip and then her balance and before I could get to her, she toppled over, crashing to the floor below. By the time I blasted the spirit and got down to her, she was already gone.'

My hands make white-knuckled fists as I remember my friend lying on that floor broken and bloody. Me helpless as I tried to bring her back. I swallow and it rings in my ears.

'Then of course there were paramedics and police making everything a million times worse. The owners of the property explained why I was in their house, suffering through the eye rolls from the detectives. I told the police I didn't see Celeste fall. I lied. But there was no evidence of it being anything other than an accident. Ghosts don't leave evidence. Eventually it was ruled a misadventure. What a word.'

'God, Holly. I'm so sorry that happened to you, and to her.'

'But that's the thing — if she'd been focused on the work instead of on all her relationship stuff, it would never have happened.' I rub my eyes with the heels of my hands. 'Max blamed himself. I tried to tell him it wasn't his fault. If it was anyone's fault it was mine. I didn't have her back. That was my job.'

My breath hitches, the memories still so clear. 'He moved back to Australia a couple of months later. I don't think he could stand it here without her. We haven't spoken since. He said he didn't blame me, but . . .' I drop my head back and squeeze my eyes shut. 'Celeste shouldn't have been there. She wasn't in the right head space. I should have seen how upset she was. I should have made time for her instead of putting work first. If I'd done that, she'd still be alive.'

After a long silence, Jason says, 'Max is right, Holly, it wasn't your fault. It was an accident.'

'Which should never have happened. That's why I can't get involved with anyone. Emotions cloud *everything*, and people die.'

'You don't really believe that, do you?'

I turn away again and watch the fire, the flames shimmering and dancing behind the grate. I don't know what I believe anymore.

'Here's what I think,' Jason says. 'You like to tell yourself you want to be on your own, but you really want the opposite. That's why you're here. You wanted a second chance with Callum. You wouldn't have said yes to him otherwise, I don't care what else was on the table, if you didn't want to see him, you would have said no. There's a connection between the two of you, and if I can see it, then I know you can feel it. He gets you and you get him and you're both secretly crazy about each other. Actually, not that secretly. Every touch, every smile, even every grumpy frown. You're both so obvious, Holly.'

I playfully whack him on the arm. 'I thought you were an architect, not a psychoanalyst.'

'I'm multi-skilled.' He yawns and stretches. 'Have you told Cal how Celeste's death affected you?'

'Nope. Apparently, I only share that kind of thing with men I hardly know.'

We both laugh.

'Can't you trust him?' Jason says.

That's the billion-dollar question, isn't it? Can I let myself trust Callum again? I hope so. Because I want to, I realise.

Jason pats my knee, not waiting for my answer. 'Sometimes you need to take a risk. A leap of faith. That's what humans do. We risk everything for the people we care about. It's part of life – the really good part.' He stands, shaking out his lanky legs. 'You should talk to Callum. He deserves to know where he stands. He thinks you think he's a massive jerk.'

I stare up at him. 'Well . . .'

He chuckles. 'I know you care about him. But you have to stop trying to save everyone. Trust that Callum can take care of himself. You deserve a shot at happiness as much as everyone else.'

*

When I get back to my room, there's a flicker of light spilling through the cracks around the adjoining door.

I put my things down and tap lightly. 'Are you awake in there?'

'Yep,' Callum calls. 'Come in.'

He's propped against the headboard, reading the book I bought him. His comforter is bunched around him, and the glow from the muted television plays out a series of colours across his beautiful face.

My heart skips so many beats my head gets light, and for once I let myself enjoy the sensation.

'Anything interesting?' I ask.

'Well, if you believe this guy, Long Island is the world centre for weirdness. But there is one thing. A missing person story from 1883. A young woman named Annie Payne disappeared from Mill Pond, which isn't far from here. She was believed to have run away, chasing a beau to California. But when the family tracked the man down, she wasn't with him. No one saw her ever again.' He lifts his brows at me.

'Are you thinking she might be our second ghost?'

'Timing fits. Could be worth digging into. Another mystery to add to the list.' He closes the book. 'Do you feel like watching something with me?' he asks, hope tinging his voice.

I shake my head. 'I just wanted to apologise for worrying you today, twice. I should have let you know we were going to see Richard. I'm just not used to involving anyone else in my decisions. I'm barely used to talking to anyone.' I smile and shrug.

He rolls onto his side to face me, propping himself up on an elbow, his T-shirt pulling tight around his bicep.

'Holly, you don't have to report to me. But maybe don't disappear on me without leaving a note when we're in the middle of investigating a violent haunting.'

I laugh. 'Fair.'

'So . . . you like Jason?'

'I really do. He's lovely.'

Callum's eyes narrow. 'How lovely are we talking?'

'Hmm.' I scrunch my mouth to the side, tapping a finger to my chin. Then I grin. 'Not that lovely.'

'Good to hear.' His voice rumbles through his smile, his eyes boring into mine.

I shuffle from foot to foot, my cheeks burning under the fierceness of his gaze.

I want to kiss him. I want to know how he tastes. I want to march across the room and crawl into his bed. Slip my hand under his T-shirt. Feel his smooth skin warm beneath my touch. For his breath to hitch and a groan to growl from his throat. I want to put my mouth to his so badly. To feel his arms tight around me. To have him press against me, hard and urgent as he kisses me back over and over. I want Callum so much I ache.

I shift my hips, heat stirring between my thighs. He watches me intently, his teeth worrying at his bottom lip. Then a gentle smile curves on his mouth, and it's so real and soft, that all the fears I'd only just been talking about, all the fears holding me back, seem to melt away.

'How's your side feeling?' I ask, because I have to say something before I actually do all those wordless things to him.

'Better,' he says, stretching his arms above his head. His T-shirt rides up, revealing hip bones and stomach and that teasing strip of hair. 'See?' He cocks a brow. 'I'd say I'm firing at about eighty per cent. Pretty soon, I'll be back to one hundred, and then, Ms Daniels, you better watch out.'

CHAPTER FIFTEEN

I escape before Callum gets up. I'm suddenly nervous to see him. Since the moment I woke, even the smallest sound from his room made my heart leap. I message him once I'm on the road, saying I have an early morning meeting at the East Mill Witch Study Center. But I left *so* early I now have a full hour to kill before the place even opens.

I know I'm being stupid avoiding him like this, but I have that awkward, day after the office Christmas party where I drank too much and made out with the boss feeling. Not that I've ever been to an office Christmas party. Or had a boss. And I didn't even kiss Callum. But I wanted to, I really, *really* wanted to.

Get out of your head, Daniels. So what if I have steamy thoughts about Callum? I'm a grown woman, I'm allowed.

I park outside the Witch Study Center, sighing so heavily I fog up my windshield. A woman with silvery hair in a long ponytail stands on the porch watering flowers that cascade from hanging baskets. She looks up and smiles.

'Holly?'

'Louise?' I call back as I step from my car. She nods. 'I'm sorry, I'm way too early. I'll just wait out here.'

'Don't be silly, I've just boiled the kettle.'

She puts her watering can down, opens the door and ushers me inside.

Louise is statuesque elegance personified: stylish in a crisp, pale lemon pantsuit teamed with ballet flats and an excessive amount of silver jewellery that jangles when she moves. She almost glides across the floor, while I clump behind her in my chunky Docs.

'I'm a descendant of one of the first women tried for witchcraft in this area,' she explains as she offers me a seat.

We settle into a pair of gold velvet wingback chairs in front of a fireplace framed by heavy wooden bookcases. A pot of tea steams on the table between us.

'Her name was Sarah Garlick,' Louise continues. 'Her neighbour, Mary Gardiner, a mere child, accused her of being a witch.' She pours our tea out into mint-green art deco teacups.

'And was she found guilty?' I ask.

'Tragically, yes, and they hung her for it. Mary had fallen ill shortly after giving birth. The poor girl was only just sixteen. She claimed that Sarah, who was unmarried and owned property, something few women did back then, had cast a spell on her out of jealousy, because Mary was married. Mary swore on the Bible that she saw Sarah at the foot of her bed with a dark shape she believed to be Satan.' Louise rolls her eyes. 'She said she'd been bewitched by Sarah, that pins were being jabbed into her skin and she was being burned from the inside out. She was probably dying of sepsis.' She shakes her head, silver earrings jangling.

'That sounds so ridiculous.'

'Ridiculous now, but not in 1657. They believed in things like that back then. Sarah denied everything, of course. By all accounts she was a god-fearing woman, but she was still taken into custody, put on trial and convicted. She maintained her innocence, even as the noose went around her neck. The Gardiners received Sarah's parcel of land as payment for her crimes against them – or rather, Joshua Gardiner did, because Mary died before Sarah hanged. I suspect he orchestrated the whole thing to get his hands on Sarah's land. The shit really hit the fan after that. Witch hysteria gripped the town, and people were accused left and right. A witch court was formed. If you've ever read *The Crucible*, well, it was like that.'

'And this was prior to Salem and their witch trials?'

'The Salem trials started in 1692, thirty-five years *after* the East Mill trials. I want to give a voice to the victims of that time, before their stories are lost to history.'

I nod. 'I'd never heard of the witch trials out here until the other day.'

'Our town has decided that part of our history should not be celebrated, publicised or apparently even recognised. But, as a historian, I believe we learn from our mistakes. It's important to acknowledge the bad alongside the good.'

I nod again. Acknowledging the bad is something I'm sensational at. I'm not so great at acknowledging the good. I need to work on that.

'How many "witches" were tried here?' I ask.

Louise explains that, according to the records, seven women were tried and hung. However, those records are less than reliable, thanks to the fire that burned through half of the town.

'Unfortunately, that fire took out some of the official town buildings, so a lot of important documents were destroyed. Not just the court records around the witch trials but also records around the town itself and the population of the area at the time.'

'Ola Hutchings mentioned that. That must make your job hard.'

'I'm working with diaries and letters, the unofficial and official accounts to try to verify what really happened here. We may never know the full story. History can be a bitch like that.' She sips her tea, bracelets rattling. 'But let's cut to the chase, shall we? You're looking into the Westerns.'

There's a touch of glee in her voice.

'The Western house,' I correct, even though she's right – by both default and instinct, we're also investigating the family. 'My colleague, Callum Jefferies, has a successful paranormal podcast where he debunks fake hauntings, and Edward Western reached out and asked him to investigate the stories of disturbances at the house.'

Louise laughs. 'That entire house and the family that owns it is a disturbance. What have you discovered so far? Have you been inside yet?'

'We haven't discovered as much as we would like, and we haven't been inside. We're waiting on more information and clearance from Mr Western.'

'Why am I not surprised? That family is so strange and secretive. You'd think there'd be plenty of available information about the Westerns, given their significance to the history of this town, but there's hardly anything. They give me the creeps, to be honest. There's something just not right about them.' She shudders as she leans in closer. 'We do know that once they were one of the most influential families in this area. Alistair and his brother Garrett came to the colonies already wealthy men, arriving around ten years after settlement was formed. The story goes that they fled Ireland prior to the rebellion, settling on family lands in England. But then had to flee again some years later, this time to America, because Garrett was under suspicion of murdering a local woman.'

'Did he murder her?'

'It was never proven. But later rumours swirled that Alistair and Garrett murdered several other women, on the Western property, under the banner of doing *God's work*. That they ran their own *private* witch trials, outside of the town's official proceedings, and that they lit the fire that ravaged the town shortly after, to conceal what they'd done.'

'And was any of *that* ever proven?'

She sighs. 'No. The Western brothers were zealots, no question, and they were up to their necks in the witch trails – as influential members of the community, they served on the witch courts. But it's hard to believe that after all this time, the fact that they were mass murderers would remain undiscovered.' She sits back, her fingertips tapping. 'Though I often wonder if we dug up that old graveyard on the Western land, would we find more bones than are marked by headstones?'

'I wondered that too,' I muse.

Louise hmms. 'Whatever the truth is, those rumours wound up tarnishing the Westerns' reputation and, consequently, their influence in this town. Even their appearance made people jittery. The entire family was unnaturally beautiful; both the men and the women. It made people uncomfortable.'

I think of my dreams, and the young woman strangled under the oak tree where I also nearly took my last breath. My chest tightens at the visceral memory. The man who snuffed out that young woman's life was so beautiful he didn't look real. And the pain that seeps from every board of the Western house – maybe the secret murders are the source of that pain.

'Louise,' I suddenly say, 'do you know of a young girl of fifteen or sixteen named Elizabeth who was possibly caught up in the witch trials?'

'Did Ola mention her to you?'

'Y-yeah,' I lie.

Louise glides towards a bookcase on the far wall. 'She would have been talking about Elizabeth Howell.' She pulls a book from the shelf. 'Elizabeth was one of the first accused of witchcraft. She was awaiting trial when she vanished. Some believed her father paid someone to get her out of jail and secret her away.' Louise looks skeptical. 'But I'm not so sure, because her father accused Garrett Western of being involved in her disappearance. He was very vocal about it.

Apparently Western had been courting the girl. But if her father had a hand in her escape, why would he draw attention to it by pointing the finger at one of the most powerful men in town?'

I palm away the cold sweat popping on my brow.

'Did you say Elizabeth *Howell*?'

'Yes . . .' Louise studies me. 'Are you okay? You've gone a bit pale.'

'I'm fine. It's just . . . the name. Howell. It surprised me. It was my mom's maiden name.'

'Were your mother's family early settlers?'

'Not that I know of. I always assumed they came here from England a few generations ago. They've all passed now. Mom included.'

'I'm sorry for your loss. But Howell is a fairly common name in this country's history.' Then she smiles and says, 'It would be an amazing coincidence, though. You should look into it. I'd be happy to help. But first,' she says, standing up swiftly, 'we need cookies. To go with our tea.' She hands me the book, then glides from the room.

I open to the chapter on Elizabeth Howell and read, hands trembling as I turn the page. Is that why the spirit is seeking me out? Because we're family? My head spins, and I sit back in my chair and squeeze my eyes shut. Elizabeth is an even more common name than Howell. This probably isn't even *my* Elizabeth. And even if it is, what are the chances that she's some long lost relative? Louise is right, it would be an amazing coincidence, and that's the problem, I don't believe in coincidences.

Gosh, I wish my mom was still here, or Gran, so I could ask her. If I'd at least spoken to Dad recently it wouldn't be totally out of the blue to ring him and say, 'Hey, about Mom's family . . .'

I reach out, eyes still closed, trying to sense something, anything. I whisper, 'Elizabeth.' But there's only silence. The same strange silence I experienced at the Western graveyard. Fear lumps in my throat. I look at the pages again. If this is the Elizabeth who's haunting me, then Garrett Western must have been one of the men in the cellar. And the man who murdered the girl under the oak tree, the unnaturally beautiful man, he had to be a Western too. How long has this family been killing people, and why the hell am I dreaming about them?

I return to the bed and breakfast with a journal full of notes and a stomach full of knots. I still haven't had a chance to speak to Callum about my encounter with the ghost of Elizabeth. Do I share this disturbing new piece of information, too? Or do I keep it to myself until I've had a moment to fully work through it? Because it's now obvious this ghost is haunting me for a reason.

I toss my bag on my bed and stare anxiously at the adjoining door. I'm suddenly swimming with the same nerves I woke up with this morning. It's like a switch has been flipped in me. Now that I've allowed myself to acknowledge my feelings for Callum, I can't seem to turn them back off. And the scariest part is, I don't think I want to.

I check the mirror, just to make sure I'm not blushing, square my shoulders, and tap on his door.

'Who is it?' Callum singsongs.

'You know who it is and I'm coming in.'

Callum's lying on his bed, grinning at me like the Cheshire Cat, his pale cheeks pink and his eyes a little red. Jason is stretched out on the floor with a half-empty bottle of whiskey sitting beside him.

I blink. 'Are you both drunk?'

Jason puts his index finger and thumb together. 'Only a little.'

I look back at Callum. 'Did you do any work today, or am I the only one who cares about this job?'

'Didn't you see my cameras set up in the hall?' I shake my head. He shakes his too, adding an eye roll. 'The manager asked me to see if I could capture George the ghost. They want me to come back out here and do a show.' He smiles excitedly.

I smother a sigh. He doesn't need a camera; I can tell him when George is around. But he's beaming at me so I swallow my words. 'I thought you didn't bring cameras.'

'Of course I brought cameras.'

'But you've been told no video at the house.'

He shrugs. 'Did I say I was going to take cameras to the house?' He flashes me a toothy grin and swings his long legs off the bed, then disappears into his bathroom, returning with a clean glass.

'Did you do any *real* work?' I ask.

'*Real* work? Of course I did *real* work. Honestly, Holly, your low opinion of me never ceases to amaze.'

'Kind of deserved though, Cal,' Jason chimes in. 'You were lying around daydreaming about ... something ... until I knocked on your door.' Now it's Jason with the toothy grin.

'Hey!' Callum gives Jason a gentle kick as he steps over him. He grabs the whiskey bottle and pours me out a measure. 'The historical society closed at two,' he says. 'We were there most of the day. I promise.' He puts the bottle back down on the floor, straightens up and crosses his heart. I follow his finger as it trails across his T-shirt. 'Then we did some filming around the area for the podcast. Then I set up the cameras. We didn't even stop for lunch. Tell her Jase.'

'He worked me all day and wouldn't let me eat.'

Callum tuts. 'Which, in hindsight, probably wasn't smart with the whiskey and all.' His lips quirk up in one corner. 'Now, stop being a party pooper. Try to relax and have some fun.'

I huff impatiently as I take the glass from him, my fingers brushing his. Sparks of heat zip crazily across my skin, and when our eyes meet a throb booms in my chest. He grins down at me and keeps grinning as he throws himself back onto his bed and links his hands behind his head.

My gaze drops to my drink as I try to compose myself. 'I'm not a party pooper ...' I huff. 'I just want to get this investigation done so we can get into the house and get out of here.'

Callum wags his finger. 'All work and no play, Holly.'

With a *tsk* I toss back the whiskey. The heat feels good as the amber liquid coats the back of my throat, loosening the knot of fear that had lodged there. 'Okay? I'm playing, alright? I'm . . . fun.'

'I never doubted it,' he says way too growly.

I squirm uncomfortably as the throb in my chest makes its way south.

'I never doubted it either,' Jason adds, hauling himself off the floor. He pours me another shot, looking down at me with a knowing smile.

I look from Jason to Callum, both tipsy, both smirking at me, and toss back another slug. I think I'm going to need it.

'Aren't we even going to discuss your investigation?' I ask Callum, already knowing what the answer will be.

'*Our* investigation,' he corrects. 'We used your notes to match a couple more names to the Western graveyard. They weren't Westerns, though. We don't know their connection. Couldn't find anything in any of Ola's info. So, there's another mystery to add to the growing list.'

I shove Callum's long legs over and wiggle onto the bed beside him. 'I've got better than that. Edward Western's ancestors may have been America's first mass murderers.' I don't mention Elizabeth Howell. I'll get to her later. Maybe.

Callum springs up. 'What do you mean, mass murderers?' He's suddenly all business.

'Garrett Western, and possibly his brother Alistair too, might have killed some people. Women, specifically.'

'They were officials on the witch court,' he says. 'That's recorded information.'

'Yes, I know, but what if they were using the witch trials as cover?'

His gaze narrows. 'To get away with murder?' I nod. 'Do you have proof of that?'

'Not exactly, just rumours and theories. But Louise Garlick from the Witch Study Center is pretty convincing.'

'But she doesn't know for sure the Westerns did anything illegal.'

'Well, no. She thinks the family is bad news, though. And I can't help but agree. People aren't that secretive unless they have something to hide, and something definitely went down in that house. Something so evil it left a stain.'

Callum rubs his chin, a deep groove forming between his eyes. 'We've still got to work with facts, Holly. But yeah, we should look into all of it . . .' His mood shifts. *Tomorrow.* He wiggles in beside me. 'Jason's leaving tomorrow, and I think we could all do with blowing off some steam, don't you?' He rests his head on my shoulder and flutters his long lashes at me.

I can smell the whiskey on him, feel the warmth of his breath on my neck and the tickle of his soft stubble on my collarbone. He teases me with a nudge, and I reflexively shake him off.

He grins wide. 'I know you want to.'

I do want to. The whiskey feels good warming my blood, and Callum's thigh feels great pressed up against mine.

Jason chimes in. 'C'mon, Holly, I have an early meeting tomorrow, so I won't see you guys before I check out. Let's all have a nice dinner together. Then you can have Cal all to yourself. Do with him what you want. Work. Play.'

'Exactly,' Callum says. 'Tonight, we relax. Tomorrow, you can ride me as hard as you want.'

I groan, rolling my eyes at his turn of phrase. 'Okay, fine. But, Callum,' I say, 'tomorrow . . .'

His eyes sparkle. 'Tomorrow I'm all yours.'

CHAPTER SIXTEEN

O'Malley's pub is almost empty. It's Wednesday night and the weekend crowd has yet to descend on the island. Only a few people sit at the dark wood tables that fill the cavernous bar. Callum and I grab a booth by the fake-cobweb-draped window while Jason gets our drinks.

'You should have booked something near the water,' I shout, frowning at the bobbing ghost decorations hanging from the ceiling. Music booms from the jukebox, vibrating through the deep brown pleather of my seat.

Callum wrinkles his nose. 'Too bougie. This is better. More fun. Besides, a lot of Irish settled around here, so this place is part of the town's history.'

I decide not to point out the sign above the bar that says, 'Established in 2002'.

Callum raps on the table in front of me. 'You look nice tonight,' he says.

I look down at my sweater. It's black with a red lightning bolt on the front. I'm not even sure why I packed it.

He points to the red lightning bolt. 'It matches your hair and your personality.'

'My personality?'

'Yeah. Power. Energy.' He smiles. 'You light things up.'

'Oh.' I look down again, this time to cover my flush, and fuss with a flyer on the table promoting the bar's upcoming Halloween party. 'So, ah . . . tell me more about what you discovered at the historical society.'

'Nuh-uh. We're not talking work tonight. We're relaxing, remember?'

'Right. Are you sure you don't just want a relaxing boys' night with Jason?'

'I know you're desperate to get away from me—'

'That's not what I meant,' I quickly interrupt, 'and you know it.'

He leans forward and places his hand over mine. 'Good. Because I want you here, Holly.'

I instinctively slide my hand away, then kick myself for doing it.

He sits back in the booth and smiles. 'Besides, I've never really seen you drunk. Oh, except for the other night – you know, when you were drooling on me in your bed.'

'*On* my bed, Callum. We were *on* my bed.'

'Who was on whose bed?' Jason asks, as he puts a pitcher of beer and three glasses on the table.

'Holly was threatening to leave us to our own devices,' Callum says.

'Bad idea, Holly. You have no clue how this guy can misbehave.' Jason slides into the booth and slings his arm around Callum's shoulder. 'He bowls all the ladies over with his charms. The stories I could tell you. Like this one time, when we were—'

Callum clamps a hand across Jason's mouth. 'Shut up, dude.' He looks back at me, shaking his head. 'All lies.'

'I'll tell you later,' Jason says conspiratorially.

'That's okay,' I say. 'I can probably live without a blow by blow of Callum's romantic exploits.'

'Jealous?' Callum says. His foot gently taps mine beneath the table.

'Green with envy,' I deadpan in response.

His eyebrows lift, his smile deepening.

I roll my eyes, but I can't contain my grin.

Two pitchers of beer and one perfectly cooked steak later, I'm more relaxed than I have been in a very long time. The guys have been laughing about everything from their days at school to driving Callum's aunt crazy by always breaking curfew, and I've been enjoying their shared jokes and stories of childhood mischief – a childhood very different from the one I had. Watching them makes me realise how much I want my own family to be in my life. As soon as I get back to town, I'm going to organise something. Maybe I could even talk Maggie into lunch or a movie.

As Jason starts another story, Callum slips down in his seat and rests his knees against mine. This time, I don't move. I embrace his touch and all the feelings it stirs inside me. He catches my eye, and everything I once saw in him, everything I once hoped for, the promise I once felt in the warmth of his lips on my cheek, is still there. A wonderful, fluttering fills my stomach, and when he smiles at me I don't just smile back, I beam.

The opening drum roll of Bruce Springsteen's 'Born to Run' roars from the jukebox.

Jason clears his throat. 'I hate to interrupt this gorgeous moment, but . . .' he stands, 'I think we should all dance.'

'Oh no.' I wave him away. 'I don't dance. I have no rhythm. Honestly.' I look up at Jason as he wiggles his shoulders at me. 'Callum,' I plead. 'A little help here?'

He shrugs. 'I learnt long ago not to get between Jase and The Boss. Sorry Holly, it's out of my power.'

Jason offers me his hand. He's not going to take no for an answer.

'Oh god,' I squeak, as I take it. I look down at Callum. 'Are you coming or what, Jefferies?'

He laughs. 'Right behind you, Daniels.'

I'm not sure that what I do could be called dancing; it's mostly laughing and when I'm not laughing, I'm struggling to find the beat. Callum is surprisingly reserved, looking almost as awkward as I feel. Jason, on the other hand, is jumping around like a bean pole on springs, his black hair flopping wildly back and forth.

When Callum suddenly stops dancing and strides away, Jason grabs my hand and attempts to spin me. I squeal as my eyes follow Callum across the floor to the jukebox. He studies the list, presses a couple of buttons, then leans against the machine smiling at me. Then Springsteen fades out and Guns N' Roses' 'Sweet Child O' Mine' fills the bar.

Jason throws his head back with a groan, then steps aside with a sweep of his arm and a grin on his face. Callum takes my hand and draws me to him.

'Callum, I really can't dance. Didn't you notice?' My voice is weirdly high again.

'You don't have to dance, Holly. You just have to sway. Unless you really don't want to?' His brows raise in question.

'No, I want to – but,' I scrunch my nose, 'Guns N' Roses?'

In one smooth move, he snakes an arm around my waist and pulls me in. The air puffs from my lungs with an *oof* as my breasts flattens against his chest. Then he dips his head, puts his lips to my ear and whispers, 'Don't knock the Gunners.'

The warmth of his breath fills me with everything from desire to terror. He must see it all flash across my face because he says, 'Don't panic. It's only a dance.' I nod up at him, try to relax and begin to sway.

Heat radiates off his body, running the length of mine as we press together, rocking back and forth, moving as one. His fingertips caress my spine and I melt into him, wrapping my arms around his waist and pressing my cheek against his chest. He quietly sings as we dance, and the words thrum through me, vibrating right into my heart.

Should I be doing this? His muscles flex as he shifts his body. *Oh yeah, I should be doing this. I should be doing this and more.* I'm so tired of arguing with myself and letting fear rule my life. Maybe it's the buzz of the beer, or the way we've laughed tonight, or maybe it's the thrill of having Callum up against me, solid and real and so beautiful, but

I feel like it might be time to take that risk that Jason was talking about. Give myself a chance at the happiness he thinks I deserve. My heart does a little skip, and I laugh giddily.

Callum looks down with a quizzical frown. I smile up at him and loop my arms around his neck. I actually see the moment his breath catches, and then a genuinely happy smile bursts across his face.

'Oh god,' I whisper. Every sensation new, and wonderful, and terrifying all at once.

When the song ends, we keep swaying, moving to a rhythm all our own, with my cheek nestled against him and his chin gently resting on the top of my head.

'I think the song's over,' I finally say, my words muffled by his shirt.

Callum takes a small step back, his gaze meeting mine. And there it is, his desire on clear display, just for me. Wide dark pupils in luscious pools of green.

'That wasn't too bad, was it?' he asks.

He leans into me, and I swallow hard as his mouth gets closer. But he just kisses my cheek.

'We should sit down,' he says, taking my hand, 'before Jason finishes all our beer.'

The rest of the night is a blur of tingly feelings and a happiness I'm not used to, and when Callum says we should call it a night, I'm seriously disappointed. I don't want this night to end.

His foot gently rubs the side of mine. 'You ready to head back, Sunshine?' he asks.

'I guess,' I say, and I don't tell him not to call me Sunshine. Because I love it when he calls me that. I've always loved it when he calls me that.

On the short stroll back to Maddison House, I relive every beat of our dance, every smile, every foot tap, every knee bump and gentle touch. Every delicious, thrilling sensation that fills my body and throbs in my heart. I can't stop grinning.

'What?' he asks.

'Nothing.'

He tilts his head and drops one of his dazzling smiles on me.

Fear flashes through me then. *Do not trust the handsome man.* What if Callum is the handsome man? Should I put these feelings on hold, at least until the job is finished and we're back in the city? But then he reaches for my hand and links his warm fingers through mine, and every thought of restraint is drowned out by a fresh wave of desire.

In the hall outside our rooms we say goodnight. Jason and Callum hug.

'What time are you leaving in the morning?' Callum asks.

Jason groans. 'Sun-up.'

'Let me know when you get home.'

'Will do, mom.' Jason turns to me. 'Next time Cal comes over for dinner, feel free to come with him.'

My cheeks tingle as I flush. 'Oh. Thanks. And thanks for . . . everything.'

'You're welcome,' he says and steps into his room. The click of the door closing behind him echoes in the hall.

Callum and I linger awkwardly.

'So, um, I'll see you at breakfast?' I dig my key from my pocket. 'We can talk over how we want to move forward.' I pause, and then quickly add, 'With the job, I mean.'

He leans in closer and whispers, 'I'm already looking forward to it.' Then he smiles and slips inside his room, leaving me breathless outside mine.

My eyes spring open. The room is icy. Even in the darkness I can see the white puff of my breath hanging in the air. There's a presence in the room, heavy and oppressive and I try to focus on it, but the energy is too forceful to shut it out. My heart quickens and I clutch the comforter, pulling it around me as I peer into the gloom. This is not George, the Maddison's benevolent ghost. This is something else.

I fumble for the lamp, the click sounding unnaturally loud in the dense silence, and recoil as light glances off the spirit of Elizabeth, standing at the end of my bed.

My racing heart shoots to my mouth.

Get a grip, I tell myself. *It's just a ghost. Just a ghost.*

I concentrate on slowing my breathing, my heartbeat, clawing back some kind of control as my gaze passes over Elizabeth's spirit, as real as if she were still alive, not dead nearly four hundred years. There's no blood on her clothes where the dagger ripped through them, and her bonnet is neatly tied. Jason would be so disappointed.

'They are close to you now,' Elizabeth says.

I jolt, still shocked to hear words coming out of a spirit's mouth and not just a ghastly howl. The way she speaks is slow and deliberate, like she has to concentrate to find every syllable, and there's an echo to the sound of her voice, as if it's layered with more than one. My mouth is so dry I can barely get my tongue to work.

'Who are *they*?' I croak out.

'We can stop them.'

'Stop who?'

'You must let us in.'

'Whatever that means, it's not going to happen.' I yank back the covers and stand in front of her. 'Are you Elizabeth Howell?'

She gives a single nod then says, 'Be warned. The handsome man . . . he is not what you think.'

'So what is he then, who is he?' I'm suddenly so angry, tired and scared I yell, 'Can't you just give me a name?'

Elizabeth suddenly glances around. Her dead eyes widen, her form flickers.

'Wait! Don't go. Are we related somehow?'

Callum bursts through the door. 'What's happening?'

I ignore him frantically calling, 'Elizabeth, I'm sorry, please!' at the spot where the spirit just stood.

'Holly!' Callum grabs my hand.

I look up at him. His eyes are wild. I look down at his other hand. 'Why are you holding your boot?'

He looks at the motorcycle boot he's clutching. 'I – I heard voices.' He quickly tosses it into his room, where it lands with an awkward clunk. 'I thought you were in trouble.'

I drop to the edge of my bed and laugh despite my galloping heart. 'You were going to defend me with a *boot*?'

'I don't know. I was asleep, it's the first thing I grabbed. What's going on?'

I scrub a hand across my forehead. 'The spirit was here.'

'Which one?' He spins around, examining the room.

'The girl from the highway.'

Callum flops onto the bed beside me and runs his fingers back through his sleep-messed hair. 'She was here?' He looks around again.

'She said—'

'Whoa, whoa whoa . . . The spirit spoke to you?' I nod. 'Like . . . words?' I nod again. 'Did she speak to you on the highway, too?'

'Is there any of that whiskey left?'

Worry clouds his face, and he disappears into the darkness of his room, returning with the bottle and two glasses.

'Do you feel like sitting by the fire in the lounge?' I ask. 'I want to get out of here for a bit.'

'Will you tell me what's going on?' he says.

'I'll tell you anything you want to know.' And for the first time in maybe forever, I mean it.

CHAPTER SEVENTEEN

A soft light spills into the hall from the lamp glowing in the corner of the lounge, welcoming any wakeful guests. Thankfully tonight the room is empty, it's late enough that everyone is tucked away in bed. Not even George is up tonight.

I snuggle into the velvety cushions of the couch, as the small fire crackles behind the grill and the grandfather clock softly ticks. Callum pours a healthy shot of whiskey into each of our glasses, hands me mine and then leans back, cradling his.

'Cute pjs,' he says, pointing at my legs. My pyjamas are covered in tiny sheet-clad ghosts.

'My sister gave them to me. I can't decide if she was being funny or bitchy.'

His shoulder rests against mine. I don't move away. 'She still doesn't get the whole seeing spirits thing?'

'No one does.'

'That's not true. I do.'

'Yeah, I guess you do.' I gently nudge him.

He pushes up his sleeves, and my gaze trails his forearm,

landing on the dark, circular tattoo just below the crook of his elbow. He once told me it was a ghost hunter's talisman.

'Do you think that works?' I ask him.

He runs his hand across it. 'Well, I'm still here so . . .'

'Maybe I should get one. Maybe it'll keep the spirits away.'

'Do you want to tell me about the spirit that's haunting you, talking to you?'

'I nearly fell over when she spoke the first time.'

'It's really never happened before?'

'Never. Not one word. Just noise. A screech, a yell. Maybe that's why they yelled – because I couldn't hear them. Or wouldn't hear them. What if they've been trying to talk to me all this time?' I take a sip of my whiskey.

'Do you think it'll change things for you?'

I consider this for a moment, then shake my head. 'I get called in because the ghosts are scaring people. Terrifying them, usually, by the time I get there. It's the living I take care of. Whether I can communicate with the spirits or not, the living and the dead should not be sharing the same space. That's not how life works. Anyway, maybe it's just this one spirit I can hear.'

'Why? Is she different somehow?'

I slowly nod. 'She's the girl from my dream, the one who was stabbed to death in the cellar. Her name is Elizabeth. Elizabeth Howell, a girl who disappeared during the witch trials. Her father accused Garrett Western of being involved somehow, but nothing ever came of it.'

'What would Garrett Western be to Edward, great uncle times ten or eleven or something?'

'Something like that.' I toss back the rest of my whiskey and hold out my glass for a refill. Callum tops us both up.

'Are you sure it's her?'

'Pretty sure. I asked her. She nodded.' I take a beat. *Am I going to tell him everything?* Yes, I decide. 'That's not all. I think she might be an ancestor of mine.'

His eyes widen. 'You think, or . . .'

'My mother's maiden name was Howell. She always said her family came over from England, way back. I just didn't think it was *that* way back . . .' I shift closer to him, chasing that safe feeling he gives off. 'I don't know for sure; I was trying to ask her when you burst through the door brandishing your boot and scared her away.' He winces, sheepishly. 'But it makes sense. More than that, it feels right. It explains why she's haunting my dreams and haunting me, and it explains why I feel a connection to this place and the house.'

'And why you haven't obliterated her.'

'Mm-hmm. I guess. I don't have anyone else I can ask about her though. Mom's gone. My grandparents are gone.' I sip my whiskey and lick my lips. When I turn to Callum, he's watching me, his gaze fixed on my mouth. He quickly looks away and quietly clears his throat.

'Can't you ask your dad?'

'I'd feel weird calling him out of the blue about this. We haven't spoken since Labor Day. We sort of had an argument. I was at his place for a cookout, but then some old family friends dropped around, and they know about my work. They started asking questions I didn't want to answer, so I excused myself and just left. I didn't even make it to the ribs. Dad was really upset about it. I went home and ate Kung-Pao beef and watched TV instead.'

'Did you at least watch something good?' he asks.

'A couple of episodes of *Dexter*. I was feeling dark.' I laugh. 'Anyway, thinking about Elizabeth has made me realise I know very little about my family history. Is that normal?'

'You're asking the wrong person.'

'Right. Sorry.'

He shrugs. 'Did Elizabeth at least tell you what she wants?'

'Sort of but . . . it's like she talks in riddles and it's up to me to piece it all together. You'd think if she wanted to tell me something, she'd tell me straight. But I feel like it takes everything for her to reach me, so maybe she can't get the words out? I don't know, the dead are so infuriating.'

Callum coughs out a laugh.

'What?'

'The *dead* are infuriating?'

'You have no idea. Anyway, what she did say was she and I, we have to stop something, or someone. She said that I have to let her in. I told her I'm not going to do that.'

'What if this whole "let us in" thing is exactly what Richard was trying to warn you about?'

'I don't think so. Actually, I think they're both trying to warn me about the same thing. It's just unfortunate that one is catatonic and the other is dead.'

Callum chuckles. 'Well, at least you have a sense of humour about it. Give me the crib notes.'

'Someone or something knows what I am – what I can do. And that might have made me a target. I have to let

Elizabeth in so we can become team-Howell and save the world or something, I don't know. I think this is why I've never listened to the dead before. They can't string together a coherent sentence.'

'As much as you're making fun of it,' Callum says, 'I don't like the sound of any of this. And I agree, you shouldn't be letting that spirit in, family or otherwise.'

I watch him throw back his whiskey, his Adam's apple bobbing. He wipes the back of his hand across his mouth and refills his glass, adding another splash to mine.

'There's something else,' I say. 'I wasn't sure if I was going to tell you . . . You've just got to promise you won't freak out, okay?'

He sits back. 'Well, if I haven't freaked out so far . . .'

'On the highway, Elizabeth told me something else. She told me, *do not trust the handsome man*. She said something similar again tonight.' I watch him as I wait for his response.

Deep lines ridge his brow. 'Why would that freak me out? Who do you think she was talking about?'

I stare at him. 'Seriously?'

His eyes scrunch shut for a moment in a wince. 'Oh. You think she means *me*?'

My gaze roams over his face, taking in his wrinkled brow and worried eyes. 'No, I don't. But I guess that's why I was hesitant to tell you.'

Callum looks away, his frown still deep, his focus on the glass in his hands. 'I'm not that handsome,' he scoffs.

'Callum. Don't. Being coy is not a good look on you.'

We sit in silence after that, sipping our drinks, the crackling from the fire filling the space between our thoughts. When Callum clears his throat again, I jump a little.

'I think we should leave,' he says.

'Oh. Okay. Sure.' I pick up my glass and go to stand. He touches my wrist to stop me.

'I mean East Mill. You're getting warnings we don't understand, I'm seeing spirits you don't see, we both feel as if something's off here. Let's just forget about it. I'll tell Western I'm not interested.'

'But this is a big deal for you. You were excited about it. Holy grail and all that stuff.'

'It's just a haunted house. There'll be others.'

'What about the money?'

'I don't need the money.'

'But *I* need the money. And I'm not going to be chased out of town by a ghost either. I can't let them win like that. Besides, that house has tormented this town for long enough.' I wiggle around to face him. 'There's something bad happening in this place, has been for years. If there's a chance we can stop it, then we should.'

He smiles, one eyebrow kicking up. 'Such a hero, Holly Daniels.'

I give him a teasing shove. 'Shut up. Anyway, you'll have my back, won't you?'

'Always, and for as long as you need me.' His eyes meet mine, holding them for too many heartbeats to count. Then he glances away, frowning again, as he looks down at his glass, spinning it around in his hands. 'I'm not sure if

I should say this or not but, if we're telling each other everything, then there's something I need to tell you.'

'Ohhhkay,' I answer hesitantly.

He takes the last gulp of his whiskey. 'I guess I wasn't really expecting this.'

'Expecting . . . what?'

His gaze remains fixed on his empty glass. His fair cheeks are flushed pink from the warmth of the fire, and the glow of the flames illuminates his skin. He practically shimmers.

'From the moment Celeste first introduced us,' he says, 'I was into you. I think you know that. Hell, I've already told you that. You're beautiful and kind and smart.' He looks up. 'With this amazing red hair.' He reaches out as if to touch a strand, then pulls his hand away, wrapping his fingers tightly around his glass again. 'Then there's your gift. Being able to see ghosts is pretty spectacular, but to expel them from this plane with just a few words? That's something else. I couldn't believe it the first time I saw you do it. We were at that old warehouse out in Brooklyn, remember? I could see the disturbance created by the entity on my screen, and then you step up, say some Latin and then *poof* – it was gone. Not even a flicker on the EMF. Nothing. It was magical. *You're* magical. I know you don't like that word, but I don't know how else to describe you.' His eyes flick to me again, as if making sure I'm still there. 'God, I'm fucking this up.' He rubs his brow.

I touch his arm. 'Keep going,' I say.

He looks up. 'Yeah?'

I nod. 'Yeah.'

'Okay. Well, I was crazy about you from the get-go. But I thought after a couple of years of not seeing each other, and after what happened between us, I'd be less . . .' He puts his glass on the table and nervously rubs his hands up and down his thighs. 'I guess I've been caught off guard by how you still make me feel. Just sitting here next to you, it feels . . . right. It feels as if no time has passed between us.'

My breath catches, my head swimming from his words. I know exactly what he means, because I feel it too. That same connection I felt when we first met. He made my heart skip then, and he still makes it skip now. But I didn't expect to hear him say *that* out loud.

I stare at my hands, willing words to come out. I can hear his breath, as shaky as mine, feel his thigh touching my thigh, his shoulder pressed against me, warming me more than any fire ever could.

I fill my lungs with the deepest breath I can and say, 'I feel the same way about you, about us.'

Callum blows out a long, soft sigh. 'That's the best news I've had in a very long time.'

His teeth tug on his bottom lip as his arm very slowly slips behind me and around my waist. My heart flutters wildly as I look into his eyes, his face glowing in the firelight. *Oh my god, he's going to kiss me. Really kiss me.* I instantly think of every reason we shouldn't be kissing, and a thousand more why we should. Then I let my gaze drop to his full, soft pout and I'm lost.

Everything slows as he leans in, lips parted, eyes already closed, and presses his mouth to mine. I shiver at his touch, so warm, so tender, better than I'd imagined, more than I'd imagined. I savour the taste of whiskey on his tongue, smoky and sweet, and breathe in his scent, the one he left on my pillow, the one that makes me giddy with desire. Then I suck on his bottom lip.

'Holy fuck,' he says as I pull back slightly. Then he clutches me tighter, his fingers digging into my waist, arms squeezing me closer, cinching me to his chest, a wall of smouldering heat – and kisses me again.

I cling to him, dizzy from the rush of blood whooshing in my ears. When he moans softly against my mouth, it's the sexiest thing I've ever heard.

Heat explodes inside me, shooting everywhere. I'm so turned on right now I think I might combust. Callum tucks his fingers into the waistband of my pjs, fluttering tiny caresses against my bare hipbone. I set my hand on his thigh and gently squeeze, thrilling when he jolts with surprise. My touch trails slowly up his leg, his muscles twitching and flexing under my roaming fingers until my hand finds the skin of his waist, so warm. Then he moans again, the sound vibrating with need. His touch, his taste, his tiny noises of pleasure, even the scratch of his stubble feels so good.

When we finally break for air, my eyes flutter open. His full mouth is pink and shiny and his pupils are black and huge, the green of his irises shining neon around them, as if he were electric.

'Wow,' he says, all throaty. 'As first kisses go, that was, ah . . .' He blows out a soft whistle.

It takes a second for my brain to spark back to life, and when it does, all I manage is, 'Uh-huh.'

We snuggle on the couch, tangled in each other's arms watching embers popping like tiny fireworks as they drift languidly up the flue. The flames and the whiskey are making me sleepy, so I curl in tighter, lifting my legs up onto the cushions and resting my cheek on his chest, thrilling at the *thump-thump-thump* of his heart. I love his heart. I love how his heart gets me. Callum gets me. I feel like I fit when I'm around him, like I'm a part of this world, and that's more important to me than anything else. More important than his beautiful face or amazing kisses. I fell hard for him once. I think I could again. I think I already have.

He touches my chin, turns my face towards him and tenderly sweeps away my bangs. Then he dusts a tiny kiss across my temple, my nose, then, ever so softly, my lips.

'I don't want to rush you,' he says. 'I don't want to rush this. I'm happy to take it slow. If we're going to do this. Are we doing this?'

I look into his expectant eyes, burning bright with hope. I try to say yes. I try to say, *Yes, we're doing this, Callum, and a whole lot more*. But I can't. Instead, I sit up, kiss him lightly, and give him the only answer I can right now. Because I'm still scared that all these emotions could trip us up at the wrong moment, like the night I lost Celeste.

'I think we should get through this investigation first,' I say. 'There's too much happening here and we need to be totally focused on that. Then let's see where we're at when we get home. What do you think?'

Callum's shoulders slump. It's almost imperceptible, but I see it and I ache knowing that I've caused it.

He dusts the backs of his fingers across my cheek. 'Of course,' he says softly. 'You're right, we do need to focus. But just remember, I'm right here when you're ready.' Then he cocks a brow and changes his tone. 'I mean, I will actually be right here. Well, not right *here* here, because at some point, we're both going to have to get off this couch.' He grins, all toothy and Callumy.

I laugh and whack his arm.

'We should go to bed,' he says. 'Um. Sleep. We should go to sleep. You know what I mean.'

'I know what you mean.'

He stands and offers me his hand. 'Ms Daniels?'

'I think I might sit for a minute and finish my drink, but I'll see you for breakfast, okay?'

'You've got it, Sunshine.' He presses his lips to the top of my head. 'But don't stay up too late. We've got ghost busting to do tomorrow.'

I watch him move towards the door. He stops and gives me a wink over his shoulder, so cheesy I snort. Then he disappears into the darkness of the hall, leaving me alone with a nearly-empty bottle of whiskey and a head full of muddled thoughts.

I'm staring at the spot in my room where the spirit of Elizabeth stood only an hour earlier. There's something gnawing at me, and it won't let up. Something I can't quite put my finger on. A bad vibe that keeps repeating like the remnants of a spicy meal. I'm used to seeing spirits, I couldn't even count how many I've faced down. But this is different, it's confusing and strange and I hate to admit it, but I'm scared. For the first time in a very long time, I'm scared of a spirit.

I glance at the adjoining door. Opening it a crack, I can see that Callum is already tucked under the covers. I look over my shoulder at my own bed, my hand still lingering on the door handle. What if Callum is right and the spirit is trying to trick me? What if it's all lies and it's laying a trap for whatever it is that wants me? I don't know what's happening here, but I know I don't want to face it alone.

I tiptoe across the floor to Callum's bed and lean over him, squinting to see if he's asleep.

He cracks one eye open, then flicks on the lamp and rolls over to face me with a sleepy smile.

'What's up? You changed your mind about me already?'

I laugh a little. 'Yeah. Because you're that irresistible.'

'I knew it.' He blesses me with one of his dazzling grins. 'Seriously, though, is everything okay?'

'I know this sounds weird and a bit damsel-in-distress – which I'm not.'

'Of course not,' he says.

'But I'm a bit freaked out by Elizabeth's spirit. I know it's stupid, but what if you're right? What if she's what Richard was warning me about? What if she lured me here? I mean, obviously *you're* the one who lured me here.' His brows shoot up. 'Because, you know, you texted me,' I quickly add, 'and asked for my help and that's why I'm here. Because of you,

I mean because of the job. Which is the house, and . . .' I stop and raise my eyes to the ceiling. 'Are you just going to let me flail like this?'

'Yep. It's kind of cute.'

I puff out a full-cheeked sigh. 'What I'm trying to say is, can I sleep in here tonight? If it wouldn't make you uncomfortable.'

Surprise flickers across his eyes, and he sits up and grabs his pillow. 'Sure. Of course. I'll sleep in the armchair so you can take the bed.'

'You don't have to do that. We're both adults. Sharing a bed doesn't mean we're going to . . .' I cringe.

There's a beat of the most awkward silence I've ever experienced, then Callum casually shrugs and asks, 'You wanna sleep head to toe? Or we can build a wall between us out of pillows. Like a fort.'

He kneels on the mattress with two pillows in his arms. It's sweet and reassuring, and it makes my heart hiccup.

'I think we can cope without a pillow fort. But no spooning me, okay?'

He chuckles and flings back the covers, and I climb in.

'I'll bet you five bucks it's you who spoons me, Daniels,' he says as he flicks off the lamp.

'In your dreams, Jefferies.'

'Every single night.'

The little sleep I manage to get is anything but restful. My dreams are filled with Elizabeth standing on the highway uttering words I can't make myself hear. Then she's on the floor at the foot of my bed, bleeding, and gurgling out a warning, a silver dagger protruding from her breast. There are strange men chanting around bodies that hang in trees, and a gaping void that howls my name from somewhere in the depths of the house. And Callum. I dream of Callum. Except it isn't him, it's someone wearing his face, and it terrifies me.

I toss and turn, desperate for rest, but I'm acutely aware that Callum is lying beside me. Every time he moves, I freeze, in case we inadvertently touch. I know I made the right call, asking if we can hold off on whatever this is for now. With something in that house possibly trying to kill us both, it's smarter to focus on that than on each other. So even though I want to press into him, throw my legs over and turn him into my very own jungle gym, I keep as far over my side of the bed as I can, waking with a jolt more than once as I almost roll onto the floor.

Now, as the morning light peeks around the drapes, I lie still and listen to him breathe – a steady, soothing rhythm that chases away my night terrors. I carefully shuffle onto my side. He's facing me with his lips slightly parted in sleep. I smile at the spattering of schoolgirl freckles that dot his nose, then my gaze moves to his mouth, and I think of our kiss. Our amazing, toe-curling kiss. I yearn to touch him. To trace my finger along the winding tattoo that swirls enticingly from his wrist. To sneak my hand inside his shirt and bask in the heat of his skin. To dust tiny kisses along the stubble shadowing his jaw, nuzzle his throat and breathe him in. To crush my lips against his, again and again so I can hear him moan. I nearly moan at the thought of it.

I roll onto my back with a sigh, smiling at the glorious ache that now pulses between my thighs. I need a shower. Probably a cold one.

I'm about to pull back the covers and slip out of bed when Callum stirs. Pressing the heels of his palms to his eyes, he rubs, then squints into the light and blinks at me. When his sleepy gaze finally focuses on my face, he smiles.

'Morning, Sunshine.' His voice is thick with early morning gravel.

He stretches out his long legs, his feet poking from beneath the sheets, and gives me a gentle kick. I smile and kick him back.

'Good morning. Did you sleep okay? I didn't disturb you, did I?'

He props himself up on his elbow. 'Best sleep I've had in ages. How about you?'

'Not so good. I had some wild dreams.'

'Wild? Were they about me?' He smirks.

I hesitate, then I decide to tell him the truth. 'You might have been in the mix.'

He arches a brow. 'Oh yeah? What were we doing?'

'Not that.'

'Damn. Do we need to worry about them?'

'No. They just felt like dreams.'

'Good.' He rolls onto his back and pats his belly. 'I'm starving. What do you say we order breakfast in bed?' He shoots me a glance that's pure mischief.

I laugh. 'Definitely not.'

'Oh well. You can't blame a guy for trying.' He shrugs, all messy hair and sparkling eyes. 'I'm going to take a shower. I'll leave the door open a little, just in case ghost girl shows up again. No peeking, though.'

I squeeze my thighs together, squishing away another rush of the heat. 'I'll try to resist.'

'Don't try too hard,' he says, and he leans in and kisses my shoulder as if it's the most natural thing in the world.

My gaze trails after him, appreciating the way his T-shirt hugs his back and how nicely his sweatpants fit the curves of his ass. I listen as the water starts running, trying not to picture what's going on in there, until first his shirt and then his pants come soaring out the door. I shake my head, laughing as I climb out of his bed. Then an old fear stirs inside me, the one that's kept me locked up for so long. But instead of surrendering to it, I think about how good it feels listening to Callum mangle 'Sweet Child O' Mine' in the shower. I choose to be happy, and it feels so strange I hardly know what to do with it.

CHAPTER EIGHTEEN

'How do you feel about breakfast to go?' I ask Callum as he pulls on his boots. 'Louise Garlick from the Witch Study Center called. There's someone she thinks we should speak to. A local who might have some personal insight into the Western family history.'

'Sounds good.' He grabs his jacket. 'Tell me on the way.'

As we walk to the car, I fill Callum in on what Louise told me. She'd been speaking with her grandmother, who had reminded her about a woman named Martha Parish. 'She's in her eighties,' Louise said, 'but she has a fine memory.'

'Apparently, the Parish family have lived in the East Mill area nearly as long as the Westerns, and Louise thinks Martha might bring a personal historical perspective to our research.'

'A different angle sounds great, and personal stories always make interesting content,' Callum says as he slides into my car.

'One more thing. Martha likes candy. The soft kind.'

'Soft candy. Got it. So, coffee, food, candy, Martha. In that order.'

I nod. 'Oh, and I meant to tell you. I had a quick look at the stuff you forwarded to me from Rosing. There were two photos of Brendin Western, one of which we've already seen, plus a few scanned articles about the house itself. But no photos of Margaret? No photos of *any* other family members. No list of staff.'

'Well, the Westerns are reclusive, don't forget.'

'Still. Can you poke him again? If we had a photo of Margaret, we might be able to see if she matches descriptions of the ghost seen in the house. She died in 1908, there must be something.'

'I'll ask again. Did you get a vibe from any of the photos?'

I flick him a frown. 'No vibes. But I noticed the numbers on the email attachments jumped from four to six. Did you miss sending me one?'

He shrugs and says, 'Nope,' as he plugs Martha's address into his phone.

'I just can't believe the family can be that photophobic. Maybe Ola can help. Nothing from her yet?'

'I'll check in with her again too.' He looks up. 'At the end of Main Street, take a left. There's a sweet store not far out of town. Apparently, it's famous. We can stop there.'

The Sweet Spot is an old-fashioned candy store, the kind with jar after jar of coloured gumballs and trays of delicate chocolates. I watch on in amusement as Callum takes his time choosing each individual piece of confectionary, while flirting shamelessly with the middle-aged woman serving him.

'So, this one is lemon?' he asks, leaning on the glass countertop and gazing up at the woman from under his long dark lashes. 'But is it sweet or sour?'

'Very sweet.' A blush colours the woman's cheeks.

'And soft?'

'Melt-in-your-mouth soft.' Her eyes drift to the pout of Callum's lips. 'Would you like to try one?'

'I'd love to, thanks . . .?'

'Betty.' She gives him a none-too-subtle wink.

'Callum,' he says in return, and I stifle a laugh when he winks back.

With a tiny pair of silver tongs, Betty places a deep yellow square into the palm of his hand. He pops it into his mouth and chews, rolling it around on his tongue with overly noisy, exaggerated enjoyment.

'This is delicious, Betty. But then, I'm sure everything in here is delicious. Am I right?' He cocks a conspiratorial eyebrow, then smiles so bright it lights up the room.

Betty and I both sigh.

'You really are shameless,' I say, once we're back in the car.

'What did I do this time?' he asks, with a confused expression.

'I'm sure *everything* in here is delicious. Callum! You and your flirting.'

He leans sideways and bumps his shoulder against mine. 'I love it when you get jealous.'

I roll my eyes.

'Anyway, Betty was lovely,' he says, 'and every woman deserves to be made to feel beautiful. If I can help with that,

I don't think that's such a bad thing.' He rests his head back against the seat. 'Besides, she threw in a few extras for us.'

Martha Parish lives in a grand house that stands at the end of a long driveway, perched above a windswept beach. Trellises covered in pink roses dot the perfectly manicured lawn, and three welcoming Adirondack chairs sit under a spectacular oak tree.

The sounds of crashing waves and gulls squawking overhead greet us as we step from the car. The beaming sunlight throws dappled shadows across the lush green of the grass, and the air is so salty you can almost see it. It reminds me of days at the beach before my mother died. Of Dad carrying me on his shoulders through the surf as I giggled hysterically. Of me and Maggie building sandcastles together. Of collecting shells along the shore with Mom. When things were good. Before the ghosts.

Callum whistles his approval, cradling a small white box tied with a pink ribbon almost delicately in his large hands. As we make our way up the path, he holds the box of candy out before him like an offering.

'I'm glad I went with the pink ribbon,' he says. 'Pink's obviously her colour.' He nods towards the roses.

'Callum, you're freaking me out a bit.'

'Why? I'm just making sure we get off to a good start. You're the one who said she likes to be bribed with candy.'

'I don't think I said bribed.'

We step onto a wide porch crowded with white wicker furniture and large pink floral cushions.

'You know,' he says, 'my aunt loved candy. I'd often swing past this little store in our old neighbourhood and pick some out for her. She really liked the chewy ones.' He smiles at the memory. 'I always got her a blue ribbon, though,' he adds. 'She loved blue.'

The doorbell rings with a musical chime, and an immaculately presented woman in a pale grey dress and sensible shoes answers the door.

'Ms Daniels?' she asks in a clipped English accent.

'Yes, and this is Callum Jefferies.'

She nods, and ushers us in. 'I'm Iris Winters, Ms Parish's housekeeper. And by housekeeper, I mean I take care of her affairs, not clean her toilets.' She looks at us sternly.

Callum and I nod politely. When she looks away, we turn to each other and smirk like schoolchildren.

Mrs Winters leads us through the house, along an antique-filled hallway and past a formal living area full of dark wood furniture and uncomfortable-looking chairs.

'Ms Parish is in the conservatorium,' she says.

She motions us forward into the room. I almost feel I need to curtsy.

'Ms Parish, this is Ms Daniels and her colleague, Mr Jefferies. They are the people Louise Garlick contacted us about. They want to discuss some local history?'

'Yes, Iris, I remember. I'm not quite senile yet,' Ms Parish says.

Iris draws a deep breath through her nose. I have a feeling her boss tests her patience.

'Please excuse me if I don't get up,' the old woman says. 'The sound of my joints creaking may send you screaming from the room. Iris, would you mind organising some iced tea for our guests, and some of that nice fruit cake you bought yesterday?'

Iris nods.

'And don't forget the lemon this time.'

'Of course,' Iris answers curtly as she leaves the room.

Martha Parish is a refined woman, who is aging with elegance. Her white hair is rolled into a neat chignon, and she wears a pale pink sweater with crisp white pants and a slick of vibrant pink lipstick that matches the colour on her nails. Silver-rimmed glasses balance precariously on her nose, and she has a half-completed embroidery lying across her lap.

Martha carefully rolls up her embroidery, places it in a basket on the small table beside her, and takes off her glasses, letting them hang loosely on a chain around her neck. With a noticeable twinkle, she eyes Callum and asks, 'What have you got there, young man? Is that for me?'

Callum steps forward. 'I hope you don't mind, Ms Parish, but I took the liberty of selecting some candy for you. I hope that wasn't too forward of me?' He hands her the box.

'Not at all, Mr Jefferies. And tied with a pink bow! How did you know that was my favourite colour?' She looks up at him, an almost sly grin making her cheeks crinkle.

He grins back. 'I just had a feeling you'd be a pink gal,' he says.

Martha casts her sharp gaze over him. 'You, Mr Jefferies, are all charm and trouble, I can tell. I'll have to keep my eye on you.' She waves her hand towards a cane lounge. 'Please, sit.'

Iris returns with iced tea and cake and arranges them on a table in the centre of the room. Callum pours a glass of tea for Martha, then puts a slice of fruitcake on a plate with a pink napkin and hands it to her.

'You have excellent manners,' she says to Callum.

'I had an aunt who insisted on good manners, Ms Parish.' He turns and holds the jug towards me. 'Tea?'

'Sure,' I say. We smile at each other, enjoying the scene.

Martha waits until Callum is settled with a piece of cake before saying, 'Now, how can I help you two?'

'We were wondering if you could elaborate on some local history,' I say. 'The kind that's passed down through families rather than found in books.'

I give Martha a quick overview of the history we already know, briefly touching on Callum's engagement by Edward Western, whose name, I note, makes Martha frown.

'We'd like some local input,' Callum says. 'We understand your family was one of the original families in East Mill.'

'We settled here about fifteen years after the first settlers. About five years after the Westerns. That's who you want to know about, correct? And the rumours that swirl around them.'

Callum and I glance at each other.

'That's it, in a nutshell,' he says.

Martha nods again. 'I can tell you the stories I grew up with, which you won't find in any books, and you can make up your own mind about them.'

She shares the tale her grandfather told her about Alistair and Garrett Western fleeing England in 1654, chased out by the locals under suspicion of murder and religious views not seen as strictly Christian. Rumours that they came to their wealth via *unnatural* means.

Callum frowns. 'Unnatural? What exactly did that involve?'

'My grandfather believed they made a pact of some kind.'

'With whom?' Callum asks.

'With *what*, Mr Jefferies,' she answers mysteriously.

She stops and takes a sip of her iced tea, her eyes dancing between me and Callum. I get the sense that she's enjoying herself.

'My grandfather believed there was someone or something they were beholden to,' she continues. 'Something that required regular sacrifices. He believed they started the witch trials themselves, installing Alistair in a position of power on the court so they could murder without suspicion. Legally sanctioned murder.'

I have to stop myself from yelling, 'I was right' at Callum.

'They must have been bitterly disappointed when a magistrate from Connecticut swooped in and finally put a stop to proceedings,' Martha adds. 'Did you know the hangings took place not far from here? The site of the old tree is on one of the trails off the highway. Not much to see now but a stump, but it's a pretty walk.'

'Are we close to where the original village was?' Callum asks.

'Yes. So you know about the fire?'

Callum and I nod.

'After the fire destroyed so much of the town,' she says, 'they wisely rebuilt closer to the ocean, where East Mill town centre now sits. That fire was an awful business. Many lives were lost.'

'What did your grandfather think about the rumours that Alistair and Garrett set the fire?' I ask.

'My grandfather had two thoughts on that. One, that the Western brothers wanted the town records expunged to make any past *illegal* activity harder to trace – no population records, no missing people, no suspicion of murder. The other was simply money. They owned a lot of the land where East Mill was eventually rebuilt, and for some years leased it back to the town.'

'Ms Parish, do *you* believe your grandfather's stories?' I ask. 'About the fire, the murders?'

She shrugs. 'I don't know. But my grandfather could certainly weave a good tale.'

Callum sits forward. 'So if we go with your grandfather's theories, the Westerns were willing to kill innocent people for power, land and money?'

'Not much has changed in the world.' Martha takes another sip of her iced tea. 'Then there was the business with Garrett Western.'

'Do you mean the disappearance of Elizabeth Howell?' I say.

'Yes. After the girl vanished, Garrett returned to England, never to be heard from again. Then members of the Western household began to die. The family says an illness swept their estate, which it probably did, but people began to believe the Westerns themselves were cursed. Longtime locals still do. No one was sad when old Brendin Western passed away. We were all hoping the town would be asked to manage the estate, but apparently Edward wasn't happy with that idea.'

'What about Edward?' Callum says. 'Do you know him particularly?'

'I know Edward a little and I'll be honest, I'm not fond of him. He has always been aloof and self-important. He didn't grow up here. His father moved to England and married a nice English girl, and that was where Edward was born and grew up. He returned sometime in the sixties with his brother Cillian. I didn't see Cillian out here much. Maybe only once or twice. Now, Edward regularly visited his Uncle Brendin,' Martha goes on, 'right up until the moment the man died. To my knowledge, Edward is the last Western standing, at least in this country. Mr Jefferies, would you mind passing me another piece of cake?'

Callum stands and places another slice on Martha's plate. 'What about female relatives, Ms Parish? No one seems to talk about them?'

She hmms as he sits back down. 'There were wives, of course. A few daughters. But the only female relative I ever remember hearing much about was Margaret. I didn't know her personally, obviously, she was dead before I was born. But by all accounts, she was a tough one. Her husband was the Western, but though she might have only married into the family, she took their legacy in this town *very* seriously.'

Callum's phone dings, and he pulls it out and glances at the screen. 'Excuse me, Ms Parish.' He shows the phone to me. 'It's from Ola,' he whispers, and then smiles at the old woman as he slips his phone back into his pocket. 'Sorry about that. Ola Hutchings is pulling a few things together for us on the Western and Rosing families.'

'Now there's an odd bunch,' Martha says, dusting cake crumbs from the front of her sweater. 'Those two families are intertwined. The Rosings have worked in some form or another for the Westerns for several generations, at least.'

'What are they, like the Renfields to the Westerns' Dracula?' Callum grins.

Martha chuckles. 'Are you an expert in such things, Mr Jefferies?'

'I read a bit. Some of the vampire myths from Eastern Europe are quite persuasive.'

I scoff. 'You can't believe in vampires.'

'Why not? There are some weird things in this world.'

I flick him a sceptical look. 'Ms Parish, what else can you tell me about Elizabeth Howell? Are there any other stories about her?'

'There was one story. Elizabeth's mother died when Elizabeth was a young girl. But the child insisted she could still see and speak to her mother long after she died. Neighbours would see her talking to thin air in the local graveyard, too, apparently communing with the dead, or so the story goes. You can imagine how well that went down in a puritan society. No wonder she was caught up in the witch trials.'

My mouth is suddenly bone dry. I pick up my tea to take a sip, but the glass trembles in my hand.

Callum gently touches my arm to steady me, takes the glass and sets it on the table. He shifts closer until we touch.

'Sh-she saw spirits?' I ask. 'She was gifted?'

'It's just a ghost story, Ms Daniels.'

I nod, but my head is spinning. If we are family, could Elizabeth have had powers like me?

'Are you gifted, Ms Daniels?' Martha studies me with a shrewd eye.

I don't answer her.

'I see,' she says.

'What about you, Mr Jefferies? Are you gifted too?'

'Not in the way you mean,' he says, tossing her a crooked grin.

Martha throws her head back and laughs.

'Callum,' I whisper harshly.

'What?' he whispers back.

I frown at him and nod to Martha.

'I'm sorry if I embarrassed you, Ms Parish,' he says. 'I can be—'

'Please,' she interrupts, 'I rarely get to flirt with a young man these days, especially one as handsome as you.' She looks him up and down, her keen gaze taking him in. 'You know, you could almost pass for a Western yourself. Such pale skin and pretty golden eyes. Where are your people from?'

'My eyes are green, not gold,' Callum corrects. 'But thank you for calling them pretty.' He smiles cheekily at her. 'I'm originally from California. My folks died when I was a kid, and I came to New York after that to live with my aunt in the city.'

'My condolences, Mr Jefferies. That must have been difficult for you.'

Iris enters the room and whispers into Martha's ear.

'Good idea, Iris. Mr Jefferies, we seldom have a man around the house, especially one who's as able-bodied as you appear to be.' Wrinkles cluster at the corners of her blue eyes as she smiles broadly. 'Would you be kind enough to give Iris a hand? We have a stubborn light bulb in the kitchen that, try as we might, neither of us can budge, and we risk our lives every time we step onto a ladder.'

A grin tugs at Callum's lips. 'I'm always glad to offer my assistance to a lady.'

'Yes, I'm sure you are,' Martha says dryly. Her eyes follow him as he leaves the room. 'I think he might be a handful, that one,' she says, once we're alone.

I laugh. 'He can be. But he's good at what he does.'

Martha quirks an eyebrow. 'You two are not a couple then? I thought by the way he touched—'

'We're colleagues,' I quickly say.

She narrows her gaze as she sizes me up. 'I never married,' Martha says. 'I've had a full and wonderful life, and I loved my freedom too much to sacrifice it for a man. But do I wish I'd taken another route? Sometimes.'

I frown, not sure where she's going with this. 'I see,' I say, not seeing at all.

Martha sighs, fixing me with a look that suggests she thinks I'm stupid. 'What I'm saying is, I think Mr Jefferies is sweet on you. He enjoys flirting, that's obvious, but he's tender with you, and you seem a good match.' She places her hands in her lap and raises her brows.

'Oh . . . um.' I realise I'm supposed to answer her. 'I mean, the thought has crossed my mind once or twice. But right now, we have a job to do, and everything else has to take a back seat.'

'How very mature of you,' she says, frowning.

We sit in awkward silence until Callum and Iris reappear.

'All done,' he says. 'Is there anything else I can help you with while I'm here?'

'Not today, but perhaps, given time, Iris and I might come up with a good reason for you to return.' Her eyes twinkle at him.

'We'll leave you in peace, Ms Parish,' I say. 'Thank you so much for your time. If we have any more questions, may we call you?'

'Of course, Iris will give you our number. And Mr Jefferies, if you're ever in this area again, please don't inconvenience yourself by staying at a hotel. I have plenty of rooms spare, and I suspect I might enjoy seeing you gracing my halls for a day or two.'

My chin drops, but Callum doesn't miss a beat.

'Thank you, Ms Parish,' he says, 'but if I take you up on your offer, I'm going to have to insist that you call me Callum.'

'Then I'm going to have to insist that you call me Martha.'

'Okay then . . .' I grab Callum's arm and drag him towards the door.

'Good luck, you two,' Martha says. 'And be careful. Watch yourself around Edward Western. If even half of the stories are true, evil is in his blood.'

CHAPTER NINETEEN

'I don't remember seeing a hanging tree in the *Ten Things to Do in East Mill* brochure,' Callum says as we drive away from Martha Parish's house.

'If the town doesn't publicise the witch trials in their history, they probably feel the same way about the place where those poor women were hung.'

'You want to go see it? Go for a *pretty walk*?'

'Okay. Which way?'

He pulls out his phone, does a search and puts the location into Maps. 'Get up to the old highway, then go left.' He keeps studying his phone.

'Is that the email from Ola you're looking at?' I ask.

He nods, frowning. 'She sent the house photos. But, she says she's also tracked down a semi-recent photo of Edward if we want it. She's just got to collect it from a volunteer.'

'Tell her yes!'

He nods, types something out then slips his phone into his front pocket. 'How do you feel about what Martha said about Elizabeth Howell?'

'Tiny bit freaked out, but it makes a lot of sense.'

'It would explain why she's drawn to you and knows about your powers.' He's somehow twisted himself around in his seat so he can face me. One long leg is pulled up and tucked beneath him as he rests against the door. 'What if that's why Garrett Western went after Elizabeth? Because she had a gift?'

'You think the women targeted by the trials were *actual* witches?'

'Or psychically gifted somehow.'

'In my dreams, the men chanted something after both murders, but I couldn't make out the words.'

'A prayer maybe? Everyone was pretty religious back then. Maybe they thought they were getting rid of evil.'

'Louise did say they were zealots, but it didn't feel like that.'

'Could you see any of the men?'

'Only the one under the oak tree. He was stunning. Pale, with light golden eyes the colour of wheat.' I glance over at Callum.

He twists back around in his seat and stretches out his long legs as far as my small car will allow.

After a few minutes of silence, I ask, 'So, what do we think about the rest of Martha's story? The pact business. Just family nonsense?'

'There's nearly always at least a grain of truth to local legends. Even with an old family yarn. Legends, and myths all have to start somewhere.'

'What if the Westerns were serial killers?' I say. 'Just run-of-the-mill psychotic murderers. Then we could pass this whole thing off to the police and wipe our hands of it.'

'They are serial killers if they killed all those people. What did Martha say about evil being in their blood?' He scrubs a hand down his face as the GPS chirps out, 'You have reached your destination.'

I turn the car into a small gravel parking area and pull up alongside a tourism map in a glass case. We study the map together.

'There.' Callum points.

It's listed as 'historic tree'.

He goes back to the car, pops the trunk and pulls a silver pistol from his duffle bag.

'What are you doing?' I ask. 'We're just going to go look at some old tree stump. And that gun's not going to do much if we come across something creepy.'

'Iron rounds.' He grins. 'They'll disperse any spirit we come across.'

'In case you've forgotten, I also disperse spirits.'

He shrugs and tucks the pistol into the back of his jeans, grabs a small EMF meter and straps it to his wrist. 'I'll be your back-up then.'

'What if it's your demon from the window? Or a vampire?' I put my arm across my face in a Dracula pose, laughing as he rolls his eyes.

'We both know Latin, and I'm sure you have holy water in your jacket pocket.'

I pull out a silver flask. 'I do, and these too.' I hold up a string of rosary beads.

'Then we're ready for anything.'

*

The air is cool and damp and leaves crunch noisily beneath our feet, our heavy boots clomping along the trail. It's not much after midday, and though the sun is high, only the occasional glimpse of it peeks through the dense branches that shadow the path.

'What about curses?' Callum asks, as he steps over one of the small rocks that litter the trail. 'Do you believe in them? Do you think people can be cursed? Say by, I don't know, family?'

'Mine would probably say I was the curse. Or were you talking about a werewolf curse or something?' I joke.

'For someone who sees dead people, you're sure quick to write everything else off. Werewolf lore goes back to Greek mythology; even Norse mythology has werewolf stories. Many indigenous people have legends of shape shifters — humans that can transform at will into an animal. There's even a condition that covers the entire body in thick hair. Imagine seeing something like that in the sixteenth century. That's where these stories start.'

'A grain of truth?'

'Exactly,' he says.

We walk on in silence after that, Callum out in front, me moving quickly to keep up. I can't help but watch how his muscles move under the soft black of his long-sleeved tee. His back and shoulders are so broad they block most of my view.

'Do you like hiking?' he suddenly asks, glancing back at me.

I quickly shift my gaze to the ground. 'I've never really thought about it. The only hiking I ever do is through Central Park.'

'We could go hiking when this is all over,' he says. 'Or, I don't know, we could spend a few days looking around East Mill. The non-spooky bits. Check out some restaurants by the water like you wanted to. Go boating. Is it whale-watching season? What do you think?'

'I, um . . .'

It's the first time we've seriously discussed actually seeing each other after all of this. I can tell Callum is trying his best to be casual about it, but he sounds as nervous as I suddenly feel.

'Sure,' I say. 'I mean, maybe, yeah, I guess.' I'm babbling. Then we're silent again.

I look up towards the treetops. The forest is quiet, except for the crunch of our boots over old autumn leaves, and the occasional croak or flutter of birds in the branches above. It's so peaceful, even my usually tumultuous thoughts are calm.

The sound of a twig cracking echoes behind me and Callum spins around. The movement is so sudden that I slam straight into his chest with a grunt, bouncing backwards and stumbling. He grabs my waist to steady me.

'Sorry. Probably just a deer. I should have put my brake lights on.'

His hands remain around me, holding me tight. I look up into his smiling face and, without thinking or overthinking or any kind of thinking at all, I push up on my toes and press my lips to his. He lets out a small, surprised puff, then draws me into the kiss. I lean against him, letting him take all my weight. His hands move from my waist to my back as he squeezes me closer. I know I'm the one who said no to this, but from the moment I woke up in bed beside him this morning, this is what I've wanted to do. So, I'm doing it.

I dig my hands into the back pockets of his jeans, my palms snug against his ass. I memorise that perfect curve, then move my hands upwards, skimming his back, roaming over every taut muscle, committing them to memory too. I glide my fingers across his shoulder blades, then the smooth skin of his neck, until they find his hair where they curl. I'm on fire again, my thighs, my cheeks, my lips, every part of me burning with desire.

I've never experienced anything like this. This kind of need, this kind of rightness. His body is hot and solid against mine and his hands are strong and confident at my back. When he pulls me closer still, I feel how much he wants me too, his hardness pressing enticingly into my hip. That really gets me, and I squeeze my legs together because it's too much. It's too much for a walk in the forest, where I can't toss him to the ground, peel off his clothes and . . .

I pull back, my breathing ragged as I stare into his beautiful, and somewhat startled face. His tongue swipes over his well-kissed lips.

'S-sorry,' I finally stammer. 'I know I said we shouldn't. I . . .'

'Please don't apologise,' he says. His arms are still around me, holding me upright.

'Okay.' I reach up and softly touch my lips to his. 'Because I'm not sorry. Not a bit.'

'Good. And if this is how nature affects you, I'm pencilling in that hike for the minute we finish this job.'

We laugh, the sound lifting into the soaring trees above us.

Callum clears his throat as his hands drop from my sides. 'Excuse me one moment,' he says, with a throaty chuckle. I don't even pretend to not watch as he less-than-artfully adjusts himself in his jeans. 'Shall we get this tree thing done,' he asks, laughter still in his voice, 'in case you get another urge to do that other thing?'

'Yep, but I still think we should keep our distance a little until we're done with the job.'

'Oh yeah, I can tell you're fixed on that idea.' He smiles wide.

I spin him around and push him along the track.

He chuckles, stumbling forward. Then, in a softer tone, he adds, 'I meant what I said before, Holly. I'll go whatever speed you need me to.' He stops abruptly and I crash into his back.

'What are you doing?'

'Just checking if you want to kiss me again.'

'Callum!' He walks on, laughing.

We continue along the trail, heading deeper into the forest. Every so often, Callum glances over his shoulder and gives me a smile. I smile back, feeling guilt licking at my insides. Because I *do* want to kiss him again, and I shouldn't be doing that, not when I've asked him to wait. We need to focus. I'll remind myself of that next time I feel—

'Is this it?' Callum asks as we step into a clearing.

It's a wide circle of grass covered with tiny purple flowers, with a tree stump sitting in the middle. The stump is dark grey, old and weathered and long dead, cracked right through the centre.

'Looks like it.'

He places his hand on my shoulder. 'Listen.'

I stop and turn my ear towards the sky. 'I don't hear anything,' I say quietly.

'Exactly. There were birds on the trail, and frogs and crickets. But here?' *Nothing,* he mouths. The EMF meter on his wrist suddenly comes to life with a screeching beep. 'What the fuck?' He lifts his hand. Red dots flash on the tiny screen. 'There must be something here,' he says. 'Can you see anything?'

The air thickens, a stale taste settling at the back of my throat.

'There.' I grab his arm and nod towards the other side of the clearing. 'A spirit of a girl. Can you see her, or feel her?'

'No,' he says, adding a quiet, 'Thank fuck.' He reaches around the back of his jeans, draws his pistol from his waistband, and points it towards the tree line. 'What's she look like? What's she doing?'

I gently push his gun down. 'Young. Pretty. A long cream dress with a buttoned bodice and a bell skirt. Oh my god, I think she's the girl from my dream. The one who was strangled under the tree at the Western house.' I look up into his shocked face and whisper, 'What was the name of the missing girl in the book I got you?'

'Annie?' he whispers back.

I steady my breathing and say, 'Annie?'

The spirit looks surprised, then she smiles and nods.

'It's her,' I tell Callum in a hushed tone.

'Fucking hell,' he says, just as quiet. 'What do we do?'

Annie points to the tree she's standing beside.

'She's trying to show us something.' I step forward until I'm standing so close to her I get goosebumps from the chill. I look to where she's pointing and feel the moment she leaves.

'She's gone,' I call over my shoulder to Callum, waving him forward.

As he comes up behind me, I brush his hand. He grabs hold, giving my fingers a squeeze.

'I have no idea how you deal with this shit every day,' he says, then he lets me go and slips his gun back into his waistband. 'I guess this means Annie definitely didn't make that trip to California.'

'Probably because one of the Westerns killed her under the oak tree on their property.' I look up at him. He's pale. 'Are you okay?'

He shakes his head. 'Nope. What did she want to show us?'

'She was pointing at . . .' I lean in and look at a small symbol carved into the tree. 'I've seen this before.'

Callum peers at it. 'What is that? Is that a triangle?'

'It was on the gate at the Western graveyard. I thought it was some kind of family crest.'

He traces his finger around the shape. 'Then what's it doing here?'

'I don't know.'

I stare at the symbol weathered into the wood, angry at myself. We should know what this means by now. I first saw this symbol days ago. We should have researched it, figured it out. We should have been working, not lying around watching movies and slow dancing to classic rock. This is not a spooky getaway! I hang my head with a huff.

'What?' he asks. 'Are you getting a vibe?'

Yeah, a vibe I need to concentrate on the job. 'No,' I say. Then I press my hand to the tree.

Energy shoots through my palm, races up my arm, surging through my veins, burning a trail under my skin, until it bursts in my chest, almost lifting me off my feet. The air rushes from my lungs. My mouth opens and closes, until I'm gulping like a goldfish. Screams swirl in the air around me. Pain and fear, so overwhelmingly powerful that I bite down on my tongue. I squeeze my eyes shut, praying that I can block it all out, but instead my mind floods with faces, images from another era flickering behind my eyes, filling my head with whispered pleas for mercy. I sob for them, tears streaming down my cheeks.

Then, just as quickly as it started, it stops.

Dizziness engulfs me. My body grows heavy as the light around me dims. I stagger backwards, away from the tree, and crumple to the ground as blackness swallows me whole. Then the words come again, but this time it's a chorus.

'Holly. Let us in.'

CHAPTER TWENTY

Somewhere in the distance, I think I hear my name being called.

'Holly!'

There it is again. I try to open my eyes, but my lids are too heavy.

'Holly. Wake up.'

The voice is louder this time, more urgent. My shoulders shake and my head flops back and forth.

'Holly? Holly!'

The voice is clearer now. Closer. Then a thunderous crack sounds above me. I flinch. Then another one comes, then another. Light flickers.

'Come on, Holly. Come on. Please . . .'

The voice is familiar, warm, welcoming. It fills me with comfort. I'm safe in that voice.

One more crack and suddenly my eyes snap open.

'Oh, thank god. Holly.'

I squint as I struggle to see. A face comes into focus. A soft face. A worried face.

'Callum? What happened?' I groan and try to push myself up.

'Hey, take it easy. You fainted or something.'

His arms wrap around me as he helps me sit, squatting behind me, and pulling me against his chest. I lean back into his warmth.

'Never touch that tree again,' he says, holding me tight to him.

'Okay,' I answer groggily.

'Can you stand? Because I think we should go.'

'Sure.' I wobble a little as I push myself up.

Callum snakes his arm around my waist and I rest against him, letting him support me as we half walk, half stumble across the clearing.

'I feel like we've done this before,' I say.

'Except in reverse,' he says, through puffs of exertion. 'You're heavier than you look.'

'Charmer.'

He chuckles, and his laughter chases away my fear.

The further we get from the tree, the stronger I feel. By the time we reach the line of pines and disappear into their protective darkness, I can stand on my own.

I stop. 'I think I'm okay now.'

'What the hell happened back there? You were screaming your lungs out, then you dropped to the ground. I thought you'd stopped breathing.'

'I don't know. There was pain, a lot of pain. In me and around me. Voices howling from anguished faces.'

His eyes are wide, filled with horror, and my stomach sinks. I knew the other shoe would eventually drop. What I can do, what I am – it scares him just like it scares everyone else.

He puts his palms on my cheeks and stares deep into my eyes. 'Listen, Holly.' I hold my breath. 'Don't die on me, okay? You can't do that. I couldn't . . .' He presses his forehead to mine.

Then his lips touch my skin, so softly they feel like butterfly wings. The lightest of tickles. My heart soars. He's not scared of me. He's scared of losing me.

Callum tosses his duffle onto the chair in the corner of his room. 'I think I should get some food into you. We haven't had anything since Martha's cake. How are you feeling?'

I drop onto the end of his bed. 'Confused.'

He sits beside me. 'Any idea what happened?'

I shake my head. 'Something moved into me, or through me, or . . .'

I try to remember the sensations that exploded inside me in the forest, but they're already drifting out of reach, the faces and the horror dulling as if they were never there. I know it happened, but I can't feel it anymore. Like the pain from an injury. An intellectual memory without the sensory recollection that should go with it. Even the fear has gone.

'I think I was supposed to know their sorrow, their terror, their grief. It's like the sickness I feel at the house. I think they want me to know their pain.'

'Whose pain?'

'The victims?'

'Maybe that's what "let us in" means. Maybe you just did it.'

'No. I didn't, because they're still asking me to. I heard them again. All of them this time. Callum, I don't know what I'm supposed to do.' I look at my hands, dirty from the forest floor. The knees of my jeans are covered in mud. 'I should wash up before we eat.'

'I'll wait here,' he says.

'I'll be fine. Why don't you sort out our food? That pizza was good the other night, do they deliver?'

'Leave the door open, okay?' he calls after me as I head for my room.

I hear him on the phone, ordering dinner as I shrug off my clothes. Something is changing inside me. Something new thrumming alongside my gift, and weirdly, I don't hate it. I never imagined there could be more to me than the thing I've always been. I've never wanted to imagine that. But what if this . . . whatever this is . . . was always there, just buried by self-loathing and shame? I've spent my life battling spirits, but I've never tried to connect with them, to understand them. I've just blocked them. What if they've been trying to communicate with me this whole time?

I should be freaking out, that would be my normal reaction, but I'm not. Because something else is going on inside me too, and it's smothering all my fears in flutters and tingles and hope of a life beyond the one I've been living. Barely living.

I scrub the dirt from my palms, my face and neck, washing away the tears on my cheeks, and close my eyes, trying again to recall the terror that filled me at the tree – to hear the wails, to feel the agony. But all I find there is the warmth of Callum's arms around me and the heat of his lips on mine as we kissed in the cool shade of the forest. *Those* sensations I can instantly remember, and they vibrate through me even more than whatever attacked me in that clearing. I can't hold back my smile. I'm *finally* opening myself up to the good, and my emotional debris is falling away as I do.

Callum is sprawled on pillows on the floor, his laptop in front of him.

'Hey,' he says, rolling onto his side and smiling up at me. 'Feel any better?'

I flop down beside him. 'A lot better,' I say. 'It's weird. It's like it never happened.' What I don't say is how good I feel, that I'm buzzing and excited, because I don't want to examine that right now. Instead, I shimmy in closer, pressing my thigh against his as I reach for my journal.

'Here's the sketch I did of the symbol at the Western graveyard, the same one we saw on that tree.'

Callum reaches for the book, a spark of desire finding me again as his hand touches mine. I need to calm down.

He looks at me, a smile twitching on his lips. 'Can I ask you something?'

I frown, suddenly worried. 'I guess.'

'Why didn't you take a photo of this thing with your phone instead of drawing it?'

'I . . . ah . . . I don't know. I didn't think of it.' I burst out laughing and snatch my journal away from him. His eyes sparkle with amusement. 'I was writing names down, and . . . Oh, shut up.'

He rolls onto his back, his hands resting on his belly, his eyes squeezed shut and a wide smile across his face as he laughs. My insides melt.

'Sorry.' He clears his throat as he rolls back onto his stomach. 'You did a wonderful job. Quite the artist. I'll just take a photo of it and see what we can find.'

He pulls out his phone and snaps.

'Okay,' he says, sending the picture to his laptop and dragging it into the search bar. 'Let's see.' Various images of the symbol fill the page. Callum clicks on one. 'This is it, right?'

'Looks like it.'

The symbol is an inverted, ornate triangle with an Egyptian ankh hanging in its centre. He clicks through a few pages, reading rapidly.

'The Poculum Vitae. The cup of power. It's an occult symbol. This says it represents the potential we all have within ourselves. It symbolises the idea that you can have anything you wish for, so long as you take it upon yourself to act.'

'That doesn't sound so bad. In fact, it sounds like good advice.'

'But wait, there's more!' Callum says, in his best TV-salesman voice. 'By drinking from the Poculum Vitae, a person attains physical and spiritual perfection and lasting life. It signifies the passage of energy through the body and the transformation of the human soul into something divine.'

'So why is it on the gate to the Western graveyard, and why was it carved into that tree?' I study my sketch again. 'Oh wait,' I say. 'Did Ola email through the photos?'

'Oh yeah, let's see.' Callum opens his email. 'Yep, here they are. Dear Callum, here are a few photos of the house, hope they're helpful ... blah, blah, blah. Wait, here's the other email. Promised photo of EW ...' He clicks, then stops, staring at his laptop screen.

'What?' I lean in.

He swings the screen to face me. 'Edward Western. Damn. How's *that* for a handsome man?'

I draw a sharp breath. 'That's the man from my dream!'

'Why am I not surprised ... Wait, which dream? The strangling one or the stabbing one?'

'Neither. The other dream, the one where I felt the pain in the house.' *The one where you asked me to trust you.*

'And you've never seen him before otherwise?'

I slowly shake my head.

'And he looked just like this?'

I slowly nod. 'Same golden eyes.'

'Well, shit. What if he's the handsome man your ghost Elizabeth was warning you about?'

I shrug. 'Could be. When was that photo taken?'

He examines the caption. 'Edward Fionn Western, 2018, at the East Mill Western property management hearing.

This must be from when the town petitioned to take control of the house after Brendin Western's death.'

'That would make Edward, what, seventy-five there?' I reach across Callum and zoom in on the man's startling face. 'He looks forty, fifty at most.'

'Poculum Vitae. Lasting life.'

'Physical perfection,' I say. Callum's foot drops over mine, and I shift my leg to meet it. Our feet tangle behind us. 'We aren't really believing this stuff, are we?' I ask.

'C'mon, Holly, why not? You see ghosts and have weirdly accurate dreams about people you've never met. So . . .'

'Those things are different.' I frown at him.

'How? Besides, every culture in the world has myths around immortality and resurrection, the soul and the afterlife. Christianity is practically based on it.'

'But they're just stories, created to keep the masses morally in check.'

'I guess that depends on what you believe. But I'm not going to have a theological argument with you right now. Like I said earlier, most myths and legends have their roots in truth.'

'Even vampires?' I snort.

'Yes, even vampires,' he says seriously. 'Those stories originated from plagues, illnesses, fear, people who drank blood believing it would extend their life. Think of leeches and how they were used in medicine, for drawing blood. Not that they actually helped. Anyway, I didn't say I believed in vampires. But I do believe there are more supernatural entities than just ghosts. I mean, look at you.'

I'm indignant. 'I'm *not* supernatural.'

'Okay, you're preternatural. You're outside of what's considered part of the natural world.' He looks at me, taking in my furious glare. 'It's not an insult, Holly. It's true and it's special and you should celebrate it. But my point remains the same. There's more in this world than we understand.' His phone buzzes, vibrating across the floor. 'Pizza's here. I'll go grab it. Are you going to be okay?'

I wave him away. 'I'm fine,' I tell him, dragging his laptop towards me.

Now I understand why Callum was approached about the case. His knowledge is far broader than mine. I do ghosts. He does immortality, theological arguments and transformation of the human soul. Even though the afterlife is part of my everyday life, I never think about it. What happens to the spirits after I do my thing, may be something I don't want to know.

I look at the photo of Edward Western again. Even in his seventies, he was a damn fine-looking man, but there's something unnerving in his appearance. The strange golden eyes even shine out of the photo. I remember Martha Parish's words. *Evil is in his blood.* I shudder.

I forward Ola's emails to myself, then move across the other open tabs, checking each page for any new snippet of information that might answer one of my hundred questions. I've opened the tab with Callum's Facebook feed before I realise what I'm doing. I go to close it, then stop, glancing at the door. I shouldn't snoop. I *really* shouldn't snoop. I duck behind the cover of the screen and start to snoop.

It doesn't look like he uses it much. In his profile picture, he's with a little girl, maybe three years old, and he looks younger – it must have been taken a while ago. He's wearing a birthday hat, and they're both pulling faces, their fingers in the corners of their mouths, dragging their lips apart. Maybe that's Jason's niece. I peek at the door again, then I open his photo album. As I quickly scroll through I see that it's mostly shots of Callum and Jason. There's one of the two of them wearing brightly coloured Christmas sweaters and overly serious expressions. Callum's hair is longer and flops messily around his face, while Jason's is shorter, almost a buzz cut. Then there's a photo of Callum holding a baby asleep in the crook of his arm. Jason's niece again? Unless he has a kid he hasn't told me about? But the next photo shows Jason holding the same baby beside a man who looks like his brother. Then there's a photo of Callum in bed, looking half asleep, dishevelled and surprised and I wonder who was there to take it. An all-too-familiar feeling begins to scratch at my insides. I quickly click back to his profile page. I don't want to look at anything more, I don't want to feel that feeling. I'm done with that feeling. And that's when I notice the post.

It's dated two days ago, under a photo of a much younger Callum standing beside a snowman.

> Hey babe, remember this? It popped up in my memories! FB is so cursed. How's the trip going? I texted you, but no answer! Playing hard to get isn't usually your style. Lol. Call me if you ever see this! xx

I click on Krissy's profile. She's pretty, with shiny chestnut hair, the kind they make shampoo commercials about. In her cover photo she's at the beach snuggling a tiny fluffy puppy.

I chew on my thumb; I should close the tab and move on. But instead I click on Callum's "photos of you" album. And there they are, Callum and Krissy, draped around each other, smiling, laughing, happy. When I see a photo of Callum, his eyes closed, his lips pressed to her cheek in a lingering kiss, dated only a month ago, my heart plummets. Because I recognise that kiss. I've felt that kiss. I know its promise. I relived it for two years.

I hear Callum at the door and quickly click the album closed, call up another tab, then push the laptop away from me, skidding it across the floor. Grabbing my notebook, I pretend to look busy.

'Dinner is served.' He has a large pizza box in his hands and a bottle of red wine tucked under his arm. 'Find anything interesting?'

I'm focusing on the page in front of me and seeing nothing as the words swim before my eyes.

'What? No,' I snap.

Callum's eyebrows pop up. 'Okay.' He puts the pizza box on the floor and ducks into the bathroom, returning with a couple of hand towels, a box of tissues, and two glasses.

I spiral, well-worn anxiety taking hold, fear and doubt rising up as everything crumbles around me. He has a girlfriend – or something. Why didn't he tell me? Why did he let me go on as if I mean something to him? As if I could ever mean something to anyone. I'm such a fool to think I could have a real relationship. Why did I trust him? He already let me down once. I'm so stupid.

I reach for a slice of pizza and jam it in my mouth. I can feel Callum's eyes on me. I can't stand it.

'What?' I say, the word muffled through cheese.

'What happened while I was downstairs? Did you see something?'

Yeah, I saw something. You kissing your girlfriend. I wipe a hand towel across my mouth. 'No, why would you think that?'

'Because I can tell something's happened and I can tell you're lying, because you're not very good at it.'

'Well, that makes one of us.' I sit up and glare at him. He stares at me, confusion pulling his eyebrows together. 'Who's Krissy?' I regret the words the instant they're out of my mouth.

Callum's frown deepens. His gaze moves slowly from me to his laptop then back to me again. He takes a deep breath and shuffles across the floor until he's sitting with his back against the bed.

'Were you snooping on me?'

'No. I was looking at the sigil and your Facebook just—'

'Magically opened up?'

There's the hint of a smile on his lips and it's infuriating.

'You haven't answered my question,' I say.

'Krissy is a friend.'

'If you have a girlfriend, Callum, you should have told me. I would never have kissed you. I don't do that kind of thing. I don't like cheaters.'

He drops his head and scrubs his fingers over his brow. When he looks up again, he shakes his head.

'She's not my girlfriend, Holly. Christ. What do you think of me? She's a friend of mine. We used to have a thing back in college, and sometimes when she's in town she stays at my place. We have a bit of fun together, but that's it. Nothing more, and neither of us wants it to be. In fact, the last time she stayed, all we did was play pool and drink way too many margaritas.'

His eyes fix on me. I look away and furiously flick through my notebook. 'Oh, okay, fine. Well, she wants you to call her. Let's do some work.'

'Holly, it's not like that.' He sighs. 'I didn't do anything wrong here.' He reaches for me, but I pull away.

'Please don't,' I say. 'I thought I could do this, but I can't. I don't want to have to scrape myself off the floor when you get a better option and disappear from my life. And you will, I know you will.'

Callum's not smiling anymore. 'You're the one who ghosted me,' he says.

'I had a pretty good reason.'

'And I'm so sorry for that, you know I want to make it up to you. But unless you give me that chance . . .' He runs a hand back over his hair. 'Krissy isn't my girlfriend. I promise.'

We sit there on the floor staring at each other for one heartbeat . . . two . . . three. A full-blown panic attack is brewing inside me. Why is it that, when it comes to anything to do with actual living people, I don't know how to handle it? With the dead, I'm brave, strong, confident. With the dead, I know where I stand. They don't scare me. But the living? They terrify me.

I flop back to the floor and stare at the ceiling. I hate this. I hate feeling like this. Weak and stupid. I'm no good at relationships, I don't know what I'm doing. I sit up again. 'I'm sorry, I shouldn't have invaded your privacy. If you want to see Krissy, it's none of my business.'

'But Holly, I want to be your business. It's *you* I want to see. It's been you for a really, really long time. But I can't go on not knowing, so if you honestly don't want this' – he points between us – 'then say something now.'

I press my lips firmly together and say nothing.

Callum sighs, his shoulders relaxing. 'I'm taking that as no news is good news.' He pulls out his phone and types.

'What are you doing?'

He holds up one finger, asking me to wait, then turns his phone to me.

> Hey K, sorry, I've been super busy. Remember that girl Holly I told you about? I think we're kind of a thing. At least, I want us to be. Wish me luck! xx

He pushes send and I almost gasp.

I stare at him in silence as he stares back at me. Then a ding echoes through the room.

Callum's eyes travel over the message, a smile lifting his cheeks. He gives me his phone and I take it with shaky hands.

> Oh, babe, that's great! I remember how obsessed you were with her. I was actually messaging to say I'm coming for a weekend next month – guess I'll have to find another couch to crash on, but maybe you can introduce me to your new girlfriend? 😉 xx

I hand him back his phone and he tosses it onto the bed.

'Are we okay?' he asks softly.

I groan and flop backwards again, draping an arm across my face. 'Why am I so weird?'

He shuffles over to me. 'You're not. Feelings are messy. I'm as freaked out as you are. It's part of the fun.'

'Your idea of fun is not the same as mine.' I laugh lightly. 'I'm so sorry. I don't mean to be such hard work. It's just difficult for me to believe things will turn out okay when they never have before and when everyone keeps leaving me.'

'Your mom and your grandmother didn't leave you. Celeste didn't leave you, just like my folks didn't leave me. Not on purpose anyway. But I know it feels like that sometimes. I feel it too. I'm terrified of losing people. Terrified I'll look around one day and everyone I love will be gone . . . You'd think that stuff would go away, right?'

'You'd think.'

'You're not the only one who's scared, Holly. And you're not the only one who just wants to be accepted and belong somewhere, to have a connection, family or whatever you want to call it.'

'So, basically what you're saying is that we're both completely messed up?'

He sweeps my hair from my face and tucks it behind my ear.

'Not completely, just a little.'

Then he smiles that smile that makes everything feel okay, and I catch myself believing that maybe it will be.

CHAPTER TWENTY-ONE

We don't mention Krissy again, or my awkward meltdown. We're eating pizza, drinking wine, looking over the photos when a notification suddenly pops up on the laptop screen. An email from Rosing.

Callum quickly opens it and reads out loud.

It relays Edward Western's stories of the haunting. Some of the sightings occurred as recently as last year, when Edward was preparing to finally move into the house after his uncle's death, while others go back generations. They match what we've read online for the most part, about the ghost of a woman who's been seen around the house, and another female spirit that stalks the grounds. He also mentions an illness that tore through the family, which could tie in with what Martha Parish told us. Multiple members of the household were struck down, he says, and the illness has often been attributed to the dark presence that haunts the halls.

'Maybe *that's* the nausea I felt at the house,' I say.

'He doesn't say anything about any violent attacks,' Callum adds, 'so that's good. It's not the horror show I thought it would be.'

'I would like to remind you that you were nearly impaled by a fence post, and I was practically electrocuted by a haunted tree.'

'True.' He rubs his eyes. 'But if we go by Edward's stories, this sounds like a fairly standard haunting.'

'What about Richard and the man he bludgeoned with the flashlight. What was his name?'

Callum checks his notes. 'Andrew Dobbs. I don't know him, do you?'

I shake my head as I drag Callum's laptop towards me. 'His website's still up. He claimed to be a powerful psychic who could connect people with their dead relatives. Hmm. He can't have been very good, though, or one of us would have heard of him.'

Callum stares at the photo of Andrew Dobbs surrounded by the letters of a ouija board. 'So going back to our earlier theory,' he says, 'that Garrett Western killed Elizabeth Howell because he thought she was an actual witch. What if that was somehow related to the Poculum Vitae thing? What if he didn't kill her because he thought she had powers, but because he wanted those powers?'

'How would that work? It's not like they're transferable, or I would have given them away years ago.'

'I don't know,' he says quickly. 'But it's a bit of a coincidence, isn't it? Elizabeth Howell believed she could see dead people. Dobbs claimed he was a psychic. Both of them murdered—'

'But the Westerns didn't kill Andrew Dobbs. Richard did.'

'Right.' He nods. 'You're right. I'm just thinking out loud.'

I wiggle forward and grab my phone, pull up a number and hit call.

'What's going on?' Callum asks.

I listen to the voice message, then say, 'Mr Rosing, it's Holly Daniels. I wanted to check your schedule for tomorrow. We'd like to organise to go inside the house and have a preliminary look around.'

Callum cocks a brow as I hang up. 'We're going in?'

'We can't just sit here throwing around theories forever, and we have information from Edward Western now. We'll go during the day and get a feel for the place. We'll be careful. But I think we've waited long enough, don't you?'

He studies me, brow creased and face serious, then he claps. 'Alright!' He stands quickly, reaches for my hand and helps me off the floor. 'We'd better get to bed then. I think you should sleep with me tonight.'

I cough out a laugh. 'That was smooth.'

'That's not what I meant.' His head tilts. 'Unless . . .' He tugs on my hoodie, pulling me closer and nuzzling my neck. 'You want it to mean that?'

I quiver from the heat of his breath, close my eyes and lean against him, as he trails feathery kisses up my throat and along my jaw. I let out a low sighing moan. I wasn't going to do this again, but . . .

I press my hands to his chest and push him away, just far enough so I can loop my arms around his neck. He smiles; his pupils already doubled in size. I like how their darkness sets off the green. I like how it sets me off too. I lift onto my tiptoes and kiss him.

The chilli from the pizza still on his lips makes mine tingle. I push my leg between his legs and he jolts, flexing against me with a tiny grunt, his fingers sinking into my waist.

Every lingering worry, every old panicked feeling, every rational or semi rational thought floats away on a wave of pleasure that's all Callum. I want this and I don't need to wait any longer.

I slip my hands up inside his shirt and trace my fingers along the bumps of his spine.

'Fuck,' he moans against my mouth. Then he gently untangles himself from me, gulping for breath.

I grab his shirt and drag him back to me. 'I think we should . . .' I glance at his bed.

'Are you sure, because you said we shouldn't—'

'I know I did, but I think I've changed my mind.' And in case he had any doubt, I crush my mouth to his.

Callum moans again, thick and throaty, the sound a hum against my lips. He pulls me tighter, twining one hand into my hair, the other splayed across the small of my back. I'm desperate to get closer and I press against him, practically grinding, loving how his arousal presses back.

'Holly,' he pleads. 'Holly, are you sure—'

I slip one hand between us and run my palm over the soft material of his sweatpants and the solid ridge beneath them to show him just how sure I am, and his groan is so deliciously needy I want to breathe it in.

Callum lets me step us across the room until the backs of his legs hit the edge of the bed and he tumbles to the mattress, taking me with him. We laugh, both of us already breathing heavily.

'You're absolutely sure?' he asks one more time.

'I'm absolutely sure I want this off,' I say, dragging at his T-shirt.

He helps me wriggle it up his body and over his head, mussing his hair that way I like. His pale cheeks glow pink and his adorable freckles pop against them. I want to kiss every one of those freckles. I want to name them and get to know them personally. My eyes dip to his lips, already red and swollen from mine. I give the bottom one a little nibble and his fingers dig into my waist with a tremble. I shimmy backwards, over his bare and beautiful chest, careful to avoid the wound on his ribs, the friction of my body against his making him grunt. Then I kiss his jaw, then his throat, then his collarbone.

I nip playfully at one of his nipples, and he gasps, then he hauls me back up to his lips, kissing me so hard I'm dizzy from it. When his hands find their way under my clothes, I shiver all the way down to my toes.

He caresses me over my bra, his thumbs swirling tiny, all-consuming circles over my hard nipples. I cling to him, bliss licking through me. Then one of his hands is between us, his fingers sliding into the waistband of my leggings.

A needy 'Yes' slips from me on a gasp.

I'm moaning and greedily kissing him, sucking at his skin, willing his fingers to get where I need them to be.

I want him to hurry up, but I also want him to take it slow, so I can enjoy every tantalising second on the way to what's about to happen.

A crackle, then a sharp beep sounds from across the room. The sensor attached to Callum's cameras in the hall bursts to life. We both turn and stare at it, then turn back and stare at each other, hair messy, and lips swollen.

'Which one is it?' Callum whispers. 'George or Elizabeth?'

I draw a breath, sensing the energy. 'Fucking George,' I say.

Callum slips his hand free from my tights and I whine with frustration. He pushes up on his elbows, his eyes on the door.

'Is he in the room?'

I turn his face back to me. 'No. Can we please go back to what we were doing?'

'What if he comes in and we're in the middle of . . .' He nods at me. 'You know.'

I huff. 'Fine. Wait here, I'll get rid of him.'

He holds me tight. 'Holly, you can't get rid of him. He's part of the place, and I'm going to do a show on him!'

I shake my head. 'No. George has to go. He's brought this on himself.'

Callum starts laughing.

I stare at him, taken aback. 'This isn't funny.'

'It is, actually. Us, being interrupted by a ghost.'

'I'll just tell him to go away.'

'Maybe we should wait until we're somewhere less haunted.'

I drop my head to his chest and grumble into his skin, 'See? This is why I hate ghosts.'

He laughs again, lifts my face and fixes my hair where his fingers tangled.

'Holly, I want to do this.' There's still laughter in his voice. 'I think you can tell how much.' I can't help but glance at the thick shape pressing against his sweatpants. He smirks when I look back up. 'I've imagined it so many times. Imagined having you in my arms, touching you everywhere, making you cry out with pleasure. What it would look like when . . .' He smiles wickedly, taking a steadying breath. 'What I would do to get you there. Everything I would do to you and with you. I can't tell you how many times I've imagined it. Even when I was hurt, even when I was angry, I wanted you and I wanted this.' He cups my face and looks deep into my eyes. 'But I want us to have time – days, weeks, so long that people will worry about where we've gone. Uber Eats containers will cover the floor because we won't be able to stay out of bed long enough to toss them in the trash. Mail will pile up at the door, because we'll be far too busy to collect it. You'll barely be able to walk. *I'll* barely be able to walk. We'll just move from the bed to the shower, to the bed, to the shower, to the bed. And when we finally come up for air, we'll start all over again.'

I breathe out a stuttering laugh. 'You've really thought this through.'

'I've had two years.'

'I'm probably going to throw the containers in the trash though, if that's okay.'

'I'll allow it.'

He lies back down, pulling me with him, and I drape across his chest, looking up into his lovely, flushed face.

'I want to take you on a date,' he says. 'Bring you flowers. Introduce you to the people in my life. Start this thing right. I'm assuming that we are starting something now?'

'I think I started the something already.'

'And I want to get down on my knees and thank you for that. Seriously. On my knees. In front of you. Both of us naked.' His brow cocks and the tingle in my cheeks is a mixture of embarrassment and wild desire.

'The way I'm drawn to you, Holly, it's like nothing I've ever experienced. I don't want to screw it up. I want you to feel safe with me.'

I drink in his words and brush my lips against his cheek. 'Okay. But you'd better come good on your promise.'

'Oh, I'm going to come good. We both are.' His eyes twinkle.

I kiss him quickly then wiggle backwards over him, loving the little hiss he makes as I move across his erection.

'Sleep it is, I guess,' I say, my voice full of disappointment. How I'm going to sleep now, I do not know.

'I'm sorry.' He pushes off the bed.

'I don't blame you. I blame Casper out in the hall.'

He chuckles as he arranges himself in his sweatpants with a shrug and a grin, then pulls back the bedcovers and says, 'Hop in, Sunshine.'

I drag my hoodie over my head, stripping down to a short, tight tank top, pushing my shoulders back and giving Callum the time he needs to take me in. He mutters 'I am such an idiot' as I slide beneath the covers. He flicks off the bedside lamp.

'Try to sleep,' I say, rolling onto my side and wiggling away a little. 'We need to be on the ball tomorrow. And Callum?'

'Yeah?'

I take a moment to find my words. Tonight has been a lot, with more emotions than I think I've ever felt in one hit. It's going to take a bit of time for what's happening between us to truly sink in. To trust the promise of that future.

'I'm sorry about tonight,' I say eventually. 'I'm sorry I'm all over the place and so constantly weird. From now on, I'll try not to be so . . . me.'

His weight shifts, and I startle as his arm swings over me and gently pulls me back against him.

'I like you. All of you. Even your weird bits.' He places a kiss on my shoulder.

'Callum,' I whisper.

'Mmm?'

'Are you spooning me?'

'Maybe.'

'Then you owe me five bucks, Jefferies.'

CHAPTER TWENTY-TWO

'Holly, wake up.'
My eyes snap open and I know something's wrong. 'What? What is it?' I squint up at Callum. He's fully dressed.

'Jason didn't check out. I went to grab coffee, and the woman on the desk stopped me and asked if I knew if he'd be checking out today.'

'What? No. He checked out yesterday morning.' I toss back the sheets and clamber out of bed.

'Yeah, well, he didn't.'

'Okay. Maybe he just . . . forgot? Have you called him?'

'Of course I called him. He didn't pick up.'

'What about his brother? Have you checked to see if he's heard from him?' I'm still zipping up my jeans as I rush back into Callum's room with my boots tucked under my arm.

'I don't want to worry Chris until I know what's going on.' He paces the floor. 'Are you ready? The manager's going to let us into his room.'

I finish lacing my boots and grab his hand. 'Come on.'

The manager is standing in the hall outside Jason's room, looking almost as worried as we are.

'We sent the cleaner in late yesterday,' the manager says, 'and Mr Wright's belongings were still inside. You'll forgive me, but the receptionist saw you all come in quite late and in high spirits the other evening. We assumed he'd simply decided to stay another day and, as we aren't fully booked, the night manager just made a note of it.' He unlocks the door and pushes it open.

'Jason?' Callum calls as he shoves his way into the room.

'He's not in there, Mr Jefferies. Just his belongings.'

'Jase?' Callum calls again. He strides to the bathroom.

'I'm sure it's a mistake,' I say. 'He probably left a few things behind by accident.' But when I look around, it's obvious something's not right.

Jason's bed is unmade. His overnight bag is on the floor, half-packed, and a pair of jeans and a sweatshirt sit folded neatly on the chair, ready to be worn. His toiletries – toothbrush, shaving cream, razor – are still sitting on the edge of the sink.

Callum stares at me terrified, his hands clasped on his head. 'He's really not here.'

I pick up a set of car keys from the top of the dresser. 'Should we check his car?'

'Fuck.' He snatches the keys from me and stalks from the room, shoving past the manager in his haste.

'I'm so sorry,' I say, then I chase after Callum.

I find him in the parking lot standing in front of an olive-green Ford Mustang, tucked behind a large black SUV.

'He would never leave his car. Never.' He stares at it. 'How did I miss this? I'm so fucking stupid.' He rushes back inside.

The manager appears, a phone in his hand. 'Would you like me to call the police?'

'Let us check with his family first,' I say. I start down the hall after Callum. When I get to his room, he's checking his gun. He slides it into his waistband and pulls his shirt down to cover it, then grabs his jacket.

'Callum, what are you doing?'

'I'm going to get him.'

'We don't know where he is.' I stand in front of him, blocking his exit. 'Callum—'

'Don't we? It's something to do with the house, Holly. It has to be.'

'Why would you think that? Maybe he met some girl at the bar the other night and snuck out to meet her and just . . . lost track of time.'

'No. If he did that, he'd message me. Besides, you heard him, he said he had to check out early because he had a meeting.'

'But why would he go to the house? We told him not to.'

'I don't know, I just know he's there.'

'You don't. Let's just call the police and—'

'Yes, I do.'

My hands go to my hips. 'How?'

'Because I can *feel* it. I'm going there now and I'm going to bring him home.'

I close my eyes and picture the Western house. 'I don't . . . Callum I don't sense anything.'

'I'm positive, Holly. Please just trust me.'

No matter what happens, you can trust me.

I search his face, see the fear paling his cheeks, his eyes determined. 'Okay. Give me five minutes to get my stuff together.'

'We don't have five minutes.' He slings his duffle bag over his shoulder. 'I'll meet you in the car.' He stops at the door, slumping against it. 'It's Jason, Holly.'

I grab his hand and give it a gentle squeeze. 'And he's smart and strong and can take care of himself.'

'If anything happens to him . . .' His voice cracks. 'He's here because of me. All of this is because of me.'

'This is not your fault. If he's there, we'll bring him home.'

Callum stares out the window as we speed towards the Western house, clenching and unclenching his jaw.

'I should've checked in with him,' he says for what must be the tenth time. 'Made sure he got home okay. We always do that. I can't believe I didn't do that.'

'Stop blaming yourself. You didn't drag him out here.'

'I did though, just like I dragged you.'

'You didn't drag me either. Jason chose to come and so did I.'

I stop at a traffic light, tapping my hand on the steering wheel as I glare at it, willing it to turn green. Then I put my foot down again, taking off with a screech.

I steal another quick glance at him. His knee is bouncing, his body tense. Every nerve in my body is alert. There's something going on here I'm not getting. How can Callum be so sure Jason is at the house? How can he *feel* it?

He turns and catches me watching him and a quick frown darkens his brow. 'When we get there,' he says, 'I think I should go in alone.'

'There is no way in hell I'm letting you go into that house alone, especially after what happened to Richard and that other man.'

'Exactly. Richard warned you. Elizabeth's spirit warned you. Maybe you should stop and listen for a change.'

I glare. 'I don't care. I'm coming in with you.' He turns away again. 'I have to call Mr Rosing. We need him to let us in.' I puff out a terse breath and dial Rosing's number.

'Rosing here.' His voice comes through the car speakers.

'Mr Rosing, it's Holly Daniels, sorry to call so early. Did you get my message last night about meeting us at the house today? If you're available, we were hoping you could meet us there as soon as possible.'

'It's no trouble, I'm an early riser too,' he says. 'The house is ready for you. I've left a key tucked above the front door jamb, and the gate is unlocked.'

'Oh great, that's great. And you'll meet us there?'

'Yes, and Mr Western. He's looking forward to meeting you both. We should be there in about thirty minutes. But don't wait for us. Head straight on in. We'll wait for you in the garden.'

'Mr Western's here in East Mill?' I turn and look at Callum; his face is the palest I've ever seen it.

'He arrived late last night,' Mr Rosing says, then he adds, 'I was driving out to pick him up when you called.'

'Then I guess we'll be seeing both of you soon.' I hang up and look at Callum again. 'I've got a bad feeling about this.'

'Same,' he says.

I press my foot to the accelerator, the car growling as it takes off.

We arrive at the Western house about twenty minutes before Mr Rosing is due to meet us there. Callum stalks to the gate.

'Callum, slow down.' I race after him, but he ignores me. 'Callum.' I reach for his arm.

He shakes me off, swings around and snaps, 'My best friend's in there, Holly!' I recoil. 'I'm sorry. I'm panicking.'

'Well, don't panic. We need to focus. We can't be emotional right now.'

'I am focusing. On getting into this cursed house.'

'Then do it with less emotion.'

'I don't do less emotion. That's your thing.'

'Hey, I don't deserve that.'

Callum stares at me, a heavy breath lifting his shoulders. 'Sorry.' He pushes the gate open. It swings back silently. 'Come on. Let's find Jase and kick some dead ass.'

I try to ignore the churning in my stomach as I walk along the path, stopping at the foot of the stairs that rise to the porch. I let out a small groan.

Callum pulls a flashlight from his duffle and hands it to me, then pulls out another, along with an EMF meter. I note the tremble in his hands.

'Are you okay?'

'Not at all.' His face is pallid, etched with fear. 'I feel like something's creeping under my skin.'

'I sense it too. The presence isn't trying to hide from me anymore.'

'But why am I sensing it?' He flicks on his EMF meter, and it squeals to life with an ear-piercing alert. Lights flash across the display – green, yellow, orange and red pulsing all at once. 'What the fuck? That's not supposed to happen.' He gives it a whack. But the tool keeps on squealing, the lights flashing faster and faster. He quickly switches it off and drops it back into his bag as if it bit him.

'Maybe whatever is here is too powerful for your tools,' I offer. 'Maybe it's so powerful that you can sense it, like you did with the woman in the window.'

His eyes flit between mine. 'Holly, I need to—'

Bile suddenly gushes up my throat. I double over, my hands on my knees, and swallow back the acrid taste. 'Give me a sec.' I take a few deep breaths, then eventually straighten up again. 'That was a rough one. Sorry, what were you saying?'

He shakes his head. 'Nothing. I'm just freaking out. This place is . . . I don't like it here.'

'Yeah, me neither.'

We step onto the porch and it sighs under our weight with a low creaking groan.

'Well, if the spirit didn't know we were here already, it knows now,' he says.

'Pretty sure it knows everything we've done since we arrived in East Mill.'

We carefully negotiate the broken pieces of wood and shards of glass that litter the porch, stopping briefly to take in the enormity of the blown-out window, before standing in front of the grand door, preparing ourselves for whatever's behind it. Callum reaches up for the key, unlocks the door and we step inside. The morning sunshine bright in the garden fades quickly.

He frowns. 'It's a bit dark in here, considering all the windows.' He flicks a light switch, but nothing happens.

'Maybe the spirit wants to keep us in the dark,' I say.

His body heaves with a heavy sigh. 'Yeah, well, I've been kept in the dark long enough.'

Baleful laughter cackles through the air, echoing off the walls.

We freeze and stare at each other.

Callum whispers, 'Was that a woman's voice?'

'You heard that too?'

'Yep. Do you see anything?'

I should be able to see it, but I can't. I shake my head. 'No. I feel it, though.'

His jaw clenches, then he points forward, moving further into the house.

'Jase,' he calls out. 'Are you in here?'

'Slow up,' I hiss.

He ignores me and keeps walking until he's standing on the bottom step of the grand staircase at the heart of the room.

'Jason?' he calls up the stairs.

'Callum, shh. Slow down. Give me a second to—'

He wheels around, his mouth twisting into a cruel sneer. 'Stop telling me what to do.'

I stumble backward. 'Callum.' There's something strange about his face. Something I don't recognise. All the light is gone, the glow, the beauty replaced by a darkness that's hard and ugly.

He slowly straightens up, lifting himself to his full height, his shoulders pressed back as he looms over me. He takes one measured step forward, then another, inching me across the room with his body.

'What are you doing? Stop it. Callum! Stop it!'

I glance over my shoulder to check my surroundings, and in that moment, he grabs me, a hand on each arm. He squeezes so tight that I yelp. He holds me in place, his fingers digging into my flesh as I squirm and wriggle against his grasp.

'You're hurting me,' I cry.

He stares at me with eyes that aren't his. They're cold and empty. The eyes of the dead. No spark, no life, no Callum. Something has control of him. I can sense its foul presence crawling beneath his skin.

I scream into his face, 'Callum, fight it!' But he doesn't even blink.

He brushes his knuckles against my cheek and coos, 'Shhh, Holly.' His voice sounds strange, unnatural. 'Everything's going to be just fine. We'll be together forever. That's what you want, isn't it?'

He takes another step forward, backing me up against a long dining table and pinning me with his thighs. The edge of the wood digs painfully into the small of my back as I struggle under his weight. He runs a delicate hand up and down my throat.

'Let go,' Callum purrs. 'There'll be no more Holly the Freak if you just let go.'

Don't listen, it's not him, it's not him, it's not him.

I clench my fists, trapped at my sides, and focus all my energy on the presence slithering inside him.

'Leave him or I'll destroy you,' I say.

A cackle bursts from his lips. 'You destroy me, you destroy him, girl,' the thing inside Callum hisses, contorting his face in rage. A second later, his expression softens. *'Please don't kill me, Holly!'* Callum's voice pleads. And then the thing inside him laughs.

It's not him.

'Focus on my voice, Callum! I know you're in there. You can fight this! I believe in you.'

'How sweet,' the thing croons, then Callum lifts a hand and, with a twisted grin, clutches my throat.

I gasp for breath as his grip tightens. 'Callum, no. Please don't do this,' I manage to croak.

His eyelids flutter, his hold on me loosening slightly, and that tiny crack is all I need to bring my knee up and connect with his groin with as much force as I can muster.

Callum howls, stumbling backward, and drops to the floor, clutching at his crotch.

Coughing, I grab a chair and prepare to launch it at him. But then he looks up at me in shock, and it's his eyes, Callum's eyes, bright green and filled with pain.

'What the hell, Holly?'

'You need to leave.' I grab the collar of his jacket and drag him behind me, sliding him over the polished wooden floor towards the front door.

'What's going on?' He tries to scramble to his feet but stumbles and lands heavily on his side.

I stop and look down at him. His face is a mask of fear and uncertainty.

'Something possessed you, Callum, and you tried to choke me. I can't trust you in this place.'

'What are you talking about?' He crawls onto his knees and stares up at me. 'I would never hurt you, Holly. Never.' He pushes off the floor and I take two quick steps back.

'You need to leave.'

He shakes his head as he rubs the place where my knee so expertly landed. 'No,' he says, and pulls his gun from the back of his jeans.

I gasp, raising my hands to protect my face.

'No, no, no. Holly, no.' He places the gun on the table and backs away, his palms up. 'It's for you. Take it.'

'Just go, Callum.'

'I'm not leaving you in here alone. No way. I don't know what just happened, but if it happens again, you can shoot me.'

'What?'

'Just try to aim for somewhere non-fatal, okay?'

I fumble for his gun, my eyes glued to him. 'Don't you remember anything?'

He shakes his head back and forth, horror now lining his face. 'No, nothing.'

'It doesn't matter. If it got to you once, it could try again.'

'Then you shoot me, but I'm not leaving you. We stick together.'

An ache bursts in my heart. I take a slow breath. I can't believe what I'm about to say.

'Stay in front of me.' I point the gun at him.

He lifts his hands in the air and turns around.

'Not with your hands up, you idiot.'

He looks over his shoulder. 'Oh, right. Of course.' His hands drop to his sides. 'It wasn't me, Holly, I swear. Whatever I did, it wasn't me.'

'I know it wasn't. I could feel it wasn't.' I touch my throat. My skin still burns from where his grip tightened.

'What did you feel?' he asks.

'Something ugly. Different from anything I've ever experienced.'

'Why didn't you do your thing and destroy it?'

'Because I couldn't be sure I wouldn't hurt you.'

'Holly . . . you might have to.'

'I won't. It caught us by surprise. I won't let that happen again.'

We climb the stairs, which creak and groan under our feet. Callum's out in front, me behind with the gun raised in one hand and a flashlight in the other. The second storey is almost pitch black, and every shadow that snakes up the wall or stretches across the floor make us stop and gasp. We edge along the hall, pushing open each door, the light from our flashlights falling on well-made beds with heavy wooden posts that are dark and austere. Most of the furniture is cloaked in sheets that drape over dressers and hide frames on the wall. I peer under one and find a mirror, jumping with an embarrassing squeal at my own reflection.

The house is neat and clean and free of dust, as if someone had been recently living here and only just closed the house up. No spiderwebs or evidence of mice or rats.

'Does this seem way too pristine for a house that no one has lived in since Brendin Western died, what, seven years ago?' I ask.

'Maybe Rosing has someone who comes in and cleans?' Callum says.

'I can't imagine anyone from town wanting to do that.'

'Do you sense anything?'

'No. It's quiet again. Way too quiet, especially after what just happened.' He visibly shudders at my words.

We find the door to the attic and climb the narrow stairs. Here, we find dust and cobwebs clinging to every corner.

'This is more like it,' Callum says as he wanders around the room, peering at old chests and leather suitcases piled onto chairs. A shard of light shines in the window and I stand on my tiptoes to look through, seeing the familiar oak tree on the hill.

'Okay, so he's not upstairs,' Callum says.

'Then he must be downstairs.' I pull up my best reassuring smile.

'Jason,' Callum calls as we step off the landing. I don't stop him. There's no point in tiptoeing and whispering anymore. The spirit is either laying low or lying in wait. Either way, our presence is no secret.

I mentally check in with Callum as we pass the spot where he tried to choke me. It's all him, but there's also something else there now, as if the spirit left something lingering behind. A trace of darkness that I'm positive wasn't there before. My grip tightens around the gun. I should have made Callum leave. I've let my feelings for him cloud my judgement and now I've put *both* of us in danger.

We don't find Jason in any of the rooms off the long gloomy hall on the lower floor. Not in the sitting room with the grand piano, the sheet draped over it hanging askew to reveal yellowed ivory keys, or the drawing room where cloaked armchairs cluster around the long-cold fireplace.

'I don't think he's here,' Callum says with a tremble as we leave the kitchen and head back to the centre of the house.

'That's probably good, isn't it?'

'But I still *feel* like he's here. We must have missed something.'

'We've checked every room.' But then a thought hits me. Ice prickles up the back of my neck. 'What about . . . the old cellar. What if it's still here, hidden under this house?'

'Where was it on the original plans?'

'At the back, where the kitchen now is. Jason said the servants' quarters were built over it. But there's nothing in those rooms, they're totally empty.'

Callum spins around and strides back towards the kitchen. I rush after him.

He shines his flashlight across the floor. 'Would it be a trap door?'

'I don't know.' I dash into the servants' quarters and check the floors and the walls. He glances up as I come back out. 'Nothing,' I say. Then I spy something. 'Callum.' I point my flashlight toward an empty sideboard. 'There's something behind that sideboard.'

He shines his flashlight to where I'm looking, then his head snaps back around to me, his eyes wide.

'Help me shift it,' he says.

We pull and push on the sideboard, wiggling it back and forth over the timber floor until we reveal a wooden door, painted the same white as the brick of the kitchen walls.

Callum wraps his fingers around the old brass knob and slowly turns. The door swings open with a long creak. Then he shines his flashlight down the steep stairs.

My heart thunders.

He glances back at me anxiously, then calls out, 'Jason? Jase, are you down there?'

A voice floats up from the shadows. 'Cal?'

Callum gasps and sprints down the stairs, taking them two at a time.

'Shit!' I slip his gun into my jacket pocket and follow him, the glow from my flashlight bouncing off his back.

'Over here,' Jason calls, and at that exact second, Callum is hoisted into the air.

He shrieks, his flashlight smashing to the ground. 'Holly!' he calls as his body rises, twisting in space before he's hurtled towards the wall. He slams against it, the air bursting from him in a loud grunt, then falls limp, bouncing on the dirt floor with a sickening thud.

I stagger backwards, falling heavily as I stumble over a wooden box. My flashlight rolls from my grip.

A spirit materialises from the darkness, a woman with jet-black eyes that glitter like pieces of coal. Her dress is long and swishes noiselessly against the ground, her hair is pulled into a stern bun, and her face is gaunt and pale. She floats across the room like nothing I've ever seen. A mass of dark energy swirls around her with inky tendrils that reach for me.

'You think you can take what is ours, foolish girl?' Her voice bounces around the cellar like a guttural chorus. 'He belongs to us.'

'Nothing here is yours,' I say, scrambling to get up. 'Your time has passed, spirit.'

'Our time will never pass, child. We are eternal.'

She flings her arms forward, and a burst of energy explodes against my chest, the force of it knocking me off my feet. I skid backwards, slamming into a wooden post, and groan at the pain that rips through my shoulder.

The spirit laughs.

I push myself up again and stand before the spirit, swallowing over the fear tightening in my throat. 'I'm not afraid of you,' I say, low and calm.

Her face twists into a sinister grin. 'But you should be.'

An invisible force shoves me down and crushes me into the ground. I gulp at the air, my lungs struggling to expand, gravel from the earth-covered floor digging into my skin. Gritting my teeth and summoning all my strength, I push myself back up again, first to my knees, then slowly to my feet, every muscle burning and shuddering under the strain.

'Is that all you've got?' I say, a slight terror-filled tremor in my voice. I square my shoulders and jut my chin, doing my best to look defiant.

The spirit appears genuinely surprised. She growls, her lips curling into a snarl as she flings her spindly arms forward again. But this time, I'm ready for her. I focus every bit of my psychic energy and hold her in place, fighting back her attack. My body shakes with the effort of it, but my eyes never leave her face. I don't even blink.

She snarls again. 'You have power, but you are a fool if you think you can best us. You cannot win, stupid girl. We will enjoy the taste of your power.'

'You talk too much,' I say. I reach down, my hand trembling, and pull my rosary from my pocket.

The spirit sneers. 'Please. You think I'm afraid of your god?'

'To be honest,' I say, 'I don't need these.' I drop the beads to the floor, shore up my focus and begin my incantation.

'Latin?' the spirit scoffs. 'Mere parlour tricks!'

'Believe me, lady, I'm capable of a lot more than parlour tricks. I dragged you out of Callum, didn't I?'

A mocking smile stretches horribly across her gaunt face.

I calm myself again, breathing out long and slow, whispering the Latin words in my mind as I allow my gift to rise. But something new rises alongside it. Not just my usual power. This is something different. It starts in the soles of my feet and surges up my legs, pulses in my chest and throbs in my temples. I stumble over the incantation in my head as heat licks across my skin, the familiar words completely leaving me as energy flows down my arms, to the tips of my fingers, where it sparks like tiny bolts of lightning. I lift my hands and stare at them in wonder and fear. Then, somehow knowing exactly what to do, I thrust my hands towards the spirit.

She twitches, subtly at first, then a violent shudder shakes her entire grotesque form. Her expression shifts from smug disdain to mild surprise, then utter fury as she rushes at me with a roar.

I step back, plant my feet and, acting on pure instinct, throw my hands out again. A force explodes from me and hangs in the middle of the room, disrupting the air. I gasp, staring at whatever is swirling there, then I push back my shoulders and do it again. Another burst of something, and this time the spirit howls. It writhes and jerks, flickering in and out. I step closer, power now pouring from my outstretched hands. Beyond the wavering glow that shimmers in front of me, I see Callum, his mouth agape. I glance at Jason and see horror on his face.

'You will never stop us!' the spirit warns as she twists and snarls.

I cock my head. 'I wouldn't be so sure about that.' And with a deep breath, I ball up my fists and punch the air with everything I have. Another shockwave booms from my body, and the spirit yowls, giving one last bloodcurdling wail before bursting into flames.

I stare at the blazing spirit in utter shock, my eyes stinging and my heart pounding. When the light finally fades and the spirit is gone, in the silence that follows, I hear Callum whisper, 'Holly?'

CHAPTER TWENTY-THREE

I'm on the floor. I guess I collapsed. My body is vibrating, my hands shake, and my ears ring like that time my sister took me to see an *NSYNC tribute band and made me stand too close to the speakers. I lift myself off the dirt and stumble to my feet. I have no idea what just happened. Normally, the spirits fizzle out or shiver a little, and then poof, they're gone. They don't hang in midair, screeching and snarling before bursting into flames, and I don't shoot fireworks from my fingertips or pulses of electricity from my palms like Iron Man. My heart thumps so hard against my ribs it hurts. I fumble on the ground, searching for my flashlight. When my fingers close around it, I flick it on and watch the beam shake in my trembling hand. I quickly shine it around the room, illuminating every corner, wanting to make sure there's nothing else lurking in the darkness even though I can sense the spirit is gone.

'Callum,' I call. I can't cover the quiver in my voice. I stagger over to him and drop to my knees. There's blood on his hand, pressed to his side. 'You're bleeding,' I say.

'Again,' he says, with a weak smile. 'Where's Jason?'

'He's fine, I think.' I turn to go to him, but Callum grabs my arm.

'What just happened?' he says.

'I got rid of it. You've seen me do my work before.'

'I've never seen anything like that. What was that light coming from you?'

I shake him off. 'What light?' I put my hand to his head. 'Are you concussed?' He stares at me, frowning.

Before he can say anything else, I turn and scramble across the floor to where Jason is. He's chained to the wall. 'Jason, are you okay?' There's fear in his face as he looks at me and my heart sinks.

'Is this what you do?' he asks.

'More or less.'

'But how?'

I shrug as casually as I can. 'It's a spell. A bit of Latin. No biggie.'

'That was more than a bit of Latin, Holly.'

Callum drops beside me and flings himself at Jason. They hug.

'Can you shine your flashlight on the lock, Holly,' Callum says to me, then turns to Jason. 'Let's get you out of here, buddy.'

Callum makes quick work of picking Jason's lock.

'By the way,' Jason says to me, 'I think those plans were wrong. This house definitely has a cellar.'

'I noticed,' I say as I stand and roll my aching shoulders. I shine my flashlight around again, this time taking in the room. I recognise it instantly. I can see the scorch marks on the wall where lanterns once hung, the rough beams that crisscross the ceiling, the dirt floor. This is where Elizabeth was murdered. The new house was built above the old cellar. But they didn't put it on the plans. This time they hid it. Then I see something else. Carved into one of the beams is the sigil of the Poculum Vitae.

'I had to pee myself, man,' I hear Jason mumble miserably.

'Don't worry about it, dude,' Callum says. 'We've all been there. Holly, come on.'

I turn to see him helping Jason off the floor. 'Yeah, okay,' I say, casting one last glance around. 'After you.' I point towards the stairs with Callum's gun, which is somehow in my hand, even though I have no memory of pulling it from my pocket.

'What's with the gun?' Jason asks.

'Tell you later,' Callum says, glancing worriedly over his shoulder at me.

As we step out of the house and into the glare of the late morning sun, we see Albert Rosing and another man waiting at the end of the winding path.

Edward Western.

He's tall and even more striking than in his photo. He's dressed in a navy jacket and cream chinos, looking half his age and exactly how he did in my dream. *Do not believe the witches, they lie.*

He raises a hand to greet us and steps forward, ignoring me and Jason and going straight for Callum.

'Mr Jefferies. It's a genuine pleasure. I am so sorry we were unable to meet before now.'

Callum shakes Western's hand and gives the man a cursory nod, then releases his grip and wipes his palm down the side of his jeans. If the older man noticed, he doesn't flinch.

'And Ms Daniels,' Western says, turning to me but not offering his hand. I'm glad not to touch him. He makes my skin crawl, and his golden eyes are even stranger in person.

'And who's this?' Western asks, focusing his attention on Jason.

I jump in, saying, 'This is our colleague, Mr Wright.'

'Good to meet you, Mr Wright.' He smiles, casting a suspicious eye over Jason. It's then I notice that Jason is in his jogging gear. He's tied his windbreaker around his waist to cover the evidence of being trapped in the basement for hours.

Edward Western's smile remains frozen on his extraordinary face. 'I'm very happy to see that you're all safe.' He turns back to Callum, his strange golden eyes fixing on him. 'Though Mr Jefferies, are you injured?'

Callum looks down at the blood staining his hand, wipes it on his shirt and tugs his jacket around him. 'It's nothing. An old injury that keeps opening up.'

'You should have that seen to. Is there anything to report? Did you experience anything unusual in the house?'

Callum and I glance at each other, and an unspoken agreement passes between us. Some events do not need to be shared.

'The house has been cleared,' Callum says. 'Holly took care of it.'

Edward Western looks at me now, his eyebrows raised. 'You did?' I nod. 'Can you tell me what you saw?'

'A woman. I would say from the late 1800s, based on her appearance. She wore a long dress, I couldn't tell you the colour, but her hair was dark and pulled back in a severe bun. Thin face. Very angry. Ring any bells?' I'm getting such a bad vibe from this guy.

His eyebrows arch, and I could be wrong, but I think I see a flash of surprise, before he smiles coolly and says, 'That sounds as if it could be the ghost that my family members have reported seeing throughout the house.'

I nod. 'Thought to be your great-great grandmother Margaret, right?' I look at Callum. He's staring at me with a heavy frown. I follow his gaze as he slowly looks back at the house. 'You've tried to sort the haunting out before, haven't you?' I say, turning back to Western. I watch him closely.

'Ah, yes. I see you've heard about Browling and Dobbs. Such a terrible thing. There was no indication of any animosity between them when we hired them, of course.' He shakes his head in disbelief. 'If only I had known about your services at the time. We could have got everything sorted so much sooner.' He smiles, and I really, really don't like it.

I size up Mr Western as he continues to talk, consulting with Mr Rosing about next steps, asking Jason if he jogs daily, discussing what Callum can and can't use on his podcast. I hope I look half as good in my eighties as he does. He's a remarkable-looking man, and extremely well preserved for his age. I find myself wondering what he looked like when he was younger. He must have been quite spectacular.

'You'll need to drop by and visit Rosing tomorrow, just to sign some paperwork he's preparing,' Western says. 'But I'll let you all be on your way. Once again, Mr Jefferies, my apologies for not being available to you sooner. I cannot tell you how much I've been looking forward to meeting you – both of you,' he adds, turning to me. 'It has been an immense pleasure. I hope our paths will cross again.'

I shudder. I really hope they don't.

We take Jason back to Maddison House and stay with him while he showers and packs up his room. Then we walk him to his car, not wanting to leave him alone for a single second. He has no idea what happened to him. He explains that he couldn't sleep after we got back from the bar, so he decided to go for a quick jog. Next thing he knew, he was shackled in the cellar of the Western house. He didn't see or hear anybody until we arrived.

'I'm sorry I can't be more help,' he says. 'There's nothing there. It's blank. I'm going to have nightmares about it.' He tosses his bag into the trunk of his car. 'You know, we should probably call the cops. I was fucking kidnapped.'

Callum rests his hand on Jason's shoulder. 'Do you really want to do that?'

Jason shrugs. 'I guess not. What would I say? A ghost grabbed me?' He laughs.

Callum hugs him tight. 'Dude, I'm really sorry you got dragged into my mess. So fucking sorry. Text me every fifteen minutes until you're home, okay?'

I give Jason a quick hug, then step away and let the two friends say goodbye. They're leaning on Jason's car and talking quietly. Going over what happened, I guess. Callum puts a hand to his forehead, shaking his head over and over. Jason pats his back, then pulls him into another tight hug. They stand locked in an embrace for several long seconds before Jason steps away and looks at his friend, his hands on his shoulders, and says, 'You've got to do it. It'll be okay.' I have a feeling they're talking about me, and I don't think I like it.

'Everything alright?' I ask, as Callum stands beside me and we wave Jason off.

'Yep,' he says. 'Happy ending, right? Just got to sign the NDA covering what I can and can't say about the family on the podcast. Then we finalise our payment and we're done.'

'Are we meeting Rosing at the house tomorrow?'

'He'll be there doing some yard work, so I said we'd swing by on our way back to town.'

I nod. 'How are you feeling?'

He shrugs. 'Bit bruised.'

'I mean . . . Do you want to talk about what happened to you at the house?'

His jaw tenses. 'Not right now. Do you want to talk about what happened to *you*?'

'Me?'

'All the glowing.'

I shrug, not meeting his eyes. 'I barely remember what happened, it was so chaotic.' I look up at his narrowed eyes. 'The spirit's gone, and we're both okay, so let's just rack it up to a job well done.' He grunts and I tug on his shirt, rolling up the corner, checking the bloodied wound dressing. 'How about you let me take you to the hospital and finally get some actual stitches into you? And by "how about", I mean, I'm taking you to the hospital.'

He laughs. 'I get all tingly when you're bossy with me, Holly.'

I roll my eyes, grab his arm and march him towards my car, happy to have something else to think about – something other than the creeping feeling that I'm missing something, and that something here is still very, very wrong.

CHAPTER TWENTY-FOUR

Callum fidgets on the paper-covered bed in the examination room, his fists clenched at his sides and his knee bouncing. His phone dings, and he holds it up to show me. It's a message from Jason saying *still alive*.

I touch his thigh to still his jittering leg. 'You coping okay?'

'Umm,' he murmurs through a grimace.

'Can I ask why you hate hospitals so much?' He immediately stiffens. 'Sorry. You don't have to answer that.'

He looks at me with anxious eyes, then his tension drains away on a soft sigh. 'It's because of my aunt. She was sick for . . . a while, and I used to spend all day in the hospital with her, reading to her as she slowly faded away. She was always this powerhouse of a woman. Full of life. This rock always there for me. It was heartbreaking to see her like that, to know what she was going through and that I was losing her, my last shred of family. I still dream about it sometimes.'

I give his fingers a squeeze. 'I get it. It happened with my mom too,' I tell him. 'I was younger, so Dad sheltered me and my sister as best he could, but I can still remember how awful it was.'

'It's the smell and the sounds, you know? All those bad memories come flooding back.'

'I know exactly what you mean.'

He draws his hand away from mine and grips the side of the narrow bed. 'Listen. Um . . . About everything that happened at the house. I, er . . .' He rubs at the scruff on his chin and stares at the floor. 'Holly, I think we should . . .'

My heart sinks to my stomach. I know where this is going; I saw his face in the cellar. It's that other shoe again, but this time it *is* dropping, and with a thud. He can't even look at me, won't meet my eyes. My weirdness is too much. The whole thing was too much. I'd run from me too if I'd seen all of that.

'It's okay, Callum. I get it. It was a lot. After what happened in that house, I totally understand if you've changed your mind about giving this a go.'

His head snaps up, his face ever tenser than before. 'That's not what I was going to say. Is that what you're thinking? Have you changed your mind about us?'

'What? No, not at all. I just . . .' I drop into a chair. 'I panicked. I'm so used to expecting the worst.'

Callum puts a hand to his heart. 'Don't scare me like that, Holly.'

'Sorry,' I say. 'It's been a bit of a day, huh?'

He chuckles. 'Yep.'

'I'm so glad this job is finally finished. I'm looking forward to getting home.' I scooch my chair closer to him and look up from under my lashes. 'Which means . . . what was it, Jefferies? Bed to shower, bed to shower?' I grin wickedly.

Surprise flashes across his face, quickly followed by a wide smile. 'You're a rollercoaster, Daniels.'

'One you're looking forward to riding?'

He bursts out laughing, grabs my face and plants a kiss on my lips, just as the doctor pushes open the door.

'How are we going in here?'

Callum looks up with a huge grin. 'Pretty fucking great, Doc.'

It's a couple of hours until we're finally back in our rooms. I head to mine telling Callum I'm going to pack for the morning, when what I really need is a moment alone to try to process what happened to me at the house. I've always known that the rosary beads and holy water were only props – bang for my clients' buck, as Gran used to say – and I've long suspected I didn't have to *say* the Latin, only think it. But maybe I don't need the Latin at all? Maybe it isn't the incantation that gets the job done. Maybe it's just me.

I drop to the bed, a T-shirt clutched in my hands. I thought I was excited about the changes happening to me, but now I'm scared again. Because what was that force that shot out of me, and what am I, if I can spark like that? Maybe it was just a one-off, brought about by my connection to Elizabeth? After all, she died in the room where my gift literally exploded.

I jam the T-shirt into my bag, suddenly exhausted. I can think about all of this when I get home and away from *here*.

That's if I'm not trapped in my bedroom with Callum, surrounded by takeout containers. The thought makes me laugh. This investigation has been frustrating and confusing and terrifying, but it's also been the best thing I've ever done.

I abandon my packing and head into Callum's room. He's angrily tossing clothes at his duffle bag.

'That's an interesting way to pack,' I say.

'Just frustrated. I want to go. Put this place behind us. I should have told Rosing to email the paperwork.'

'It's only one more night.'

'One more night I could do without.'

'I have a theory on Jason,' I say. 'If you want to hear it?' He looks up. 'What if he was possessed like you were and went to the house and chained *himself* up, and that's why he doesn't remember how he got there?'

'Could be.' Callum hangs his head and sighs. 'I need to talk to you about what went on at the house.'

Oh shit. My stomach clenches. I'm not ready to talk about that. I still haven't wrapped my head around it myself. How do I frame what happened in that cellar in a way that won't terrify him, when it terrifies me? But I don't want to hide what happened from him either. I want to share everything with him, even the freaky stuff. Just maybe not tonight.

His worried eyes search mine, his teeth tugging on his bottom lip, and I suddenly get that it's not my electric fingers he wants to talk about, it's what he nearly did to me. I don't want him feeling guilty for something he had no control over. It wasn't his fault; I should have sensed the spirit was there. I'm the one who failed. I'm the one who didn't have his back.

'We'll talk about all of it,' I say. 'I promise. But can we do it later? When we're more relaxed. I'm kind of wiped out.' I smile.

He chews his lip for a little longer, then finally nods. 'Okay. Why don't you go take a nap?' he says. 'I'll wash up and come join you.'

'Would you overthink it if I napped alone?'

'Umm. Probably.'

'I just know that I won't nap if you're with me.'

'Really? What will you do?'

I walk over to him and wrap my arms around his neck. 'This.' Then I stretch up and kiss him.

He moans that lovely moan of his, low in the back of his throat, his hands instantly everywhere. Pulling my hips, stroking my arms, dusting the edge of my breasts, slipping below my waistband. I've never been kissed the way Callum kisses me. So hungry yet so tender. It feels like he was made to kiss only me, as if his lips were created to fit perfectly with my own.

I slip my arms from his neck and press my palms to his chest, gently pushing him away. 'This is why I can't nap with you.'

He smiles and kisses the top of my head. 'Okay. Go nap, Sunshine. I'll shower and . . . er, amuse myself somehow.' He gives me a lopsided smirk and flick of his brows.

'Oh god. Too much information,' I say, but I can't deny the heat that image prompts between my thighs.

CHAPTER TWENTY-FIVE

The room is familiar to me, as if I've been there before. A large oak table is elegantly set with four golden dishes and sparkling crystal glasses, and a grand staircase soars towards the floor above. I walk down the hallway, studying the paintings on the wall. There are five remarkable portraits – four men, all of them strikingly handsome, and one woman, her expression stern. The sound of voices drifts towards me, and I follow it, stepping into a drawing room. Three men and a woman look up as I enter, and I understand immediately that these are the people in the portraits I was just admiring. A fourth man is seated with his back to me. When he stands and turns, I'm surprised to see it's Callum.

'Hey,' he says, with a sweet smile. He takes my hand. 'Come meet everyone.'

I shuffle backwards. Something doesn't feel right.

'What are you doing?' he asks. 'Why are you embarrassing me?'

'Please let me go, Callum,' I say, tugging my hand from his.

He looks down at me and his smile transforms into a sneer.

I recognise the sneer. I recognise the room. I'm in the Western house, and the man before me isn't Callum anymore.

'It doesn't have to be like this,' the man says. 'You could have made it easy on yourself. Wouldn't you like to be normal, even if only for a moment?'

'I am normal,' I say, still backing away.

'You are anything but normal, Holly. You're extraordinary.'

I turn and start to run, but the man trips me, and I hit the floor with a thump. I scramble forward along the hallway, fighting for traction on the polished boards. Someone grabs my shoulders and flips me onto my back. The man who was chasing me drops to his knees and straddles my chest, pinning me beneath him.

When I stare into his face and his strange golden eyes, I finally understand. Callum has become Edward Western.

I hit him, punching his chest, my legs kicking, trying to fight him off. The others gather around, each grinning in a way that fills me with horror.

The woman puts her face near mine and sneers. 'I told you you could not win, stupid girl.'

It's the spirit I fought in the cellar, now alive and standing in front of me, her hair pulled back tight and her long dress swishing on the ground. I scream.

Edward Western wraps his fingers around my throat and squeezes tighter and tighter. I thrash against the floor, hips bouncing and feet skidding, fists lashing out, while the others loom above me, hissing unintelligible words. My pulse pounds in my ears. Then the room starts to dim.

I'm dying, I think, as my arms flop limply to my sides. Then I hear someone calling my name, and my body jerks.

My eyes snap open. Callum is hovering over me, his hands on my shoulders. I scream again and hit out, my fist connecting with the side of his face as I scramble away from him.

He yelps and lurches back, his hand flying to his injured cheek.

'Holly, it's me! It's Callum. You were dreaming. You were having a nightmare.'

I look around the room, dazed and disorientated. 'What?'

'You were having a bad dream.'

I'm in my room at the bed and breakfast. I'm in my bed. 'Oh,' I breathe out, and slide back down the mattress as my body relaxes. I run a shaking hand across my forehead, wiping away the slick of sweat. 'I – I was at the h-house,' I manage to stammer.

'What the hell was happening? What did you see?' He looks as scared as I feel.

'It was just the spirit,' I quickly lie. 'The one I exorcised in the cellar. I was reliving everything, I guess.'

He frowns. 'You called out my name.' He looks so worried.

I reach for the water beside my bed and hold onto it with two hands, but the liquid still splashes over the side of the glass.

'Of course I did. You got hurt.' I force a smile to my trembling lips. 'What time is it? Did I miss dinner?'

Callum exhales deeply, shakes his head, and checks the time on my phone. 'It's five am,' he says. 'You've been out for about . . .' He quickly does the math. 'Fourteen hours.'

'What?' I push a shaky hand back through my hair. 'I guess I really was tired. Go back to bed, get some more sleep.'

'Do you want me to stay with you?'

'No,' I say, a little too hastily. 'I'm okay. Go back to sleep. Sorry to wake you. Stupid dreams.'

He slowly nods, his eyebrows pulled tight. 'Okay. Call me if you need me.' He kisses my forehead.

I somehow manage not to flinch.

Morning brings with it a fresh perspective. Last night's dream was just my brain's way of processing everything that happened at the house and the unanswered questions bouncing around my mind.

If Jason was bait, then for what? The spirit mentioned something about enjoying the taste of my power. Is that why Jason was here, to get me to the house? Was that what Elizabeth and Richard were trying to warn me about? What if Callum's theory about the early-settler Western brothers, who instigated the witch trials, is right? That they wanted to kill the witches not to destroy them, but to somehow take their powers, and the spirit who dwelled in this house was still trying to carry out their wishes in some dead, misguided way. Then I remember Annie and the beautiful man on the hill. What if the Westerns never actually stopped wanting those powers? A shudder runs through me, but I shake it off. We're going home, the house is no longer haunted, and hopefully Annie's spirit can rest now, too.

I can hear Callum moving around in his room, so I push open the door and say, 'How long until we head off?' He spins around, his face dark and his mouth taut. 'What is it? What's wrong?'

'Sit down,' he says, and he sounds so serious I drop straight into a chair. He pulls another chair closer to me, sits and wrings his hands in his lap. 'Before we go sign the papers, we need to talk.'

I manage a tiny nod and whisper a nervous, 'O-okay.'

'Before I start,' he says, 'I need to know you won't be angry with me when I tell you what I'm going to tell you.'

That feeling I've been having that something's not right starts barrelling up my spine.

'I can't promise you that,' I say, 'until I know what you're going to tell me. But now I'm worried.'

He runs a hand over the back of his neck, then puts his palms on his thighs and breathes deeply. 'I want to preface this by saying, like you and your dreams, I needed time to process this information before I spoke to you about it. But we said we wouldn't keep things from each other, and with everything that's happened between us, and everything that went down at the house, I know I should have said something earlier.'

'Okay. Now I'm scared.'

His gaze drops. 'When Rosing sent me the photos, there was one I didn't show you. It was a portrait of a woman. When you noticed there was a photo missing, I, ah . . . I lied about it. The portrait was of Margaret Western. Who, from your description, sounds like the ghost you faced in the house.'

'Okay . . . But as we already thought the haunting might have been her, why would you hide that from me?'

He takes another deep breath. 'Because I panicked. Because Margaret Western looked exactly like my Aunt Aideen.'

I frown. '*Exactly* like her,' he adds. 'And . . . a hell of a lot like me.'

'I'm confused, Callum. What are you telling me?'

His gaze lifts to my face and he stares at me for a long moment, then he looks down again, twisting his fingers anxiously.

'As I told you, I don't know much about my family. My mom and dad were gone before I even knew who they were. I didn't know my grandparents, and Aideen never talked about family, even when I pressed her. When she insisted that I learn everything about myths and legends and the paranormal, I thought she was just being her eccentric self, but now I think she had a different reason. I think she wanted me to be prepared.' He stops and swallows.

Fear prickles over my skin. 'Prepared for . . .'

'I think I'm related to the Westerns.' The words leave him in a rush.

It takes a second for this to sink in. Then I shake my head. 'No. That's . . .' He looks up at me, his eyes locking on mine. 'That's . . . ridiculous . . .'

I take in his face as if seeing him for the first time. Uncommonly green eyes with flecks of gold circling the pupils. Fair skin that I've always thought seemed to somehow glow. A striking beauty so casually worn it's easy to see past it. But I know the man he is inside and . . . My pulse quickens. *Inside.* I flash back to yesterday at the house and the dark stain I sensed within him after the possession. Was it always there and I just never noticed it? *Oh god.*

'I'm not one hundred per cent sure,' Callum says. 'Actually, that's not true. After yesterday, I am sure. I can feel my connection to the family. I think that's why the spirit could show itself to me that first night. Why I *knew* Jason was at the house. Why I sensed the spirit and felt its energy under my skin, as if it was part of me. Because it was part of me. There was something when I shook Western's hand, too. I can't explain it. It was like a knowing, an understanding. A link.'

'But . . .' I'm looking for something, anything to prove he's wrong. That this is just as stupid as it sounds. 'Then why did something try to scare us off on that first night? Why were *you* attacked?'

'Maybe it wasn't so much me being attacked as you being protected. The same spirits that were making you sick, stopping me going any further, stopping you from following me into that house.'

My heart thunders in my ears as what he's telling me truly sinks in. 'How long have you been thinking about this? How long have you suspected? We got those photos days ago, Callum.'

'It's been creeping up on me,' he says. 'At first, I thought I was being crazy, that the job was getting to me. I didn't think—'

'You've been lying to me for days?' I can't catch my breath. My head is swimming. I squeeze my eyes shut for a moment, trying to slow everything down.

'Not the whole time, and not exactly lying,' he says. 'I – I wasn't sure. Like you and your dreams, I thought I was seeing something that wasn't there. But then Jason—'

My eyes snap open again. 'Jason knows?'

'No. I mean, not really. Before he left, I said something to him, expecting him to tell me I was being an idiot, but instead, he told me that when Aideen was dying, she asked him to make sure I never looked into my family history. That I didn't go searching for them. He'd never told me that before. My guess is this is why.'

I spring to my feet, my fists clenched tightly. 'This is why you said it was all your fault, what happened to Jason and me. I thought you just meant because you took the case, but you meant because you were lured here, and you lured me and Jason here with you.'

'I didn't *lure* you, and I wanted to tell you everything yesterday, I said we needed to talk, but you kept fobbing me off and kissing me.'

'Oh, so your lying is my fault? I was trying to be kind. I didn't want you to feel bad about what you did to me at the house. I thought it was out of your control. But it wasn't. It was why you were brought here. Because you're one of them.'

'We don't know that for certain, and it *was* out of my control.' He moves towards me, and I shrink from him. 'I'm sorry. I know I should have told you as soon as I suspected something wasn't right, but I wanted to dig into it more, investigate it properly, see if there was anything in Aideen's storage.'

My body trembles – filled with rage and horror and excruciating heartbreak. 'You've been in my dreams, right there, next to the Westerns because *you're one of them*.'

His face pales. 'You didn't tell me I was with the Westerns in your dreams.'

'I thought they were dreams, Callum. Because of everything that was being stirred up inside me. Because I'm falling—' I bite my lip and take a shaky breath. 'You think you're related to a family that murdered women like me to somehow steal their psychic powers. Wasn't that your theory?'

'It was just a crackpot theory, which you told me can't be correct.'

I think of the whispering men standing over the dead bodies of the girls. What if their whispers were some kind of spell?

'The spirit in the cellar told me, "We will enjoy the taste of your power." You delivered me to that thing on a silver platter, and you nearly got me killed.'

'Holly, no, never in a million years could I have thought something like that would happen.' He reaches out for me again. 'I would *never* hurt you.'

I pin him with a glare. 'But you did. You did hurt me, Callum. You laid your hands on me. Why didn't you tell me what was going on?'

'Because I wasn't sure.'

'That's not good enough. We're supposed to be a team. We're supposed to be more than that, we're supposed to be—' My words catch.

He stares at me. 'You haven't told me everything either. My part in your dreams, and what really happened in the cellar. I saw the light coming out of you. I'm not the only one keeping secrets.'

'Is this why you're drawn to me, because of what I am? Is it some weird connection to my gift?'

'Oh my god, no Holly, no. I'm drawn to you because of you.'

'How can you be sure? How can *I* be sure? Oh no,' I moan. 'You *are* the handsome man I can't trust.' Tears well in my eyes, and I rub at them with my knuckles. 'Oh god.'

'You should sit down.' He takes my hand.

I snatch it away. 'Don't touch me.'

'I'm sorry.' His voice is desperate. 'I didn't know for sure. I had a feeling, a weird feeling, but I've never experienced anything like this. I honestly hoped we could get the job done and just go home. That we could be together. That I could look into it in my own time, or just bury it in another box inside me. What's another box, right? But I knew I wouldn't be able to do that, not if there was even a chance. It's too big.' Tears run down his cheeks.

'If you'd have just told me, we could have worked it out together.'

'I'm sorry,' he says, 'I didn't want to hide it from you. But I also didn't want it to be true. I don't want to experience these weird sensations. I don't want *them* to be my family. I don't want to be whatever they are. I don't want to be a supernatural fr—'

The last word is swallowed in a gasp, but I know what he was going to say.

'A supernatural what?'

He drops his gaze to the floor.

'A supernatural what, Callum? A supernatural freak, like me? Right. Got it. You talk a good game; I'll give you that. Pretending you're fine with who I am, what I am. But god forbid you should be anything like me.' I press my fingers to my temples. 'You meant it when you agreed with Peter that I was a freak, didn't you? You weren't just trying to shut him down.'

He looks up, his eyes rimmed red. 'No. I didn't mean it, I swear.'

'It doesn't matter. Because it's obvious now how you feel.' I scrub my palms across my tear-stained cheeks. 'I'm glad I found out who you really are. That you're a liar and a coward.' I pick up my bag. 'You can find your own way back to the city.'

'Holly, please don't go. I didn't mean for any of this to happen. I'm still trying to figure this all out – I don't know who I am anymore.'

'If you'd have told me, the one person who might have understood . . .' I push my shoulders back. 'But I can't help you now. Goodbye, Callum.'

CHAPTER TWENTY-SIX

I descend into the glowing room, placing each foot carefully on the old wooden boards. Voices drift up from the darkness below, and I cling to the walls, sheltering in their shadows. In the middle of the cellar, a man is kneeling on the dirt floor. An older man looms above him, whispering a series of words. He empties an ampoule of liquid into a small bronze chalice engraved with a triangular sigil balanced in the younger man's hands. A lamp hanging from the beam above him illuminates his features, and I stifle a shocked gasp. The man looks like Callum. His hair is lighter, blond rather than Callum's brown, and a little longer, curling around his nape and over the collar of his shirt, but his face is just as beautiful.

He rises to his feet and whispers something in the older man's ear. I lean forward, desperate to hear, and my foot slips. I grab at a shelf to stop from falling, sending tins clattering to the floor. The men's heads snap towards me. I hold my breath, waiting for one of them to rush at me, to grab me, to take me. But they don't move. It's as if their unnerving golden eyes can't see me.

Then Elizabeth Howell whispers, 'Your work is not done yet, Cousin. Let us in.'

*

It's not like I hadn't already figured out that Elizabeth and I are family. But since leaving East Mill, every time I've closed my eyes she's there whispering 'Cousin' in my ear. We're always in the cellar of the Western house. Always watching a ceremony I don't understand. Side by side. She doesn't scare me anymore. We are the same, Elizabeth and I. We are blood. We are both Howells and we are both gifted.

The first two days after I walked away from Callum, I cried so much I began to wonder if I could dehydrate from the amount of fluids I was losing, if someone could truly die from a broken heart. For a while, it felt like that was happening. My heart ached so fiercely I thought it might stop beating. Callum hasn't called, hasn't sent so much as a text. Which is good, because I don't want to speak to him. I never want to see him again. At least, that's what I tell myself. What's one more lie between my heart and my head? But today . . . today I woke up and decided I'd cried enough. It's time to do what I always do. Shove my feelings down and get on with my life.

I pour myself a strong coffee, drop onto the couch and call Mrs Tyler to follow up on her haunting. It's hard to believe it's been less than two weeks since I sent her husband's spirit packing, less than two weeks since I first heard from Callum again, and only three days since I left him in East Mill. It all feels like a lifetime ago.

'Just checking in to confirm that there haven't been any more disturbances,' I say to her.

'Not a peep,' Mrs Tyler says.

'Great. I like to follow up and make sure my clients are doing okay.'

'I'm very well, sleeping a lot better. How are you, Ms Daniels? Is everything alright with you?'

I rub my forehead so hard I'm sure I leave a welt. 'Everything's great,' I say brightly. 'Don't hesitate to call if you need any more help.'

'No offence, dear, but I hope I never have to speak to you again.'

Next, I busy myself checking my emails, requesting more information for a possible new client. When my phone rings I'm distracted enough that I answer without checking the caller ID.

'Holly Daniels,' I say, all business.

'Holly. It's Jason. Don't hang up.'

I sit up straight, my body tense.

'Holly?' he says again.

'I don't want to talk to you, Jason.'

'Cal's missing. I haven't heard from him for two days, and that's not like him.'

I'm silent as his words sink in. Then I shake them off. 'I'm sure he's fine. He's quite capable of looking after himself, and only himself.'

'I know you're hurt. He told me what happened. All of it. He made a mistake. A really big one. I was caught up in his lie too, remember. But I still love him, and I don't know who else to turn to. He's not answering his phone or emails. Holly, we don't ignore each other ever. He wouldn't do that. Something's wrong. I think he's at the house.'

I close my eyes. All I want is to put East Mill and Callum Jefferies far, far behind me. Except I can't, because my dreams won't let me, and no matter how angry I am with Callum, neither will my heart.

I heave out a giant sigh. 'What would make you think he's at the Western house?'

'Because he called me. He told me you'd left, that you'd had a fight. Said he was going to the house to sign some papers, and that's the last I heard from him. I thought I was giving him space. But . . .'

'Have you called the bed and breakfast?'

'He checked out the day you left.'

'Have you called the police?'

'He'd kill me if I did that, he'd want me to call you first, because he trusts you. I'm in the city today. Can you meet me at his apartment?'

I look to the heavens with a shake of the head. 'I'll meet you there in an hour.'

I arrive at Callum's apartment block just as another resident is leaving. He holds open the heavy glass doors, allowing me to slip under his arm.

'Great security,' I mutter to myself.

At Callum's door, I thump and call out, 'Callum, if you're in there, you'd better open up now.' I press my ear to the door and listen to the silence.

Jason arrives minutes later with keys in hand. His hair hangs messily around his worried face.

'Thanks for coming,' he says, as he unlocks Callum's door and calls out, 'Callum, you here, man?' He races inside. 'Callum,' he calls again as he disappears up the hall.

I glace around the living room. It's exactly as I first saw it. Spotless, cushions fluffed, books neatly piled on the coffee table, weird things on the shelves, his framed degrees. Little bits of Callum all around me. A pang throbs in my heart.

I start after Jason and find him in the kitchen, holding onto the countertop as if it's the only thing keeping him upright.

'I was hoping he was sulking or something,' he says, 'but he's really not here.'

'Why did you want me to come?'

'I don't know. I thought you might feel something if something weird had happened.' He looks at me, hopeful.

I shake my head and give his arm a gentle squeeze. 'Do you know if Callum keeps any of his aunt's stuff in this apartment?'

He looks confused. 'I think he's got a few boxes in the spare room. But otherwise it's all in storage across town. Why?'

'Where's the spare room?'

He nods for me to follow, and we start back down the hall.

'What are we looking for?' he says.

'Anything about his parents. Photos, letters, family documents. He thinks he's related to the Westerns, he told you that, right?'

'He told me. And I told him to tell you.'

'But you didn't know before East Mill?'

'All I knew was that Aideen didn't want him going looking for family after she died, but I didn't know why.'

'Because they might be mass murderers.'

'That's a pretty good reason.' He takes my hand. 'He's crazy about you. He has been since you first met. That's never changed.'

I draw my hand away. 'I don't want to talk about it, Jason.'

'I know he fucked up, but Holly, he's frightened. I've never heard him like he was when he called me. I don't want to make excuses for him, but—'

'Then don't,' I snap. 'What about those?' I point to a pile of carboard boxes in the corner of the room, sealed tight with old yellowing packing tape. The word 'California' is printed neatly across the top.

'Looks like he still hasn't got to these,' Jason says, as he uses his keys to slice through the tape. He digs around inside the first box, pulls out a plastic tub, and hands it to me. Then he opens box number two.

I peel back the lid of the tub. It looks like years of old bills. 'I don't think this is anything,' I say quickly looking through it.

'This could be something.' He puts his tub on the dresser top and hands me a pile of paperwork.

'Has he not gone through any of this?' I ask shuffling through what Jason gave me.

'He's been slowly going through Aideen's storage. Very slowly. I think he finds it too much to deal with, anything about his folks, you know. The whole orphan thing is a massive part of his psyche, you have no idea. And I don't think Aideen helped with that. He always felt different, and all he ever wanted was to feel normal. Fit in with the crowd. I think that's why he attached himself to me, because he wanted the kind of normal family I had. Not a couple of dead parents and an eccentric aunt.'

Jason's words slice through my heart. I understand all of that. Oh boy, do I. I now also understand that if you let those feelings fester, they can infect your entire life, just like they infected mine. It's taken me nearly twenty years to figure that out, and Callum is part of the reason that I did.

'I hate the word "normal",' I say. 'What does it even mean? No one's normal. We're all different. *Normal.* Such bullshit.' I pick up a file and flick through the contents. I knew there were similarities between me and Callum, even some shared neuroses, but I had no idea how deep it went. Why hadn't I been able to see that part of him? Was I so caught up in my own sob story I couldn't hear anyone else's?

Jason studies a piece of paper. 'Got something. His mother's birth certificate.'

I take a breath and refocus. 'Great. What's her last name?' I ask.

'Iarthar. Niamh Iarthar. Same last name as Aideen.'

I feel a surge of relief. 'Not Western. That's good.' We both continue to rifle through the documents, quickly scanning the pages.

'Hey, here's his folks' wedding certificate,' Jason says, looking surprised.

'Let me see that.' I look over the document and shrug. Niamh Iarthar married Lyle Jefferies in 1989. Two signatures at the bottom. Nothing jumps out at me. I pick up Callum's mother's birth certificate. It's faded, and a deep crease makes it difficult to read, but there's one thing I clock straight away. The name of Niamh's father, Callum's grandfather: *Cillian*.

'Shit,' I whisper.

'What?' Jason asks.

It doesn't say Cillian Western. It says Cillian Iarthar. But surely it couldn't be a coincidence. What would the chances be that Callum's grandfather would have the same first name as Edward Western's brother? I think back to Mrs Parish's house. If Callum reacted to hearing the name I didn't notice it.

'What is it?' Jason asks again.

'A woman we met in East Mill mentioned a Cillian. Edward Western's brother. Niamh's father was Cillian. Has Callum ever mentioned his grandfather to you?'

'Only that he was dead. That's all he ever knew as far as I know. He stopped asking Aideen questions after a while. She made him believe he didn't want to hear the answers.'

A photo slips from the file in my hand and flutters to the floor.

Jason reaches down and picks it up. 'It's an old photo,' he says. 'Not sure who?'

He hands it to me. It's black and white, and a little blurry. A man in light pants and a sweater stands by a dune, a windswept beach stretching out behind him. 'Not Callum's dad?'

'No. Hang on, I think I spotted one of him earlier.' Jason rummages through the box again. 'This is Lyle Jefferies.'

He shows me a Polaroid of a tall man with brown hair like Callum's and hazel-green eyes.

'And this is his mom,' he says, handing me another photo.

The woman in this photo is stunning, statuesque with pale skin, long, dark blonde hair, and bright eyes the colour of caramel.

'I wonder who this is, then?' I look at the old black and white photo of the man on the beach again. It's difficult to make out his features.

'There's something on the back.' Jason takes it from me and flips it over. 'Here. See? You can make out *E* and *1967*.'

I snatch it back from him and stare at it. 'Oh my god. I think this is Edward Western.'

'But the guy at the house was, what, fifty? How is this him in '67? He wouldn't have even been born.'

'Edward Western is eighty-two,' I say.

'The guy from the house? No way! Are you sure this is . . .' He looks over my shoulder. 'Shit, I think you're right, it is him.'

We're both silent as we let that sink in.

'So, it's true,' Jason eventually says. 'Callum is somehow related to the Westerns.'

'What I still don't get is the Cillian thing,' I say. 'If Callum's grandfather is Edward Western's younger brother, why are he and Niamh listed as Iarthar on Niamh's birth certificate?'

I frown, typing *Iarthar* into Google on my phone, then turn it around to show Jason what I've found. Iarthar is Gaelic for *West*.

We stare at each other, then again at the old photo of Edward.

'We know that Edward and Cillian's father relocated to England,' I say, 'married there, and that's where his children were born. Edward and Cillian weren't raised in East Mill. But what if their father also changed his name. Then when the brothers came back to the States, Edward reverted to Western, but Cillian kept the name his father gave him.'

'Trying to distance himself from his ancestors?' Jason says.

'I would, wouldn't you?' I look up at him. 'That might explain why Callum's aunt was so anti-family, if she was raised by a father who didn't want anything to do with them. Maybe that's where she learned not to talk about them.'

'So Callum is a Western.' Jason leans heavily against the wall.

'No, Callum is an Iarthar and a Jefferies, but I have a feeling Edward Western would like to change that.'

'When he was telling me everything, he mentioned he thought he could be psychic in some way. You don't really think he could be, do you?'

'He saw a spirit at the house, and if his theory about the Westerns and why they murder is true, then yeah I think he could be. My grandmother was psychic, and so am I. If his family are in any way paranormal or psychic, or whatever we want to call them, it could be in Callum's blood too.' *Evil is in his blood.*

Jason is ashen. 'He's in trouble, isn't he?'

I gather up the documents and the photo. 'I've got to go.'

'I'm coming with you,' he calls after me as I rush down the hall.

'No, you're not.'

'I'm not letting you go to that house on your own.'

'I don't need you to be my hero, Jason. It's bad enough that I have to worry about Callum. You'll just be another distraction.'

'Let me do something. I can't just sit here.'

'Okay, this is how you can help. Text Callum. Tell him you've spoken to me and that I'm still furious. Tell him I never want to see him again. Tell him you understand he needs time out and you're here for him when he's ready. Make it sound as if you're not worried and no one is coming for him. That way no one will know that I *am* coming for him.'

'But Holly—' The elevator doors close, blocking him out.

CHAPTER TWENTY-SEVEN

The late afternoon sun is throwing deep shadows across the lawn as I pull up outside the Western house. If Callum's theory about what this family has been doing for centuries is correct, I might as well have tied a big red bow around myself. Edward must have thought all his Christmases had come at once when Callum showed up with me as his sidekick. The only positive to hang onto is that he has no idea of my connection to the spirit of Elizabeth, and no idea that connection has supercharged my powers. At least, that's what I think has happened, but I don't know for sure, and I don't know if it matters. Because I've never used my powers on anything other than a ghost, and Edward Western is very much alive.

I grab my flashlight, rosary, and hip flask full of holy water from the trunk, turn and cast my eyes towards the house. Then I look down at my old tools in my hands. I don't need these props anymore. All I need is inside me. I toss everything but my flashlight back into the car and slam the trunk closed.

As I step through the imposing iron gates and onto the cobbled path, Mr Rosing emerges from the rose garden.

I gasp and take a quick step back, bracing myself, though I don't know what for.

'Ms Daniels, what are you doing here? Is everything alright?'

He seems genuinely surprised. Concerned even. Maybe I was wrong about him. Maybe I'm wrong about everything.

'I'm wondering if you've seen Callum around?' I linger by the gate.

He looks puzzled. 'You think he's here at the house?'

'I'm not sure.' I glance over my shoulder at the shadowy building. 'But I was hoping to go in and just double check if he's—' I hear hurried footsteps behind me, then something sharp stings the side of my neck. My hand flies to my throat. 'What—?'

'You *are* going in, Ms Daniels,' Mr Rosing says, standing back. There's a small syringe in his hand. 'But I'm afraid you won't be coming back out.'

My knees buckle as the world tilts.

Mr Rosing grabs my arm. 'The Master knew you would come,' he whispers in my ear. 'A woman in love is so predictable.'

I'm sprawled across the dirt floor, the side of my face pressed to the cold ground and my knee twisted painfully beneath me.

I groan.

'Ms Daniels,' a man's voice drawls. 'Are you with us?'

My eyes flicker open briefly, then I sink back into darkness.

'Ms Daniels?' the man says again.

My memory comes rushing back. Mr Rosing. The garden. The syringe. *A sedative?* 'What did you do to me?'

'There you are. I was beginning to think Albert accidentally killed you.'

I carefully shift my aching body and squint towards the voice. Edward Western is leering down at me.

'I knew you wouldn't be able to resist coming back here,' he says. 'You hero types are all the same.'

I shrink away from him and his strange eyes and quickly assess my situation. I'm back in the cellar of the Western house with my hands and feet bound. Across the room, Callum kneels in a corner, his head hanging.

I call to him, my voice a scratchy rasp.

He looks up, his eyes filled with sorrow. 'I'm so sorry, Holly,' he says. 'I'm so sorry . . .'

I turn back to Edward Western. 'What are you going to do to us?' I croak.

'Give the poor girl a drink, Albert, can't you see she's parched?'

Mr Rosing holds a bottle to my lips, and I drink greedily.

Western shoos him away with a dismissive flick of his hand.

'Untie me.' I sound a lot braver than I feel. Everything inside me is shaking like Jell-O.

'Not until we've had a little chat,' Western says, all politeness.

I peer around him to Callum. 'Has he hurt you?'

Callum's eyes meet mine. 'Why did you come? You shouldn't have come.'

'Don't be an idiot. I'm here to rescue you.'

Western's laugh chills me to the core. 'How adorable,' he says.

I glare up at him determined not to show fear. 'What are we doing here?'

'Shall I break it down for you, Ms Daniels, do the big villain reveal? Though I have a feeling you already know what I'm going to tell you. First, I want young Callum here back in the family fold. He was stolen from us and hidden for far too long. And to *truly* make him one of the family again, I need your power. Or should I say, Callum needs your power.'

'I don't want anything to do with you, you fuck,' Callum spits out at his great-uncle.

Western stalks across the room and slaps Callum hard across the face. Callum tumbles sideways, his head smacking into the ground.

'Stop it!' I yell.

'The boy needs to learn some manners if he's going to be one of us,' Western says coolly. 'The fact is, Ms Daniels, your gift won't work on me, because I'm human, for the most part. So, this is how it's going to go. You will voluntarily offer your powers to me, which I will then transfer to Callum, and your death will be painless. One dead witch, one immortal Western. If you choose to fight me, I will slit your boyfriend's throat in front of you and let you live just long enough to watch him bleed out.'

'You won't,' I say. 'You want Callum.'

'He is no good to me like he is, and you both know all my secrets now. I can't let the two of you walk out of here happily-ever-after.' A cold smile splits his face, and I shudder. 'Of course, I would prefer for Callum to survive. I have so little family left, and he's my great-nephew, after all. It would be such a shame to waste what could be a promising future. My guess is you'd rather he survives too. I mean, Holly – may I call you Holly? What do you have to live for? No one cares about you. Why would they? You're an abomination. A freak.'

'Don't listen to him, Holly,' Callum calls out. 'You have your family. You have me.'

'So very touching,' Western jeers.

'Why don't you just *take* my power?' I say. 'Isn't that what your family does, steal power from others?'

'We don't steal, we procure, and I've already tried that. You would not release them to me, even when you were close to death.'

I suck back a sharp gasp.

'Yes,' he says. 'Under the oak tree. For a moment I thought I had you. I was ready to taste you, but you just would not let go. I knew then and there that there is something extraordinary inside you. I hoped Callum himself would have better luck, that maybe he could convince you to release your gift.' He grunts out an impatient sigh. 'My great-great-grandmother assured me she could make him do it. But she underestimated his feelings for you, and overestimated her own power, arrogant creature that she was. I'm pleased you sent her to hell, or wherever she ended up. She was of no further use to me. Just an ugly, narcissistic presence tarnishing my magnificent home.'

I take a furtive glance around the room. There must be a way out of this. I need time to think. He likes to talk about himself. I'll keep him talking.

'What are you, then? You said you're *mostly* human?'

'Something so old there isn't a name for it. We're worshippers of the Poculum Vitae, the transformers of life's essence into power. You could call us psychic eaters. Like soul eaters . . . but with less soul.' He chuckles at his joke. 'In better times, we were revered by religious men, who sought our help to control what they saw as evil. That would be people like you – the ones they didn't understand. We sucked those poor souls dry. Slowly, the powers we consumed changed us. They made us stronger and more beautiful, allowing us to live longer. We became better than human. Once we truly understood what we could become, we left the fools of the church behind. People like you have brought us a great deal of wealth and influence over the years.'

'You do this for money?' I roll my eyes. 'That's kind of pathetic.'

Western bristles. 'Don't forget the immortality, Holly. You'll be dead soon, and your essence will swirl through Callum's being. For centuries, the abilities we have seized have nourished us, prolonged our lives, given us power. History has been shaped by us. We came to the Americas to make this place ours, just as my ancestors had with Europe. But we underestimated this fledgling country's thirst for justice. In more recent times, the law has thwarted us. Getting away with murder has become so bothersome.' He sighs extravagantly.

'So, my family crumbled, a dying lineage from a dead world. Imagine my joy when I discovered that one of my brother's children had a son. That is how the legacy is passed, you see, through the sons. Here was a second chance to rebuild my family's birthright. My brother Cillian was a fool, weak and afraid of power. He raised his daughters to fear their own blood, poisoning their minds against their family. But in the end that worked against them, because it meant they failed to tell Callum who he really was.' He turns to Callum and smiles. 'I managed to eliminate your parents, but Aideen snatched you up before I could get my hands on you. That woman could have been such a gift to this family. But if she really wanted to protect you, she should have told you who you are.'

I feel Callum's rage burning from across the room. He tries to stand but falls back to his knees, flinching in pain.

'You killed my parents?' His voice is eerily quiet.

'Not me personally. Albert saw to that. He found just the man for the job – a man with terminal cancer and medical debts he could never hope to repay. He needed money for his family. So we took care of them, and he got in his car and took care of your parents.'

Callum howls, falling forward, his shoulders shaking with his pain-racked sobs. My heart breaks as I watch him shattering into a million pieces. I can't see how we're going to get out of this cellar alive. Even if I die and give Callum my power, he wouldn't survive – not really – because he would no longer be Callum. The goodness in him would be replaced by the evil at the heart of the Western family. But there's no way I can watch him die.

There's only one thing left for me to try.

I unfurl my senses, reaching out to Elizabeth. But there's nothing. Just the same strange silence that envelops this cursed house.

'Fine,' I say, 'take my powers.'

Callum groans. 'No, Holly. Don't do it. I don't want to be like him!'

'And I don't want you dead,' I say.

'It's not your choice. *I* decide if I live or die. *I* decide who I am, and I'm not like him.'

'Exactly,' I say. 'You decide who you are, with or without my powers, and you don't have to become what this maniac wants you to be. I'm a goner either way, but at least you'll get to live.'

I wish I could crawl across the room and hold him one last time. Look into his beautiful eyes and see the spark that dances there. Gently touch my lips to his and say goodbye.

'What do I need to do?' I ask, turning away from Callum's anguished face. Edward Western looks at me, unbearably smug.

'I knew you'd make the sensible choice,' he says.

He draws a weapon from his jacket, and I gasp. I know that weapon, I've seen it before. I can just make out the engraving on the blade. It's the symbol of the Cup of Power, the Poculum Vitae, with Latin words surrounding it, etched into the silver metal. It's the same dagger that pierced Elizabeth Howell's breast in this very cellar.

He moves towards Callum, unties his great-nephew's hands and lifts one of his arms in the air.

'Get away from me, you son of a bitch.' Callum struggles, trying to yank his arm back.

Rosing puts a small bronze chalice on the floor. I've seen that before, too.

'I'm going to kill you,' Callum seethes at Rosing, hissing the words through clenched teeth. The man gives him an obsequious bow.

'I look forward to serving you, sir.'

Western drags the knife across Callum's arm, leaving a long, deep gash. Blood oozes from his wrist, dripping into the vessel below. But Callum doesn't flinch; his jaw is clamped tight, his face stony.

Edward Western gathers up the bowl and whispers some words over it. I finally get to hear the mysterious chant, and it's definitely no prayer. It's a language that I don't know, but I recognise it as something old. A thick, guttural growl rolls over his tongue with throaty clicks.

He puts his lips to the edge of the bowl and drinks, dabs his mouth with a handkerchief, then turns the knife on himself, drawing blood from his own arm.

'Hold him, Albert,' he says.

Rosing pulls Callum's head back and wrenches his mouth open as Western pours the blood down his great-nephew's throat.

I gag as Callum coughs and splutters, spitting frothy blood across the floor.

Western tosses a piece of cloth towards Callum, who holds it to his arm, his face dark with fury, blood dripping from his chin.

'Now it's your turn,' Western says, as he moves towards me. 'Untie her please, Albert, and help her stand.'

My heart thunders. I'm in real trouble. I reach out for Elizabeth again with a desperate plea. *Elizabeth. Cousin. I'm here but I don't know what I'm supposed to do. If you want this to stop, you have to help me. NOW. We can do this together. Cousin, talk to me. Come to me.*

Rosing hauls me up, and Western presses his nose to my throat and breathes deeply. I recoil, my stomach roiling.

'I smell the power on you,' he says. 'You are strong. I don't think you even know how strong you are.' He glances over at Callum with a self-satisfied smile. 'It was worth the years of waiting to find this one for you, boy. You are incredibly lucky. You will have power like you can't imagine. You will finally have a family again.'

'I had family. You killed them.'

'I am your true family.'

Callum sneers. 'You really need to let that go, old man. You're obsolete.'

'You are wrong. This has been the role of every man in my family and those who have devoted themselves to us, like Rosing here. It's time to restore the Westerns to what we should always have been – policymakers, presidents, kings. I will be the one to do it, and you will carry our name forward through history.'

'My name is Jefferies.'

'That's your father's name. It is not yours.'

Callum's gaze flicks to me and I see exactly what he's doing. Needling Western. Distracting him, to give me time to do whatever I'm going to do. As the men joust, I call out to Elizabeth one last time.

Elizabeth, I'm ready to let you in. I'm ready to let in the spirit of every woman this family has murdered.

I stand perfectly still, frozen in hope, my shoulders slowly slumping with each passing second as nothing happens. Then, just as I'm about to give up, something crashes into me.

The air explodes from my lungs as I hurtle backwards. I plant my feet firmly in the dirt, clench my teeth and ball my fists. Wind rushes around the room, my hair lifting and swirling as the spirits slam against me, one by one entering my body. I shake uncontrollably as faces flash through my mind, their hearts thumping as one with mine, their voices wailing in my ears. Then an inky haze descends over my eyes.

I hear Callum calling my name over and over, but I can't answer him because I can't speak. There's so much power coursing through me, I feel like I could burst from it. I didn't think this through. But it's too late, the spirits are a part of me now, roaring and screaming and thrumming inside me. I press my hands to my ears, trying to block out their howls, the pounding in my brain almost unbearable.

I plead for them to stop, for everything to stop. *Please, I can't take this. Please, please stop.*

The voices fall silent, then I hear Elizabeth's voice in my head, *Cousin, he is ours.*

Edward Western charges towards me. Then he stops, freezing to the spot, as horror and fury fight each other, contorting the beauty of his face.

'Grab her, Albert!' he yells.

Rosing whimpers as he edges towards me, then he squeals as my arms slowly begin to rise. He's lifted into the air, suspended above me, his neck bent as his body presses against the wooden beams that run the length of the ceiling.

He lets out a strangled cry.

Don't make me kill him. Please don't make me, I beg the spirits.

Another squeal, and he falls to the floor, landing with a nasty crunch. He screams in pain.

'I will not show you that kind of mercy,' Western rails. 'Whatever you are doing, woman, stop it. Now.' He has the silver blade to Callum's throat.

'Do whatever you have to, Holly!' Callum calls. 'Stop him—' He sucks in a shocked breath as Western presses the knife edge into his pale skin, and a bead of blood collects on the blade. He is prepared to kill his own family to save himself. No surprises there.

Help him!

The knife begins to vibrate, then it's ripped from Western's grasp and shoots across the room, embedding itself in the wall.

Western throws his head back and roars. He rushes at me with his hands outstretched.

'You will not leave this house alive!' he screeches. But as the words leave his proud lips, he crumples to his knees with a wretched cry.

He tries to stand, his body quaking, but his legs buckle below him again as an invisible force pushes him to the ground.

A stomach-churning snap rings out, and he howls in agony as his leg breaks.

A chorus pours from my mouth, forming one voice: '*We will make you suffer for the sins of your family. For all of us, trapped for centuries.*'

The broken man drags himself towards the stairs. But as his fingers touch the first step, my arms lift again, and Western's body rises. With fear now taking the place of pride in his eyes, he hovers in the air, his torso twisting unnaturally back and forth, strangled cries falling from his lips, until he suddenly drops, landing heavily on the wooden steps, his mouth wide open in shock.

'You can't s-s-stop us,' he groans. 'We are power. We are eternal. We will—' But before he can finish what will be his final words, his golden eyes glaze over, and he slumps forward, silent at last.

CHAPTER TWENTY-EIGHT

I'm drowning in my own body, fighting for every breath, choking as I struggle to see through the blackness that floats in front of my eyes. I'm sure I'm dying, or already dead, or worse. Entombed in my own body, forever the vessel for the spirits that writhe with fury inside me.

But it doesn't matter. Because nothing matters except that Edward Western has been stopped and Callum will live. He will live because I saved him. I finally saved someone I love. If I die now, it will all be worth it.

As my consciousness slowly fades and darkness surrounds me, a gentle voice inside my mind whispers, *We are free*.

My eyes flicker open, and I roll onto my back and hungrily fill my lungs with air, sucking in deep breaths while blinking clear my vision. Rosing lies directly in front of me, broken but alive. Edward Western is a heap at the foot of the stairs, his once intense eyes now blank and unseeing, while Callum sags against the wall, his arm stained with streaks of red.

I crawl across the floor towards him, touch his chin and lift his face.

He looks up. 'You're back. Holly . . . I thought you were dead.'

I kiss him. First on his lips, then on his forehead, then on his lips again. 'I'm not that easy to get rid of.'

I gently pull his hand away from his throat. There's a small slice where Western's knife was pressed against it.

'I hear guys with scars are considered sexy,' he says.

'Always with the jokes, Jefferies. Let me look at your arm.'

'Your eyes went black, Holly. They were black.'

'Okay,' I say, wrapping the cloth back around his wound. 'You'll live. You've had worse.' I untie his bound ankles.

'Did you hear me? They went black. Your eyes.'

I nod. 'I heard you.'

He puts a hand on either side of my face, his eyes darting between mine. 'Is it just you in there?'

'Just me. Everyone else is gone. Passed on, finally. Free. Come on, we need to go.'

I help him stand. He stumbles towards a table and picks up his gun.

'I have to do one thing first,' he says, and points the gun at Rosing's head.

Mr Rosing raises his hands in defence, whimpering, 'No! Please!'

I rush forward and grab Callum's arm. 'Callum, you can't.'

'He killed my parents.'

Rosing moans on the ground. 'I didn't. It was the driver.'

'Who you paid.'

'Mr Western—'

'*You* organised it. You die. Let go, Holly.' Callum tugs his arm free.

'Please don't do this,' I say. 'You'll never forgive yourself.'

'Oh, I think I will.'

'No, you won't. I know you. This isn't you.'

'This is me. Didn't you hear anything Western said? I come from a long line of murderers.' His voice shakes, the gun trembling as he aims it at the man cowering on the floor. 'My parents died because of me, and now he dies because of that. You don't know who I am. Even I don't know who I am.'

I touch his chin and turn his face towards me. 'You can't blame yourself for what Western did, and I do know who you are. You're Callum Jefferies, son of Lyle and Niamh, nephew of Aideen, friend of Jason, and someone . . .' I swallow. 'Someone I love. You're not a murderer. I couldn't love anyone who would kill like this.'

He blinks, then blinks again and shakes his head, as if clearing his mind.

'You love me? After what I did? Knowing what I am? You love me?'

'Yeah, I know. Amazing. But your fucked-up family is not your fault.' I cup his cheek. 'I know how scary everything is right now, but this,' I touch the gun, pushing the barrel down, 'is not you.'

'You love me?' he says again, this time with a small smile.

I laugh. 'I'm going to stop loving you in about thirty seconds if you keep asking me that.' I gently unwrap Callum's fingers from the gun and take it from him. Squatting beside Rosing, I ask, 'Do you have a phone?'

He nods, wincing as he indicates his jacket pocket.

I reach in and pull it out. 'Mr Rosing, I'm going to dial 911, and you're going to tell them there's been a terrible accident. Mr Western took a tumble down the stairs into the cellar and grabbed you as he fell, taking you with him. Got it?'

He nods again.

'Good. You're a bit beaten up, but you'll survive. But if I hear anything from you ever again, I won't stop Callum from putting a bullet in your brain.' I dial 911 then hand the phone to him, watching as Mr Rosing relays my story.

'What about Western?' Callum asks.

'He's still breathing. But whatever the spirits did to him, I don't think he's coming back from it. I think he's trapped, like they once were. It would be sweet irony if he ended up in Lakeview Hospital.'

'We should keep tabs on him,' Callum says, tapping his great-uncle with his foot. 'I don't trust this fucker.'

'We will. But we need to go now, before the paramedics get here.' As I step over Edward Western's motionless body, his pale skin now grey, his unnatural glow dimmed, I bend down and whisper in his ear, 'You underestimated the women you murdered, and you underestimated me, and together we beat you.'

I'm almost certain hatred flickers across the surface of his glazed golden eyes.

*

As we jog up the path away from the old house, there's energy all around me. The buzz of old life, whispers of voices once lived, the kind of vibrations I'd expect from a place that has been a home for nearly four hundred years. The veil that had been suppressing the sounds of the dead has been lifted, and now they babble in my ear. For once, I'm happy to hear them.

'Can I . . . get a ride home?' Callum asks with a sheepish smile.

'First I have to save you from demonic immortality and now I have to *drive you home?*' I grin, then press a soft kiss to his lips. 'You're going to be okay.'

'I've got a lot to digest, you know?'

I do know. I know all too well, I think as sirens ring out through the night.

We don't talk much on the way back to the city. Callum mostly sleeps and I wonder how long it's been since he was able to do that.

I drop him at his apartment. 'You sure you don't want company?' I ask.

He looks down at the gash on his arm. 'I think I should get this stitched up first. That's right, I'm going to a hospital voluntarily.'

'I could come with you.'

'I'd rather do it on my own, if that's okay? Just need a minute to decompress.'

'Of course it's okay. It's good you're going somewhere in the city. If you went back to the doctor at that local hospital he'd probably report you for gang violence . . . or having a knife kink.' That makes him laugh, and his laugh makes me smile. 'Callum, you're going to need some time to understand what's happened to you. But just know that I'll be here when you're ready to talk.'

'I know. Get some sleep, hero, I'll see you tomorrow.' He smiles then kisses me and climbs out of the car. 'Oh wait,' he says turning back around. He leans in the door again. 'I love you too.'

When I finally close my apartment door I lean back against it and sigh, never so glad to be home. I toss my backpack to the floor, fish out my phone, and send a quick text to Jason to let him know we're safe, though I suspect Callum has already done the same. As I stumble up the hall, I unbutton my jeans and shrug off my jacket, letting it fall to the floor. I'm more tired than I've been in my entire life, but I'm happy. *Happy? What the hell is that?* I laugh. My hands have yet to completely steady, and I'm still trembling a little from a force I don't fully understand, but I feel pretty good, all things considered. In fact, I feel kind of great.

'Maybe I really am the Ghost Whisperer?' I say to myself in the mirror. Then I scrunch up my face and laugh. 'Nah.'

I flop onto my bed, wishing I'd gone to the hospital with Callum. I don't like the thought of him being on his own with all that must be churning through his mind. It's hard enough slowly discovering your supernatural self. I can't imagine what it would be like to have it come crashing down, obliterating the life you thought you knew. I send him a text to let him know I'm thinking of him. He answers with two heart emojis, and I hug my phone to my chest.

Gathering my laptop from the floor beside me, I prop myself up on a pile of pillows. There's something I have to do. I start an email.

> Hi Dad and Maggie.
> I know I've been distant and useless at staying in touch, but I'm going to do better, I promise. Can I come for a visit? Or dinner? I don't care whose house. I could even do something here if you don't want the bother, though I might need some help with the cooking part. Or we could get takeout. Anyway, let me know. I love you guys so much. Miss you.
> Holly xx

I wipe away the tears that have caught me off guard and press send with a trembling hand, then grab a tissue and blow my nose so loudly I make myself laugh. To my surprise, it only takes a minute for a reply to come back. It's from Maggie.

> Hey Hol!
> You're always welcome here. Call me. I promise to be nicer than my last text.
> Maggie xxx

I'm drifting off to sleep, my laptop still open on my chest, when Dad replies.

> Honey, this is your home. You never have to ask. I'm thinking of firing up the grill on the weekend if you're hungry for some spicy ribs?
> Love, Dad.

Fat tears splash onto my keyboard. I slide down my mattress, clutching my covers tight around me as my body shakes. It's as if everything I've hung on to for years, everything I buried inside me releases all at once, freeing me, just like the spirits I helped to free. Anger and hurt, fear and self-loathing pours out in huge, snotty sobs, gulps of breath and hiccups of laughter. It feels so good to let it all go.

I run my palm down my wet face, sniffling as I shake my head. *If this is your doing, Elizabeth, thank you. I hope you've found your peace too.* Because that's how it feels – peaceful. My usually churned-up insides are at peace. At least for now.

I close my laptop and gently place it on the floor, pull the covers back up and smile. It's starting to look like I won't be found alone eaten by rats after all.

I wake up feeling wonderfully light. Is this what happy is? I check my phone and see that I have two messages from Callum. I quickly let him know I'm awake and okay, then climb out of bed and pull back the drapes. The sun streams in, and I bathe in its light, enjoying the warmth of a brand-new day. I've been imbued with new knowledge that Elizabeth and the spirits left behind, whispered words that float back to me as if I'm living someone else's memories. They drew me to East Mill. They fed me clues, trying to keep me safe until they knew I was strong enough to break the bond that had trapped them there. Strong enough to contain the fury of the murdered. I hate the thought of how long they had to wait. How long Elizabeth had to wait for her family to show up for her.

I make coffee and toast, drop onto the couch with a satisfied sigh, grab the TV remote and flick on the local news. Immediately, my jaw drops. There's been a fire in East Mill; a historic home has been razed to the ground. The owner is in an unresponsive condition in the hospital, and another man has been seriously injured. Local fire personnel fought hard to save the house, but tragically, the building was lost. I stare at the images of the smouldering ruins.

My phone rings, and I know who it is without even looking.

'Put on the news,' Callum says.

'I'm watching it now. You didn't go back and burn it down, did you?'

'I was about to ask you the same thing.'

'Not me,' I say, thinking, *Elizabeth?* We watch in silence until the end of the report.

'So,' he says, as the news moves on to the latest in sports. 'How'd you sleep?'

'Like a log.' I'm not exaggerating. I woke up in almost exactly the same position I was in when I shut my eyes. 'How did you go with the doctor?'

'Just a couple of stitches in my arm.'

'Good . . . and . . . how are you feeling today about . . . things?'

He's silent for a few seconds, then says, 'Angry, tired, and a whole lot of other stuff. But I don't want to talk about it right now, if that's okay?'

'Of course it's okay.'

'So,' he starts, his tone brighter, 'are you busy tonight?'

'No. I mean, I assumed I'd be seeing you . . .'

'I'll pick you up at seven.'

'You'll pick me up? Like a date?'

'Exactly like a date. I told you; you and me, Holly, we're going to start this thing off right.'

CHAPTER TWENTY-NINE

At two minutes past seven, my intercom crackles to life. I press the button. 'You're late,' I say, laughing.

'C'mon,' Callum says. 'It's like two minutes.'

'I'm coming down.'

'No. Buzz me in, I wanna come upstairs and get you.'

'Callum.'

'Buzz me in, Holly.'

I buzz him in.

'Who is it?' I tease, when he knocks on the door.

'Are you always going to be this much work, Daniels?' he calls to me.

I laugh again as I turn the lock. 'You know I'm hard work.'

He pushes the door open, swoops in, gathers me in his arms and says, 'Lucky I like to work.' He presses his mouth to mine.

When we finally part, he smiles down at me, positively radiant.

'I think you just ruined my lip gloss,' I say, patting my lips.

'It was delicious. Strawberry?'

I roll my eyes and point at the flowers in his hand. 'Are those for me?'

'Beautiful flowers for a beautiful woman.'

'Oh, shut up and give them here.' I take them to the kitchen, grab a glass from the cupboard, fill it with water and jam them in.

Callum frowns. 'Remind me to bring you a vase next time.'

'Don't judge me, I've never needed one. I can't think of the last time someone bought me flowers.'

'I'm going to have to change that,' he says as he looks around.

'My apartment isn't as big as yours,' I quickly say, 'or as nice. And it's messy, sorry, and I don't have lots of degrees on my walls, or art.'

I watch him take it all in. The brown leather couch that fills up most of my living room and the cute retro kitchen table with the pale blue chairs. He admires the photos of New York that stretch down one wall, then points at a tiny green shrub in a pot on the kitchen counter.

'Is that a plant I see? I thought you said you weren't good with the living?' His lips twitch at the corners.

'Shut up. Maggie gave it to me for Christmas. The card said she thought I needed something to take care of other than myself. I'm not sure, but I think it might have been her not-so-subtle way of saying I'm a loner.'

Callum laughs. 'Ouch. I always thought it would be fun to have a sibling, but now I'm not so sure.'

'It's been hard at times. But I'm still glad I have her. We're going to catch up for dinner soon with Dad. It's a new development. And you've got Jason,' I add, 'he's like your brother.'

'True. He came over last night. Crashed at my place, listened to my tragic story. Gave me some perspective. He's always been good like that.'

'Are you okay?'

'Honestly, no. But right now, I've got far more important things on my mind.' His eyes lock to mine. 'Holly, I'm so sorry about everything.'

'Callum, you already—'

'Please let me get through this.' He blows out a soft breath. 'I know that after all that's happened, I've got a lot of work to do to earn your trust back, but please know the only thing that I've ever thought you are is amazing. I've *never* lied to you about that. Ever. I swear it. I know I've failed you twice now, but I will not do it again. You make me feel like I belong somewhere, and I intend to cherish that, and cherish you. I'm so sorry that we lost two years.'

He stops and takes another shaky breath.

'Callum, we don't—'

'Just one more thing, please, I need to clear up one more thing. I don't want to be like the Westerns, I don't, but I'd be happy to be like you. I'd consider myself lucky if I was even half the person you are. Kind, patient, strong and determined. I will never put you in danger like that again. If you let me, I will keep you safe forever. I promise.'

He looks at me with fear and hope and love, so open I see it shining clearly in his eyes. I see the whole world in his eyes.

I'm so tired of hiding and always expecting the worst. I don't want to do that anymore. I want to be the person he thinks I am. I want to be the hope in his eyes. Feelings are messy, but I'm not going to shy away from that any longer.

I rest my hand on his cheek. 'How about we keep each other safe, and move forward from all our stuff? No more hanging onto the past.'

He kisses into my palm and whispers, 'Thank you.' And as I look up at him, the warmth in his smile tells me this is right.

'So, forward,' he says. 'I like forward, it happens to be my favourite direction. Shall we start by moving forward to dinner?'

I bite my lip. It's time to get messy.

'Or . . .' I say.

'Or?' He tilts his head.

I grab the waistband of his jeans and tug him closer. 'Or we could move forward up the hall to my . . . bedroom.' My knuckle grazes the warm skin of his belly and his breath hitches in surprise.

'I'd need . . . to cancel . . . our reservation,' he says, in a halting voice.

I shove my hand deep into his front pocket and fumble for his phone. He gasps.

'Jesus,' he mutters as he takes the phone from me, his eyes locked to mine as he dials. 'Mrs Chen? There's been a change of plans. I'll bring Holly by another night. Sorry for the late notice.' He stifles a laugh. 'Oh yeah, I'll make sure I eat something.' He hangs up and tosses his phone to the couch. 'You are a bad influence,' he says with a devilish grin. 'That woman is like family, and now she's worried I'm going to starve.'

I squeak as he lifts me into the air, my legs instinctively hooking around him.

He nuzzles the crook of my neck. 'Is this more what you had in mind, Daniels?' he murmurs against my skin.

I shiver. 'It's a start, Jefferies.'

We giggle like teens as we stumble up the hall, bumping into the walls, my legs still wrapped low on his hips. He gently lowers me to the bed, and I watch him strip his T-shirt over his head, a cheeky smile across his preposterously handsome face. My gaze drifts over him, taking in his smooth pale skin and tight stomach, his broad chest, that tantalising strip of hair disappearing into his jeans, and his smile. That smile that makes my heart leap from my chest like something from a cartoon.

'So, we're doing this?' he says, with one perfectly arched eyebrow.

I pull him onto the bed beside me. 'You promised me when we got back to the city . . .'

He laughs. 'And I don't want to break any more promises to you ever.'

I nip a tiny kiss on his throat just below where Edward Western's silver dagger nicked him, then trace a finger along the edge of the bandage on his arm. My touch drifts down to the wound dressing beneath his ribs.

'Are you sure you're up to this?' I ask.

'Oh, Holly, I'm up . . . to it.' His grin is the widest I've ever seen, and I laugh. 'Just be gentle with me,' he adds, laughing too.

I pop the button on his jeans. 'I'll do my best.'

I pull his zip down nice and slow.

He watches me, his lips pressed tight together, his chest shaking with each trembling breath.

'You're not going to help at all?' I ask. My heart is thumping against my ribs.

'I was waiting to see where this was going.' He gently tugs at the bottom of my sweater. 'May I?' I enthusiastically fling my arms into the air and he laughs, saying, 'I'll take that as a yes.' He swiftly slips my sweater over my head, then lets his gaze linger on my body. 'Goddamn, Holly. You're gorgeous.'

He leans in and I close my eyes, enjoying the sensation of his soft lips tickling my skin as he kisses along the edge of my bra. Then he slips a hand behind me and unhooks the clasp in one smooth movement.

I hold my breath as my bra falls away. He moans loudly, his eyes alight with desire.

He tugs me towards him and I fall against his chest, skin on skin, so much heat. Then, holding me tight, he rolls me slowly onto the mattress. Dipping his head, he places a quick, tender kiss on my lips, before his mouth finds my neck, then my shoulder, then the delicate skin of my breast. He lingers there, the heat of his mouth making me quiver, until, ever so slowly, he sucks me in. My gasp turns into a soft moan as his tongue swirls and teases one nipple, while his thumb rubs back and forth over the other.

Then his kisses move down to my stomach.

'I love a plaid skirt,' he says. 'This one's super cute.' He pulls the side zip down, and I lift my hips. 'Looks even cuter when it's sliding off.' His voice is already pure gravel.

I squirm; his hands soft on my skin as he very slowly wiggles the material down. Then he does the same with my underwear, until I lay naked in front of him.

He sucks in a breath and whispers in what sounds like wonder, 'Wow.'

I push up on my elbows and ask, 'How come I'm naked, and you're not?'

He grins, sliding backwards off the bed, kissing my thighs, my knees, my ankles along the way. Then he stands and with one quick movement, he shoves down his jeans, steps out of them and stands in front of me in his boxer briefs.

'Oh. Hi there,' I say, as I stare at the thick, rigid outline in the soft black material. His already wide grin spreads ear-to-ear.

I wriggle to the end of the mattress, hook my fingers into his waistband and drag his briefs down over his thighs, my eyes on his.

Then, as his last piece of clothing falls to the floor, I dare to look down.

It's been a while since I've seen a man naked. Callum is magnificent. Thick and long and . . . I touch his length, and his stomach tightens. I run a finger along a vein and he lets out a ragged breath.

'Wait a sec,' he says.

'What?' I say, looking up.

'Hang on.' He digs out a small, slightly crushed box from the pocket of his puddled jeans and with trembling hands, pulls free a strip of condoms. 'Okay, I know this looks bad,' he says with six condoms hanging from his fingers, 'but I stopped on the way here. I was being responsible. We don't have to use them all.'

I snatch them from him. 'I think we should try.'

I inch back on the mattress, and he whispers 'fuck' as he crawls towards me.

His eyes are all pupils again, just how I like them, and he smoulders down at me, his hand gliding over my stomach until it's between my legs, finally. He cups my heat, crushes his lips to mine and slips his fingers inside me. I arch up, moaning against his mouth, lifting my hips to meet his hand as he gently moves in and out. I gasp when his thumb finds just the right spot, pressing down in circles, coordinated in expert precision with his fingers curved within me, until I'm making noises I never knew I could. My eyes squeeze shut as the pleasure builds and builds, every muscle tensing, every breath now a gasp, every bit of me on fire, until I let go with a cry, grabbing at his back while my toes stretch out. My body goes limp, my hands shaking as they fall to my sides. I blink open and I see his eyes, his beautiful eyes. I still have the strip of condoms clutched in one fist.

I lick my parched lips. 'Let's get one of these on you.'

He sits back on his heels looking slightly stunned, and I tear open one of the small packages. I pull the condom out and hold it in my still shaking hands.

'Do you want me to do it?' he says.

'Maybe. I'm feeling a little weak right now.'

He chuckles as he takes it from me, and I watch as he slowly rolls it down his length.

We stare at each other for a long moment, at least fifty beats of my racing heart, then I put my hands to his chest and press him back onto the mattress. His eyes widen, blinking over and over as I straddle his hips, take him in my hand and lower myself onto him. A groan rumbles from his throat, my name on his breath, his grip tight on my waist as he sinks deeper into me and we start to slowly move.

I like him like this, because I can see him. His eyes, his lips, his whole face, neck and chest. I can look down and watch him moving in and out of me, and I can watch him watching that too, his eyes flicking from my face to the spot where our bodies meet.

We're gentle at first, a slow roll, languid and smooth. But I need more, so I pick up the pace raising and falling faster and faster. I watch him watching me, his tongue flicking over his lips until I can't keep my eyes open anymore, because a shimmering heat is building inside me. My stomach tightens, my thighs tremble, all my already tender parts are filling back up with pleasure. Then I'm coming again and I'm gripping his arms, my body stretched around him as needy sounds pour from my open lips.

I don't have time to refocus before he's growling out, 'Oh fuck, Holly,' his hands sliding up my back as he flips me carefully to the mattress.

'Is this okay?' he asks.

I just nod, no words forming, barely any breath left.

Maybe *this* is how I like him, because I like his weight on me, heavy, solid, real, here, and I like him looking down at me with fierce eyes, and I like his thrusts. I like them a lot.

He gently pulls my knees up beside his waist, one at a time, sinking so deep, I cry out. Lights pop behind my eyes and I'm not sure if this is something new or if I'm still reeling from the time before, because it can't be happening again, but it is, and it thunders over me, so intense that I have to clench my jaw to stop from screaming out thanks to the universe. I grab at the sheets, bunching the soft material into tight fists.

He groans again, slamming his mouth to mine, and I kiss him as if I can't get enough – because I can't.

He breaks our kiss with a sharp hiss and presses his face into the crook of my neck, breathing out tiny grunts. I squeeze him tight to me, not wanting this to stop, not wanting it to ever stop. His idea about us disappearing into a bedroom for months suddenly seems like the perfect plan. I'm sore and I'm sweaty, and it feels so good, the best I've ever felt in my entire life. He lifts his head and looks at me, smiles and touches his lips softly to mine. Then his hips stutter, and the sound that he makes is the most beautiful thing I have ever heard.

Callum opens his eyes with a series of blinks as if he's trying to focus.

'Wow,' he breathes out all ragged. 'We're really good at this.' He has a giant smile and his voice is deliciously rough.

'I bet we're even better the second time,' I say, my own ragged breaths matching his.

'Imagine the third.'

'The fiftieth.'

He laughs, and it's all husky and sex-soaked. 'I can't wait to find out.'

If I had enough energy left, I'd swoon.

CHAPTER THIRTY

I wake to gentle kisses and strong arms. I fold into them, the grogginess of sleep giving everything a warm glow. Callum's skin is hot and smooth against my hands, his body firm and his touch soft. He rolls himself on top of me, then leans down and kisses me, deep and wet and messy. I pull him closer, arching my hips into him. The weight of him is a comfort, hard in all the right places.

Our hands are everywhere, our bruised lips crushed together again. Legs tangled, feet rubbing against feet. Nothing has ever felt so perfect. He slides down my body, kissing along my rib cage and across my belly until his mouth finds its way between my legs. I sigh softly as his tongue teases and swirls, back and forth, over and over while I wriggle and gasp. Then I'm bursting to life, bliss reaching every part of my body as I pulse against his mouth. He gazes up at me with mussed-up sexy hair, sparkling eyes and a smile so proud and pretty I almost forget how to breathe.

'Morning, Sunshine,' he says, his voice croaky with sleep.
'Hi,' I barely squeak back.

'I hope I can give you many more mornings like this,' he murmurs into my skin, then softly kisses my belly. 'Every morning. All the mornings.'

'Do we call this morning?' I say, with a laugh. It's still dark out.

'Oh, I woke you.'

'I'm not complaining.'

He checks his phone by my bed. 'Shit. It's not even five. Guess I couldn't wait.'

'Again, not complaining.'

'Go back to sleep,' he says.

'Only if you promise to wake me the same way?'

'You got it, Sunshine.'

I curl into his chest as his arms encircle me, and I feel him kiss the top of my head as I drift back to sleep.

When I finally open my eyes again, the sun is creeping into my room. I stretch, sleepy and happy and kind of sore, in the best possible way. My legs reach for Callum, but all they find is empty sheets.

I sit up. 'Callum?'

Sliding out of bed, I push open the bathroom door, finding it empty. I stand still and listen. The apartment is silent. My heart begins to thud.

I pull on clean underwear and grab a T-shirt from the floor, dragging it over my head as I move down the hall.

'Callum?' I call again.

By the time I get to the kitchen, I'm in full panic mode and it only took me about thirty seconds to get there. That's when I spot a note on the kitchen table. I snatch it up, then smile at the blocky black writing surrounded by tiny, scribbled hearts.

Morning, Sleeping Beauty. If you wake before I get back, DON'T PANIC! I've gone to grab us coffee and food (you need to go to the store and get something other than frozen pizza!). I should be back by 9.30. If I'm not, PANIC. Kidding. See you in a bit xox

I let my head flop back and breathe out a relieved sigh that quickly becomes a pitiful groan. I hope I'm not going to be like this every time he leaves the room. *He's not going anywhere and you're not going anywhere.*

I pour myself a glass of water and gulp it down as a rush of hunger hits my stomach. No dinner and a whole lot of sex has left me starving. I check the clock on the stove. It's just before nine. I don't think I can wait for Callum, so I make a slice of toast and crunch into it as I flop onto the couch. I grab my laptop and flip it open, heading straight for my emails. There are two that make me sit up straight. One is from Ola Hutchings. The other is from someone I've never met: Katherine Browling. I put my toast on the table, steel myself and open Katherine's first.

Holly,
I found your card in Richard's office. I thought you might like to know that Richard has started talking. Not just a word or two, really talking. It feels like a miracle. I wanted to tell you because I understand you visited him, and he seems to think his recovery has something to do with you. He asked me to let you know that he's okay. I don't know what

> will happen next, but if this is because of something you did, thank you. You've given me my husband back, and my children their father.
>
> Katherine Browling

I smile so wide my cheeks ache. Whatever I did in that cellar with Elizabeth and the other spirits, it released Richard too. I know it's not over for that family, but at least Richard is speaking again. I close the email, making a mental note to reply later, then with a steadying breath, I open Ola's. It's addressed to both me and Callum.

> I'm assuming you heard about the Western house being destroyed by a fire. Sadly, there was nothing to be saved. A tragic loss. But somehow a relief. We just have to hope no more Westerns come out of the woodwork to rebuild! Not sure if you need these now, given the circumstances, but my colleague found them at the bottom of a box when logging documents for our new website. They were with some information from the local paper, wrongly filed.
>
> Hope to see you out here again one day,
>
> Ola.

There are three photos attached.

The first image is labelled 'Young Edward'. A shiver rolls through me. The photo looks as if it was taken around the same time as the black and white one I found at Callum's apartment, but this one is in colour. His golden eyes pin me back against the couch with a chilling intensity, and I have to remind myself that he can't hurt me or Callum anymore. I quickly close it and move on.

The second photo is labelled 'Brendin Western 1959'. He's standing in the garden, flower beds in bloom around him, with a man who can only be Albert Rosing's father. Equally bland, equally beige looking and equally creepy.

The third attachment is labelled 'Cillian Western/Iarthar'. Edward's brother. Callum's grandfather. The photo is dated to the '70s, which would put him somewhere in his thirties in this photo; around the same age Callum is now. I click on it, curiosity buzzing inside me. My hand slaps over my mouth in horror. If there was ever any doubt Edward Western was telling the truth about Callum's heritage, this photo completely blows it away. Callum's grandfather was almost a double of his grandson. The same sparkling eyes, the same smile, the same soft face.

I close Ola's email and slam my laptop shut. I really don't like the fear that just surged through me. Rubbing my eyes as if I can rub it all away, I take the last bite of my now-cold toast and head for the shower. Of course, the moment I squirt shampoo in my hair, Callum calls me.

I drip across the bathroom floor to the basin, where I left my phone, wincing from the suds stinging my eyes.

'What are you wearing?' Callum asks.

'Shampoo.' I think I hear him splutter. I pull a towel off the rack and wrap myself in it.

'Send me a photo.'

'No!'

He laughs. 'Did you check your emails?'

'Ola's message? Information we could have done with sooner, right? I mean, the photo of your grandfather.'

'Yeah, quite the looker, huh?' He laughs again, but this time there's no humour there. In fact, his voice has a quiver. 'Why wouldn't Aideen tell me? I'm trying really hard not to be mad at her right now.'

'Callum, no. She loved you and she wanted to protect you.'

'I know. I do. But Holly, it's not just the photos. I got another email, this one from a lawyer in London, about Western's estate. I've already spoken to him briefly. He's calling me back in a couple of hours.'

'But how does he even know about you?'

'That's the thing. Edward left instructions that in the event of his death or if he was deemed no longer capable of making decisions for his estate, the lawyer should get in touch with me. And no, my great-uncle isn't dead. Yet. I checked. But there's been no improvement, and the doctors aren't expecting one. He's locked in his body. Sweet justice.' Callum sighs heavily. 'Anyway, I'll know more when the guy rings back.'

'That's . . .'

'Yep.'

'I don't think I like it.'

'Me neither. I've also got to figure out what I'm going to do about my show. I promoted the crap out of a special on that house. But what the hell do I even say? Yeah, it was haunted, by one of my relatives as it turns out, and the ghosts of the women my family murdered . . .' He trails off.

'Maybe you can tease out something on Maddison House instead? Tell them about George the friendly ghost. Did your cameras pick anything up that night?'

'Nah. It was probably a moth or something.'

'Well, that's annoying, considering what that moth interrupted.'

'We made up for it,' he says, all gravelly. 'Anyway,' he sighs deep, 'I need to spend a bit of time on all of that today. I have sponsors to answer to. I know I promised you coffee and food, but would you be okay if I drop it by on my way back out? I need to sort some shit. We could do takeout and watch a movie later.' There's a short silence. 'Or, you know, something . . . else.'

'We can do all those things,' I say.

I hang up and stare into space, shampoo dribbling down the side of my face and goosebumps popping coolly across my skin. A feeling I don't like is growing inside me, and if there's one thing East Mill taught me, it was not to ignore my feelings.

Callum arrives around four that afternoon, carrying a large duffle bag. 'Are you moving in?' I ask. 'That's a lot of baggage.'

'I think we both have a fair amount of baggage,' he says with a grin.

He drops his bag on the floor and gathers me into his arms. My feet lift off the ground as he pulls me to him with a grunt.

'I forgot how heavy you are,' he says, quickly putting his lips to mine before I can complain.

'Mmmpffh,' I manage to protest before the tip of his tongue touches mine and stars explode behind my eyes.

Callum waddles us across the floor and I laugh as he collides with my coffee table, sending books skidding to the rug. He gently lowers me to the couch and wiggles in beside me.

'We need to talk,' he says.

'Though first we should kiss more, don't you think?'

I trace a finger across the muscles of his forearm, along the weaving black ink of his tattoo, drifting slowly up and over his bicep. He moans, as I trail up the side of his neck, finger dusting the scruff on his jaw, before toying with the hair on his nape.

'I like your priorities,' he says after another soft moan. Then he stills my hand. 'But we *really* need to talk. I spoke to the lawyer in London. It seems Western created a living will about a year ago, and made me his sole beneficiary.'

'He'd been planning this whole thing for a year?'

'I think he'd been planning this my entire life.'

'I guess he thought his vision for you was a sure thing.' Callum drops his head to his chest and sighs, and I know he's thinking about what very nearly happened to us in that cellar. I take his hand and squeeze it tight, then press a soft kiss to his cheek.

He links his fingers through mine.

'A trust exists for any medical care Western needs,' he says. 'And when he dies I get everything. The house in East Mill – which, of course, burned down, but I get the land. His apartment in the city and some money. Quite a lot of money.'

'What will you do with it all?'

'I'll give the land to the town council. Let them turn it into a park. I thought I might donate the money to Louise Garlick and her research. I'll sell the apartment in the city. I'm going to talk to the lawyer about getting all this in place so when Western finally fucks off, it'll all just happen and my name won't be involved. There's one other thing, too . . .' He runs a hand through his hair. 'A property in Ireland.'

'In Ireland?'

'Yeah . . . and the cherry on top, there's more of them, Holly. More fucking Westerns. Spread out across England and Europe. The lawyer is currently reaching out to as many as he can – he has to, because of the will.'

'I guess it makes sense there'd be more Westerns over there,' I say. 'We know Garrett Western returned to England after Elizabeth Howell disappeared. Who was definitely related to me, by the way.'

Callum looks down at our hands, our linked fingers squeezing each other tight. 'So . . . My ancestor killed your ancestor.'

'I feel like that's something we probably shouldn't overthink.'

He nods slowly. 'Agreed. Who would have guessed checking out that old house would open this can of worms? I wish we never went.'

'If we never went, you wouldn't be here, sitting next to me.'

'Well . . . I suppose that makes it all worth it.' He gives me a teasing bump with his shoulder. I roll my eyes, but I bump him back. 'Anyway,' he says, 'the paperwork should be through to me in a few weeks, and he's going to keep in touch about everything else.'

'You're not going over there?'

'For now, I'd feel better dealing with all of this from a safe distance.'

I sigh out the enormous ball of tension that had jammed itself in my chest. I was sure he was going to tell me he was leaving.

'So, you don't want to go and kick some evil British butt?' I tease.

He laughs. 'Absolutely I do. But I think we should steer clear of my family until I know who's evil and who's not. And I think you especially should steer clear.'

'You're not going to start being all hero-guy again, are you? Let's remember who saved who.'

'Oh, I remember.' He lifts my hand to his lips with a kiss.

Though he saved me too, from myself, and from a lonely future consisting of ghosts, takeaway phở and ravenous rats. I curl into his chest.

'Listen,' he says, 'I know you didn't sign on for this, and I know that being close to me could prove dangerous to you. Pretty soon, other Westerns are going to know about me, if they don't already, and I can't be sure one of them won't come at me again. I hope you can see past my family, and I hope you won't look at me differently because of them, but I get it if you do. It's a lot. What they were. What I might become. But I'm hoping now that I know what I know, I'll be able to protect us, and I'll be ready. Knowledge is power, right?'

'Power is power too, though, and I seem to have a fair bit of that. How do you plan to find out who's who?'

'I happen to be a paranormal investigator. I knew that dubious skill would come in handy one day.' He grins, all crooked charm. 'But I want you to think about what you might be getting into. With me. Given what we now know about who I am.'

'I already know who you are. So, you're going to have to get used to me being around.'

'Holly, I'm crazy about you. I love every part of you. Even the parts that you don't think are worthy of love. In fact, I love those parts most of all.'

I press my lips to his cheek and let them linger there, then I sit back and point at his bag. 'I thought you were going somewhere. I thought you were leaving me.'

'Nope. That's my laptop and a few work things, some clothes.'

I tilt my head. 'You're not going to ask me for a drawer, are you?'

'I could probably do with some hanging space too.'

'Damn, Jefferies. You're high maintenance.' I dust a kiss across his still-smiling mouth. 'I don't care who your family is,' I whisper. 'I only care who you are.'

He smiles at me, a brilliant, beaming smile that I feel deep in my soul.

'So,' he says, 'you still want to watch that movie? I was thinking . . . *The Conjuring*.' His eyes twinkle.

'Um. No.'

'*The Exorcist*?'

'Can you just stop it?'

'Wait, I know – *Ghostbusters*!'

I grab a cushion and whack him with it. He shakes with laughter.

'To be honest,' I say, 'I'm not much in the mood for a movie.'

'Okay, what are you in the mood for?'

I glance up the hall.

'Oh,' he says. 'Ms Daniels, are you trying to seduce me?'

'Like I'd have to try.'

I stand and help to pull him off the couch. He grabs his bag and slings it over his shoulder.

'There'd better be more condoms in there,' I say.

'Why do you think it's this heavy?'

I laugh and take his hand. 'But you can't keep me up all night this time. I have a job tomorrow. I've got some *real* ghostbusting to do.'

'Wait.' He spins me around and tugs me to him. 'Do you need backup?'

I frown. 'Of course I don't need backup.' Then I look up into his eyes, vibrant green, filled with kindness, humour and mischief, a perfect reflection of who he is, and I smile. 'I don't *need* backup, but I'd like it.'

EPILOGUE

CALLUM

My tech setup illuminates the kitchen with an eerie green glow. I check that the night vision camera pointing towards the pantry is recording.

'The spirit is supposed to hang around in there,' I whisper to Holly. 'Both the current owners and the previous owners of the house have reported poltergeist activity in the pantry. Food thrown around, boxes spilled, that kind of thing.'

'I'm picturing Slimer from *Ghostbusters*,' she whispers back. 'With hotdogs hanging out of his mouth. But he's not in there now.'

I squint at my monitors. 'Yeah, I can't see anything either.' I catch her eye. 'Don't look at me like that, this gear works. You've seen it work.'

'I'm not looking at you like anything.' She rubs my back. 'Stop being so sensitive.' She bends down and plants a squeaky kiss on my cheek. 'Now, want me to flush the spirit out for you? Drive it this way so you get the money shot?'

'Sounds like a plan,' I say. 'I'll have your back.'

In the months since the events of East Mill, Holly and I have become a team. In every sense of the word. We've tried to make up for the two years we missed. We went on that hike we'd talked about and decided it probably wasn't for us. Too much nature for a couple of people who spend hours in the dark with the dead. We've done lots of talking, gone on lots of dates and of course, had lots of sex. Lots. Holly even did the math on how much sex we'd missed out on during the two years we were apart. We're trying to catch up. We're also trying to forget about my great uncle, lying in a bed in Lakeview Hospital. That part hasn't been as easy. I've visited him more than once. Compelled to see him for some reason, standing beside his bed, looking down at him, his face unsettlingly like mine. I've scoured the internet and old books trying to find anything on the Westerns, what they are and what I could have become. But I keep coming up with a big nothing, and it's killing me. All I know is I hate the man in that hospital bed, and whenever I'm near him, that hate bubbles in my blood. At least I think it's the hate. God, I hope it's the hate.

'Callum, behind you!' Holly suddenly yells.

I spin around, my eyes darting between my Structured Light Sensor camera and the darkness all around me. 'I can't see it!' I call. But then I do – a crazy, fluorescent green stick figure on my screen rushing towards me. Energy slams into my chest and I soar backwards, landing with a thud and skidding across the glossy wood floors until I slide into a wall.

'Coming through,' Holly calls as she vaults over me.

I hold my camera up, trying to catch the action, but the stick figure image of the spirit changes course and darts out of frame.

Then there's a shimmer of light, and a crackle and pop and Holly yells, 'Got it!'

She walks back towards me with her arms out and says, 'This house is clean!' Then she flicks on a hall light and we both wince. 'I tried to get it to go to the pantry, so your camera would record it. But Slimer wouldn't play. You alright down there, Jefferies?' She offers me her hand.

'More of a heads up would have been nice, Daniels.'

'Not my fault you move so slow. Did it hurt you?'

'Just my ego.' I rub my ass.

She laughs and loops her arms around my neck. 'Your place or mine, ghostbuster?'

In the small studio I've set up in my apartment, I quickly type out the notes on the spirit Holly saw. She turned out to be a senior, resplendent in '80s-style gym gear. I guess all the aerobics made her hungry, even in the afterlife. And strong enough to kick my ass. The humiliation is complete.

When my phone vibrates on the desk and the words 'Lakeview Hospital' glow on the screen, I know what I'm going to hear before I even answer. Because I feel it.

'Got it,' I say when the doctor finishes his report, 'my lawyer will be in touch soon.' I send a quick email, to get things in motion.

I sit with the news for a moment, staring into space, then explode from my chair and race down the hall calling, 'Holly?'

'What is it?' She barrels up the hall to meet me.

I skid to a halt, breathing like I've just sprinted a marathon not twenty feet.

'He's dead. Edward's dead.'

She grips my arm. 'How do you know?'

'The hospital just called me.'

'But how? How could he be dead?'

'The doctor said his body finally gave out. I guess it's hard to suck on psychic souls when you're in a coma.'

'He's definitely dead?'

'Definitely dead. There's some paperwork, but I've already contacted the funeral home and told them to start enacting the plans I put in place.' Which is cremation with no service, no death notice, no acknowledgement that the man ever existed, nothing. His ashes can go to landfill for all I care.

'Ding-dong, Western's dead!' Holly sings out.

I laugh, even though for some reason I'm not feeling her level of joy. I wanted him dead. If he'd had plugs I would have unplugged him months ago. But he didn't. He just lay there stubbornly living. But not anymore. So why aren't I happier, and why do I have this weird feeling like a nest of wasps has just moved in under my skin, buzzing and stinging? I roll my shoulders, trying to shake off my uneasy vibe.

'Hey.' Holly grabs my hand, obviously noticing. 'It's over now. You're free of him.' I nod but I mustn't have convinced her, because she firmly adds, 'It is, and you are. It's been months, and no other Western has come knocking on your door. And now Edward's finally gone. It's done; I can sense it. I know he was family and—'

'Holly, that man wasn't family. You're family. Jason's family. Hopefully your sister and dad will one day be family.' The surprise that flashes across her face. 'I just mean . . .' I quickly add. 'That hopefully one day Maggie and your dad will actually like me.' I'm not their favourite. They haven't yet forgiven me for hurting Holly two years ago.

She puts her hand to her heart. 'Don't scare me like that, I thought you were about to drop to one knee.'

'What would you do if I did?' Not that I'm thinking about it. Not so soon, that would be crazy. But it's not like I'm *not* thinking about it either, because I know I'm going to be with her for as long as I'm kicking, if she'll have me, which I think she might.

'I'd tell you to get up,' she says. 'We're a team, you never have to kneel in front of me.'

'Really? Because . . . I thought you liked it when I knelt in front of you, Daniels?'

Her cheeks flush. Then she wiggles closer, pressing herself against me.

'Well, that depends, Jefferies,' she says, all breathy, 'on what you're doing while you're down there.' All my blood rushes south.

She squeezes my fingers tight. 'I've been thinking lately, you still haven't come good on that promise you made to me in East Mill. Not once have we been listed as missing persons because we've stayed too long in bed.'

I chuckle. 'My bad. Did you want to start now?'

'I think we should,' she says.

'Do we need Uber Eats?'

'Yes we need Uber Eats, it's part of the plan. Besides, I'm hungry.'

'Of course you are.' I can't hold in my grin.

'Don't judge me!'

'No judgement.'

'Lucky, because I'd just *hate* to have to bring up how you got your ass handed to you tonight by Ms Aerobics 1982.'

'Thanks for not bringing that up.'

Holly laughs, lifts onto her toes and kisses me in that way of hers that makes me feel like she can't get enough, and I kiss her back the same way, because I know I can't.

I get that she's trying to distract me, and I love her for it.

I love her like crazy.

I'll love her for the rest of my life . . . and afterlife.

I don't need to be psychic to know that.

ACKNOWLEDGEMENTS

This is a pinch me moment. A core memory kind of thing. To be writing an acknowledgement for my paranormal romance that is now an actual book *insert exploding head emoji*! Not that I ever stopped believing in this story. I always trusted it would find its way into the world somehow. I just had to be patient. Its time would come. I was sure of it.

I've always loved a good ghost story. When I first started telling people I was writing a paranormal romance they'd say, 'Vampires?' and I would tell them, 'No, ghosts!' I was usually met with surprise and confusion followed by a slightly sad-for-me face. Ghosts were obviously not in at the time. But you've got to write what you love and what's in your heart and this is the story that was nestled there. And so, I wrote it, ghosts and all, and here we are.

Thank you, as always, to my wonderful team at Simon & Schuster and Atria Books Australia for helping my dreams become reality. To Anthea Bariamis for her brilliant eye and bang on ideas. Lizzie Levot for being my masterful edit-guardian-angel once again. And Vanessa Lanaway for helping make my nonsensical sentences make sense. These amazing, talented, fabulous women have been a gentle, positive guiding hand across all my books, and I'm so blessed to have them in my corner.

I also want to thank Cassandra DiBello for seeing something in my stories right from the start and then seeing something in *this* story. I kept saying to her, whenever we were talking future books, 'Oh . . . and . . . I have this paranormal romance . . .' downplaying it, knowing the chance of it ever getting a shot was pretty slim. But then the strangest thing happened. Paranormal romance started to have a moment again, and I happened to have one, and Cass asked to see it. My story's time had come. Just like I believed it would. The day she called to tell me it was going to be my next book was . . . well, I bought champagne, and I think I cried. Who am I kidding, of course I cried. I cry a ridiculous amount when talking about this book. Which is fair warning if you ever see me and we discuss Holly and Callum. Please bring tissues.

To my family and friends who have heard me going on and on about this one for a few years now. I'm still going on and on about it. I will never stop! Never! Some of you have read it. One of you has read it in every incarnation *cough* Hazel *cough*. I appreciate all your endless encouragement and continued faith that this story must have deserved how fiercely I believed in it.

To the Romance Writers of Australia aspiring group, thanks for getting behind these characters. Your enthusiastic embracing of my Holly and Callum flash fictions helped me trust that I might be onto something with their love story.

The wonderful book community really has been the biggest surprise in all of this. I'm so thankful to have met so many of you – readers, authors, booksellers – you're all so welcoming, and I'm so grateful for your support.

And of course, my mum. You know, every time I would speak about one of my books, she'd just assume I was talking about this one. She'd say, 'The ghost one?' I'd say, 'No, mum. That's not getting published.' She'd say, 'Well it should be! That's your best one!' Spoiler alert: she hadn't read it. She just knew how much I loved it, so she loved it too. She's always been Holly and Callum's most vigorous champion and has always been mine.

I love this story with all my heart. All of me is in all its pages. It's the story closest to me, the one that started my author journey, the one that grafted itself to my soul so firmly that I upended my life to write it. It was never far from mind, never far from my fingertips. As other well-loved stories poured out of me and miraculously made their way to bookshelves, this one was always there in the background, haunting me, nudging me, reminding me to believe in the extraordinary.

Like Holly, there's a part of me that has always felt a little out of place. As if I don't quite fit. That I'm too different. The quirky side character. In the margins, not quite part of the main story. That I can be easily forgotten, looked past, edited out, regardless of evidence to the contrary. I'm not sure those feelings ever go away. In fact, I know they don't, and I know I'm not alone in occasionally feeling like this. But I also know that, like Holly, I do fit. We all do. It's just we all fit a bit different. Thank you for helping me feel like I fit, for reading this book and being here at the end of its miraculous journey. As Callum would say, 'I like you. All of you. Even your weird bits.'

Amy xox

ABOUT THE AUTHOR

Amy Hutton is an award-winning author and television producer. When not plotting delicious romantic trials for her characters, she is an enthusiastic traveller, an animal advocate, a Disneyland aficionado, and a lover of tattoos. Amy lives in Sydney, Australia with her rescue dog named Buffy. For more visit amyhuttonauthor.com or find her on Instagram @AmyHuttonAuthor.